THE
Merry
Lives OF
Spinsters

Also by

Rebecca Connolly

The Arrangements:

An Arrangement of Sorts
Married to the Marquess
Secrets of a Spinster
The Dangers of Doing Good
The Burdens of a Bachelor
A Bride Worth Taking
A Wager Worth Making
A Gerrard Family Christmas

The London League:

The Lady and the Gent

Coming Soon

The Spinster and I

THE Merry Lives OF Spinsters

REBECCA CONNOLLY

Phase Publishing, LLC
Seattle

Cover art by Tugboat Design
http://www.tugboatdesign.net

Phase Publishing, LLC first paperback edition
May 2018

ISBN 978-1-943048-53-3
Library of Congress Control Number 2018941170
Cataloging-in-Publication Data on file.

Acknowledgements

For Alicia, my very own Georgie. I would totally have done this with you if we'd thought of it then! Thanks for being one of my people, love!

And to my favorite TV show, Timeless, for highlighting powerful women and characters throughout history, and showing that smart women can do incredible things. Also for the laughter, and all the swooning. Especially the swooning. Perfectly willing to be cast as an extra or test read scripts or run lines or fetch people's lunch or hold things… Call me.

.

Want to hear about future releases and upcoming events for Rebecca Connolly?

Sign up for the monthly Wit and Whimsy at:

www.rebeccaconnolly.com

Prologue
Mayfair, 1815

"Elizabeth Daniels was nearly compromised last night."

Georgiana Allen looked up from her cherry wood writing desk to gape at her currently breathless cousin with wide eyes. "She was? By whom, pray tell?"

"Marcus Ramsgate." Isabella shivered and looked a little pale, still panting from her hasty entrance. "They were found in the orangery at Fulston House. By the marquess."

Georgie winced and set her pen down. Lord Hartley was undeniably a kinder, more forgiving man than his father, the duke, but even he would not have looked kindly upon that. And Marcus Ramsgate? "That upstart with more charm than coin," Aunt Charity had once called him, without any hint of the virtue for which she was named.

She was not wrong.

It wasn't that Mr. Ramsgate wasn't attractive or enticing or a decent enough candidate for matrimony, if one were to look at him objectively. He had all the makings of a gentleman. It was just that he chose not to employ any of them.

Elizabeth Daniels should have known better. She *had* known better, as of their conversation last week. She wanted a calm and kind man, and a quiet, happy life for herself.

Well, that was all rubbish now.

"That's the fourth girl this season," Izzy whispered as if that were some great secret.

Fifth, actually, but there was no sense in revealing what was not commonly known, particularly when Georgie only knew because Anna Maxwell had secretly confessed it to her at the wedding breakfast.

And as Anna Maxwell was now Anna Lambert, Isabella's sister-in-law, that confession would remain between the two of them.

Georgie shook her head, setting her jaw. "We'll not let another go. Not one more."

"We?" her cousin asked a bit timidly.

She nodded once and forced a grim smile. "Get Emma and Charlotte. We have work to do."

Chapter One

———————————— ❦⊱⊰❦ ————————————

It is a rare woman that can find her own path in life without a man to instruct or direct her. Which seems odd, as most of the men of this world seem to need help with instruction and direction themselves...

-The Spinster Chronicles, 10 May 1816

"This meeting of the Spinsters, with a capital S, is now called to order."

Georgie looked at her friend with as much derision as one could lovingly express. "Really, Charlotte, must we resort to formality? We are not an official organization, nor is this a meeting."

Charlotte Wright, a rather attractive brunette with dark eyes and a fair complexion, and a determined spinster at the age of twenty-four, grinned without shame. "No? I think by now we are formed into enough of a body that we could become official."

"It does feel like something official," Georgie's cousin, Izzy, sadly an acknowledged spinster of twenty-six, replied with an impish grin. "Should we elect officers?"

"No!" Georgie retorted firmly, rolling her eyes. "This is only an afternoon tea!"

"We're English," Prudence Westfall, most assuredly a spinster at twenty-five, pointed out, flashing a rare grin. "Everything comes with a good tea."

"I don't think this is very good," Charlotte sniffed, sipping carefully. "Passable at best."

"Don't let my mother hear you say that," Izzy chortled, fingering one of her copper ringlets. "She thinks a mild tea soothes the digestion and is far better suited for young ladies."

"Then she'd better find something else for us," Grace Morledge, a charming beauty who was inexplicably a spinster at twenty-five, offered dryly. "We are only once-young ladies here, and a strong tea is preferred."

Georgie shook her head and sipped her perfectly acceptable tea without comment. There was no arguing with the group once they had decided to focus their attention on a topic, and if they wished to spend their time discussing the strength and quality of this particular tea, she would let them.

After all, she had no news to share. Everything was as it should be. Ever since she had gathered the others to take up her cause three years ago to prevent ignorant young women from ruining their lives with forced marriages, and to encourage proper thought and independence, they'd been able to prevent some truly disastrous moments simply by being watchful and sharing their wisdom with those who did not know better. Their weekly newssheet was now extremely popular, and they regularly heard girls quoting sections at each other and eyeing potential suitors with more wariness than they had in years past.

It had not worked out every time, of course, but they had discovered that there were a remarkable number of young women that knew absolutely nothing of the world or of men.

Not that any of them knew much about men, except perhaps Charlotte, who was quite proud of the number of proposals she had refused. But, with their combined number of years in Society, at whatever level or experience, they had observed and learned quite a lot.

In fact, if Georgie had ever truly wished to navigate the workings of Society as most of the other women did, she was convinced she would have done a marvelous job of it.

But that was neither here nor there.

The Season was well under way, and there was a fresh crop of girls hoping for good matches, and oddly enough, all of them were behaving with far more maturity and respectability than the girls in the last three seasons combined. Nobody had been ruined so far this Season, or even come close to it, and she couldn't even claim to have had a hand in that. There was every opportunity, but thus far, the unmarried members of Society had behaved themselves remarkably well. She was not naïve enough to believe that this would last, or that somehow her attempts to thwart forced marriage, particularly from ruination, had begun to change opinions on the idea.

She rather thought it was only because everyone was feeling the same way she was.

Bored.

There was an absolute boredom about London this time, and she couldn't attest to why. Everything was the same as it always had been. The same events were occurring, the same people were in attendance, and the same expectations surrounded her. She would not be courted, she would rarely dance, and she would end the Season with no husband.

It was all the same.

Aside from her increasing years, and the increasing popularity of their recent project, The Spinster Chronicles, absolutely everything about Georgiana Allen was exactly, unequivocally, and impeccably the same.

No wonder she wasn't married.

She would bore herself to death if she wasn't careful. She was more than halfway there already. Bored with herself, bored with their mostly unfounded reputation, bored with the effort she had put into this venture… Bored with it all. But she couldn't say anything about that; not to anyone.

"Georgie, why are you staring at the wallpaper?" Izzy asked suddenly, a smile in her voice. "It's the same horrible mossy green it's always been, and you heard Mama this morning."

Georgie looked at her cousin with a grin. "'It is absolutely, perfectly fine, and exactly as I would wish it'," they recited together, mimicking Izzy's mother with near perfection.

Charlotte coughed a laugh into her tea and set it aside, dabbing at her mouth with a table linen. "Did she really say that?"

"She always says that," Izzy told them with a heaving sigh.

"About everything," Georgie added, nodding for effect.

"The tapestries," Izzy offered.

"The livery," Georgie drawled.

"The menus."

"Her gowns."

"Her daughters."

"Her sons."

"Ha!" Charlotte burst out laughing, surprising all the rest. It took her a moment to collect herself, as it usually did when she was truly amused, and she finally wiped at her eyes as she settled. "Your mother… thinks your brothers… are perfect?"

Izzy shook her head in a pitying fashion. "No, she simply finds them all 'exactly as she would wish,' which means absolutely nothing anymore, and given my brothers are thirty, twenty-seven, and twelve, I find her indifference disconcerting."

"At least she finds no fault with you," Prue suggested in her gentle, mild-mannered way. "That's quite lovely, isn't it?"

Georgie smiled at that. Prue was the dearest and sweetest creature on the planet, but with all the timidity of twelve shy girls rolled into one. If she became even the slightest bit flustered, she grew tongue-tied, or stammered, or turned a remarkable shade of pink. She came from a family that cared little for her and seemed to only heighten her struggles rather than improve them.

Domineering mothers have that effect on shy daughters.

"I suppose it must be," Izzy allowed with a slight smirk, "but where I am concerned, she may follow up her usual line with 'Other people may say you lack,' and then she follows it up with something very detailed and specific, always assuring me that I am 'absolutely, perfectly fine' in her eyes." She lifted her eyes in a dramatic roll that brought laughter from all around. "She never did that with Catherine, and I have never heard her do so with my sisters-in-law."

"Well, Anna is perfect, isn't she?" Charlotte offered with a shrug. "And Jane is above imperfections, so what is there to criticize? Except, perhaps, their choices of your brothers, but that is an issue of personal taste, so one cannot fault it."

Prue, never perfectly comfortable with Charlotte's outspoken ways, looked torn between defending William and David Lambert and laughing along with her. Her brow furrowed slightly, and she opted to fidget with her faded blue muslin instead.

"Aunt Faith has no compunction in advising me," Georgie brought up, smiling for all, "but I am not a daughter, and so there is no need for me to be as she wishes it. She only asks me what my mother would think and leaves it at that."

Grace, who was the newest addition to their little group, smiled in bemusement. "And what would your mother think, Georgie?" she asked without any hesitation.

Of all the girls present, she alone did not know the nature of Hope Allen, or she would not have asked such a question. The others grinned at each other and sat back in preparation for Georgie's response.

She mulled over her answer, preparing an adequate, if entertaining one.

"My mother," Georgie began, keeping her voice perfectly mellow, "is one of three sisters, ironically named Faith, Hope, and Charity, and in that order. And each of those sisters has an interesting take on each of those virtues. Aunt Faith, for all her lovely hospitality, only has faith in her own opinions and tastes. Aunt Charity, to no one's surprise, has never managed charity. And my mother, Hope, does not know the meaning of the word, particularly where her daughter is concerned. Her sons, both still at Eton, are apparently going to rule the world if they manage to receive passing marks in any of their classes, where they are apparently not being properly instructed to their esteemed level. And it is a pity that their only sister, who is *significantly* older, has not managed to secure a husband for herself, despite having all the proper mentoring and training, and is destined to plague those sweet, innocent boys with her care for the rest of her miserable life."

"The word she used was hopeless," Izzy pointed out, beside herself with laughter. "Not miserable. Hopeless."

That sent the others into complete stitches, and Georgie gave her cousin a polite nod of acknowledgment. "Quite right, Izzy. My mistake."

Grace looked shocked but laughed along with the rest. "Is she really so against you?"

Georgie sighed with a hint of laughter. "Oh, she's not against me at all, Grace. Just disappointed. I don't know what she expected, I'm neither a great beauty nor particularly graceful, and I don't need any fingers at all to count the number of potential suitors I've had." She shrugged lightly, grinning at her newest friend. "She always wonders why I'm not more like Izzy."

Izzy howled at that and even Prue had to giggle, while Grace merely smiled her very pretty smile. "I think Izzy is delightful," Grace told her.

"So do I, to be sure." Georgie grinned at her favorite cousin. "If I were more like Izzy, I might, perhaps, have gained a husband."

"Yes," Izzy snorted with a flick of her hair, "because I've had so very many husbands."

Georgie shrugged again and sipped her tea. "Ah, well. Their loss."

"Hear, hear!" Charlotte crowed, helping herself to a crumpet.

"Oh, Charlotte," Prue sighed, shaking her head.

Grace still looked disgruntled. "I don't understand, I'm afraid. Are all your mothers this way? So meddling or disapproving or ridiculous?"

"Yes," Georgie and Izzy said together.

"Mine's given up on me entirely," Charlotte admitted, saluting Grace with her cup of tea, which she still drank, despite her aversion to it.

Prue's head dropped, and she suddenly focused very intently on her needlework. "My mother may be the worst of the lot," she murmured. "If I can say such a thing."

"You can," all the others assured her as one.

Even Grace knew that, having witnessed what Marjorie Westfall was like for herself only last week.

"I still can't believe she criticized your gown in front of so many," Grace said with a scowl. "I thought you looked lovely."

Prue lifted one shoulder, still not looking up. "Pink is not my color, I should have known better."

Georgie gaped and looked around the room, finding similar expressions on the others' faces. "Prue," she said, sitting forward. "You have the sort of coloring where you can wear almost anything and look perfectly fetching. There was no cause for her to make a scene like that."

Again, she gave a small shrug. "She likes to make a scene."

"Prue, your mother is a bully," Charlotte snapped, her mouth tightening. "If I didn't think you would die from embarrassment, I would tell her off with quite a bit of flair."

Prue's pale eyes widened, and she clamped down on her lips.

Charlotte made a noise of distress and flung a hand out. "You see? Even the thought of it makes her want to faint!"

"I'm s-sorry," Prue stammered weakly.

Grace leaned over and put an arm around her slender shoulders. "That was not a criticism, love. Charlotte is only a very passionate defender. You know that."

Charlotte practically bounded from her seat and placed a perfunctory kiss on the top of Prue's head. "I'm sorry, little lamb. I shouldn't have suggested it."

Prue managed a smile, though it wavered. "I app-preciate the thought." She looked over at Izzy and Georgie and her smile broadened. "Well, we certainly know why *I* am a spinster, don't we?"

It wasn't like Prue to tease herself, but since she was smiling, they all laughed.

"Come now, Miss Westfall," Georgie intoned formally. "We all know why each of us are spinsters." She shot a dirty look at Grace. "Except for Miss Morledge, of course."

Grace grinned sheepishly and shrugged. "I don't know either, I simply am!"

"I'm plain," Izzy offered. Then she wrinkled up her nose. "And 'nice,' it seems."

They all winced accordingly.

"I'm too fastidious," Charlotte announced without shame.

"I'd rather talk with a plant than a person," Prue admitted, still smiling, "and I'm probably better at it."

Grace turned to Georgie expectantly. "And you? Why are you a spinster, Miss Allen?"

Georgie smiled indulgently. "Well, I'm just unpleasant, and that's all there is to it!"

The rest of the girls protested quite nicely, and Georgie did her best to be properly demure about the whole thing, but remained firm in her position because, in truth, she was rather unpleasant. Or had become unpleasant. At twenty-seven, it was rather difficult to say. She had always known her own mind, but as she had grown older, she seemed to share it more, and apparently that was a fault.

One of many, but more than likely her primary one.

She was nothing if not honest where she was concerned.

"I'm here! I'm here!" A girl with light brown hair in slight disarray almost fell into the room, breathless and red-faced, her arms filled with small, leather-bound books.

Almost as one, the Spinsters, with a capital S, raised their brows at each other.

"Welcome to the meeting, Elinor," Charlotte drawled without any hint of the welcome the others had received.

Elinor Asheley, aged eighteen, had absolutely no business associating with them. She was far too young to be a spinster, with or without a capital S, and far too innocent to turn to cynicism as they all had. But she was determined to be part of their group, and to be a spinster herself, and her sister had been one of the founding members, as well as a very great friend to Georgie, so they allowed her, for Emma's sake.

Emma had married in the autumn to a kind widower with two children and had only a fleeting interest in the group as it was now, but she did still share the latest gossip with them. And she was frankly terrified of what Elinor would get up to and begged the girls to mind her when she was not in London to do so herself. As Mr. Partlowe favored country life over all else, they had begun minding Elinor all the time.

Unfortunately, the girl did not see their influence as any sort of guardianship so much as adoption, and she was the most willing puppy to ever grace a gathering.

Elinor's eyes lit up. "Oh! Are we having official meetings now? That would make my mother feel better. If I could put down a committee meeting regularly in my social calendar, she would not be nearly so stuffy."

"I doubt that," Georgie muttered under her breath, fixing a very polite smile on her face. She liked Elinor a great deal, and adored Emma, when she was not slightly irritated that her best friend had married and left her to her unending spinsterhood alone. But Mrs. Asheley was not her favorite person in the world. Nor, as far as she was aware, was she anybody else's.

"It's an idea," Charlotte told Elinor with a devious little smirk.

Georgie almost groaned and heard Izzy actually do so. Charlotte loved encouraging Elinor, and the results were always disastrous.

"I'm in favor!" Elinor chirped, sitting herself down with a swish of her white skirts. "We will need it with all of the information I've collected for this Season."

"Secretary," Izzy, Charlotte, and Grace all said at the same time.

"No," Georgie ordered again, giving them each a severe look. They most certainly did not need anything official to encourage Elinor further in her delusions.

"Welcome, dear," Prue said kindly. "Have some tea, it is still warm."

Elinor wrinkled up her nose at it. "Did Mrs. Lambert have it made according to her instructions, or did Izzy order it?"

Izzy grinned with all the fondness in the world. "Mother did, Elinor."

The girl shuddered too-knowingly. "Just a biscuit for me, please. I'd fancy water straight to that sort of tea."

Charlotte grinned over at Georgie. "I like her. Can we keep her?"

Georgie scoffed softly. "Last week you wanted to be rid of her. Something about a boarding school, I believe."

"Finishing school," Charlotte corrected, shaking her head and letting the loosened curls dance a little. "The child is in desperate need of finishing, anyone can see that."

"So are you, but we keep our mouths shut about it," Grace broke in with a sweet smile that belied the words she'd just spoken.

Izzy choked on her tea and Georgie thumped her on the back as she sputtered with laughter while the others chuckled with the good-natured fun they always did.

"And what is it that you have discovered, Elinor?" Georgie asked once the girl was seated, doubtful it would be anything of real use.

Elinor's fair eyes lit up and she chewed quickly on the biscuit she had just bitten into. "Lord Sterling's cousin has returned to London."

Charlotte groaned and rolled her eyes dramatically. "Which one?

There are about twenty-seven Sterling cousins, and none of them have ever been worth our attention before." She narrowed her eyes at the rest. "Which was the one who jilted that Scottish girl?"

"Mr. Andrews," Izzy and Georgie said together.

"And the one who was caught dueling?"

"Mr. Parkerton."

"What about the Sterling cousin who had the pet monkey?" Grace asked, sitting forward. "The one who claimed to have wed a daughter of the maharajah?"

"Mr. Newell," Charlotte answered with a laugh. "He also claimed to have killed a tiger, though I don't suppose he could have done that unless he'd sat on the poor creature and broke its head."

"Lovely thought," Prue mumbled, looking pale.

"The point is," Georgie overrode loudly, turning back to Elinor, who was wide-eyed with shock, "that we are not inclined to think very much of any Sterling cousins, given their history."

Elinor swallowed, nodding.

"But just for the sake of being thorough," Izzy offered, smiling kindly, "tell us who it is, then."

"Captain Anthony Sterling."

"Well, I like the sound of a captain," Charlotte chortled, sitting back.

"It didn't help Captain Cary last year," Izzy muttered.

Charlotte glared at her quickly. "You wouldn't have accepted him either, Isabella Lambert, and you know it." She sniffed and looked back at Elinor. "Go on, Elinor, give us the details."

She turned to her books and pulled a thin journal from it, flipping open a page. "Second son of Lord Sterling's uncle, served under General Robinson, and he went to school with Mr. Partlowe."

It was the most unimpressive description she could have given the man, whoever he was, and they looked around at each other with the same mild disappointment.

"That's it?" Charlotte asked when Elinor did not go on.

Elinor glanced up, then back down at her paper, her finger tracing the words carefully. She looked up and nodded. "Yes, that is all I have."

Charlotte blinked, then turned to the others. "She's not even hired as a secretary, and I'm already dismissing her." She swung back around to Elinor, shaking her head. "What sort of introduction to the man is that?"

"It's all I could find out on such short notice!" Elinor protested, her voice growing louder in its defensiveness. "He only just returned yesterday!"

"And he went to school with your sister's husband?" Charlotte demanded. "Who is in London at the present?"

Elinor scowled and snapped the journal shut. "I don't see why you care, Miss Refuses-All-Proposals. No one meets your high and mighty standards."

Georgie groaned and looked over at Izzy, who was shaking her head.

It was always this way; Charlotte making exorbitant demands of Elinor simply because she was eager and willing, and then becoming disgruntled when the information did not match her expectations.

No one knew what she was actually looking for, but Georgie highly suspected she did not either.

"Would you mind asking Mr. Partlowe to share some insight with you, Elinor, dear?" Izzy asked in her best tone, which had soothed everything from horses to old crones. "We would be so grateful."

Elinor looked at her with an almost-pout, and then nodded. "Of course. He's still so keen on being accommodating so I might think well of him, he might even be willing to give me an introduction."

"Oh, that would be lovely for you," Grace teased, setting her tea down. "Perhaps you'll have the captain for yourself, Elinor."

"I shall not!" Elinor protested hotly, apparently mortally offended by the notion. "I am determined to be a spinster, and nothing shall dissuade me."

Nearly the entire room groaned, and Georgie shook her head. "Well, regardless, Elinor, it would behoove you to find out what you can about the man, so we might have better insight into him. The last soldier who returned to London turned out to be a blackguard and I had to send letters to no less than six families to warn them of his interest in their daughters. I don't even like the Thomkinses, but that doesn't mean I care to see Catherine deluded into a match with a man like that." She shuddered at the memory and sighed. "We should try to discover that much, at least."

The rest nodded in agreement, their expressions somber.

They would never pretend that there was anything particularly noble in their work, for in truth it was more interference than anything else. They were well aware that they occasionally made quite a nuisance of themselves, and at least half of their efforts were either not needed or in vain. Their intentions were good, but their reputation had become one of nagging, fussy women who saw every man as a villain and every young woman as naïve.

Nothing could have been further from the truth, but there was no point in explaining any of that.

"And if Captain Sterling happens to exceed expectations?" Grace asked with a calculating look.

Charlotte shrugged, grinning. "I vote we give him to Georgie. Let her cut her teeth on that uniform and see how he fares."

That earned her a resounding round of laughter, and Georgie smiled indulgently.

"Would you take him, Georgie?" Elinor asked, her eyes wide. "Would you really?"

Georgie sighed heavily and turned to Elinor, keeping her expression and her tone mild. "I am not willing to write off any man without knowing his situation and nature, Elinor. I am in no position to be particularly selective. But I can honestly say that there is nothing about the name Captain Anthony Sterling that makes me in any way inclined to make his better acquaintance, good or bad."

Chapter Two

———⸙❧ ❧⸙———

It is impossible to say if there are truly any benefits to a man being in uniform or not. While it may enhance whatever physical attractiveness he may possess, in my experience, I have never found anything of heightened attractiveness of nature because of it.

-*The Spinster Chronicles, 3 March 1817*

Captain Anthony Sterling yawned as he surveyed the room, not entirely accustomed to the finer things in life now that his time in the army was done. He had no regrets about resigning his commission; it had been the perfect time to do so.

But he'd intentionally avoided being one of those officers that used their uniforms to influence others, and as such, he'd not had much interaction with anyone outside of his regiment and the other officers. Oh, there had been the occasional country dance that their regiment had been invited to, but Tony had always found a very good reason to avoid going. He preferred the battles on the field to the battles in a ballroom.

There was no particular reason for it. He was no tragic hero and he really was quite a congenial fellow with the opposite sex. He could dance rather well, he could converse with ease, and he had always done the utmost to behave as a gentleman no matter the circumstance.

He simply did not enjoy it.

His older brother Benedict had chosen, probably for the best, to avoid that necessity altogether by becoming a physician and situating himself in a small coastal town in Dorset. He never came to London, and rarely left his own county. Tony had just come from spending a month there, and while the experience had been invigorating and enjoyable, he'd rather felt as if he'd spent weeks convalescing by the seaside.

It hadn't suited.

So here he was, back in London and feeling even more uncomfortable for it. His uniform certainly drew enough attention from the young ladies in the room, and he wished he'd thought twice about wearing it. Technically, he no longer had to. But it was far more comfortable for him than his rarely used eveningwear, so that had decided everything for him.

What exactly had possessed him to choose a ball for his first foray back into Society? He should have just gone to a club and spent some time with the other gentlemen, it would have been far better suited to his level of comfort.

But alas, he was here, and he couldn't leave when he'd only been here half an hour.

So, he would just stand here.

And yawn.

"Now is that any way to behave at a ball, Captain? You have so much potential, it would be a shame to waste it."

Tony didn't bother hiding the smirk he felt as he turned to face the only person he was likely to know at the ball this evening. "My Lord Sterling, I shall consider your word a command."

That earned him a dry snort. "Don't do that, then I would have to consider myself a person of some importance, and I doubt my wife would like that very much."

Tony held out his hand, grinning outright. "It is good to see you, Francis."

His cousin gripped his hand firmly, clapping him on the shoulder. "And you as well. I'd heard you were in Dorset with Ben for a while, how did that go?"

Tony sighed heavily, shaking his head. "I am not meant for a simple life by the coast like he is. Ben was always the more easy-natured of the pair of us, so it's perfect for him."

Francis grunted and took up position next to Tony, surveying the room with his usual blank expression. "Has he got a wife yet?"

"Lord, no." Tony chuckled and took a drink from the footman nearest him. "Half of the village girls are in love with him, though. You would not believe how many calls of 'Doctor Sterling' we received every time we were out."

"Knowing Ben, I can believe it." Francis folded his arms and nodded to himself. "He won't be easily snatched up, though. He's far too selective."

"Says the man who swore to remain a bachelor for the entirety of his days," Tony reminded him with a smile.

It was amazing to see the transformation that came over Francis at that reminder. His expression changed from bland politeness with a hint of smugness to a warm irony, his features softening as his eyes fixed on a dark-haired woman across the room, completely unaware of them, chatting with other women around her.

"I thought I would," Francis murmured, still staring at his wife. "Janet was… unexpected."

Tony scoffed softly as he watched them, Janet now returning the look from her husband, and coloring at it.

"And to think she once hated you," Tony mused, almost to himself, as his cousin wasn't listening.

Francis let a corner of his mouth lift in a crooked smile, Janet looked away quickly, smiling herself. Then his cousin seemed to shake himself and looked back at Tony. "As I said, too selective."

"How odd," Tony said with a smile. "Must be a family trait."

That earned him a scolding look. "I'll have no sarcastic judgment from you, sir, who cannot sort himself out enough to remember how to behave in decent society, and probably never did anything unless directly ordered while he served, am I right?"

Tony frowned at his cousin. "Hardly fair. It was my job to obey orders."

Francis scowled playfully. "No one is commanding you now, are they? And without a command, you don't know what to do with yourself."

If only it were as stupid as it sounded, but that was too accurate for Tony's comfort. He didn't know what to do anymore, and a command would have been quite welcome right now. Preferably one to leave the ball and take up his recently resigned commission to get him back to familiar ground.

But that seemed unlikely. Particularly since he'd gone through so much trouble to get out, and his stepmother Miranda had been so pleased by that he hadn't the heart to change it.

"Good heavens, Tony, it was only a joke," Francis scoffed, nudging him. "No need to look so despondent. It's a ball, not a funeral."

"I've never felt so out of place in my life," Tony muttered.

"With that expression, you look it."

Well, that was certainly helpful.

"There was a time," Francis continued, looking amused as he moved in front of Tony, "when you were very good at being the gentleman. Shame about that."

Tony barely hid another scowl. "Are you abandoning me to my pathetic fate?"

Francis gave him a sardonic look. "Only for the time it takes me to claim this dance with my charming wife, who is far more attractive a companion than you, and of whom I happen to be fonder than you. So, if you can bear it, I will proceed accordingly."

There was really no course but to let him go, and Tony moodily watched as his cousin did just as he said he would, and the smile it brought to his wife's face was something to behold.

Tony had never thought of Francis as a particularly romantic person, and most of the time considered him quite the opposite, but there was no doubt in anybody's mind that Lord and Lady Sterling were a love match, which was absolutely not a common occurrence. Tony didn't know Janet well, but he certainly liked her well enough. He had no doubt that, now he was in London, he would come to like her better than Francis.

At this particular moment, he was sure he would.

"Tony!"

He turned quickly to see his cousin Hugh, Francis' younger brother, coming towards him with a wide grin. He looked almost nothing like his brother, who was darker and more brooding, while

Hugh was fair and lively, but in features they were alike enough to keep anyone from asking inappropriate questions. Tony remembered that when they had chosen to let their hair grow unfashionably long in their more entertaining youth, they each had developed an astonishing amount of perfect curls that spawned envy in several of their female cousins.

It was a useless piece of information, but Tony was sure somewhere he could employ it as he saw fit.

"Hugh!" He reached for his cousin's hand and embraced him warmly.

Hugh thumped him on the back and held him at arm's length, looking him over. "My, you're looking rather robust. I'd almost consider you a sailor, you're so tanned."

"If you spent any time out of doors, you could have some color in your face as well," Tony teased, reaching out to pinch his cousin's cheeks.

Hugh slapped his hand away with a laugh. "I get out! I ride and hunt as much as the next gentleman."

Tony pointedly looked at the gentleman nearest him, who was pasty-faced and rotund. He frowned and murmured, "That doesn't seem to be very much."

The gentleman didn't seem to notice Tony and Hugh's snickering, which was no doubt due to his inebriation and the distraction of several pretty girls in his immediate vicinity. None that paid him any mind, granted, but they were still present.

"If that is what I can expect from returning to Society," Tony muttered, "I'd rather leave now and avoid it altogether."

Hugh snorted, shaking his head. "You won't. You're not Mr. Talbot, and it would take you years to even come close. Just dance at these things and keep to your riding. Perhaps fence, if you like."

"I do fence, and quite well," Tony offered with a faint smile. "Would you care to test me?"

"Not even a little," Hugh replied swiftly. "I am no fool."

That was to be determined. Hugh had always been a bit of a fool, especially when compared to his brother, but Francis was wise, and Hugh was not.

"Pity." Tony scanned the room without much concern,

wondering if any of his friends would have returned to the area. He'd lost track of most of his schoolmates, and he'd been in the army for so long that most of his friends were there, or had been. Lieutenant Henshaw might be the sort that would come to London eventually, but he was undoubtedly still in Bristol with his family. That ought to get him racing off to London, certainly, as he had seven younger sisters.

If that was not enough to scare a man to Town, nothing was.

"How long have you been in Town, Tony?" Hugh asked him. "You should have called."

"Only a few days," Tony assured him, "and I intended to call once I was settled."

"Settled." Hugh scoffed loudly, drawing a few surprised looks. "You're not going to be settled until you've secured a country house with extensive grounds and your only neighbors are the foxes you hunt."

Tony tossed him a scolding glare. "I'm not a recluse, nor a confirmed bachelor."

Hugh's eyes widened, as did his smile. "Don't say that too loudly."

"Nor am I inclined to make a match any time soon." Tony shook his head. "Truly, there must be something else that Society cares about besides the availability of a man and the size of his fortune."

"If there is, I've yet to hear of it." Hugh took a long drink of the punch he held, then looked back at Tony with a brighter expression. "Say, how much did you make in the army? I'll wager it was a pretty penny."

Tony's collar suddenly felt tight and it was all he could do to avoid tugging at it. "Enough," he evaded.

Truth be told, he had made quite a good deal, and he no longer had any concern for his future. It was, in fact, enough for him to be a decently tempting prospect for the young ladies of Society that did not aim for the peerage. He was not in any particular hurry to become a target for any young woman, or her overeager mother, but he knew full well that he ought to at least begin to consider the idea.

It was about the only thing there *was* to do these days.

He began a slow scan of the room. There were several very pretty young ladies about, some dancing while others mingled, but Tony could honestly say he did not know a single one of them. That was disconcerting, to say the least.

"Whatever happened to Margaret Lister?" Tony asked Hugh as he sipped his drink again.

Hugh grunted. "She married Tobias Morgan. Has a pair of boys now, God help her."

"And Elizabeth Warren?"

"Fancied her, too, did you?"

Tony gave his cousin a look. "It is only a question, not an insight into my interests."

"She was a very pretty woman," Hugh admitted, holding up his hands in surrender. "Not passing any judgment. I was far too young to be interested in her myself, but…"

"What happened to her, Hugh?" Tony overrode.

"To whom?" Francis asked as he appeared with Janet. "Asking after women, are we, Tony?"

Tony groaned, but smiled. "Not anymore, you've brought the best of the lot." He bowed to Janet and took her hand. "My Lady Sterling, you are lovelier than I recall, and bear the burden of your unfortunate husband so well."

Janet dimpled a warm smile, allowing him to draw her hand to his lips. "We all have our crosses to bear, Captain, and I try to bear mine with little complaint. Please, call me Janet."

"As you wish." He smirked at Francis's expression, and released Janet's hand. "At least he's learned to dance, which must help matters."

"I always danced!" Francis protested.

"No, you didn't," Tony and Hugh said together.

Janet gave a merry laugh and looked up at her husband with a broad smile. "That explains a lot."

Francis narrowed his eyes at her, then turned to the others with a suspiciously clear expression. "Whom was Tony asking about, Hugh?"

"Elizabeth Warren," Hugh answered almost gleefully, his eyes alight. "I was just about to break his heart with the news."

Janet tilted her head at Tony with a curious smile. "You weren't one of the sad fools trailing after her, were you, Tony?"

He shook his head at once. "Not at all, she was simply the most popular name on gentlemen's lips when last I was about London Society."

"Well, she's not about Society anymore," Janet told him quite plainly. "Poor thing got saddled with Charles Hartley after an unfortunate house party incident."

Tony winced at that. Charles Hartley was neither intelligent nor kind, and only his fortune and Grecian profile gave him any credence with anyone.

"I think you'd better stop asking after the girls you once knew, Tony," Francis sighed, looking around himself. "The only ones you might possibly recognize would be in that far corner, and I doubt any would be of interest to you."

Tony followed his cousin's gaze and saw a plain, diminutive girl in a cream dress trying to make herself smaller as she sat between a rather large woman with an excessive number of ruffles and an older woman, whose wrinkled visage Tony recalled all too well.

"Lady Hetty Redgrave is still about?" Tony laughed, turning to his cousins.

"And thriving," Hugh grumbled, casting a sour look at the woman. "Last week she called me an insolent puppy who was in want of training."

Tony choked on a laugh while Francis shrugged. "She's not wrong."

Hugh chose, probably for the best, to ignore them. "And now she has her very own batch of admirers to encourage her on in her insolence."

"Can a woman over seventy be insolent?" Tony asked the rest. "I rather think they have earned something by that time."

"I adore Lady Hetty myself," Janet offered, smiling fondly at her. "And it is good to see others pay her some respect."

Tony watched as two other girls came to the corner, one sitting next to Lady Hetty and the other sitting behind the plain girl, leaning forward to speak to her. Lady Hetty turned to say something to them, then she and the three younger girls laughed, while the larger woman rose and moved to the other side of the room.

"Miss Westfall must be delighted," Hugh said. "She may now breathe freely on her right side. Perhaps now someone might dance with her, given the opening."

"She's small enough that it makes no difference if Mrs. Guntrip sits there or no," Francis commented. "And she's one of the Spinsters, so I don't know that she expects to dance at all."

"Would you dance with her, the way she stammers on?" Hugh snorted softly. "Like trying to converse with a very small goat."

Janet rapped Hugh on the arm sharply, her jaw tightening. "I demand you take that back, Hugh Sterling, right this minute. That was a beastly, cruel thing to say, and I would properly crown you if we were not in public and expected to behave."

"Oh, come off it, Janet..." Hugh protested, coloring slightly.

"Do it," Tony told him, his voice tight. "I nearly crowned you myself, and I don't know Miss Westfall from anyone."

"Fortunate man."

"Hugh!" Francis scolded, looking rather put out. "Were you raised by heathens and schooled by scoundrels? Or did you misplace your manners somewhere with a sensible weskit?"

Hugh looked like an irritated schoolboy, then grumbled, "I apologize to all of Miss Westfall's champions for my uncalled-for harshness with regards to her character."

Janet nodded her approval, and then swept away with a warning look at her husband.

"However true it might be," Hugh continued under his breath.

Tony glanced at his young cousin in disbelief. Hugh had never been so cynical or harsh before and had always spoken of young ladies with some measure of deference, if a trifle humorous. Now he was rude and reckless, and nothing good-natured to be found.

Hugh caught his gaze and misread it. "Janet disapproves of me," he muttered, keeping his voice low so Francis could not hear. "She thinks I lack taste and honor, or something. It's very rich coming from a woman who..."

"Careful," Tony warned. He glanced at Francis, who miraculously hadn't heard. "I don't know her well, but I will absolutely thrash you if you go on." He leaned closer and hissed, "Have you no sense, Hugh? What has gotten into you?"

An odd expression crossed Hugh's pale face and he blinked almost unsteadily. "Rest easy, soldier," he drawled. "This is no war. You don't have to defend *every* woman in London."

Tony's brow furrowed with concern and some distress, when Francis turned to the pair of them. "Talking about women again? Between Hugh and myself, we can give you a fair scope of the current flock."

"Capital idea," Hugh replied, almost too loudly. "Anyone catching your eye, Tony?"

He wasn't at all pleased with the change in topic, but Tony allowed it, making a mental note to keep a closer eye on Hugh in the coming days. "I wouldn't even know where to begin looking, were I truly inclined towards romantic pursuits."

"Well, take a look, then," Francis urged, laughing to himself. "We seem to be the only sensible branches of the family, so it would behoove us to keep things proper."

Tony raised a brow at him. "And a proper wife would do that?"

His cousin shrugged. "It'd be a proper place to start."

"And a proper way to die, if you choose poorly," Hugh grumbled, giving Tony a knowing look.

He didn't want to start a discussion on young ladies in London, whether they would suit his tastes or not. But he must start somewhere, and if his cousins wished to give him some insight here, he might as well take them up on the offer. It was better than nothing.

He could safely ignore the dancing young ladies for present, so he focused on those currently not. A very fine-looking woman with dark hair, dark eyes, and a decent collection of men gathered about her drew his gaze. She was listening to them all, he was sure of it, but not exactly engaging with them. She looked rather bored, in fact, but nothing in her behavior was enough to dissuade any trying for her. And if one fell away, there was another to take his place.

"Who is that?" Tony asked his cousins, indicating her with his chin. "Do you know her?"

Hugh shuddered visibly. "Charlotte Wright. She's an heiress, and a Spinster."

Tony looked again, surprised. "She doesn't look like a spinster. There are plenty of men about her. Surely she's got offers enough."

"Oh, not that kind of spinster," Hugh assured him. "Spinster with a capital S."

That made no sense, and Tony didn't bother hiding his confusion. "What?"

Francis rolled his eyes. "Oh, I cannot bear a discussion of them. Janet adores them and their column, and if my brother and cousin are going to discuss them, I'll say something out of character." He bowed a little and left them without delay.

"Even Francis is a coward when it comes to them," Hugh acknowledged with a sigh. "But it only makes him wiser. You can't blame him."

"I won't, I'm sure," Tony said, "when I have any idea what you're talking about."

"The Spinsters." Hugh cast a quick glance around, then took a small step closer. "Have you read any of the London papers lately?"

Tony shook his head. "Should I have?"

Hugh waved a dismissive hand. "It makes little difference. Next time you have a chance, pick up one of the gossip columns. In it, once a week, you will find something on the second page called The Spinster Chronicles."

Hugh's tone was a tad too dramatic for Tony's taste, and he really couldn't understand the need. "So, a column is being published for spinsters?"

"Not *for* spinsters," Hugh retorted defensively, "*by* spinsters. *The Spinsters*, to be precise. And it's grown now to the entire page, not just one column. They have a commentary on everything relating to London and Society, men and women, fashions, courtship… As if anybody should listen to them on those topics when they obviously have no success in them. And they are positively ruining London for everyone."

"Oh, come now…" Tony groaned, folding his arms and smiling a little. "How can one little column ruin anything?"

"Not the column," Hugh spat, truly upset. "Them! They are interfering in everything! A man can't get a bit of flirting in with a young woman unless he's got the most pristine pedigree and behavior ever known to man. They're encouraging young women to be just as prudish and independent as they are, and I would place money on the notion that they've all memorized that dribble from Mary Wollstonecraft."

Tony hummed a soft laugh. "You speak as if that were a new publication. Young ladies have been reading that for some time now."

Hugh turned to him, not at all amused. "It is no laughing matter! Thomas Perkins tried to have a go with the second Garnet girl and was herded off as if he were a badly-behaved sheep."

"If Thomas Perkins is anything like his brother Harry, I'd herd him away from young women too," Tony quipped, truly finding this whole thing rather amusing.

His cousin seemed to consider that, then made a noise of irritation. "All right, it was a poor example, I grant you, but for the rest of us?" He shook his head in disbelief. "It's impossible, Tony!" Hugh's brow furrowed, and he stared at him for a long moment.

"What?" Tony asked slowly as suspicion suddenly flooded him. "What are you thinking?"

"You're bored out of your mind."

Tony grunted. "And I was trying so hard to hide that, shame you sniffed it out."

"You could put a stop to this."

Tony's humor fled at that, and his smirk faded. "To what?"

"All of this." Hugh smiled suddenly, and it spread until it filled his entire face. "You could break up the Spinsters."

It was the most insane proposition he had ever been given, and he began to laugh, not out of humor, as it was the furthest thing from amusing, but out of sheer disbelief at its stupidity. "What?"

Hugh seized his arms in excitement. "It's a brilliant scheme! You are a soldier who takes orders and dangerous missions."

"Not so dangerous…"

"You would have dealt with dozens of evil forces."

"Well, now, as to that…"

"You could disband their little troupe without any trouble whatsoever!" Hugh laughed, squeezing his arms. "It's a stroke of genius! You can save all of us, Tony!"

"Stop!" he ordered, freeing himself from his cousin's grasp. "Stop right there. First, it's a group of young ladies, not a band of French rebels. Second, there is no reason to suppose that what they are doing is causing harm or detriment to anyone and may actually be improving the morality of the upper class. Third, no."

Hugh tilted his head, confused. "No?"

Tony shook his head very firmly. "No. Absolutely not. I refuse."

"You can't!" his cousin gasped. "The gentlemen of London need you, Tony!"

"To save them from a bunch of meddling spinsters?" he asked with all the derision he could muster, which was a sizable amount. "Then the gentlemen of London have grown remarkably soft in my absence. Excuse me." He gave his cousin a bow and turned to go.

Hugh grabbed his arm, his eyes wide and disbelieving. "Where are you going?

Tony gave him a condescending smile. "To pay my respects to Lady Hetty and ask for an introduction to Miss Westfall. I fancy a dance with a very small goat, and I expect to be quite charmed by her. Perhaps I'll even marry her and give you more torment for your relations by marriage."

He shrugged out of Hugh's hold and strode away, making a direct path for Lady Hetty, who had always slightly terrified him, and for Miss Westfall, who looked as if everything terrified her. He pitied her, poor girl, and her friends had abandoned her yet again, save for Lady Hetty. He might have it in him to give her some enjoyment in the evening, provided she would not fear him. He could be imposing, with his somewhat towering height, but he'd been told he had a kind smile, and he prayed that was still the case.

Even so, he was a soldier, with duty and honor to uphold, he had the uniform to prove it, and if he could do a service to her, he would not feel his evening wasted.

And he would be lying if he said he was not a little curious about the Spinsters, whoever they were, and what they were about.

But that was another matter for another time.

He approached Lady Hetty with caution, a polite smile on his face. "Lady Hetty," he said reverentially as he bowed before her. "It is an unexpected delight to see you again."

She peered up at him, her dark eyes twinkling slightly. "Unexpected because you are surprised that you've missed me, or unexpected because I'm not dead?"

"Whichever makes you think better of me, madam."

She wheezed a laugh. "Captain Sterling, you've not changed at all, and that's a fine thing, for a change. Do you know Miss Westfall?" she asked, indicating the girl next to her.

"No, madam, but I would be quite pleased to make her acquaintance, if you'll give me leave to do so."

Chapter Three

⁓⁓⁓

First impressions are a tricky business. It often happens that what one sees is not, in fact, what one gets. Anyone can act for five minutes, and far too many do. The question is how accomplished an actor are they, and why are they acting a part? Take a second look, if not a third, and if a third is not enough, give them an impression in return to remember.

-The Spinster Chronicles, 17 July 1816

He'd read the page four times in an hour, and then a further three more times that afternoon, chuckling to himself at times, nodding in agreement at others. It was well written, each article possessing just the right amount of wit to keep it entertaining. It was hardly shocking, despite what Hugh had said. The lead column the week before had borne a completely different tone, one with far more cynicism, but when addressing the subject of conversation at balls, it was perfectly fitting.

And downright hilarious.

Between the two of them, and the few others he had managed to track down, he'd almost come to a decision. He needed further information, however. Which explained why Tony was now on the front step of his cousin's home, debating whether he could actually go through with this. It would probably end up being far more than he bargained for, but with nothing better to do and no one to dissuade him, this was his best course of action.

He raised his hand to knock when the door opened, and he had to step back.

Hugh stood there, hat on his head and gloves in his hands, looking all-too surprised to have Tony on his front step. Then his brow furrowed, and he turned mulish. "Good day, cousin. Have you come to berate me further about my behavior, or have you procured a commission for me so that I might find the order and maturity that I seem to lack?"

Tony frowned at his cousin. "No…"

"Oh." Hugh's expression changed to one of mild confusion. "Then what brings you here?"

"I came to…" Tony winced, shaking his head. "I came to ask about the Spinsters," he mumbled.

Hugh grinned slowly. "Ah, piqued your interest, have I? Well, you are in luck. I am about to attend a card party where all of them should be in attendance, and you shall accompany me."

"Oh, that's not necessary," Tony protested, hastily backing up. "Another time will do."

"Not at all." Hugh stepped out of the house and turned Tony in his direction. "The best way to learn about them is in person, and the sooner you begin the better."

"I'm not agreeing to anything," Tony warned him.

Hugh gave him a knowing look. "We'll see about that."

"I'm only curious."

"Of course."

"Because I read the column."

"Naturally."

"It raised questions."

"I suspected it might."

Tony frowned as Hugh entered the carriage. "I'm only asking for more information, Hugh."

Hugh gave him a bemused smile. "Yes, I know. Get in, we'll talk on the way."

This was destined to be a very bad idea, but there was no help for it. Tony boarded and situated himself across from his cousin, sighing in resignation. "Whose card party is it?" he asked. "Will they mind an uninvited guest?"

"Not at all." Hugh fussed at his berry-colored coat and gold waistcoat with a furrowed brow. "It's Mrs. Wilton. She has three unmarried daughters, though only two would be considered of an eligible age. She'll be quite delighted to see you." He looked him over quickly, smirking. "Doubtless she will be disappointed at your lack of uniform, but there's nothing to be done about that, and you look smart enough for a card party."

Tony looked down at himself in confusion, not thinking there should be anything lacking in his general appearance. "Thank you, I suppose." He narrowed his eyes at his cousin. "She's not going to be insufferable about it, is she?"

Hugh shook his head quickly. "Not at all, Mrs. Wilton is the sanest mother of daughters I have ever met in my life. And her daughters are perfectly proper and respectable, pretty enough, and the fortune is admirable. A bit bland, but doubtless they liven up on better acquaintance."

"Then why have the third out if she is so young and the mother not aggressive about marrying the girls off?" Tony asked. Really, was it not enough to have the trouble of two unmarried daughters? The complexities of Society and its concerns were overwhelming, and often unfathomable.

"As I understand it, the youngest Miss Wilton is determined and opinionated, rather unlike her sisters." Hugh shrugged and looked out of the window. "She's probably only out to avoid an all-out battle with her mother or sisters. I'd avoid that one, if you can."

Tony shuddered. "I don't need to have a child bride, thank you very much."

That caught his cousin's attention, and a sly smile appeared on his face. "Then what sort of bride would you like, Captain?"

Tony glared a warning at him. "One when I am ready, which is not at this moment."

His words had no effect on his cousin's expression. "Yet you want to know more about the Spinsters."

Tony let the sounds of the carriage fill the silence, and then turned a sardonic look on him. "Would you like me to marry one of the Spinsters, Hugh?"

For a moment, his cousin looked pale and slightly ill. Then he laughed and retorted, "You'd never. They're all tyrannical and interfering busybodies who can't get husbands for themselves, and their bitterness about that has led to a campaign to prevent any young woman from anything remotely romantic. They're all destined to be hags who huff and puff in the corners of ballrooms for the rest of their lives."

"That's very eloquently put," Tony snorted. "Pity you didn't have that passion and penchant for speech when you were in school, you might have received better marks."

Hugh grinned rather smugly. "There is nothing like a cause to properly motivate a man to action."

True, Tony thought. *Very, very true.*

But he doubted his cousin's cause and his own would be the same. Unless Tony witnessed some great maneuvering in a military fashion from these women in a way that directly affected him, he had no intention of putting a stop to anything. His cause right now was sheer curiosity and fascination. And for now, that was enough.

Most of the spinsters he had known in his life had been shy, retreating creatures; wallflowers who never danced; blatantly plain or sometimes downright unattractive women with nothing else to recommend them; heiresses with higher opinions of themselves than of any man who might have tried for them. To be perfectly blunt about it, he'd not known too many spinsters who were under the age of forty. But most of them shared one thing: they were all exceedingly bitter about their state. Very rarely, in his admittedly limited experience, had he met a spinster that seemed comfortable with her situation, if able to find humor in it. The Spinsters, and their articles, seemed to be proof that such women existed.

Why that should interest him, he couldn't have said, but he couldn't deny that it did.

His dance with Miss Westfall had certainly proven something along those lines. She was the same sort of timid creature that he would have expected her to be, and the sort that was understandably, if unfortunately, a spinster. Yet as he had spoken with her, and eventually obtained consent for a dance, she had proven to be just as sweet-tempered as any other shy creature he'd ever met, spinster or not. She had only found difficulty with her speech for the first few minutes of their association, and it had eventually tapered off into something he barely noticed, once she'd grown accustomed to him. The embarrassed flush on her cheeks never dissipated, but the smile he had coaxed from her by the end had only been the sweeter for it. She did not pity herself and had even praised his patience and stamina for enduring her, laughing when she'd done so. A girl like that would have made someone a most excellent wife, and certainly a loyal, devoted one.

Not him, she was not his sort, but certainly someone.

It actually perturbed him now that no one had done.

They pulled up to the Wilton's address and were shown up to the card room with remarkable haste and energy, which made Tony doubt Hugh's claims of a sensible mother in Mrs. Wilton.

Yet her greeting of them was perfunctory at best, though perfectly polite. Tony caught a hint of a scheming look in her eye, but no daughters of hers descended on him after he'd left her, which was a pleasant surprise.

He and Hugh wandered about the room, making polite conversation and introductions as needed, and then took up position near a tall window with sheer curtains.

"Right, then," Tony muttered, sipping at the tea he'd been offered. "Point out these Spinsters and let's get on with it."

Hugh chuckled quietly and indicated a far table where four women sat. "Two of them are there. The red haired one is Isabella Lambert, generally thought of as being a good sort, but without beauty or fortune, she has no hopes."

Tony frowned at that. Miss Lambert wasn't at all unattractive, and he would never have said she was without beauty. Why, when she smiled, as she did now, she had a very pleasing countenance. She did not have the universal attractiveness and charm of her friend, Miss Wright, he would allow, but neither was she so very plain as for it to draw comment.

"To her left is Grace Morledge," Hugh went on, evidently not having anything further to say with regards to Miss Lambert. "Daughter of Lord Trenwick. Fortune enough, pretty enough, and accomplished enough."

Tony looked at his cousin in surprise. "So why is she a spinster?"

"No idea." Hugh shrugged as if it made no difference to him.

"She simply is."

This was becoming increasingly confusing. By everything he could see, Miss Morledge was everything a young woman could wish to be, and the idea that there was something lacking in her enough to be a spinster seemed laughable. Surely, if she had faults enough to remain unmarried, Hugh would have known about them and informed Tony of their existence.

"Miss Westfall you already know," Hugh went on, indicating her in the corner, her eyes lowered as if she had been scolded. "Timid creature, and that would be a paltry description."

"Be kind, Hugh," Tony warned. "I like the girl."

Hugh gave him a sidelong look. "But you see why she is a spinster."

He had to nod at that, but he did so grudgingly. "I only think higher of the rest of them for including her," he muttered.

His cousin groaned in annoyance. "Don't think kindly on them. Miss Westfall is a very good girl, I'll grant you, but none of the rest of them can be trusted."

Tony would not believe that, coming from Hugh, but he would remain silent about it. "And then Miss Wright, correct? Does she round out the lot?"

Hugh scowled and shook his head. "No, I only wish it were so easy. The one you need to worry about is that one right there." He gestured unmistakably to a tall blonde woman in a green sprigged muslin, currently speaking with another woman, similar in appearance, though her hair was darker, and she was not as attractive.

"And she is?" he asked, watching her with interest.

"Georgiana Allen." Hugh shuddered for effect, which was not called for. "She is the most tyrannical, and their leader. A shrew in the making, if ever I saw one. The woman she is speaking with is Emma Partlowe, who was formerly Emma Asheley, and she was one of the Spinsters, too, before her marriage last year."

Tony glanced at his cousin quickly. "Partlowe? As in Thomas Partlowe?"

Hugh turned to him, mildly surprised. "You know him?"

He nodded, looking back at Miss Allen and Mrs. Partlowe. "I used to. We were at school together. I hadn't heard he'd remarried."

"Well, he has," Hugh retorted as he turned back to scan the room, "and he chose the tamest of the lot. She is close friends with Miss Allen, so it really should have disrupted everything. Unfortunately, I think the Spinsters are only emboldened and embittered by the change. I'm surprised Miss Allen is actually talking with Mrs. Partlowe after such a betrayal."

Hugh continued to ramble, but Tony ignored him to the best of his ability.

Miss Allen was a handsome woman, anyone could see that. He wouldn't call her beautiful, that was not his place and he couldn't see her well from his position. But she certainly was not plain, and there was a hint of a smile when she spoke that made her countenance rather pleasing. She paused whatever she was saying and looked across the room, her eyes narrowing.

Tony followed her gaze and saw Elliott Harker speaking to a young woman that seemed rather taken with him. Harker was from a good family, but he couldn't have said if the man himself were someone of merit. The girl, however, looked a trifle too young for him, and by her looks, she was undoubtedly one of the Wilton daughters.

The youngest one, if he were to put money on it.

Even if Harker had been one of the best men in England, he would have balked at the idea of him courting a girl of fifteen. But flirtation was not courtship, and he would be very interested to see if Miss Allen or the Spinsters would react in any way.

It could be very telling.

Another girl sitting at the card table suddenly stood and made her way, very nonchalantly, towards them. No one else in the room would have noticed had they not been watching, but Tony smirked when the young woman, who could not possibly have been considered a spinster, came alongside the Wilton girl and began taking part in the conversation. There had been no command to act, no distress noted on any of the faces of any Spinster he had seen, yet the situation had been diffused before it had become anything at all. That was not to say that there would not be further encounters between Mr. Harker and Miss Wilton, but at least there would now be extra care taken with her.

Tony glanced back at Miss Allen, who was smiling more fully in her renewed conversation with Mrs. Partlowe, and that smile made him wonder. It was not a superior or smug smile. There was no haughtiness in it, nothing to suggest a vindictive nature or any sort of bitterness. She looked perfectly at ease, laughing now with her friend, who had, by all accounts, surpassed her in all worldly respects.

What sort of spinster was she? And why such a reputation for their group? What was their aim? Surely Society was not so far gone as to require guardians of feminine innocence and virtue such as they were portrayed to be. Why not leave the rest of the young ladies to their follies, whatever they were, and let the consequences follow?

Why involve themselves at all?

What bound such a diverse group of women together?

And why did all the men in London seem to despise them?

"I'll do it," Tony heard himself say.

"What was that?" Hugh asked absently.

"I'll do it. I'll investigate the Spinsters." Tony nodded slowly, his eyes fixed on Miss Allen while the rest of him filled with an odd sense of anticipation, rather like before a battle.

Hugh stood in front of him, eyes wide. "You'll do it?"

Tony gave him another firm nod.

His cousin clasped his arms, looking far too jubilant at the prospect. "Tony, you have no idea how pleased this makes me."

"I believe I have some," he replied, stepping out of his hold. He gave Hugh a warning look. "Do not spread word of this, Hugh. I will stop at once if I am ever approached on the subject, mark my words."

Hugh raised his hands in surrender. "They're marked, they're marked!"

Tony didn't believe him for a second, but there wasn't anything to be done about that. He exhaled sharply and looked back over at the Spinsters, who were dissipating into conversations with others present. "Now, what would be the best plan of attack, in your estimation?"

"Take out the leader."

He glowered briefly at his too-eager cousin. "Yes, thank you, but *how?*"

"Oh." Hugh frowned and turned to look across the room. "If

you want to get to Miss Allen, you need to go through Miss Lambert." Hugh nodded thoughtfully, a small smile on his face. "Yes, Miss Lambert would be the way."

"Really?" Tony considered the copper-haired girl with the easy manners with interest. He wouldn't have thought Miss Lambert to be so key in all of this, she seemed rather ambivalent in nature. "Why would that be?"

"They're cousins," Hugh replied. "And Miss Allen is living with the Lamberts while her parents enjoy the continent. I think Miss Lambert's good opinion would allow you access far more easily than anything else."

It was a good thought, and certainly a strategic one.

"Think of it as an attack from the side!" Hugh suggested, brightening at the idea. "You're a soldier, you know how to maneuver when you see opportunity."

Tony didn't need his cousin, who had never even managed to play soldiers successfully, to tell him how to maneuver or that he could accomplish this task because of his training. He knew full well how strategic he'd need to be, and while he might not know the particulars of what he would do, he had a fairly good idea, and a knack for acting on his instincts.

And his instincts were always infallible.

Hugh sobered, looking speculative. "How long do you think it will take?"

Tony raised a brow at his cousin. "Are you anxious for the Spinsters to be disbanded for some reason? Is there a young woman you are being prevented from pursuing?"

His cousin shuddered, and he looked almost offended. "I should say not. I am in no hurry to be tied to a wife of any sort. I would rather enjoy several years of sowing my wild oats like any other gentleman."

"I think you'll find that there is nothing gentlemanly about sowing wild oats," Tony informed him, disapproval rife in his tone. "No matter how popular the idea."

Hugh tossed back the remains of his tea. "You spend your time in your way and leave me to mine." He nudged his head towards Miss Lambert, who was preparing to sit for another game, though they were in want of another set of players. "Get to it."

"I make no promises," Tony warned him. "I cannot ensure anything."

Hugh scowled grumpily. "Convenient."

Tony put a hand on his cousin's shoulder. "Come, I have need of you."

That got his attention and Hugh looked at him with a mixture of horror and confusion. "For what?"

"Introductions," Tony said with a smile, "and whist."

Much later, Tony reentered his apartments with a tired sigh, rubbing at his eyes. He hadn't set up a house for himself yet, and he saw no need to do so in haste. As things stood now, he only had to greet the porter at the gate and perhaps say a word or two to his valet, Rollins, and that would be the end of all required conversation at the conclusion of a particularly long day.

Tonight, he didn't even have that.

Rollins had asked for the day to visit his sister in Richmond, and Tony had allowed it without a second thought. Rollins had served him the entirety of the war, and beyond. He had been an exemplary soldier as well as valet. Tony considered him more a friend than a servant, though Rollins would balk at being referred to as such. He was a bit particular about the distinction of rank, and while Tony had assured him that there was no rank to his name or his family, Rollins insisted that it remain.

At any rate, it was a relief to have Rollins gone for the evening.

Tony removed his jacket and draped it over the bed, loosened his cravat, and unbuttoned his waistcoat before dropping himself into a chair by the fire with a groan. The card party had not gone on long, but Hugh had dragged him along to his club and forced him to meet several other gentlemen, most of whom Tony had not been particularly impressed with.

It occurred to him now why his cousin seemed so changed from when he'd known him before. He'd spent too much time with these puffed up fops who had no idea of the ways of the world and only cared for their own interests. There was nothing of substance to any man there.

Now Hugh had become one of them.

But all of them, every single one, had spoken to him about the Spinsters. If he had any interest in pursuing a woman, he would need to be cleverer than the Spinsters, they'd warned him.

He thought it best not to tell them that he would have kept each and every one of them from any respectable young woman himself, with the conversations they'd been having.

Copious amounts of alcohol had never made a man better than he was, and it was never more proven than when combined with other men under the same influence.

Tony had kept his opinions to himself on several subjects, especially in conversation with his cousin. Hugh was so delighted that Tony was going to take on the Spinsters that it was as though there were no further problems in his life and he had nothing else to wish for.

Pity Hugh had no notion that he would derive no satisfaction from Tony's efforts.

He could not say for certain until he met the Spinsters as a whole and had gained their trust, but he was of the opinion that there was no need for such a strongly bound group of women to be forced to give up their amusements, particularly when there was no harm being done. Harm to the pride of fools did not count, nor was it worth the breath to even say the words. And he saw no need to get in the middle of the affairs of young ladies of Society, nor did he think any man ought to.

More than once since he'd told Hugh he'd get involved, he'd thought better of it. There was nothing to be gained by it, not for him. But he was curious, and for a man with no desire to find a wife for some time, there was not much else to do but indulge in his curiosities. Until he was more settled in his post-military life, this would be it.

He was a misfit in Society at present, so why not look into another group of misfits and see what could be gained by it?

Tony grunted a humorless laugh to himself as he reflected on his card playing this evening with Miss Lambert. Hugh had remained for only two rounds, then begged leave to associate with others in the room. Miss Lambert's partner, the second Miss Wilton, had also abandoned them, but at the behest of her mother, which had made the girl roll her eyes and smile indulgently. Left without partners, Tony and Miss Lambert were able to begin a real conversation without any pretense until other guests came to join in the card playing.

It hadn't been anything extraordinary, he'd had dozens of similar conversations with young ladies before. He'd found Miss Lambert to be a charming girl, warm and kind, exceedingly polite, yet in possession of a hidden wit that made very brief appearances. She was absolutely without cynicism and knew every single person in the room.

He'd been completely upfront with her about not knowing very many people, now he was returned to London, and she had most kindly given him names and pertinent details of every guest without saying a single negative word about any of them. He suspected she knew less than savory details about some from the way her mouth quirked at times when speaking of them, but such words never crossed her lips.

And this young woman was supposed to be part of a group of meddlesome, bitter spinsters who were unable to mind their own affairs?

The idea was absolutely ludicrous.

Which only made everything more confusing for Tony, and, unfortunately, convinced him that his course of action was something to see through to the end.

Whatever that end was.

He would not be breaking up the Spinsters, he could say that without reservation. But it was entirely possible that he could diminish the extent of their meddling, if they truly were doing anything of the sort. Having made the acquaintance of both Miss Westfall and Miss Lambert, he highly doubted it. But having seen Miss Wright with her suitors, there were some questions. He could say nothing for Miss Morledge or Miss Allen, he only knew what he had been told, and nothing he had witnessed had supported the more outrageous claims.

He was undoubtedly mad for even considering this, and his fellow officers would have laughed in his face had they any knowledge of it. Was this what he had come to? Using the skills he had so proficiently honed through his years of service to investigate a passel of females because they bothered a few would-be rakes?

It sounded pathetic, even to his ears.

Tony rubbed at his eyes with another sigh. Tomorrow, if Miss Lambert's careless words were correct, she and her friends would gather for tea. He would pay a call upon her, as if it were no more than that, and let events unfold as they would.

He did not suppose that Miss Allen would be as naïve as her cousin, having seen the calculating expression she wore, as if he could see her mind whirling. He knew that she would be the greatest obstacle for him for even gaining admittance into the company of the Spinsters, let alone their trust or confidence.

He needed to be sharp and be on his guard, and he needed to be perfectly above reproach. One did not have opportunity to undo a first impression most of the time, and while his conduct with Miss Lambert and Miss Westfall had been near perfection, they were only two out of the five. And most likely the easiest to sway.

It shouldn't be too difficult to accomplish. He wasn't much of a rogue even on his most wicked days, and he wasn't stuffy enough to be intolerable. He was, by all accounts, the perfect man for the job.

All because he was bored and in need of a purpose.

Only time would tell if the Spinsters would be the cure for such an affliction.

Chapter Four

———— ⌒⟡⌒ ————

A gentleman with honorable intentions has no need to be false in any circumstances. He has no need of secrets. A young lady, however, is destined to have many secrets and cannot be expected to be fully forthcoming. Any man who takes issue with the discrepancy, which this author is fully aware of, ought to take his concerns to his mother and see how she responds to his complaint.

-*The Spinster Chronicles, 24 October 1815*

"You do not mean to refuse him, do you, Charlotte?"

"Of course, I do. Are you mad?"

Georgie groaned and leaned back against the divan, shaking her head in disgust. They'd been over this repeatedly, but Charlotte was unmoved. She had so many suitors and did not discourage any of them unless they were truly distasteful for one reason or another, yet when any of them proposed marriage, she turned them down with swiftness and certainty.

All in the name of love, it appeared.

"Charlotte," Izzy tried in her most placating tone, "we all approve of Mr. Dale immensely. He is a perfect gentleman and is very well set up. He is handsome and kind…"

"And yet my answer will still be no," Charlotte replied, looking thoughtful. "Hmm. I wonder why that could be."

Izzy looked around at the rest of them in desperation. "It's hopeless."

"That's exactly what I thought," Charlotte said with wide eyes. "It's hopeless. How can I consider marrying a man when it would be a perfectly hopeless match?"

"I highly doubt that's what Izzy meant," Grace muttered, shaking her head.

Izzy laughed softly. "It's not."

"Why is Mr. Dale hopeless?" Prue asked with an innocent look of concern.

Charlotte huffed irritably and adjusted her skirts. "*He* isn't hopeless, to be sure. He's a good man, and a kind one, but there's no affection between us. I'm fond of him, but I can hardly marry a man I'm only fond of. I would be destined to dislike him within a week."

Prue's brow furrowed, and she looked at Georgie with a frown. "I'd like to marry a man I'm fond of. I think that would be delightful."

"It's not good enough!" Charlotte protested.

"It would be for me," Prue admitted. "It's more than I expect."

"Me, too," Grace murmured as she picked up her embroidery. "In our society today, that is all we can hope for. Affection, desirable as it is, is not a requirement."

"No!" Charlotte half-shouted, her color rising. "No, I refuse to accept that! We should expect love, not just affection! No more polite matches or eligible matches or fortunate matches. We should demand love!"

"Hear, hear!" Elinor echoed passionately from her chair near the corner.

The rest of the room seemed to sigh in resignation. "Not all of us can afford such luxuries, Charlotte," Georgie said as gently as she could manage.

It was as if the thought had never occurred to Charlotte before. She blinked slowly and stared at each girl in turn. "What do you mean?" she asked carefully. "Do you mean that you... you don't expect to find love?"

Each of them seemed to shrug, and Elinor looked astonished by the revelation. Charlotte frowned and looked at Georgie expectantly, as if she were somehow supposed to resolve this issue.

"I'm sorry, Charlotte," Georgie told her, as she sat up, smiling for effect. "I don't expect anything anymore. But I think I would take a good match if I could."

"I'd need a man to be interested before I could even think about matches," Izzy broke in with a laugh. "Let's start with the basics, shall we?"

That broke the odd tension that had filled the room, and they all laughed in relief.

Georgie exhaled slowly, grateful her cousin had such a way with people. Charlotte had never come out and said it, but she had little patience with the others for not seeing the world in the same way she did. She had a fortune and a family that indulged her whims, she had no need to marry at all, if she chose not to.

The rest of them, apart from Grace, perhaps, would come down in the world rather sharply with no husband to provide for them. It was harsh reality, but they all lived with it. Being a spinster was not something that one ought to envy or idolize, as Elinor had begun to. It was a miserable existence, if one thought about it too much.

Which was why Georgie never did and continued on as she always had done.

"Pardon me, Miss Lambert," a maid asked from the door to the parlor. "But you… have a caller. A gentleman caller."

A hush fell over the room and everyone stared at Izzy with wide eyes.

She had… a *what?*

Izzy's mouth worked soundlessly, and she looked at Georgie in complete and utter bewilderment.

Georgie felt her pain. Izzy was a bit helpless when it came to things like this, having such limited experience, though she was warm and comfortable enough with anybody in social situations. But callers she did not have, especially of the male sort, and the idea that one should suddenly be at her door was nothing short of terrifying.

"Who is it, Bessie?" Georgie asked, putting a hand over Izzy's soothingly.

"Captain Anthony Sterling, Miss Allen."

Charlotte barked a surprised laugh, then covered her mouth quickly.

Georgie looked at her cousin very slowly. How, exactly, had her cousin come to know a man well enough for him to call upon her without telling her about it? They lived together, for pity's sake! They had adjoining bedchambers!

Izzy shook her head quickly, her eyes still wide and her skin paling.

"Did he say what he wants?" Grace asked with all politeness, eyeing the cousins curiously.

"No, ma'am. He did say he understood it to be a little against custom, but as he is newly returned to London, he thought he might prevail upon Miss Lambert for a brief time this afternoon, as he knows nobody else."

"He knows his cousins," Georgie snapped. "Why not prevail upon them?"

"Now, now, Georgie," Charlotte soothed with a mischievous twinkle in her eye. "If our good captain has taken a fancy to Isabella, we mustn't restrict his attempts."

"I've only met him once," Izzy whispered, still looking a bit windswept. "He was… he was very polite, very kind, and seemed genuinely interested in what I had to say. But it was never anything to suggest… He wanted to know about the other guests, and I told him. And then we played whist, and that was it!"

Charlotte clapped her hands, then rubbed them together. "Send the man up, and let us see what we have."

Georgie shook her head at once as both Izzy *and* Prue looked utterly terrified at the thought. "No, he has come to call upon Izzy. I will accompany her as chaperone, and the rest of you will stay put until we return." She looked at her cousin for confirmation, which was given in a brisk nod.

They rose as one and Izzy turned to Bessie. "You may show Captain Sterling into the drawing room, Bessie. Georgie and I will see him there."

Bessie bobbed quickly with a soft "Yes, Miss Lambert," and then turned to do as she was bid.

Georgie took Izzy's arm and the two of them moved from the room while the other girls began to titter softly amongst themselves.

"Steady, Izzy," Georgie murmured. "It's only a call, not a proposal."

Izzy snorted a soft laugh. "This is true. Poor man probably

thought I expected it. I shall have to disillusion him slowly."

"And very gently," Georgie added. "These soldiering types may not understand propriety. He might be very confused by all of this."

Izzy gave her a scolding look. "Now you've made him sound pathetic."

She shrugged one shoulder. "He might be, you never know."

"I've met him, remember. He's not."

Georgie bit her tongue and restrained a sigh. There was no point in pressing the matter, and Izzy was no longer nervous, so she had accomplished what she'd intended. Whatever Captain Sterling wanted, it was bound to be something to tell the other girls about, one way or the other.

They waited only a few moments for Bessie to bring Captain Sterling to the drawing room, and Georgie was surprised by the sight of him.

He was handsome, almost remarkably so, and very tall, which she had always appreciated. He wore the usual garb of a gentleman rather than his uniform, which instantly made Georgie more inclined to approve of him. Soldiers who had resigned their commission ought not to pretend to still be in possession of it, particularly when the sole purpose was to attract young women who were easily swayed by regimentals.

He bowed very smartly, and wore a small, polite smile, but nothing out of the realm of politeness.

Very odd.

"Miss Lambert," Captain Sterling said in a warm tone, "I hope you'll forgive the impertinence of my calling unexpectedly like this. I know it is not done, but I hoped I might further our acquaintance, and I did not know how else to go about it."

Izzy smiled with fondness, as she usually did. "I don't mind at all, sir. Do you know my cousin, Miss Georgiana Allen?"

He turned to Georgie and his smile broadened. "I do not. A pleasure, Miss Allen."

Georgie curtseyed, as was polite. "Thank you, Captain."

"Please, Captain, do be seated," Izzy said, gesturing for him to do so.

He nodded and moved to the couch, and Georgie watched him

carefully. There was something about him she did not trust, but she would reserve judgment until she had cause.

"It is actually quite fortunate that you are here as well, Miss Allen," Captain Sterling began, still smiling. "I know very little of the members of Society, which is my primary reason for calling today. I had the pleasure of meeting Miss Lambert yesterday at Mrs. Wilton's card party, and she knew so much about the guests there, I felt sure she would be an excellent choice to help me find my way about London."

The words rang with truth and politeness and were certainly the things that Georgie would want to have said about Izzy. But she couldn't give him the satisfaction. She tilted her head. "Would not your cousins be able to give you a fair introduction wherever you needed? They've been about Society long enough and know you far better than Isabella would."

Izzy stiffened beside her, and Georgie saw her mouth tighten a little.

Captain Sterling, however, only raised a brow. "My cousin, Lord Sterling, is lately married, Miss Allen. I did not think Lady Sterling would appreciate my interference as they adjust to married life."

"They've been married for over a year," Georgie pointed out, not bothering to moderate the cynicism in her tone.

"And still quite besotted, Miss Allen. Trust me, I am safer here. Besides, I think Lady Sterling wishes me to marry, and I've no desire to let her choose a bride for me at every opportunity."

Georgie nearly reared back in shock, and she fought a laugh. A man who did not wish to marry was calling upon a spinster for social introductions? It was so beyond anything.

But she kept her composure. She mustn't let on that she found him amusing, if a little ridiculous. "And your cousin Mr. Hugh Sterling?" she prodded, still sounding doubtful. "Surely he could be of some help."

Captain Sterling suddenly looked so sardonic, it was all she could do to maintain a straight face. "Would you want my cousin to give you any sort of social introductions?"

Georgie made a face. "I'm afraid not, but I don't know Mr. Sterling well enough to say much."

"Clearly enough to say something."

"He's not my relation."

Captain Sterling smiled slyly. "No, Miss Allen, he is mine. And because he is mine, and I know him so well, I am here instead of there, because I have it on very good authority that between you and Miss Lambert, I am destined to find a far better introduction to Society than anything my foolhardy cousin thinks worth his while."

Georgie heard Izzy give a very small laugh beside her and glanced over to find her cousin clamping down on her lips hard.

Well, *that* was not particularly helpful.

She gave Captain Sterling a hard look. "Why would a pair of spinsters be able to give you any better social advice than anyone else? Surely you've heard about us."

He raised his brows in surprise and crossed one leg over the other, seeming to relax into the couch. "I have. And I stand by what I said. More than that, I've read the Spinster Chronicles, and I found it insightful, witty, and altogether too true." He cocked his head, his smile fading back into a small one she could not read. "And written by more than one author, if I am not mistaken. Do you share the duties or is one of you the primary writer?"

"We share it," Izzy answered before Georgie could tell him off. "Differing points of view, you know."

He nodded sagely. "Very wise."

"I'm sorry, Captain Sterling," Georgie interrupted, sitting forward, "but what exactly are you doing here?"

He considered her for a moment, then let his lips curve into a more attractive smirk than she would have expected from him. "To be perfectly candid, Miss Allen, I came to offer myself to the Spinsters. With a capital S."

Now Izzy did laugh, though it was more of a squawk than anything else, and she clamped a hand over her mouth.

Georgie stared at Captain Sterling with narrowed eyes, altogether too suspicious to find any amusement in his words. "And how would offering yourself to a group of well-educated, well-bred, well-adjusted young ladies be of any help at all?"

"Because most of London complains about the lot of you, despite rather enjoying your column, and I think there is a massive misunderstanding that needs to be explored." He shrugged and folded his hands neatly over one slender knee. "I think you need someone to vouch for you on the other side."

"You don't even know what we do," Georgie pointed out.

He considered that for a brief moment. "True, which would mean you would have to bring me into your confidence, at least partially." He shook his head in a pitying sort of way. "Trust me, the impression of Society in general is much exaggerated and fairly skewed."

"How would you know?" Georgie demanded, wishing she had the ability to raise only one brow so she might look more disconcerting. "You've only just met me."

Captain Sterling's look was rather frank. "And you've left an impression. One I am inclined to consider as your true self. Not to mention that I have met Miss Lambert and found her to be a perfectly agreeable young woman, which conflicted sharply with what I'd been told of your group. I knew the general consensus had to be incorrect." He smiled blandly. "Except perhaps for you, Miss Allen, but as you said, we have only just met. Perhaps that will change."

Georgie ought to have been offended. She ought to have stormed out of the room and demanded he leave her aunt's house this very moment. She ought to have done any number of things. But heaven help her, she quite liked his frankness, and all she wanted to do was grin outright.

Which she could not do.

"Hmm," was all she managed to say.

Captain Sterling quirked his brows at her, and Georgie let her glance slide to Izzy, who could barely contain herself, her cheeks flushed with emotion.

Georgie held up a finger and rose as gracefully as she could, which was actually quite graceful, and moved to the hallway. "Elinor?" she called, grateful the parlor wasn't so far away that her behavior would be considered unusual.

"Yes?" came the almost frantic response, which told Georgie that the girls had been trying to listen without actually leaving the parlor. Soon enough, Elinor's head appeared through the doorway, a would-be innocent expression on her face that could not contain her eagerness.

Georgie gave her a rather devious look. "What do we know about Captain Sterling?"

Elinor's eyes widened, and she dashed out of sight.

"I beg your pardon?" Captain Sterling asked from within the drawing room.

Georgie turned to look back at him patiently. "One moment, Captain, if you please."

He turned a quizzical look to Izzy, but she was as loyal as ever and only smiled indulgently.

"Captain Anthony Sterling?" Elinor called back.

"That's the one," Georgie replied, rolling her eyes. "Unless you know of another Captain Sterling."

The man in question snorted softly, and Georgie gave him a warning look, which prompted him to put up his hands in surrender and compose himself.

"Single," Elinor said as she appeared in the doorway, her journal in hand.

"Well, there's a surprise," Georgie muttered.

"I heard that," Captain Sterling protested.

She ignored him.

"No outstanding gambling debts," Elinor continued, "a commendable record with the military, no courtships of note, no jiltings, and no scandals." She scanned down the page with her finger. "Let me see… Suspected fortune of around seven thousand a year, which has yet to be confirmed. One brother, a doctor in Dorset. His stepmother is still living, and there is an aunt, her sister. High marks at school, a fair rider, and…" She broke off with a hiss.

"What?" Captain Sterling called from his seat. "What was that for?"

Elinor wrinkled up her nose and gave Georgie a look. "No houses. Not a one."

Captain Sterling groaned. "I'm a younger son! We don't have houses!"

"Captain Sterling," Georgie scolded firmly, "if you cannot behave yourself, you will remove yourself from the room."

He glared at her. "Am I to receive poor marks based solely on the order of my birth? I haven't had time to secure permanent lodgings for myself, because I have been *in the army.*"

Izzy cleared her throat. "This is true, Georgie."

Georgie looked at her cousin with narrowed eyes, then turned to the impertinent captain on her aunt's couch. "Captain Sterling, I congratulate you. You have attained a status of approved gentleman, which means that should you have been interested in courtship or marriage, we would consider you a respectable candidate for any of the young ladies looking for a suitable partner."

He looked mildly surprised, then his brow furrowed. "Are you... matchmakers?"

"Sometimes," Izzy chirped with a laugh. "You'd be surprised how many young ladies come to us for advice. We know quite a lot, particularly about the eligible members of Society."

"The men?" he asked with genuine interest.

"Oh, the women, too," Izzy replied. "Sometimes we are approached to assist in finding a young woman that would be suitable for a man we have approved of."

"Do they know of your approval?"

Georgie scoffed loudly. "Of course not. We don't need to have people parading about for our good opinion. I didn't mean to encourage you or puff you up. I only wanted..."

"To demonstrate what you were capable of and intimidate me in a show of force," he finished easily. "Yes, I could see that, and it was masterfully done. But it does not answer the question as to whether or not I could be of use to you." He adjusted his coat and smiled very politely. "I have stated my reasons, and you have the resources to know of their certainty. If you feel you must leave to discuss the offer, please feel free to do so."

Impertinent man.

Georgie glowered and was preparing a rather excellent vitriol when Izzy surprised her by rising and curtseying. "Thank you, Captain," her traitorous cousin said with all warmth and gentility. "We shall only be a moment."

Georgie sputtered as Izzy took her arm and pulled her from the room and back into the parlor with their friends, where she quickly gave them the basics of the situation.

"He wants... to be one of us?" Grace asked as she looked around in confusion.

Charlotte's brow was furrowed in thought. "Or is he offering to be our spy?"

"I have no idea," Georgie sighed, shaking her head. "It's one of the most ridiculous things I have ever heard. Clearly the man is absolutely bored and looking to have a laugh with some of his idiotic friends, all of whom are tired of our interference and determined to put a stop to it. I was going to turn him out of the house, but Izzy seemed to think it was worth some discussion."

As if on cue, each of the girls turned to look at Izzy.

She stared at them and shrugged with a small smile. "What? He is very nice. And terribly witty, you should have heard the way he talked to Georgie."

That piqued their interest, and now they all turned to Georgie. "Really?" Charlotte asked in a blatantly suggestive tone, a small smirk on her lips.

Georgie huffed a little. "He didn't let me have my own way, if that makes you feel any better."

"Oh, it does," Charlotte assured her.

"I had a very good impression of him from the card party," Izzy said now, her tone apologetic. "And if he is willing to help us, I don't see why we shouldn't let him."

"Because we know nothing about him!" Georgie protested hotly. "Of course you had a good impression of him, he was *trying* to leave a good impression! Anybody can be polite for the course of an hour when it suits them!"

Grace made a pained face. "That's very true."

Even Charlotte looked unconvinced. "I have to agree, though I'm still inclined to let him try purely for the sake of adventure."

"He was very kind and considerate with me," Prue broke in softly.

Whatever anyone else was going to say died at those words, and they all stared at Prue in shock.

"Prue," Izzy murmured, her eyes wide, "you... you know Captain Sterling?"

She nodded with a very small smile, her cheeks coloring slightly.

"We were introduced at the ball the other night. He came over to pay his respects to Lady Hetty, and she introduced us. He sat beside me and talked to me as if I were anyone, and it was as if my nerves and stammer did not bother him one bit. And then he asked me to dance, and he was quite good at it. Very patient, considering I'm so shy." She smiled further. "Lady Hetty likes him, she told me afterwards. And I did, too."

Georgie stared at Prue in wonder, then frowned and looked back at Izzy. "Well, I can't very well refuse *both* of you," she muttered, frustrated at being so perfectly foiled, and at the warmth that had spread through her at Prue's story. She rose and moved to the door. "Captain Sterling!"

Moments later he appeared in the doorway of the drawing room, not venturing into the corridor. "Miss Allen?"

"One further question." She folded her hands before her, clearing her throat. "We must ask it, you understand, as you will take on much by joining with us. What would make you a proper candidate? By your own accounts, you're not particularly well-known in London currently, nor are you likely to be, aside from altering your personality."

Captain Sterling smiled. "You forget, madam, that I was a soldier for many years. There were numerous times when I was of service in less... obvious ways to my superiors. I am more than qualified to collect gossip on candidates of your choosing for the good of Society." His smile grew on one side. "And I'll admit, I'm anxious to see what you and your Spinsters are all about, and how you operate."

Georgie stared at him for a long moment, then sighed heavily. "Oh, all right, come on over here and meet the rest of them."

He inclined his head without the slightest hint of victory and came over to the door.

"Captain Anthony Sterling," she intoned flatly, "may I present the writers of the Spinster Chronicles? Miss Westfall and Miss Lambert you already know. In the pink is Miss Morledge, in the blue is Miss Wright, and the girl in the yellow is Miss Asheley."

Captain Sterling bowed perfectly, and each of the girls behaved appropriately as well. "Delighted to make the acquaintance of you all," he said, sounding as if he truly meant it.

"A pleasure, Captain," Grace replied with her usual charm and grace.

He nodded at her. "So how does this work, ladies? How does one become part of your group? There are several unmarried ladies in and about London, yet only six of you."

"Five," Georgie corrected quickly. "Miss Asheley is not of an age to be a spinster."

Captain Sterling looked at her in surprise. "Yet she is here."

Georgie nodded and gave Elinor a scolding look. "She refuses to accept that she cannot possibly be a spinster before three-and-twenty. And even that is a stretch."

"I don't see why not," Elinor grumped, folding her arms petulantly. "I am not going to marry any sooner than any of you, so that should make me just as much of a spinster as anyone."

They all groaned again, and Charlotte reached out to pat her cheek. "When you have lived as long as we have, darling, you might understand."

Elinor scowled and batted her hand away.

"Elinor is very helpful," Izzy said quickly, no doubt desperate to make up for the poor impression. "We value her insight greatly, and she has been useful in helping us find topics for our column."

"No doubt," Captain Sterling murmured, still eyeing the girl with some hesitation.

"I'm not sure I mind being a spinster so much," Grace mused thoughtfully. "It's all I know, so it's really quite comfortable."

Now Captain Sterling frowned. "So, you're all spinsters... on purpose?"

Georgie turned to him with all seriousness. "No, Captain Sterling, not on purpose. Unless it is a unified plot by all of the men in England to abjectly avoid us. None of us chose our situation."

"I did!" Charlotte proclaimed proudly with a wave of her hand.

Now Georgie rolled her eyes. "Except for Miss Wright, who is wildly unconventional and very disillusioned. Ignore her."

Captain Sterling chuckled, and it was unfortunately a rather warm and pleasant sound. "Determined to be independent forever, Miss Wright?" he asked, considering her with a teasing smile.

Charlotte dipped her chin playfully. "Naturally. But it does not follow that I must remain unmarried. I simply refuse to settle with anything less than a man brought to his knees for love of me just as I am, and for my own heart to be inclined the same."

Grace coughed in surprise, and Prue flushed at once.

"Oh, is that all?" the captain replied mildly.

"Don't encourage her," Georgie muttered. "She's turned down five proposals already, and a sixth will come next week, and apparently she has decided to refuse that one as well."

"Too right!" Charlotte crowed with a clap of her hands. "Nothing but the very best for me!"

"Which leaves a boring monotony for the rest of us," Prue pointed out, giving Charlotte a serious look.

"I don't plan on being boring," Grace responded. "Married or not, I'd like to be exciting. Or at the very least, entertaining."

"It's a right sight better than being 'nice,' I'd imagine," Izzy chimed in, making a face.

Georgie sighed, shaking her head. "This is who we are, Captain." She cocked her head at him and put her hands on her hips. "Are you going to run for the safety of home now?"

He stared at her for a long moment, then slowly smiled, and something in Georgie's chest gave a little at the sight. "On the contrary, Miss Allen. I don't think there's any place I'd rather be."

Chapter Five

———⁙⁂⁙———

True understanding requires complete openness in conversation and a willingness to listen intently. Without either of those, hope is lost. If, however, partial understanding is all that is required, one must only share what one wishes to share, and listen with politeness. Respond when it is required. Nod on occasion. And then promptly forget the whole thing.

-The Spinster Chronicles, 30 June 1817

Life was bound to change once he had gotten himself accepted into the Spinsters, but Tony hadn't really anticipated exactly how much.

The first thing to go had been formality, and he chafed at the idea. He wasn't stuffy, and had no compunction against familiarity, but it was one thing to be able to call at someone's home when one wished and another to be able to call someone by whatever name one wished. He doubted it would ever be natural for him to call any of them by their shortened names, but it was especially awkward when they had not been acquainted for long.

"There's no point in following polite rules of Society," Charlotte had told him the day before. "We've transcended all the rest, so why not do away with that as well?"

"But won't it raise suspicions if I call you Charlotte instead of Miss Wright?" he'd asked in confusion. "People do love to gossip."

She snorted softly. "They do, and they will, but not because you call me Charlotte. Loads of people call me Charlotte, and without my permission. They'll talk because you are being seen with the Spinsters, and no one will know what to make of that."

Tony had already determined that he was not going to be effusive with any of the girls, nor was he going to sit around with them as if he were one of them. He was going to behave just as he always had, and as any particular situation called for. He was not *joining* the Spinsters; he was only investigating them. Helping them, if he had to, and quite honestly, amusing himself.

He would do all in his power to limit any conversation connecting him to them, not because he was ashamed or wanted to hide it, but because he didn't think it needed to be talked about. They certainly didn't need to be talked about more than they already were, and he refused to give Society reason to increase that.

Most of the Spinsters had insisted that he call them by their Christian names, with the only exception being Miss Westfall, who was too shy to do anything remotely resembling an encouragement of familiarity. While he knew her name was Prudence, and the others called her Prue, he would not until she was more comfortable. He may think of her that way, but he could not, in good conscience, verbalize it.

Miss Allen appeared to be ambivalent to absolutely everything where he was concerned. She'd frowned a little at everyone offering up their Christian names for him, and only shrugged when the others suggested she do the same. It was not a refusal, but it certainly was not encouragement. He might prod her, though, and test her proprietary bounds where familiarity was concerned. He rather liked her name and found himself trying not to smile whenever someone said "Georgie".

He, of course, had given them all power to call him whatever they wished, whether that be Captain or Sterling or Tony. He did insist on never being Anthony, however, as only Miranda called him that, and only when she was being cross or superior.

They were all agreed, however, that propriety must be observed in public settings. They did have a reputation to live up to, and they really ought not to scandalize everyone when they were trying so hard to be of use to them.

The other thing that had struck Tony about being so adopted by the group was that his social calendar suddenly became quite demanding. He wouldn't have thought it, but this particular group of spinsters, no capital S required, was highly sought-after and were invited to practically everything. Not necessarily all of them, but between the group, there were opportunities everywhere.

And when one or two were invited, they were sure to have Tony added to the list of invitees. He'd told them it wasn't necessary, as he was quite able to obtain his own invitations, but they insisted it was no trouble. Miranda and his aunt Arabella had trained him long ago to never argue with women, and Tony was convinced he had lived a much longer life than he would have otherwise by adhering to that wisdom.

This morning, for example, he was to attend a small garden party hosted by Mr. and Mrs. Galbraith, whose two grown daughters were catching the eye of every eligible man in England, not just London, and they were being notoriously conservative about which of those gentlemen they admitted into their acquaintance. It was astonishing enough that Tony had managed to be so included, let alone that he had managed by himself. He attributed that small victory to the fact that Mr. Galbraith had been a military man, and they had been introduced a few days before the invitations had been sent out.

No doubt they were hoping that an honorable man with a similar military background would jump at the chance to make a match with one of their daughters.

They would undoubtedly be mistaken.

There was yet another shift in his life that association with the Spinsters had brought him rather quickly. He could no longer make his own impressions about people in Society, as he would be given a complete profile and background on any individual of interest. He had been fully briefed on both Galbraith sisters in the days before the party, as well as who their most likely suitors were, and their profiles as well.

He knew far more about the regular members of Society than he suspected anyone else did within their circles, and he was beyond impressed with the skills of his newfound associates. If all of this turned out to be as accurate as he suspected it was, he would have to consider recommending them to the Home and Foreign Offices as potential operatives.

He pulled up to the Galbraith home and was shown in without question or a word of greeting, once his invitation had been presented. After a silent march behind the designated servant along two different corridors, he was brought out to the terrace, in full view of all the other guests.

Mr. and Mrs. Galbraith awaited him, smiling warmly. That confirmed his suspicions. They wanted him for their daughters.

A pity, that. The girls had made him so aware of the nature of the Galbraith daughters that, although well-bred and well-off, he had no desire to pursue either of them. And if what he had heard of the sisters was true, they would not want him either.

Still, politeness was important.

Tony smiled as he bowed in greeting to his hosts, made polite conversation for the briefest of moments, then proceeded forth as the other guests were doing. Only now most of the guests were staring at him.

Brilliant.

He exhaled slowly, carefully maintaining his pleasant demeanor, and searched for anyone he knew. Conversation would be key for making the staring cease, unless he spoke with someone rather shocking.

That ruled out any of the Spinsters, then. At least for the first few minutes.

What he wouldn't give to have some of his friends and comrades here now. Henshaw, at least, would have been a comfort and found amusement in it. Morton would have been just as uncomfortable as Tony was, but he would have come anyway. He would have been pleased to see either of them, probably more than he ever had in his life.

He took a glass of punch from a footman's tray with a nod, then moved in the direction of the other guests, not quite knowing his destination.

His cousins were not here.

He couldn't talk to the Spinsters yet.

Which left...

Lady Hetty.

Perfect.

She watched him come, as there really was no mistaking the fact that he was heading in her direction. She had no one directly around her, and it was clear she did not care one whit about it. The teacup and saucer in her hand were carefully placed on the small table beside her while she shook her head slowly from side to side.

"Hopeless," she croaked, coughing slightly. "Absolutely hopeless."

"What is hopeless, my lady?" Tony asked after bowing politely.

Lady Hetty gave him a droll sort of look that was impossible to mistake. "You are hopeless, Captain."

Tony smiled in spite of himself. "Am I? How so?"

"You did not come to a garden party to converse with a crotchety old spinster like me, and yet here you are." She waved a hand at him wildly. "Conversing with me, despite the fact that no one else is doing so."

"Perhaps I like conversing with you, Lady Hetty," he offered mildly, "despite your self-proclaimed crotchety spinster state."

She coughed once in disbelief and reached for her tea again. "Nobody likes conversing with me, Captain Sterling."

He shook his head at her. "Not true. I could make a list of people who do enjoy conversing with you."

"They'd all be lying."

"Not all, surely." He looked around and saw Izzy not too far away. "I'm sure Miss Lambert enjoys conversing with you."

"She doesn't count," Lady Hetty protested with a snort. "She probably enjoys conversing with everyone."

Tony bit back a laugh at that, because it was so true. Izzy was a very agreeable person, and she was far too kind to ever pretend that she found anyone otherwise. He suspected she was not quite so nice as everyone believed her to be, but she was not doing anything to alter that perception of her.

"You should go speak with her," Lady Hetty continued after taking a careful sip of her tea. "She would enjoy that."

"But you just said she enjoys conversing with everyone," Tony reminded her. "That's not much to induce me to join the throng."

Lady Hetty scowled at him. "You will never marry if you talk like that. And you will never marry if you stand here speaking to me."

Tony shrugged and sipped his punch. "At the moment, marriage is not of great concern to me. Perhaps I will just marry you, my lady."

That made the older woman laugh heartily and drew several pairs of eyes in their direction.

"Oh, Captain Sterling," Lady Hetty said, once she had recovered herself. "That would not help your case at all."

Tony sighed heavily. "So, I shouldn't ask for your hand?"

She beamed at him, her lined face creasing further still. "No, indeed, but you have earned the seat beside me, should you wish it."

He inclined his head. "Thank you, my lady. I do." He took the indicated seat and crossed one leg over the other, surveying the gathering. A few still stared at him, wondering at his choice in companion at the moment, no doubt, but the rest seemed to mind their own business.

The Galbraith daughters were surrounded, as they ought to have been, though it did not appear that there were any forerunners for the position of husband to either.

"So, who will win out, do you think?" Tony asked her, indicating the group with a nod.

Lady Hetty snorted softly. "None of those fools, I can promise you that. They may appear to be fine candidates on paper, but the reality is far less enticing."

"The girls or the men?"

Lady Hetty hummed an almost laugh. "Cheeky, Sterling. That will do."

"For what?"

"Your own prospects."

Tony gave her a wry look. "I have none."

She returned his look very frankly. "An attractive army captain who earned a pretty penny from his service? I'd call those some fair prospects."

He rolled his eyes a little, smiling. "I mean potential candidates, my lady. I have none. I am not looking."

"Well, they are, so you'd better watch your step." She took up her tea again, making a face. "This isn't that good. I would have thought Lucinda Galbraith capable of better."

Tony was almost taken aback by that. Not that Lady Hetty saying such a thing was so extreme, for it really was quite tame for her, but the idea that a woman should be capable of a better tea. Was that a mark that ought to have distinguished a woman?

Whether or not Miranda's tea had ever been noteworthy wasn't something he had ever noticed, he just drank it.

Who noticed things like that?

"Why should Mrs. Galbraith do better?" Tony asked, puzzled by the thought. "Is the tea that bad?"

Lady Hetty shook her head, frowning at him. "No, it isn't. It's simply not that good."

"And Mrs. Galbraith?"

"She was the most accomplished girl in her time," Lady Hetty explained, leaning closer to impart the secret. "Everybody said so, and she never refuted it."

"And making a good tea is a mark of accomplishment?"

Lady Hetty reared back, her expression almost scandalized. "Good heavens, man, are you really so ignorant as to what makes a woman accomplished?"

Tony chuckled helplessly and shrugged a shoulder. "I didn't think so, but apparently I've missed a few marks there. Tell me, then, and relieve me of my ignorance."

"Making tea isn't an obvious accomplishment, I grant you," Lady Hetty commented with a soft grunt of approval. "It is simply one of the finer points. Any woman can be taught to dance or to sing or to draw, and the intelligent ones may speak French or German, if not both. Any accomplished girl will possess the appropriate mannerisms, poise, and comportment, while the truly gifted may also have grace, and elegance."

"And all of that is supposed to be customary?" Tony inquired, no longer quite so amused.

She nodded, giving him a wry look. "You truly know nothing of accomplished women?"

Tony smiled apologetically. "I have no sisters, Lady Hetty, and my stepmother never said anything on the subject. I do have one female cousin, but I have always considered her a child in my mind, so I cannot say anything about her accomplishment other than the fact that she apparently is so." His smile turned wry. "I think you will find that most men know absolutely nothing about what makes a woman really accomplished."

"Well, that's no surprise, is it?" Lady Hetty cackled a laugh to herself, seeming quite pleased with her wit. "Any woman can be accomplished, Captain, and on paper, so many are. But it is really in the finer details that you will find the important matters."

"As in a good tea?" he suggested, not bothering to hide the note of derision.

She looked back at him, trying not to smile. "Now you are teasing me, Captain."

"I would never."

"Oh, you would, and it is one of your own finer points." She patted his hand warmly. "You're not puffed up like so many other men of your age and station. A more ridiculous conglomeration of pincushions I haven't seen in years."

"One would ask how many," Tony murmured with a smile, "but I am not so naïve."

Lady Hetty ignored that comment, as was undoubtedly too kind. "You should be associating with more young people, Captain Sterling, not wasting your time on an old woman like me."

Tony grinned at her, even though she was frowning now. "Perhaps I enjoy your company, my lady."

"Be that as it may," she scolded, her eyes twinkling despite her frown, "we can do better for you. Go and speak to someone within a decade of your age."

"That would require me to be acquainted with anyone present that met those conditions," Tony sighed. "Alas, I am not. My cousins are not here, nor is your friend Miss Westfall. I haven't made many acquaintances since my arrival, and I cannot say that I am particularly social. I haven't even been introduced to the Galbraith daughters, only the father and mother."

"It is not worth being acquainted with the daughters," Lady Hetty assured him with another pat to his hand. "Lacking in more of those finer points I mentioned, despite being accomplished enough. Too brash, too silly, and too comfortable with their fine way of life. And I can say this, being a relation."

"Are you really?" he asked with interest. "I had no idea."

She nodded, pursing her lips a little. "I'm a cousin of Mr. Galbraith, though not from the side of the family with ties to the peerage, much to their dismay. Not that it stops them from claiming to be cousins of the Duke of Rothsbury. Thirty years ago, it was true, but my brother couldn't figure out how to produce legitimate offspring, and so the title fell to our cousin and his heirs, who reproduce remarkably well." Lady Hetty shook her head in disgust. "He had one duty to see to that mattered, and he couldn't manage it. Poor Henry."

Sensing she was rapidly losing track of the conversation at hand, Tony cleared his throat. "So, you maintain this connection with the Galbraiths?"

Lady Hetty looked over at him as if she had forgotten he was there. "Someone has to remind them of the true nature of their station. And, as you see, I am still invited out of politeness. I am their only distinguished relation remaining. Why else do you think I would have come to this silly soirée of theirs? Family duty. Now I needn't attend at Christmas, for which I am vastly relieved."

Tony coughed a laugh into his fist. There was something utterly refreshing about holding a conversation with a woman who had no false modesty or reserve, who had no qualms about saying exactly what she thought and did not care what anybody else thought. Granted, he was quite sure that Lady Hetty had not been nearly so outspoken in her younger years, no matter what degree of cynicism her thoughts might have carried. Age had emboldened her, as did her comfortable station in life.

Some found her to be somewhat tyrannical and intolerable, but Tony rather liked her frankness and open temperament. She did not tolerate fools, nor did she hesitate to identify them, and that alone made her a favorite of his.

It helped that his stepmother had always admired Lady Hetty and had frequently said so. As Tony had always regarded Miranda as someone worthy of admiration, her good opinion carried much weight with him.

And thus, Lady Hetty would as well.

"Give me your opinion, then, Lady Hetty," Tony murmured,

leaning forward to speak further in confidence. "Whom should I bring into my acquaintance at this gathering?"

She glanced around the garden with a speculative look. "Well, there's not many, I can tell you that. My relations have always allowed the most peculiar mixture of people into their society. I am far more selective."

That was certainly putting it mildly, but Tony thought it best not to bring that up.

"Hmm." Lady Hetty's eyes narrowed as she continued to scan the gathering. "Mr. Sandford is a fair fellow. Quiet man, which speaks well of him, but very polite, which says nothing at all. You could liven him up, I have no doubt."

"Thank you for your vote of confidence," Tony muttered.

"Mr. Shaw would be your sort," Lady Hetty went on without marking him. "Agreeable man, and the younger brother of Lord Radcliffe. Keeps to himself, tends to his duties, and doesn't mind talking with the old women. Probably because his aunt is one, and he dotes on her prodigiously, but we mustn't fault him for Augusta. And he also seems entirely uninterested in marriage, which would make the two of you quite a pair."

Tony looked at the man she was indicating, who stood just outside of a group of people without looking as though he were being excluded. He could have taken two steps to his left and been in their midst, and yet he remained where he was, his expression one of careful vacancy. There was no telling what he thought, but he did not look particularly displeased.

He knew nothing of Shaw, but he did look like the sort of man Tony had come to appreciate, the sort of man who would be a wise and intelligent man of sense.

He'd consider that one.

"But as for the women..." Lady Hetty continued, her tone turning more intrigued.

"Don't go selecting potential wives for me, Lady Hetty," Tony warned. "I get enough of that from Miranda and my cousin, Lady Sterling. I couldn't bear it from you as well."

Lady Hetty turned her gaze to him, quirking a brow. "You don't have to marry them, Captain, but it wouldn't hurt you to talk to them.

And you'll have far less rumors floating around about you if you do. Otherwise people will wonder what in the world is wrong with you."

This really was too much, and it was all Tony could do to keep from laughing. "Well, we couldn't have that."

"Certainly not." Lady Hetty rapped her walking stick on the ground then. "Come, take me for a stroll, Captain. I shall make your introductions."

"Oh, no, Lady Hetty," Tony protested at once. "I couldn't. You must sit here and take your ease."

She wagged a ringed finger under his nose suddenly. "Don't you say one word about my age or condition, Captain Sterling. I am still on this earth and I will continue to act as though I am. I'm not asking you to drive me around in a phaeton. Walk me around the garden."

Tony knew better than to argue with a woman possibly twice his age about what she could and could not do. He rose and held out his hand, which she promptly took, hauling herself out of the chair with his aid. She nodded, looped her hand through his arm, and indicated that they should move on.

Despite her small frame and increasing years, Lady Hetty had lost none of her posture. She still held her head high, glided as proudly as any fine woman, and Tony was positive that if he let her walk on her own, she would have done so without any tremor or unsteadiness in her step. She dipped her chin with surprising modesty when acknowledged by others, yet at the same time she lost none of her poise.

"Not there," she suddenly barked, yanking on his arm a little. "I don't want to endure Mrs. Davies or her insipid daughter, and neither do you."

"Apologies," Tony said in a quiet voice, keeping his smile polite. "Where do you suggest we go?"

She pointed her walking stick towards a small group near a carefully trimmed hedge. "That's a sensible group. Take me there."

Tony steered her in the direction she'd indicated. "What makes that particular group sensible?" he inquired.

"Miss Allen is part of it," Lady Hetty said bluntly. "She brings good sense everywhere."

That hadn't exactly been Tony's experience with her, but he

wasn't about to bring that up. "Does she, indeed?"

"Do you know Miss Allen?" Lady Hetty asked in return, no doubt hearing the doubtful note he failed to hide.

"A very little," he admitted. "That is… We have been introduced."

His response was apparently lacking, for Lady Hetty grunted softly to herself. "And you said you were not acquainted with anyone here. So like a man. You mark my words, Captain Sterling, you couldn't do better for a wife than Georgiana Allen."

"I am sure she is a very…"

"And I do mean you, sir," she interrupted, intentionally stabbing his toe with her walking stick. "I'm not speaking generally. *You*, sir, could not do better."

Tony chewed his lip in irritation, wishing he had chosen to stand alone in a small patch of sunlight instead of conversing with Lady Hetty. Curse his unsuspecting naïveté. Of course she would be a champion for Georgie; they were so alike in temperament and wit.

But to choose him specifically? For her? It was beyond anything.

"Then it is fortunate that you are taking me there, my lady," Tony managed to say, giving her a wry look, "so that I may plead my case to her."

Lady Hetty chuckled and grinned up at him. "As I said, cheeky. You'll do well for her. But you'll have to wear her down first, Captain. She's a mite feisty."

Tony smirked as he looked over at the group, now aware of their approach, and at Georgie herself, who was watching him come with disapproval and warning.

"Feisty, you say?" Tony murmured. "Dear me."

They were upon the group now, and Lady Hetty gave him a fair introduction to all present, ending, ironically enough, with Georgie.

"And I believe you are acquainted with Miss Allen, Captain," she said, smiling almost dotingly at Georgie.

"We are, my lady, a little," Tony replied, bowing politely to Georgie. "How are you, Miss Allen?"

"Well enough, Captain, thank you," Georgie told him, somehow managing not to snarl, though he suspected she was dismembering him in her mind. "The day is a trifle warm for my taste."

He nodded knowingly, composing his features into utter politeness. "It is rather, is it not? I do feel so for you ladies in all your finery, coming out in weather such as this. It must be positively plaguing to you all."

The other ladies in the group smile and blushed, while the men looked as though they had never considered that but decided to be sympathetic anyway.

"That's not the only plaguing thing," Georgie muttered, picking at her white muslin skirts.

"Captain, did you see much of the war when you were in the army?" one of the girls asked with an unmistakable glint in her eyes. "It all sounds very heroic."

Tony shook his head. "No, ma'am, I did not. We had our share of scuffles, to be sure, but the true heroes were in other companies than mine and are far better men."

"I don't doubt that," Georgie added under her breath, coughing and smiling for effect.

"Why do you not wear your regimentals, Captain?" Miss Wells asked, though her arm was linked through a slender man beside her. "They are so very fine."

"Not that fine," came Georgie's retort with another light cough.

Tony turned to her with a concerned look. "Miss Allen, are you well? Come, let me take you for a glass of lemonade."

Georgie glared at him, but she knew better than to snap at him when he had personally addressed her. She gave him a false smile. "Thank you, Captain."

He turned to the man beside him. "Mr. Greensley, would you see to Lady Hetty? I hate to abandon her."

Greensley, surprisingly, did not seem to mind at all. He seemed close to grinning outright. "Indeed, sir. I shall offer my arm." He did so, smiling now at Lady Hetty.

"As if that's a comfort," Lady Hetty grumbled, taking his arm and smiling anyway.

Tony offered his now free arm to Georgie, and she reluctantly took it, letting him steer her away.

"Claws in, for heaven's sake," Tony muttered through a smile. "No one else needs to know of your spite."

Georgie's jaw tightened, and she looked up at him furiously. "You used Lady Hetty to make friends? My spite for that knows no levels."

Tony sighed patiently, nodding at the passing Galbraiths. "I happen to like Lady Hetty a great deal. I apologize if that makes you uncomfortable."

"She is seventy years old!" Georgie protested as they reached the punch, reaching for a glass despite his offer.

"And still more enjoyable to associate with than you..." he mused.

She whirled to him with a gasp. "I am perfectly pleasant!"

Tony gave her a look. "You've yet to be pleasant with me, Miss Allen, and unless you are prepared to make introductions for me yourself and prove me wrong, I will continue to use the only allies I currently have. No matter what age."

Georgie stared at him for a long moment, her wide green eyes turbulent. "I find you perfectly insufferable," she muttered.

Tony shrugged. "We all strive for perfection in some way. It's a pleasure to know I've attained mine."

That amused her, he could see, though she tried desperately to hide it.

He offered his arm, which she took without reluctance this time, and led her back. "You can laugh, you know," he whispered loudly. "It won't offend me or anyone else here to see you laugh. Go on, laugh. It was quite a clever comeback."

"You are ruining it," she retorted softly, fighting a smile.

Tony smiled down at her. "Well, that's no surprise, is it?"

Georgie nodded thoughtfully, and then smiled back. "No, it really isn't, Captain."

Chapter Six

———— ❦ ————

Assumptions are a delicate matter, particularly where people are concerned. You must never think you may safely assume to know someone's mind or true feelings, for you may find that they just might surprise you. People are peculiar, and assumptions even more so.

-The Spinster Chronicles, 30 January 1818

From then on, Georgie was the one introducing Tony at various events, and it was astonishing how many people she seemed to know.

For a spinster, no capital S needed, her circles seemed to know no bounds. Card parties were now opportunities to widen his own circles. Balls were used to learn the names and faces of as many young ladies as possible. Musical evenings were spent mingling with influential individuals whose good opinion Tony would need to accomplish anything.

But it wasn't Georgie alone. Charlotte took him around to meet more people, Izzy was nearly a fixture at his side, which ought to have started rumors, but oddly did not, and Grace seemed to always know when he needed rescue from an unfortunate social situation. Even Elinor had adopted him, though she was too young to be of much help anywhere. The only one who hadn't taken up his banner with fervor was Prue, but at least she was no longer quaking when Tony came into the room.

Tony would consider that progress, and happily.

Despite becoming increasingly fond of his merry band of

Spinsters, it was Georgie who intrigued him most. Not because of anything Lady Hetty may have said about her, as he was choosing to promptly forget all about it, but because Georgie seemed a mystery. She was a lovely woman in appearance, and seemed rather accomplished, though he couldn't have said if she could draw or play any sort of instrument. But she was well-informed and intelligent without being a complete bluestocking, which he considered to be a mark of good judgment, whether or not it was considered a popular accomplishment. He'd always struggled to find something praiseworthy in the girls who had no ability to carry on a conversation that strayed from the topics of weather, fashion, or gossip.

Georgie rarely spoke of any of those things.

Not that they'd shared much conversation of significance. She seemed to be keeping him at arm's length, keeping to superficial banter, which she was quite skilled at. But then, he'd known that from the first moment they met. She had wit and she had no reservation about letting anyone see it.

But not in public. He'd seen her behavior at the garden party with the other guests, and at two other small gatherings, and she had been all politeness. Not in any way simpering or missish, but in the way that might encourage interest and give one a good opinion of her. She behaved perfectly, it seemed, and one would struggle to find fault in her.

Yet she had no suitors. Rare was the sight of a man conversing with her, though one or two might be nearby. He hadn't witnessed her behavior at a ball or dance, so he could not attest to the number of dance partners she had, but he would wager that she had few.

Why, he couldn't have said.

He'd have danced with her, even if she might have criticized his every step. He was fairly certain he could convince his cousin to dance with her, although Hugh would probably flee to the opposite end of whatever room they were in to avoid it. Francis had more sense, and a wife to contend with. He was by far the easier man to sway.

Would that have been enough to spur others to do so?

Despite his new forays into Society and his new acquaintances, he had yet to truly discover what people thought of the Spinsters, as he was always in the company of the Spinsters when he was making said acquaintances. He was only now beginning to earn invitations on his own merit, and he was glad for it. He'd had enough of being forced into teas and card parties, making small talk for the sake of gaining admittance. He would rather take things at his own pace, and his too-social female acquaintances were draining him of energy and spirit.

He'd begged off attending a luncheon with Charlotte and Grace today in favor of waiting upon Francis, and he was grateful for the chance to be relaxed and in the company of a man who understood him.

Being surrounded by women was surprisingly intimidating.

But it seemed he had come too early in the day. Francis was not yet ready for him, so Tony paced the grand entryway at his leisure.

Sterling House had been in the family for generations, and it was rare that any changes were made to the interiors, aside from the color of rooms and arrangement of furniture. The woodwork around him was still as pristine as it had been the day it had been carved, and its intricate artistry fascinated Tony just as much now as it had when he was a boy. The tapestries spun tales of brave knights and bold heroes, echoed by the suits of armor on guard along the corridor.

It was a rather imposing setting, Tony considered as he wandered along. One without a familiarity with the family might have found themselves wondering about the utter masculine nature of it all, but the Sterlings had never shied away from that sort of thing. A historically male-dominated family would tend that way, especially when the wives usually favored the country houses to London.

Janet, on the other hand, adored London, so he anticipated having a very different sort of arrangement in the future, once she decided to take it up. Of course, Francis was so infatuated with his wife that he would let her do anything she wished.

Alas for their poor ancestors.

Tony grinned at the small, almost imperceptible mark on one of the suits of armor along the row. He and Francis had been exuberant knights in their imaginations once, and that mark was a reminder of a particularly good day, given that they hadn't been caught, and no one had ever known how carried away they had been.

Escaping a deserved punishment was always something worthy

of celebration.

"Don't look at that too closely, someone will figure it out."

Tony laughed and turned to see Francis descending the stairs, brushing at the sleeves of his jacket. "After all this time? I highly doubt that. You don't even have the same staff as was in those days."

"'Course I don't," Francis snorted. "I had to get rid of any potential witnesses, didn't I?" He stepped forward and shook Tony's hand hard. "How are you, Tony?"

"Well, thank you. I am sorry to have called so early, I thought…"

Francis cut him off with a swift nod. "Usually, I would have been up long before now, but I returned late from my business in Bath, so I am behind my time. Janet is still abed, but come, take breakfast with me." He didn't wait for Tony to reply and turned him towards the breakfast room.

Once he was seated, and a plate of food before him, Tony turned to his cousin. "Business in Bath? What business?"

Francis rolled his eyes as he chewed. "Janet's sister has it in her head that we're all going to come to Bath in the summer for some weeks. I went to see about lodgings and the like."

Tony frowned at him, ignoring the food for a moment. "Francis, you're a peer, and a man of fortune. You could have sent a man for that, or at least sent inquiries."

"I needed to get out of London," Francis explained with a shrug. "Why not see to the matter myself?"

"Is London so plaguing for you?" Tony asked with a laugh, helping himself to his food.

Francis gave him a look. "With my brother behaving like a fop with no manners and refusing to listen to reason? And a wife who is more social than I have ever been in my entire life? Yes, London plagues me. And I don't see Bath being any better."

His cousin's consternation amused Tony and he fought a grin. "One might ask why you remain in London at all if it is so displeasing, and why you chose a social wife."

"She chose me," Francis pointed out, smiling to himself. "I simply chose not to argue the point. And I rather fancy keeping her pleased with me before she realizes that her choice of husband was a horrible mistake."

"I could enlighten her, if you like."

"You could also get out of my house before I crown you with a candlestick."

Tony chuckled and continued to eat.

Francis said nothing for a long moment, then cleared his throat. "I understand you have become acquainted with the Spinsters."

Tony looked at him sharply. His cousin's face was devoid of suspicion, but there was a hint of mischief in his eyes that Tony didn't trust at all. "I've become acquainted with several people in the last few days, and I believe some of them are spinsters, if you must call them such."

"Not just any spinsters," Francis pointed out, his tone turning just as teasing as his look. "*The* Spinsters. Writers of the Spinster Chronicles, protectors of the innocent, defamers of marriage, haters of men. Those particular spinsters."

Francis's words struck Tony hard, and he stared at his cousin without responding for a moment. "Is that how they are seen?" he asked carefully, ignoring the way his stomach clenched and his blood boiled.

"How else should they be seen?" Francis asked in return, sitting back in his chair. "Isn't that what they do? We all read their articles, though one could hardly call them newsworthy. The commentary is witty, I'll give them that, and they seem to have found their audience, but at what cost? You should hear how the fathers of eligible daughters talk about them."

"Should I?" Tony murmured, choosing to cut his meat rather than spear his cousin.

Francis nodded, apparently missing the way Tony gripped his silverware. "And you must know the young men are up in arms about it. I don't believe half of their claims, as I've never seen anyone whisk young ladies away from them in the name of protection, but obviously something had to happen or else the stories would never have started."

"Hmm," was all Tony could muster, shoving his face with more food to avoid saying something he might regret.

The faster he finished his meal, the sooner he could depart without incident.

"Well?" Francis prodded, pushing his empty plate aside. "Have you met them, or haven't you?"

"You seem to already know I have," Tony replied easily. "Why ask?"

"Because I want to know the details." Francis banged on the table a little. "Come on, Tony, Hugh says…"

"I don't very well care what Hugh says on the subject," Tony snapped, surprised that his tone was actually fairly mild. "As you said, he's becoming a fop with more arrogance than taste, and with the circle of friends he has chosen for himself, I'd wonder at your listening to his opinions about them as well."

Francis looked at him with a furrowed brow, clearly not expecting that reaction. "You do know them."

Tony rolled his eyes and set aside his silverware roughly. "Oh, very astute, my lord. And I was going to come here to seek your advice and insight, but as you've already given me a fairly clear picture of where you stand, I believe I no longer need to." He rose from the table and bowed, then went to move past him.

"Hang on a minute," Francis barked, grabbing his arm as he passed. "Stop!"

Tony looked down at him, raising a brow even as his jaw clenched.

Francis indicated the chair. "Come on, sit back down."

"And if I don't?"

"I'll tell Alice what you did to her favorite doll when she was six."

Tony hadn't expected blackmail from his cousin, and he blanched at the thought. Alice was Francis and Hugh's younger sister, a girl of high spirits and short temper. Her grudges tended to last a very long time and remain quite passionate. She was eighteen now, but he had no doubt she would rail about that for at least five years if she knew.

His indignation abated slightly, and he moved back to his chair, sitting down roughly. "Fine. I am once more seated."

"And you are still furious."

Tony inclined his head a little, not seeing the need to deny what was obvious.

"Tell me why," Francis said, folding his arms and looking intrigued.

Was it worth the effort, knowing his cousin felt the same scorn Hugh did for them, though at a milder level?

He did not have much of a choice, he supposed, considering the only other man he could confide in was Hugh, and that would have been much worse. He didn't have to tell Francis how he came to be acquainted with them, or to what extent, but he could be honest in other respects.

Mostly.

"I have come to know them," Tony allowed with a heavy sigh. "We've met several times at various functions I have attended, and a few of them have been very kind to introduce me to some of their associates."

"Oh, they must approve of you, then," Francis offered with a slight smile. "Fortunate man."

Tony gave him a hard look, which made Francis sober and hold up his hands in surrender.

"I have not seen anything worthy of the sort of contempt that you seem so filled with for them," Tony observed, frowning.

"I have no complaint against any of them personally," Francis insisted as he sat forward. "I barely know a single one of them. I only protest that they fill nearly every conversation I wish to hold with anyone."

That was fair, and Tony acknowledged it with a nod. "I have found each of them to be accomplished, kind, considerate young women, some of them remarkably so. As a group, they seem supportive of one another, which I find commendable, considering their situations, and I have yet to hear them disparage anyone, male or female." Tony looked at his cousin steadily then. "They deserve better than what anybody says about them, and I'll thank you to refrain from expressing such opinions in my presence."

Francis looked surprised but nodded straightaway. "Fine, I can manage that. Lord knows, Janet applauds them, and that ought to be indicative of some good sense. But Tony…" He considered his words carefully, his eyes narrowing. "How much time have you spent with these women?"

"Enough," Tony said, shrugging lightly. "I don't see the need for anyone to judge them so harshly, and I'm determined to do what I can to stifle it."

His cousin whistled low. "I don't envy you that task. I think you'll find it harder to accomplish than you realize, given the heated nature of things here. But you may consider me an ally, if you need one, provided I don't have to make grand gestures or pronouncements. I do have some dignity, you know."

Tony snorted. "Not much."

"I pretend at it."

"Now that's true." Tony winced and gave Francis a hopeful look. "You won't tell Hugh, will you?"

"Lord, no," Francis said at once, looking disgusted. "The less Hugh knows about any of this the better. He thinks the Spinsters are the devil incarnate, though I can't imagine why. He's never pursued any woman, as far as I know, so it's not as though they've thwarted him personally."

Not yet, no, but if Hugh continued pursuing the path he was on, Tony would not be surprised if it happened sooner rather than later. And if Georgie caught Hugh in her clutches after something like that, the poor lad wouldn't stand a chance. Tony's money would be on Georgie for that one. No question.

"Can we speak of other things now?" Francis asked, cringing a little. "Really, I hate talking about the Spinsters. They're everywhere."

Tony laughed at that. "Yes, they tend to be. Very well. How is Janet, then?"

"No, you cannot put that in there."

"Why not? It's the truth!"

"Charlotte, be reasonable."

"She *did* look like a pumpkin!"

"But that doesn't mean you have to say that!"

"It makes me wonder what you'd say about me if we were not friends."

Georgie winced with an audible hiss, and she was not the only one to do so at Prue's soft words.

Writing day was always a challenge for their group, given the difference in their personalities and abilities, but it was especially difficult when Charlotte was in a rage. She had volunteered to take on the Fashion Forum portion this week, and no one had suspected why, despite her usual aversion to the topic.

Now it was quite clear, and they were left with the crisis of shutting her down without losing much time.

"That is hardly fair, Prudence," Charlotte protested, looking rather wounded. "I would never say anything about you."

Prue shrugged a little in her pale green muslin, hard at work on her own section about the events of the coming week. "It's easy to say that now, but if you did not know me and I had come in an ensemble my mother had chosen for me that did not suit, it is entirely possible that you would without a second thought."

That was probably true, Georgie supposed. Charlotte was the sort of person who said whatever came into her mind, regardless of the effect it might have. She was not intentionally malicious, only a little thoughtless, and often had no idea what injury she caused with her words or actions.

Prue, on the other hand, was the sort of girl who always seemed to be on the receiving end of the careless words and actions of others, though never Charlotte specifically. No one ever considered Prue very much except for their particular circle. She was the type of quiet creature that became invisible far too easily, and it left her exposed for comments.

Charlotte huffed loudly now and crossed out a line of her work rather dramatically. "Very well, then. Nothing remotely resembling any vegetables in here, and I will even go so far as to remove all indication of a name. I would hate to offend anyone by commenting on the idiocy of garment choices, despite the fact that quite literally everyone was saying exactly the same thing."

"Why not just say that?" Grace offered from her position in the window seat. "Comment on the color…"

"Oh, I have," Charlotte muttered, widening her eyes meaningfully as she scribbled some additional things. "Thoroughly."

"Specifically," Grace continued as if Charlotte had said nothing, and glanced across the room at her. "Not just orange."

Charlotte made an irritated noise. "I hate orange."

"My hair is orange," Izzy chimed in from her lounging position on the divan. She had finished her piece already, opting for the Society Dabbler, which was always tamer with her behind the pen.

Georgie grinned at her cousin's quip, knowing Charlotte would hate it.

"Isabella Lambert," Charlotte protested loudly, setting her pen down. "Your hair is a glorious shade of copper, and I suspect it flows like a river that cascades down your narrow shoulders in a most enticing way. Don't you dare reduce it to a boring thing like orange."

Izzy stared at Charlotte in surprise, then looked at Georgie with a small smile. "Remind me to have Charlotte instruct any potential suitors on the proper way to gain my affections."

The room laughed at that, and the tension was diffused, just as it always was when Izzy put her mind to it.

Georgie would have loved to have such a gift. Oh, she was pleasant enough, and had heard quite often that she had a lovely temperament, but she became irritated quickly and simply could not tolerate fools. It wasn't in her nature.

It did not explain why her mother continued to have such an effect on her, but that was unimportant. One could hardly tell off one's mother in the same way they could anyone else.

Not that Georgie was in the habit of telling off individuals on a regular basis, much as she may have considered it. She always behaved properly.

If only just.

"It would serve Mrs. Renfrew right to be publicly scolded for her ensemble," Charlotte muttered, though she smiled now. "And by name. It was ghastly. Even Prue has to admit that." She looked at Prue rather pointedly in expectation.

Prue seemed to glow with the violence of the pink that stained her cheeks, her eyes wide as saucers. Then she ducked her chin and her hand shook as she strove to continue writing. "It was not particularly flattering on her, no."

"Ah ha!" Charlotte crowed as she held out her hands in victory.

"There you have it."

Grace threw a scolding look in Charlotte's direction. "You can't get her to say such things by force!" She got up from her seat and moved to Prue, rubbing her shoulders gently. "There, there, lamb. It's all right, Mrs. Renfrew won't hear of it from us."

"No doubt she heard it from several others, though." Charlotte sighed as she returned to her work. "Someone surely ought to have told her, for her own protection."

"Considering her two daughters look just like her and are trying for the Morris brothers," Elinor announced from the corner where she had been studiously compiling her latest information into a more organized fashion. "I would think there are several things she ought to be told for her protection." Elinor looked at Georgie in outrage. "Can you believe I had to convince Mary to not accompany Mr. Morris to his private box at the theater? I don't know what she was thinking, but I highly doubt she can be trusted. She seemed to actually be keen on the idea, and to take her aunt with her as chaperone. Her aunt is almost completely blind!"

"I say let her get on with it," Charlotte offered with a dismissive wave of her hand. "If Mary Renfrew wishes to be Mary Morris by such means and doesn't care about the implications or consequences, let her ruin herself quickly and be done with it."

"That's a bit harsh," Izzy said with a frown. "Mary may only be ignorant, and desperate to marry."

"If I had her mother, I'd be desperate to be married, too," Charlotte retorted.

Georgie shook her head slowly, going back to work on her own article, but her heart wasn't in it. Usually she adored the chance to write the main article of the Chronicles, using it as an opportunity to vent her frustrations and dispense advice that she'd been wanting to for the younger generation of misses.

But lately, even this all had become a bit staid.

She knew full well that things had gotten out of hand as far as the gossip and comments of others. They'd not done half of what was said about them, and she doubted anybody could have managed such things.

And that went for the young girls who held them to such an

extreme standard of goodness as well.

They had never stopped any elopements, nor had they discovered anyone in the middle of a tryst. Georgie had never argued with a parent over the treatment of their daughter, and Charlotte, for all her refusing proposals, had never done so purely to remain a spinster. Georgie had never challenged a man to a duel to protect the honor of a girl in her protection, nor did she actually have any girls in her protection.

She wasn't fully aware of what those who did not approve of them were saying, and that ignorance ate away at her. People could be entirely too cruel in general whenever something they did not understand or did not approve of was the topic. It made no difference that many of these people had known Georgie since she was young. They perceived her as being something of a hoyden, as if she had somehow grown inappropriate in the years since her own coming out.

She'd never intended any of this to happen. All she'd wanted was to impart some of the wisdom she'd gained in her twenty-seven years of life, many of them spent waiting for the spark of life to come to her, with other girls who could find themselves in her situation.

She had been tired hearing of girls who were too naïve with the opposite sex and lost themselves in the moment, swept away by dreams of romance and what might have been. She'd been distressed when she heard about girls who had agreed to marriages with men that they had absolutely no affection for, purely to avoid being a spinster. She was disturbed by those whose only goal was financial gain or improvement of station. Unlike Charlotte, she did not insist that love was required, particularly at this point in her life, but she did feel that there ought to be some sort of compatibility between a husband and wife.

Not that Georgie had any sort of knowledge or experience of those things, nor should anyone actually take her advice on the subject seriously, but she had some opinions. She had seen a great deal from her vantage point in the corner of every ballroom she had ever been in.

Georgie looked around at her friends, sighing a little. All she had ever wanted was to give people pause in their hasty decisions to avoid what they saw as a horrifying alternative. Spinsterhood was not as terrible as was often feared, and she wished she had known that before.

She wished everyone knew that.

Including the women in this room.

But what would be said of her if she backed out of their schemes now?

None of them knew of her doubts and her regrets. She hadn't said a word about it. They were all in the midst of whatever purpose they imagined for themselves and enjoying every moment of it. She could not confide in a single one of them.

If spinsterhood could get lonelier than it already was, it had done so for Georgie.

"Pardon me, Miss Lambert," Bessie said from the doorway. "Captain Sterling is here."

Izzy sat up with a yawn and looked around. "Everybody done with their articles?"

They answered in the affirmative and handed them over to her.

Izzy nodded and stuffed them between pages of a book. "Show him in, Bessie."

"Why we aren't getting Tony's opinion on these is beyond me," Charlotte muttered as she sat back in her chair.

Prue paled quickly. "I would hate for him to see mine, knowing I was the author."

Georgie smiled at that, albeit briefly. They kept the author of each article anonymous for the sake of protecting their reputations, though everybody knew they wrote something in the Chronicles. It might not have been much, but it saved them some trouble, and no one had ever outright asked them if they were the authors.

So, there was that.

Loud footsteps echoed in the corridor, and they all turned to the doorway expectantly.

"All right," Tony boomed as he appeared, smiling despite his tone, "who the devil put my name in the Society Dabbler?"

Chapter Seven

————— ❧ ❧ ❧ —————

A ball is the perfect opportunity to test the young man of your choice. Mark his attentions and his behaviors, but also his eye. The most perfect of gentlemen by appearances might act his part flawlessly, but his eye will never lie. Also, one can always trust a man who trods toes. No blackguard would be foolish enough to make such an obvious misstep and risk it all in such a shoddy way.

-The Spinster Chronicles, 4 August 1815

"Oh, lord, her mother chose her ensemble."

"Don't you dare say anything, Charlotte Wright."

"As if I would. Poor little Prudence would faint clear away if one of us said a word about it. Never mind that others will say all sorts of things."

"I don't very well care what anybody else says about our Prue, but we must do what we can about that."

"Oh, I didn't think she could look so ill. Not with her complexion."

"And I wrote that nasty piece about orange. Everybody's going to pay attention now. Curse my sharp tongue."

Georgie stared at Prue shamelessly, as did everybody else in the room. It truly was the most horrid shade of orange she had ever seen, and it put Mrs. Renfrew's ensemble quite to shame. And Prue's cheeks were flaming already, which only made everything worse.

Despite Prue's diminutive stature, her mother was anything but.

They could not have been more different in appearance and in nature, and Mrs. Westfall had the utmost contempt for her daughter, but nobody knew why. There were no other children, and Mr. Westfall had been dead for years. But rather than cling to her daughter, Mrs. Westfall had turned tyrannical, and there was no apparent end in sight.

Mrs. Westfall wore a dark shade of blue, far more flattering to her coloring, and she paraded about the room with a preening sort of look. Prue followed behind dutifully, her eyes lowered, unable to look at anyone. But she could not have missed the whispers or the snickering of those around her.

Georgie certainly didn't miss them.

She heard every single one of them.

"Lord have mercy," Izzy whispered next to her, sounding choked up and emotional. "Please let the dancing begin or someone else do something foolish."

Georgie nodded without speaking. She couldn't have managed a word herself.

She noticed a movement out of the corner of her eye and her breath caught as she saw Tony striding forward, dressed in pristine eveningwear. He had the audacity to bow to Mrs. Westfall, to whom he had not actually been introduced.

She looked up at him with her usual haughtiness, her face turning mottled.

Georgie would have given a fortune to hear what Tony was saying, but he was too far away, and not even Mrs. Westfall could manage a volume that would reach across the room.

"What is he doing?" Charlotte muttered under her breath. "Marjorie is going to pop off his head."

"Hush, Charlotte," Izzy hissed, waving a hand at her.

Georgie watched intently, ignoring the way Charlotte called Prue's mother by her given name. She was always saying that when Mrs. Westfall behaved as the mother of Prue ought, she would give her the courtesy of her proper address.

She could hardly blame Charlotte for that, but she could not bring herself to do the same.

Impossibly, Mrs. Westfall's expression cleared, and she turned to her daughter, quite literally dragging Prue forward.

Georgie bit back a smile as Tony bowed to her and extended his hand.

"Take it, Prue," Charlotte hissed. "Come on and take it."

"Her mother will crown her if she doesn't," Izzy muttered. "Come on, Prue."

Georgie wasn't minding Prue as much as she was Tony. Was he truly so bold as to stand before an entire room of whispering gossips and take the hand of the most timid creature of them all? He didn't seem the slightest bit put off by Mrs. Westfall, nor by Prue's hesitation. Instead, his hand only seemed to grow more and more steady, his intent constant.

Prue needed consistency. And patience, understanding, warmth…

In short, everything her mother was not.

Prue's trembling hand reached out and took his, and he was quick to whisk her away, leading her towards the line that was forming for the first dance of the evening.

Charlotte exhaled noisily, fanning herself quickly. "Well, that was smartly done of Tony. Prue's going to be a stammering storm the entire time, and undoubtedly after they're done. Izzy, go see if Lady Hetty has arrived yet and make sure there's a chair for her. Georgie, find Grace, she's always managed to set Prue to rights."

Georgie wrenched her gaze away from Prue and Tony, dancing rather well, if silently, and looked at Charlotte with a raised brow. "And what will you do, Charlotte?"

Charlotte dimpled a smile at her, her dark eyes twinkling. "Distract everyone from Prue's ensemble."

"Oh, Charlotte," Izzy moaned, "don't do anything foolish!"

Charlotte scoffed loudly. "Oh, sweet Izzy, haven't you learned by now? I never do anything foolish. I always know exactly what I am doing." She nodded at them both and glided away, heading directly for a small group of gentlemen, all of whom watched her cream and gold swathed figure approach with interest.

"What do you think she's going to do?" Izzy hissed to her, fidgeting with her blue muslin that was two seasons old.

Georgie shook her head slowly, watching the dance again. "I

haven't the faintest idea, Izzy, and I am glad for it." She sighed, allowing herself to smile more. "I think we'd better prepare a spot for Prue. She looks done for already."

Izzy chuckled a little. "She looks better away from her mother, and if Tony is half the man I think he is, Prue will actually smile. In public."

With a small hum of satisfaction, Izzy turned and headed off in another direction.

Georgie stayed where she was, despite Charlotte's instructions. Grace was about somewhere, and she would take note of Prue's distress easily enough and come all on her own. Elinor would flutter about trying to do something useful, but only make more of a fuss.

All of that could transpire as it would, and Georgie wouldn't care overly much.

She watched Tony dance with Prue, smiling as warmly as he might have done with any other young woman, one without a terribly unbecoming dress and a terribly unflattering mother. He danced well, which must always be appreciated, and no one would ever have suspected that a rescue had taken place. Prue did not talk much under usual circumstances, but when dancing she was sometimes worse.

Not this time.

Her embarrassed flush was rapidly fading, and Tony kept up a steady stream of words, though none of them could be heard over the music. Prue looked more at ease than Georgie had seen her in months, if not years. She had never known that Prue was such a lively dancer, nor would she have expected it.

Had Tony known that, too?

He couldn't have. As far as she knew, he'd only danced with Prue once, shortly after meeting her, and she would not have been so comfortable with him then.

Georgie would never claim to know much of men, but she had never met one who acted the part of a true gentleman with a good heart and pure motives. Not even Grace's brothers, or her cousins, could fall into that category.

She'd always wanted someone to prove that such men really existed outside of the overblown imaginations of young ladies, but she never thought she would actually find one. Truthfully, she was not entirely convinced that Tony was such a man either, nor could she claim that he was some grand epitome of gentlemen. All she knew was this was a good deed, and she was feeling something rather significant about it.

If it was sincere.

And she intended to find that out the moment Prue was secure in Lady Hetty's care.

She glanced across the room to see Izzy chatting warmly with Lady Hetty, who watched the dance with an almost wistful expression, despite the customary frown she wore. But she nodded at something Izzy was saying and answered accordingly, making Izzy laugh. Grace was already hovering behind them, a vision in a rose-colored gown, yet nobody seemed to take notice.

Georgie would never understand how Izzy and Grace had escaped the notice of every man in England, given their caring natures and warm hearts, not to mention their pleasant features and possession of all the fine accomplishments of young ladies. They would each have made any man a perfect and charming wife.

But that was another set of cares for a different time.

The dance finished to general applause, and the musicians started to converse about the next piece as the dancers dispersed. Georgie watched Tony and Prue, who moved to the chairs near Lady Hetty, purposefully situated in the exact opposite direction from her mother. Prue looked as contented as she ever was, perhaps the slightest bit self-conscious, but perfectly comfortable on Tony's arm.

And then she smiled.

Good heavens.

Georgie looked over at Izzy in shock, who had seen it and was barely containing her own smile of pride. Prue smiling in public was not a completely foregone conclusion at any given time. Usually, however, she smiled only when surrounded by the rest of them or when Lady Hetty had said something particularly witty. Never, as far as Georgie could recall, had it happened in the presence of a man.

She wasn't sure she liked this, but she was also near to tears.

The conflict of emotions and impulses was setting everything awry.

Tony saw Prue seated next to Lady Hetty, who said something

to him that made Tony grin. He responded, bowed to each of the girls, and then left them all, heading in Georgie's direction.

Well, not in *her* direction specifically, but generally speaking.

Georgie moved quickly to intercept him before he could do anything else.

He saw her coming, took in her expression, which she had not thought to be so very imposing, and heard him groan as she approached. "Oh, now what? What could you possibly disapprove of now?"

It was all Georgie could do to avoid making a very unattractive face at him. "I beg your pardon?"

Tony lifted one of his brows at her, making her envious that she could not reciprocate the motion. "You are determined to find fault with me, despite my having absolutely no ulterior motives, and I really am growing quite fatigued with defending myself at every turn. Might I spare myself the trouble of this conversation?"

Georgie was fully aware that people were staring at them, no doubt wondering what the dashing Captain Sterling would do after dancing with Miss Westfall, but she could not make herself move. "No," she said firmly. "No, you may not."

He sighed a little too dramatically and tilted his head at her. "Then would you, perhaps, accompany me to the north corner of this ballroom? There is a footman with beverages there, and I would very much like one."

She scowled up at him but nodded and turned to proceed with him in that direction. "Do you have to sound so polite about it? Anyone hearing you would think me a shrew."

"I am always polite, Miss Allen," Tony replied with ease, clasping his hands behind his back. "I find it to be the mark of an exemplary gentleman."

Georgie looked up at him in disbelief. "I don't believe that for a moment."

"No, really, I do feel that way."

She rolled her eyes, knowing he was deliberately provoking her, and hating how good he was at it. "I'm sure you do, but it does not follow that you are always polite. That is what I doubt. Especially given our acquaintance."

"And yet you introduce me to nearly everyone," he mused, looking thoughtful. "Clearly you must have some good opinion of me, or you would not be nearly so keen."

"It is because I pity you," Georgie snapped, keeping a bland smile on her face for the benefit of those watching. "Poor, pathetic creature you are, and in such want of friends and associates." She tsked and shook her head sadly. "It is almost more than my generous heart can bear."

Tony snickered under his breath, coughing into a gloved hand slightly, then turned a warm smile to her. "Generous heart. That is exactly how I would describe you, Miss Allen. Please, ask me your questions."

Georgie shook her head, exhaling in what was almost irritation, but not quite. "Why did you dance with Prue?"

"Because I like her."

"We all like her, Captain," Georgie reminded him firmly.

"Yes, but it would be odd for any of you to dance with her at an event like this."

She had to try her utmost to avoid covering her face with her hand. "You know what I mean."

"Oh!" Tony said, as if the realization had only just dawned on him. "Oh, why did I go to her almost immediately after her entrance and practically steal her away from her mother?"

Georgie gave him a patient nod.

He straightened up a little. "Well, it seemed the thing to do. Everybody was just staring and whispering, and I know how sensitive Prue is. My feet were moving before I had really thought about it, so I can only say it was my first instinct."

Instinct. His instinct had been to go to Prue and save her from her embarrassment.

Her heart gave a weak flutter in her chest, which she quickly shushed.

"What is her mother like?" Tony murmured, lowering his voice, though his expression remained perfectly composed. "I have a fair idea, but I want to hear it from you."

"Well," Georgie started, exhaling quickly, "that could take quite a long time, and the language required might not be entirely appropriate for such a distinguished setting."

Tony laughed. "Try."

She smirked, inclining her head at her aunt Faith, who watched her with a suspicious expression. "Mrs. Westfall has the sort of personality that makes one wish for a firearm."

Tony coughed in surprise, putting his fist to his mouth, though the curve of his lips could still be seen.

Georgie nodded, smiling. "She berates Prue whenever she can, in public or out of it, and can be heard to complain quite vocally about everything that is wrong in her life. If you are so fortunate as to converse with her, you will find that there is nothing that is going well. Particularly not with her eligible daughter, whom she finds to be the very worst trial of all."

Tony grumbled under his breath unintelligibly, but the meaning was clear.

"Quite," Georgie quipped, looking over at Mrs. Westfall, who sat in a chair with a cup of punch that was clearly not her first, and was watching Prue with distaste. "The mercy of it all is that she does not care what Prue does, so we are able to steal her away quite often."

"Would that someone would permanently steal Prue from her mother," Tony muttered, his brow furrowing darkly. "That would solve everything."

She slid her glance to him slyly. "Are you offering, Captain Sterling?"

That made him smile, and he shook his head. "Alas, Miss Allen, I think Miss Westfall deserves far better than me. But I'll see what I can do about it."

"I've tried myself," Georgie admitted with a sigh as they reached the footman with beverages. "I can't convince any man to consider it, not even the ones I think highly of. I don't know why."

Tony gave her a quick look.

"Oh, all right," she snapped with an impatient flick of her wrist. "I know very well why. But it isn't her fault, and it shouldn't detract anyone from trying for her. If they tried, they might just find out how sweet and good she really is and forget all about everything else."

"You say that as if patience were a virtue all men were blessed with." Tony sipped from the beverage he held and shook his head.

"It's not."

Georgie snorted softly. "Really? I'd have thought..." She trailed off instantly, a sight catching her eye that made thought and word vanish.

Lucy Wilton was heading for a side corridor, her hand clasped tightly in that of Simon Delaney, who she knew was not only a scoundrel but was also supposedly courting Caroline Briggs. There was no reason he should be tugging Lucy anywhere, especially since she was all of fifteen and too young and too silly to be out.

"Georgie?" Tony asked, his voice somehow far away.

She seized his arm in a crushing grip. "Tony," she gasped, her eyes fixed on Lucy's flushed and excited face.

No one marked the pair of them. They weren't making any sort of fuss about their escapade, and everybody was watching the dancing. It was the perfect escape opportunity.

Tony followed her gaze, and his eyes narrowed. "Wait here," he growled.

She held his arm tightly. "What are you going to do?"

He looked down at her hand, then smiled a little at her. "I'm going to rescue the damsel. And perhaps thrash the villain. The moment I bring her back, do something with her."

Georgie nodded quickly and forced herself to release his sleeve. "I'll get Jane Wilton to come. She's the one Lucy will listen to and will be discreet."

Tony gave her a short nod. "Go, Georgie. Go now." He moved away from her with ease, seeming to weave between the guests without any sort of hindrance. He exited out the same door the couple had, and Georgie had to restrain a shiver.

Lord only knew what he would face.

But she had her marching orders, and she wasn't about to disobey them. She scanned the room in search of Jane Wilton, careful to keep her composure and act without the appearance of haste. There wouldn't be any good in drawing attention to the situation. It would only harm the Wiltons, and it wouldn't help the Spinsters at all either.

Charlotte saw her and left her four gentlemen, stepping discreetly to her side. "What's happening?" she asked in a quiet voice, taking Georgie's arm with a fond smile. "I can see the look in your eyes, even if no one else can."

"Lucy Wilton," Georgie hissed quickly through her teeth. "Simon Delaney."

"No!" Charlotte gasped, if one could gasp without changing expression.

Georgie nodded once, smiling at Mrs. Westfall, who did not return it. "Tony's gone after them, I'm to fetch Jane and we'll keep everything as quiet and contained as we can."

"Of course," Charlotte replied a bit distractedly. "Of course. I'll alert the others. Quietly, of course. Tony should be able to set things right before anything untoward occurs."

"But will he?" Georgie murmured before she could stop herself.

Charlotte gave her an odd look. "Georgiana Allen, have you taken leave of your senses? Or have you really become such a skeptic that you can't see one of the good ones right before your eyes?" She lifted a dubious brow, then moved away, seemingly perfectly at ease.

Georgie watched her go, her brow furrowing. She knew Tony was a good man, certainly, but what did that matter? Good men behaved in ways not becoming them all the time, and despite Tony's clever wit and kindness where they were concerned, she could not know how he would respond. She would like to think he had good motives, both for helping Prue and for helping Lucy Wilton, but...

Well, it hardly mattered at the moment. He was helping them for the time being and that was the most important thing.

She spotted Jane in conversation with Mr. Greensley, which was unfortunate, as that was a rather good pairing. She hated to break it up, but surely there would be more opportunities for them. Mr. Greensley was a good sort. He would undoubtedly try again, if Jane were the woman he wanted.

"Miss Wilton," Georgie said with as much warmth as she could. "Mr. Greensley. I wonder if I might steal Miss Wilton away for a moment. I desperately need her advice on a gift for my cousin, and she is so good at these sorts of things."

"Of course," Mr. Greensley replied with a smart bow. "Please."

Jane looked at Georgie with a bewildered expression as she pulled her away. "Miss Allen, surely by now you have heard that I am dismal when it comes to presents. My sisters talk about it constantly."

Georgie nodded quickly. "Yes, I am well aware. I need your presence more than advice on presents. Come with me."

They strolled back around the side of the room, apparently deep in conversation, though it was all a pretense. The moment Jane had the slightest understanding of what her sister had done, Georgie was charged with keeping her restrained and at her side, so she wouldn't march off to confront Lucy and Delaney herself. A fuss such as that would only cause more gossip, and it would be a miracle if the secret could remain a secret if such a scene were to occur.

Lucy came through the doorway then, looking perturbed but not altogether distressed or disheveled. Georgie released Jane's arm and watched as she took her sister by the hand and hauled her away, Jane's jaw set while Lucy looked merely resigned.

No one would pay any attention to that sort of sight. The sight of older sisters dragging wayward younger ones was quite commonplace, and Lucy Wilton had already earned herself the sort of reputation that would make nobody question what was happening. No one would suspect anything untoward.

Georgie allowed herself a silent sigh of relief, and glanced back at the doorway, wondering where Simon Delaney had gotten to, and what Tony was about. But so long as Lucy was safe and out of the way, she was perfectly content.

She smiled to herself and skirted around the edges of the room to join the others and Lady Hetty.

Charlotte, as usual, was not with them. One could only expect her to be engaging her usual collection of men, all of whom were doomed to fail in their pursuit of her.

"What's happened?" Izzy murmured beside her.

"It'll keep," she replied, patting her cousin's hand. She took a deep, cleansing breath. "It'll keep."

"Oh no, it won't!"

Charlotte was suddenly before them, looking excitable and lively, her dark eyes dancing, her dimple making an appearance.

Georgie looked past Charlotte for a moment, then back at her. "Where did you come from?"

"Everybody always asks me that," she quipped, adjusting her

gloves. "I never know quite what to say."

Grace heaved an irritated sigh. "Not generally speaking, Charlotte. Where did you just come from at this moment? Specifically."

Charlotte looked behind both shoulders as if anybody was listening, which they were not, then leaned forward. "I've been eavesdropping on Tony and Simon Delaney."

Izzy gasped. "Simon Delaney? Is Tony a friend of his?"

"If he was before," Charlotte retorted with a little smirk, "he certainly isn't now!"

She quickly related to them what she had heard, which was only the tail end of the conversation, in which Tony had scolded Simon Delaney for taking advantage of a young girl's nature. Simon had insisted that Lucy Wilton had professed to know exactly what she was doing. Two questions further had revealed that Lucy had *not*, in fact, known what she was doing. Tony had sent her back into the ballroom and told her that if he did not have her as a partner for a dance in ten minutes, he would send out a search party.

"So that's why Lucy looks as though she's eaten lemons," Grace mused.

Lady Hetty harrumphed. "She always looks like that."

"Thank the Lord for Tony," Izzy breathed, putting a hand to her cheek. "That could have been disastrous."

Prue was too shocked and flushed to even manage a stammer. Poor dear.

"That's not the best part," Charlotte added, looking rather smug. "You should have heard what Tony said to Simon Delaney."

"Oh Charlotte!" Izzy squealed softly. "Can you recall it?"

"She can always recall it," Grace and Georgie said together.

Charlotte shrugged. "I can. Simon Delaney was most put out and said many things that I will not repeat out of feminine delicacy."

Georgie snorted at that.

Charlotte ignored her. "Then Delaney said something about seeing her a spinster like us. And Tony, oh, he was magnificent. He said, 'Better a spinster like them than ruined by a toad like you.' And Delaney said, 'You don't even know her!' Rather put out he was."

"What did Tony say to that?" Prue asked, her voice awed.

It was the first time she'd called him Tony, and they all knew it. That seemed significant somehow.

Charlotte smiled warmly at Prue. "He said, 'No, nor do I need to. And if I see you anywhere near her, or any other female not bound to you by blood or marital ties again, I will make certain you are run out of London by more powerful men than you could ever think to name'."

Georgie's heart felt as though it was bursting in her chest at the repeated words, and she couldn't manage to draw a proper breath. Tony had said exactly the words she could have wished and more. He had taken up their cause for his own without anybody instructing him.

"And Tony looked so tall and powerful," Charlotte was saying almost dreamily.

Lady Hetty laughed once, leaning in. "He *is* tall."

"And strong," Grace reminded them.

Izzy nodded at them both. "And probably influential considering…"

"Yes, yes," Charlotte replied quickly with a wave of her hand, "but he was full of vigor and energy and…"

"Charlotte," Georgie interrupted gently, finding her voice at last. "Is that exactly what he said?"

Her friend looked almost outraged. "Yes. Exactly, Georgie. You know I never lie about eavesdropping."

She did know that. They all knew that.

"And he didn't know you were there?"

Now Charlotte looked mortally offended. "Of course not! What kind of eavesdropper would I be if people knew I was there? He marched straight out and joined in the waltz with his cousin's wife without seeing me. I promise you, Georgie, he was not saying it for my benefit."

Georgie looked out at the dancing now, where the waltz was coming to its conclusion. Tony escorted Lady Sterling off the floor, then turned and walked to Lucy Wilton, who was appropriately waiting and looking much chagrined. He never gave her a hint of a sour or superior expression. He was warm and engaging, smiling the entire time.

Lucy Wilton would be in love with him before the night was out.

And this was a man she was not sure she could trust? He had proven himself to be beyond what she had initially expected, and more than equal to the tasks they had given him. He was a fine ally for them and a fine gentleman besides. He'd treated Prue with kindness, he'd borne Lady Hetty's eccentricities with ease, he'd bantered with Georgie skillfully, and he'd taken care of Lucy Wilton beyond imagining.

If Georgie couldn't trust him, then she was beyond hope of ever trusting anyone.

She watched him thoughtfully for a moment. Perhaps he would not think so ill of her as others might, if she were to confide in him.

Rising from her seat with a wordless murmur to the others, she proceeded around the edge of the room again, stopping near the spot where Tony danced with Lucy. Her heart pounded so hard it began to pain her, but she could not back down now. Someone had to know, help her decide, set her mind at ease, and it was better that person be an outsider than one of the Spinsters in truth.

The dance concluded, and Tony bowed to Lucy, who, sure enough, beamed at him too fondly. He returned her to her sister, then saw Georgie coming towards him. He looked surprised but smiled and met her as the next dance continued.

"Come to ask me to dance, Miss Allen?" he asked.

She shook her head, trying to smile at him, but failing.

He frowned at once. "Georgie? What is it?"

He said her name so easily, and without any hint of rancor or teasing. She needed that, and she used it to buoy her wavering confidence.

"May I speak to you for a moment?" she queried.

He nodded and gestured towards the window nearby. Once there, he looked at her more carefully. "Georgie, Miss Lucy is secure, you saw me dancing with her just now. She's a bit embarrassed, perhaps foolish, but she is well and whole. No lasting harm done."

Georgie smiled, shaking her head quickly. "No, it isn't that, you were marvelous with her. I am most appreciative. It's just..." She straightened a little. "Tony, I've misjudged you and I am sorry for it. You have proven yourself worthy of trust, and to be a very fine man indeed. I should like to be friends with you in earnest, not just for the

Spinsters."

Tony's brows rose, and he smiled. "I'm not sure I like where this is going, Georgie. You're complimenting me, and that leaves me quite terrified."

She laughed at that, the tension in her chest easing. "Yes, I fear I am a difficult person at times."

"But only in the best of ways," he assured her. "And I accept your friendship readily."

Georgie chewed her lip for a moment. "Tony, if you want to know the true state of the Spinsters, I have… That is… may I confide in you about something? As a friend."

He sobered, and his brow furrowed a bit. "Of course, Georgie."

"Promise not to tell a soul?" she demanded.

He nodded once. "On my honor."

Georgie stared at him, exhaling slowly. "I sometimes regret ever assembling the Spinsters. And I'm wondering if it isn't time to end things."

Chapter Eight

A voice of reason is essential to any young lady, no matter if she be married or not. It is preferable if that voice of reason is her own, for convenience's sake if nothing else. But if one does not possess a voice of reason herself, an outside voice will do. Reason must always be objective, and that voice must be clear and impartial. Partiality can never be trusted as reason.

-The Spinster Chronicles, 2 September 1817

She wanted to end things? *She* wanted to end things?

She had started the Spinster Chronicles in the first place out of her own righteous indignation, and now she wanted to end things?

Hugh would have been dancing in the streets if he knew.

Fortunately, Tony had the good sense not to say a word about Georgie's extraordinary claim the night before. In fact, he hadn't even let Georgie get into any details about what she had said. If it were anybody else, he would have thought they were being dramatic or having a fit of capriciousness.

Not Georgie.

He'd seen her face, could see what it cost her to say it, but more than that, he had come to know her, at least a little, and she would never have admitted such a thing unless it had occupied her thoughts for some time. She was entirely serious.

But a ball surrounded by gossips and opponents of her group was hardly the place to have that discussion. He'd managed to persuade her not to do anything rash, which made her snap at him about never doing anything rash, a retort that he absolutely believed.

Georgiana Allen would have made a perfectly laid out plan that she was determined to see through to the very end. Nothing ill-conceived or hasty in any way, shape, or form.

He wasn't sure if that was a comfort or not.

If she would always proceed with thought and care, giving every aspect due consideration, she would not have approached him lightly. She could already have a plan for making a proper retreat from the situation she had created for them. It was even conceivable that the strategy was already being implemented, whatever it was.

That was a terrifying thought.

He was convinced that the others had no idea Georgie was having these regrets. The fact that she came to him, of all people, to confess them ought to have been proof of that. And she had done so in confidence, at that.

Which meant he still had time.

For what, he was still unclear about.

His cousin, and most of the men in London, wanted the Spinsters to be disbanded so they could return to their previous way of thinking and doing things. They wanted no interference from others in their pursuit of young women, and they did not want the young women of London to have examples of independent thinkers to look to. They wanted the naïveté to return, the thirst for a husband of any sort, the ease of their way to the altar.

They undoubtedly wanted other things as well, but he refused to consider those with any real thought.

It was not worth the effort.

Hugh had begged him to break them up, to do something about the mess, and he had agreed. He hadn't actually planned to do anything about the situation other than investigate, but now there was a chance to accomplish the original intention without causing anyone personal injury or doing any harm.

Georgie wanted the Spinsters to be ended, at least in some way. Tony had come to them for the same purpose, though none of them knew it. It was too easy to see how both parties could have their desired result and make many others happy in the process.

Except Tony couldn't think of a single reason the Spinsters ought to have been disbanded.

Not a one.

That perplexed him exceedingly.

He had no idea what Georgie would say further on the subject, but, as her friend, he had agreed to meet her today so that they might have a discussion on the topic. They were to walk in Hyde Park, though he wasn't entirely sure how that was going to be orchestrated. Georgie had said she would see to all the arrangements, whatever that meant, and he could only pray she was not planning to stage some sort of illicit assignation.

He was willing to go to many lengths for these women, he knew, but that was beyond anything. A gentleman could only endure so much talk before something began to stick.

Tony sighed as Rollins helped him into his jacket, then proceeded to brush the sleeves for him. "I'm going to have a private conversation with a woman today, Rollins."

"Congratulations, sir," the valet replied, focused on his task.

"I doubt that's the correct sentiment." Tony craned his neck, tugging at his cravat. "She's going to confide in me."

"My condolences, sir," Rollins replied.

Tony frowned at his valet in the mirror. "I don't think *that* is the appropriate sentiment either."

Rollins met his gaze. "I have sisters, sir. Trust me, it is absolutely the correct sentiment." He patted Tony's shoulder firmly and turned to the bureau.

"She trusts me, Rollins," Tony insisted, tugging at his weskit and examining his reflection. "It's a mark of honor."

"If you say so, sir," came the dubious reply.

Tony gave up the argument. It was obvious that Rollins wouldn't agree, and Tony's attempts to insist that this was a good thing were weak, even in his own mind.

"God help me," he muttered, tugging at the cravat again.

"That about sums it up, sir," Rollins concurred as he fixed the cravat that Tony had just mussed.

Tony scowled at him. "Thank you, Rollins. That will be all."

The valet almost smiled and nodded. "Yes, sir. Good luck, sir."

He bowed and moved to leave the room.

Tony frowned as Rollins left. "You needn't make it sound as though I am riding off to battle."

Rollins paused at the door. "Aren't you, sir?" He gave him a knowing look, and then departed.

Insubordinate servant. Tony shook his head, exhaling sharply.

"Captain Sterling, sir!" came the voice of the landlord. "Rider come for you, sir, with a missive."

Tony rolled his eyes and strode for the door to his apartments. The man could never slide the missives under the door like other landlords. He always felt the need to announce the messages, desperate to find out anything he could about the business of his tenants.

He opened the door and took the note, handing over a few coins. "My thanks to the rider, and thank you, Mr. Lawson." He shut the door before Mr. Lawson could begin to make inquiries, and broke the seal on the note, opening it quickly.

Mr. Partlowe is going to be taking his wife on a walk in Hyde Park around eleven this morning. Mrs. Partlowe has invited me along. It would be best if you happened to come upon us. We will be taking the south path.

Georgie

It was interesting, but the flourish with which she wrote the G in her name made him smile. It was quite different from the neat simplicity with which she had written everything else. Georgie was a no-nonsense sort, with a surprising wit and an intriguing side of mischief, but never anything resembling embellishment.

Except, apparently, for one letter in her name.

He chuckled and folded the note, stuffing it into his pocket.

There was a sharp rap on his door and he looked at it curiously. "Come," he called, not entirely sure if he should.

The door opened rather suddenly, and Hugh entered, his eyes widening at the sight of Tony so near. He looked as though he had slept poorly, or perhaps just minimally, and had undoubtedly had too much to drink the night before.

It was not his best look.

"Cousin," Hugh clipped, blinking his reddened eyes almost separately as he entered the apartments.

Tony nodded in greeting, closing the door when his cousin failed to do so. "You look terrible, Hugh."

"As well I might," Hugh laughed harshly, rubbing a hand over his face. "A night of gaming and drinking after the ball."

That wasn't promising, but it explained his cousin's rumpled appearance. "And how did you fare?"

Hugh looked almost amused. "I won, and I lost, and neither of those in extreme."

"And the drink?"

There was a slight wince at that. "Perhaps to the extreme."

Tony nodded, though it really was quite obvious. "I see."

Hugh stared at him, his eyes narrowing, his mouth tight.

Tony returned the look with a rather mild stare of his own, not saying anything.

The silence continued on, the only sound the grandfather clock in the corner ticking.

Just when Tony thought his cousin might have fallen asleep on his feet with his eyes open, Hugh exhaled roughly. "Dammit, Tony, what were you thinking last night?"

"Last night?" Tony frowned at him, shaking his head. "I don't see why you are so opposed to my dancing with Miss Westfall…"

"I'm not talking about Miss Westfall!" Hugh snapped loudly. "I don't care about Miss Westfall. Devil take Miss Westfall!"

"Careful, Hugh," Tony warned him, his tone turning dark and dangerous.

Hugh huffed and slapped his gloves into an open hand. "I did not intend for you to make things more difficult when I asked you to investigate the Spinsters, Tony, but last night…"

Tony gaped at him incredulously. "Surely you're not speaking of Delaney and Lucy Wilton."

"Of course, I am!" Hugh laughed again as if that should be obvious. "Delaney is a close friend of mine since school, a very good sort, and an excellent card player."

"Which is exactly what a gentleman should aim for," Tony

scoffed, folding his arms. "I suppose you don't mind that he fancied taking a fifteen-year-old girl to the orangery unaccompanied."

"He was doing no such thing!" Hugh protested. "The girl was feeling weak and he offered to escort her to get some air."

Tony barked a hard laugh. "Is that what he told you? That's how he described it? Painted himself as the perfect gentleman, did he?"

Hugh sputtered noisily. "So, he might have given her some innocent flirtation! What harm is there in that?"

"Innocent flirtation?" Tony shook his head in disbelief, not altogether certain he was above beating his cousin to a bloody pulp. "Hugh, I saw them with my own eyes! Lucy Wilton was not faint, she was not in any distress at all, and Delaney was not playing the gentleman with her. She is a child! A naïve little thing that had no idea the sort of trouble she could have been in had anybody else in the world seen them alone together. They were not going for air, they were going towards the orangery, *away* from the night air."

A flash of distress crossed Hugh's face, cracking his outraged expression slightly. "No, surely not. Delaney swore to me that you had to play hero, that somehow the Spinsters got to you."

"You believe Delaney's account of things, do you?" Tony nodded in thought, a heaviness settling in his stomach. "Your own cousin. You believe him over me."

"Were the Spinsters involved, Tony?" Hugh asked, his voice no longer so indignant. "Was Miss Allen?"

Tony gave his cousin the barest sort of smile he could manage. "And what if they were? Does it make one bit of difference who saw the danger first?"

"There may not have been danger," Hugh suggested. "But if it was Miss Allen, you can be sure the whole thing was overdone, and you might have had the wrong impression."

"No one gave me an impression of what was happening," Tony snarled. "I took my own stock of the situation and acted. If Miss Allen happened to be involved, it would have been in a manner befitting a woman of Society with a general concern for one of its own, which is more than I can say for so many others."

Hugh did not miss the implication, and he stiffened in response. "Delaney will spread this all over Town, you know. He will put the word out that you are helping the Spinsters, and that you are against us all. Every man will look at you with contempt."

Tony shook his head again. "I'd rather bear the contempt in their eyes all my days than see a moment of distress in hers. Look to your priorities, cousin. Miss Allen has the right of it."

He clipped a brief nod and left the apartments, storming his way down the stairs.

A walk in the park would undoubtedly do him some good. It would give him time to think how he would convince Georgie to keep the Spinsters alive and well and offer whatever he could to help them do even more.

"Captain Sterling!"

Tony smiled broadly at the approaching Partlowes, looking the very picture of a proper English couple. Georgie walked beside Mr. Partlowe in a simple green walking dress and spencer, her bonnet ribbons loose and trailing. She saw him at once and widened her eyes meaningfully.

He had no idea what she was trying to say, but surely he could manage this bit without being wrong.

"Partlowe," Tony greeted, reaching out to shake his hand. "A pleasure to see you again."

Mr. Partlowe, always a man of some reserve, inclined his head at the compliment, then turned to his fairer wife. "I don't believe, Sterling, that you are acquainted with my wife."

Tony bowed to her, smiling further still. "Alas, I am not. Your servant, ma'am."

Mrs. Partlowe returned his smile, but it was reserved as well. "How do you do, Captain?"

"Much better for having made your acquaintance at last."

She grinned outright at that, taking him by surprise. "Now I see what my sister Elinor has been going on about. You're quite a character, aren't you, Captain?"

"Emma," Mr. Partlowe murmured quietly, seeming a trifle

uncomfortable with her quip.

"No, no, Partlowe, it's quite all right," Tony assured him, wondering why he had seen the need to correct her for something so slight. "You must remember that I can be a character at times, and there are stories from school to prove it."

Partlowe looked almost as uncomfortable at the recollection, but he tried for a smile.

"I had forgotten that Mrs. Partlowe was formerly Miss Asheley, and I am acquainted with Miss Elinor a little." Tony looked back to Mrs. Partlowe, still smiling. "She is a lovely girl, Mrs. Partlowe."

She laughed once. "I think you mean lively, sir. So, are you acquainted with Miss Allen here, then?"

The look on her face told Tony that she knew exactly how acquainted he was with her, and with others, but it seemed her husband did not. That was curious, but he knew Partlowe, and he could not say that he blamed her there.

Tony bowed in greeting to Georgie. "I am, yes. Good morning, Miss Allen. How are you?"

Georgie curtseyed prettily, managing to smile. "I am well, thank you, Captain Sterling. And yourself?"

There was a slight bite to her tone, but if the others noticed, they gave no sign. Tony managed to keep his smile contained. "Very well, indeed."

"Where are you headed, Captain?" Mrs. Partlowe asked him.

He glanced at her as if pleased by the question. "Nowhere in particular, ma'am. I am simply enjoying the fine day."

"Perhaps you will walk with us," she suggested brightly, looking at her husband for permission. "Then Miss Allen would not be awkwardly grouped with the pair of us."

"Oh," Tony replied, looking at both Mr. Partlowe and Georgie, "that would be very fine, indeed, but only if Mr. Partlowe can bear the thought of only having one fair companion instead of two."

Partlowe laughed at that, smiling at his wife with the first real warmth that Tony had seen in him yet.

"And if Miss Allen does not mind the company," he added, giving Georgie a look.

Her expression was playfully disgruntled, but she cleared it before the others could see. "I have no complaints."

"There now," Partlowe stated as he politely released Georgie's arm. "Join us, please."

Tony did so, then waited for the Partlowes to precede them along the path before following at a respectable distance.

"Good lord, Tony," Georgie hissed once it was safe. "I could have choked on your manners."

"Just being gentlemanly, Georgie," he replied, keeping his tone low as hers had been. "Wouldn't want to raise any suspicions."

"You could have made some fairly obvious insinuations and it still would not raise any suspicions for Mr. Partlowe," Georgie told him, staring at the couple ahead of them with a hint of distaste.

That was true, but he was surprised to hear her speak so about her friend's husband. "I was under the impression that you and Mrs. Partlowe are the best of friends."

"We were," she responded, flicking her gaze to him quickly. "What of it?"

"You don't like her husband." He shrugged a shoulder. "That seems odd."

Georgie made a soft noise of irritation. "I don't dislike Mr. Partlowe. He's decent enough, but so sedate. So reserved, so proper."

"And that's a bad thing?"

"For Emma, yes." Georgie shook her head, the yellow ribbons dancing with the motion. "She didn't used to be so demure and tiresome. She was more like Elinor, but with sense. I didn't think she minded being a spinster with the rest of us, but then she…" She waved her hand at them.

Tony nodded in thought, beginning to understand her point. "She married for comfort."

Georgie bobbed her head quickly. "I should have been happy for her. I was happy that she was happy, but I did not think she particularly was. It didn't feel happy, Tony, it felt like surrender."

"Not everyone is as independent as you, Georgie," Tony reminded her. "And not every woman is comfortable with being a spinster, as you are."

She stopped just then and looked up at him. "Comfortable. Is that what you think this is?"

Her words startled him, as did the rather straightforward tone. He suddenly felt as though he were the one being investigated. "My apologies. Apparently, I am wrong."

"Hmm." Her brow furrowed slightly, and she began walking again, smiling when Mrs. Partlowe looked behind her at them. "Comfortable. It's not wrong, I suppose, but it's not the word I would choose. Accustomed, perhaps. Resigned, certainly. But comfortable?" She shook her head quite firmly. "There is no comfort in being a spinster, Captain."

"Oh, it's Captain again?" he teased, suddenly anxious for her to be brought out of melancholy.

Georgie gave him a sidelong look. "You called me a spinster, Captain."

He returned her look. "And? Are you not?"

She sighed, and he heard the weight of it. "No, I am, and probably quite soundly so at my age. But no one likes to be reminded of the fact. We haven't forgotten what we are, but you don't see anyone else in Society being defined in the same way. There's no spite in being a bachelor or a miss or an heiress, yet we all know to whom those titles refer."

"Again, I apologize, Georgie," Tony said, taking a risk by moving just a bit closer. "I didn't mean anything by it."

"I know that," she allowed, smiling a little. "I doubt anybody does. But that's just it." She considered her words with care, then dipped her chin. "It is one thing for us to call ourselves spinsters. It's another thing for anyone else to."

Tony looked at her then. "Why is that?" he asked gently.

Her smile turned sad. "We laugh when we say it. Or smile. We know the truth."

"What truth?"

"That those women called spinsters, whatever the reason, have private moments of crippling loneliness. Mind-numbing insecurities. Pillows drenched with tears. And the smiles we bear, as with the titles, hide the fact that we hurt all the time. We laugh because we understand each other." Georgie's throat worked on a weak swallow. "No one else does."

Tony had never acted in any way that would have been

considered forward or untoward, but he had the maddest desire to take Georgie's hand at that moment. She sounded so lost, so alone and helpless. He'd never imagined that a woman as vivacious and bold as Georgie could suddenly be as vulnerable and exposed as she was.

"Georgie..." His fingers reached out just a little but didn't quite make it to her.

She shook herself quickly and looked up at him. "Apologies, Tony. I didn't mean to grow maudlin."

He exhaled slowly, relieved she was returned to him, though not at the sudden defenses she had thrown up. "I didn't find you maudlin in the least. It was very honest, and I like that."

Georgie laughed as she toyed with her bonnet ribbons. "If you like that, you should take more opportunities to speak with me. I'll be so honest you will run to your stepmother for comfort."

Tony grinned at the image that brought up. "I don't think Miranda would be overly fond of my running to her for comfort. She'd laugh in my face if I did that."

"I like her already."

"You would."

They smiled at each other briefly, then looked away. "So," Tony said almost briskly, "you are considering disbanding the Spinsters, with a capital S?"

Georgie chewed on her lip for a moment. "Considering, yes. But not straightaway. It's just... Well, it's gotten so out of hand. It was never supposed to be like this."

"Like what?" Tony asked, not following.

She reached into her reticule and pulled out a note, handing it to him. "This is from Ruth Ainsley, thanking me for all of the work I've done. She's envious that I have the strength to endure my spinsterhood so proudly, and she's not going to accept a proposal she had previously been considering because she finds it no longer suits her. I apparently gave her the strength to defy her parents' wishes."

Tony hissed a wince as he scanned the lines quickly, the flowery language painful even to him.

Georgie shook her head slowly. "I never meant for people to envy me, nor to prevent girls from marrying if they so chose, nor to defy their parents. What is there to envy? We don't live in a world where a single woman may do as she pleases and have all the advantages of life. I did not mean to become someone others wished to emulate. I only wanted to reassure others who might find themselves in a situation like mine that it is not as dismal as it seems." She sighed and looked down at the path as they walked. "But the truth is… it can be dismal. Sometimes it is very dismal. And when it is, I find I cannot feel so harshly about Emma's decision after all."

This was beyond anything that Tony had anticipated when he'd agreed to meet her today. There was so much more to the situation, to the Spinsters themselves, than he'd thought. And there was so much more to Georgie. Whatever he'd thought or felt about her before, it was as if he were seeing her clearly for the first time now.

And he was somehow more intrigued.

"I'll help you," he vowed without shame.

Her nose wrinkled up in confusion as she turned her attention to him again. "With what?"

"This," he said simply. "All of this. Managing your expectations, understanding what you want, finding your way through whatever this has become. Whatever you need, whatever it takes. I'll help you, if I can, even if you just need someone to talk to."

Her lips curved into a slight smile, and he saw amusement dancing in her eyes. "I may lash out at you."

"Well, there's a surprise." He returned her smile easily, clasping his hands behind his back.

Georgie's smile spread, and she managed a light laugh. "You're a good sort, Tony Sterling."

He sighed in resignation. "Yes, I know. It is my one failing."

"Oh, give me time," Georgie assured him. "I am sure I could find more."

"You may try."

"And try I will."

He nodded at that. "I look forward to it."

And the oddity of it all was that he truly did.

Chapter Nine

—⁂—

Loyal friends are a rare thing indeed. It is difficult to know if a person can be trusted with secrets of the heart or any sort of confidence, and only time and experience can give this to you. If anyone, particularly a man, attempts to gain your confidence and you do not feel assured of this trust, you are in no way obliged to tell him anything. In fact, it would be better to give him nothing at all, or to even lie. A woman's trust is a sacred thing.

-The Spinster Chronicles, 10 February 1816

"I don't understand why I cannot be there on Writing Day."

"Because they are private writings."

"That are then circulated about London days later?"

"They are private when we are writing them. Then we read them to each other and get approval, and *then* they are circulated."

"So why may I not give my approval?"

Georgie sighed and discarded a card from her hand, giving her partner a scolding look. "Because you are a man."

Tony looked back at her, shaking his head. "That is not my fault."

Grace coughed a surprised laugh and took a quick sip of the lemonade beside her. "That's true, Georgie."

Georgie glared at her. "Not helpful. Discard, if you please."

She did so with an apologetic shrug at Tony, who only barely glanced at her, keeping his gaze steady on Georgie. "Am I to be punished for a circumstance over which I had no control?"

"Discard," Izzy reminded him, her smile growing.

"Circumstance?" Georgie repeated with a short laugh. "Is that what you're calling the fortunate nature of belonging to your sex?"

Tony laid down a card and smirked a little. "I am not about to get into a debate about the benefits or consequences of being a man or a woman, Georgie."

"That's a relief," Grace muttered, widening her eyes as she examined her cards. "I think you would lose."

He looked at her in disbelief. "What? Why would I lose?"

"Don't!" Izzy warned with a laugh. "Don't say another word, Tony."

Grace smirked at him, fluttering her lashes playfully. "Because you cannot see clearly how very much better your lot is in life than ours, and until you can, you will never understand the discrepancy."

Tony blinked at her, then looked at Georgie and Izzy. "I understand that there is a discrepancy, and I know where it lies as well. I'm not an idiot."

"Well, thank heavens for that," Georgie told him.

Izzy shook her head and laid down a card. "I'm going to have to separate the pair of you to save us all an argument."

Tony chuckled, sitting back in his chair. "Grace took part, too."

"Then we'll separate her, as well." Izzy shrugged without concern. "I'll not have anybody quarreling at my card party."

"That's never stopped anyone before," Georgie reminded her fondly. "Somebody always quarrels when the Lamberts gather."

Izzy threw her a scolding look. "It is not that bad."

She laughed once and gestured to the room in general. "Do you see who is here? Give them ten minutes, Izzy. Your brothers alone would be cause for concern, but with Charlotte and Grace's brothers? Not to mention…"

"All right," Izzy overrode, her cheeks coloring a bit. She huffed a little sigh and turned to Tony. "My brothers are not easy-tempered and have strong opinions. Charlotte's brother enjoys starting debates of any kind with them, says it is always an adventure to see which brother will take which side, but really it is just very loud and blustery. And Grace's brother…"

Grace groaned and set her cards down. "James is so high and

mighty, one would think he had already inherited the title, and it's not even a very grand one. No one can tolerate him for five minutes, not even me."

Georgie laughed easily and looked at the over-trimmed Mr. Morledge, engaged in an animated conversation with Izzy's father, who had taught his sons everything they knew about argument, though he had more restraint than any of them.

"So, the spirited nature of your group is hereditary," Tony mused aloud. "What a comfort."

Izzy snorted, and Grace rolled her eyes. "All except for Izzy, you forget. She's never fought with anyone in her entire life."

"Not true!" Georgie and Izzy said together, making the rest laugh.

"Please tell me there are stories," Tony begged, leaning forward to rest an arm on the table. "I am desperate to know when Izzy lost her temper."

Izzy hooted a laugh and looked at Georgie expectantly. "Would you care to disillusion the dear captain, or shall I?"

Georgie scowled at her. "It was always my fault," she admitted reluctantly. "Izzy would only defend herself, or me, as the case usually was."

Tony moaned in disappointment, shaking his head. "I knew it. I just knew it."

"I beg your pardon?" Georgie demanded, grinning outright. "What did you know?"

"That it was your fault," he replied at once. "It would have to be, wouldn't it? You're you, and Izzy is Izzy."

"And I am gracefully escaping wherever this conversation is headed," Grace interjected as she scooted her chair back, making them all laugh again.

Before she could rise, however, Prue appeared at their table, looking almost sickly.

"Prue?" Georgie moved to get up, but her friend waved her back down gently.

"Miss Westfall, are you ill?" Tony asked as he rose, his face a mask of concern.

Prue shook her head quickly, giving him a faint smile. "No,

Captain, I am well. I've just…"

"Little lamb, what is it?" Charlotte came up and took Prue's elbow. "I saw your face when you came in, and it quite terrified me. Was your mother insufferable again?"

"No m-more than usual," Prue managed, stammering a little.

Izzy gave her a warm smile. "That's the first time I've heard you truly admit that she is so."

Prue swallowed with a small nod. "It's fairly o-obvious, isn't it?"

Georgie frowned at that. It wasn't like Prue to be cynical in any way, and yet there was a bitter edge to her words that unnerved her. "What is it?"

Prue laid a hand on the card table, her mouth tightening. "We've had word from my aunt and uncle Howard. They are bringing Eliza into town at the end of the m-month."

Georgie, Izzy, and Charlotte hissed in pain and Georgie covered Prue's hand with one of hers at once.

Grace looked bewildered. "Who?" she asked them, her tone apologetic.

"Prue's cousin," Izzy explained, rising from her seat and going over to Prue. "She makes everything infinitely more difficult for Prue out of spite. I can't think of a single redeeming quality about her."

Coming from Izzy, that was quite a damning sentence.

Grace's eyes widened, and she looked at Prue almost wildly. "Darling, I am so sorry."

Prue nodded quickly, letting Izzy hug her. "I d-didn't think they were coming this y-year. And I was s-so pleased…"

Izzy and Charlotte looked at each other over Prue's head, and turned her away from the rest, leading her to a quiet corner. "It's all right, lamb," Charlotte soothed in a very motherly tone. "Don't fret yourself."

Grace put a hand to her head with a soft moan. "Are these Howards people of importance in any way?"

"Some," Georgie replied, suddenly feeling mildly unwell herself. "Her mother is sister to Mrs. Westfall, and they are very similar in nature and appearances. But her husband was a member of Parliament before he was replaced last year, and he's never stopped making noise about it. They seem to be absolutely everywhere when they are in London."

Grace muttered something under her breath that made Tony jerk in surprise. "That means I'll have to admit them into my association, and undoubtedly invite them to our ball." She made a noise of disgust and rose quickly. "I'll have to speak to James about this immediately. If I can persuade him to take my side, perhaps we can convince Mama not to include them."

Georgie looked up at her in surprise. "Would they intentionally cut someone like that?"

"Papa wouldn't," Grace said with a shake of her head. "But he's on the Continent for who knows how long. Mama is less determined, and rather indulgent of her children. There is a chance. Not much of one, but I have to try." She nodded to them both, then swept away with more elegance than Georgie could have managed in her life.

Tony looked at Georgie then, fiddling with the cards absently. "Is it really going to be so bad?"

She looked across the table at him. "You remember what I said about Mrs. Westfall?"

He nodded, saying nothing.

"I would rather endure Mrs. Westfall every day for a year then spend five minutes in Eliza Howard's company," Georgie informed him without any hint of shame.

He gaped at that for a moment, then shook his head. "I have difficulty imagining that."

"You will see for yourself soon enough." Georgie made a soft noise of amusement as she stared at Tony for a moment. "She's going to try for you, you know."

That seemed to take him by surprise. "You think so?"

She nodded with confidence. "Oh, yes. Eliza is a very conniving creature and being a handsome captain with a rather respectable fortune will be all the enticement she needs. Don't secure a house for yourself yet, that would set her quite firmly on your scent."

Poor Tony looked thunderstruck and a bit horrified at the prospect. That would only grow worse when he actually became acquainted with the wretch.

But then Tony smiled slyly, and it caught Georgie in her chest, surprising her with the pleasure-pain it invoked. "What?" she demanded, trying to tamp the sensation down.

"I didn't know you thought I was handsome," he told her in a rather smug tone.

Georgie groaned and shook her head, rising from her chair. "Don't do that."

"Do what?" he asked as he rose as well.

"Pretend not to be fully aware of your own appearance." She glared at him and started a slow turn about the room. "It is most unbecoming in a man."

Tony was at her side quickly, hands clasped behind his back. "I would never pretend at false modesty, but I also cannot admit to anything. The trap of being a gentleman."

Georgie rolled her eyes and turned her attention to the room in general. "I'm not going to listen to you complain about your difficulties in life, Tony. I acknowledge you probably have some, but they are not that dire."

"I cannot see that yours are at present either," he informed her in a light tone. "You are well cared for by your aunt, your parents have set you up well, and no one is casting you off."

Was he really so dense as that? Or was he trying to provoke her yet again? She looked at him in suspicion, and he returned her look easily.

Dense it was, then.

"I receive a letter from my mother no less than once a month telling me what a disappointment I am," Georgie informed him in a quiet voice. "She despairs of my ever amounting to anything useful and cannot see why she ever bothered with my education and accomplishment considering the way I have turned out."

"What?" Tony's voice was a little too loud, and she shushed him, looking around quickly. Only Charlotte seemed to notice, and she gave Georgie an odd look, but went back to her conversation with Prue.

"How long do you think my aunt will continue to be generous?" Georgie hissed to Tony, now watching her intently. "Or Izzy? How long do you think we have until we must do something with ourselves, or seclude ourselves in the country in a small cottage that our parents will reluctantly provide?"

Tony stared at her, eyes wide, not even a sound of response from him.

"Or perhaps I could become a companion to my mother," she went on, letting all her pent-up derision seep into her words. "I have no doubt she would see my uses then, as I would be free for her every criticism and forced to endure her ordering me about to avoid being sent away."

"Georgie…" Tony tried, his voice rough.

"There is no place for a spinster without a fortune or title," Georgie snapped, looking at him again. "I am not as fortunate as Grace or Charlotte. I have endured the world's pity and its scorn, knowing that the one purpose I am supposed to fulfill in my life is kept from me, though God alone knows why. I will never be able to become the sort of woman Lady Hetty is because the world would not look as kindly on me if I were in her position. I would have nothing but its disdain, a burden to all who had any concern for me. That is the nature of my difficulties, Tony. Will you complain about yours now?"

He said nothing, and Georgie felt herself seething, the anger rolling off her skin as a billowing cloud.

"What can I do, Georgie?" he finally inquired in a low tone. "Tell me."

His sincerity quieted her distress and allowed her to draw an easy breath again. She even managed a smile, breathing deeply once more. "Forgive me?" she suggested. "I seem to be lashing out more than usual lately, and it's not becoming."

"Georgie, you have every right to your feelings," Tony insisted kindly, "and nothing to apologize for. I can take a lashing, if you must call it that, but it's my own fault for being careless with my words. I don't understand your position, but I should like to. I don't know how to put this except bluntly, but I should like to be your friend in truth, not just in name and because of our connections."

Georgie smiled without having to force anything at all. "We are, Tony. We are. Which is why I really must apologize for my behavior. One does not treat friends this way."

"I already gave you full leave to give me whatever verbal beatings you see fit," he replied. "Stop apologizing before I grow vexed and tire of your company."

She chuckled and stopped at a window that looked out over the back garden of her aunt's house. "Consider it done. I would hate to truly become disagreeable to you."

Tony nodded sagely and took up position on the other side of the window. "It is enough to bear with your temper, I couldn't imagine what you'd be like as disagreeable."

She pretended to kick his shins, and he pretended to wince at it.

"Why aren't you married, Georgie?" Tony asked without any preface, his dark eyes almost speculative. "I'm not being insensitive, but you are a handsome woman with no small amount of charms, no matter how spiteful your temper can get."

She narrowed her eyes at him for that, which made him smile.

"And I understand that your fortune is respectable…" he went on.

Georgie made a face. "That would be putting a favorable light on it."

"It's not off-putting," he reminded her. "Certainly not enough to make you a poor prospect. So why?"

"That is the question of a lifetime," Georgie sighed. "One many people have asked, including my mother, though not with your curiosity."

"Don't put me off, Georgie," he scolded, lowering his voice. "Come on now, why are you unmarried?"

Why, indeed. She'd asked the same question hundreds, thousands of times over the years. She'd wondered what she lacked, how she could improve, and why there had never been any interest in her. She'd done everything right, the same way every other girl had, and yet she had come up lacking.

She'd asked everyone, including her mother and her cousin, and each of those inquiries had proven utterly useless.

Why was she unmarried?

"I don't know, Tony," she admitted frankly. "The best response I can give you is that nobody ever asked."

Her answer didn't seem to surprise him at all, and he watched her still, looking at her as though he could see something that intrigued him. What that could be, she couldn't possibly say, but she could not say that she minded. After all, he was a rather handsome man, and she did not have one of those staring at her often.

"But the answer I usually give is that I'm naturally unpleasant," she quipped, suddenly feeling a mite breathless.

Tony chuckled at that. "Well, there is that, yes."

Georgie scowled, wishing she felt more outrage at his lack of refute than she did. "You could defend me, you know. A gentleman would have."

He shrugged one shoulder. "I've never seen the need to rise up in defense of a woman when it was her own words that provide the reason. Counterproductive, I find it."

She fought the urge to laugh again at his extraordinary statement. He was always saying things like that, no doubt for the shock effect as well as for amusement, and his timing was near perfect every time.

Georgie was growing quite used to that. She and Tony had not spent much time together since their walk in Hyde Park the other day, it was simply not possible to do so without raising suspicions. Neither of them wished to have rumors start about them, so they had to be mindful of opportunities and settings.

Here at her cousin's home, it was much safer. They had invited only close friends and associates, so they could converse without speculation.

Of course, he still called on them when the Spinsters were gathered, but not every time, again for the sake of reputation.

He'd said that he would not mind anyone speculating on his having an attachment with Izzy or Georgie if it would help, but they'd assured him it would only make him more of a spectacle.

That had made him pause, and the subject had never been brought up again.

"Any further thought on…?" he prodded, leaving the thought unfinished.

Georgie was grateful for that. The room was not large, and with all the girls here, they could easily be overheard. It was a small mercy that Elinor had not come, as she would have undoubtedly been trailing behind Georgie the entire time.

She shook her head in response. "Not really. I mean, it is always on my mind, but nothing has changed since we spoke last. You?"

He considered that, his head tilting slightly in thought. "Some. Nothing definitive, but it might help to parse out what exactly you no longer enjoy about it. Is it the girls?"

She scoffed at that. "No, not at all. I adore them. They are true friends, undoubtedly for life. You saw how we all banded together for Prue just now, and nothing's even happened yet."

Tony nodded, smiling over at Prue, who was seated next to Izzy, though not engaging in conversation. "There is a special bond among you all, that is obvious. Was it always that way?"

"Almost," Georgie replied, thinking back on it. "There was Emma and Izzy and I, obviously. And Charlotte was a good friend of ours. We adopted Prue almost at once, she was so timid, even then. Grace has only recently joined us, but she adds so much to our group."

"And you never included anyone else?" Tony straightened against the wall, looking around. "Surely there are more spi... that is, unmarried women about."

Georgie smiled at his correction. Since their conversation in Hyde Park, he had never called them spinsters again, unless indicating the capital S. It was really very sweet, though she wished she had not scolded him for it.

She was entirely too sensitive on the subject, and it would only further damage their fledgling friendship.

"No, we never thought to widen our circles," she confirmed, smiling at Charlotte, who was attempting to put off Grace's brother from conversing with her. "We didn't even think to replace Emma when she married."

"No designs to take the Spinster Chronicles to the entire country?" Tony teased with a laugh.

Georgie shuddered and pushed off the wall, seeing the speculative look in her aunt's eyes as she watched them. "Heavens, no. Walk with me, my aunt grows suspicious."

Tony looked where she indicated, then nodded once, gesturing for her to lead the way. "Shall I look cross to throw her suspicions into disarray?"

"I would be most grateful, yes," she replied, only half in jest.

He immediately furrowed his brow, his mouth forming a perfect frown.

Georgie had to force herself not to laugh. "Very good. So convincing."

"Too much?" he asked, shaking his head slowly as if Georgie had said something wrong.

"Rather perfect, actually." She managed to look over at her aunt again, who looked almost exasperated. "I'll be hearing about this for days."

"You have experience with this." It was not a question, nor did it have any tone of disapproval in it.

Georgie gave him a sidelong look as they walked. "Most men tend to wear that expression in my presence. I have yet to determine why."

"You cannot think of a single reason?" he persisted, a brow rising in disbelief.

"Oh, all right," she blustered a little, frowning without having to pretend. "I speak to most people the way I do with you, but only when provoked. I can be very well-behaved when I wish to be."

"I'm sure you can," Tony replied in the most unconvincing voice she had ever heard. "Though I imagine hating men has something to do with it."

Georgie turned to him, her hands on her hips now. "I do not hate men! I like them quite a lot!"

"Don't announce that too loudly," he suggested, looking around them.

"I do!" she insisted. "I simply hold them to a high standard."

He looked doubtful. "Do they know that?"

"They would if they asked," she quipped, "but none ever do."

"It's not the sort of question one asks a lady," he pointed out, forgetting to furrow his brow.

She shrugged her shoulders easily. "Then I suppose I will have to write about it in my next column."

That caught his attention and he nodded in thought. "I shall have to give my approval to the article. As a man with a vested interest in the column and its successes, you must allow me that."

Georgie shook her head at once, smiling smugly. "Not a chance, Tony. It was a good try, though."

He scowled at her in earnest. "Come on, Georgie. Let me help."

"Not with the column. If you want to help, find out what the gossip really is about it, and me, and then report back to me." She gave him a daring look, wondering what he would say to that.

Tony straightened up, then stared her down. "I will. And I won't protect you from what I find, Georgiana Allen. If you want me to do this, if you really want to know, I will tell you exactly what I hear, word for word."

Clearly, he thought this would intimidate her, but she was made of stronger stuff than that. Years of practice had given her a far thicker skin than anyone expected. Necessity had dictated she must gain that, at least.

"I accept." She stuck out her hand, as a man might have done. "Are we agreed?"

Tony looked down at her hand, then back into her eyes. He reached out and clasped her hand. "We are," he replied simply before drawing her hand up to his lips for a quick kiss.

She barely had time to gasp at the bold gesture before he was gone, sitting down at the card table with Charlotte and two others.

Georgie looked around quickly, praying no one had seen that, for there would be no easy way to explain it. No one marked her, so she seemed safe. She rubbed her hand almost absently as she moved back to the window, suddenly feeling rather warm.

Much, much too warm.

Chapter Ten

—◦⌘◦—

The trouble with gossip is that it is sometimes very useful, but other times only hurtful. A clever woman is able to discern the difference, but a silly one will repeat it all without thought. A good woman knows there is absolutely no benefit to gossip whatsoever and avoids it at all cost. A man, however, does not care about gossip. He already knows everything anyway. Or so he presumes.

-The Spinster Chronicles, 25 April 1817

"Are you a praying man, Francis?"

"I've been known to bow my head on occasion, but I'd hardly call myself religious. Why?"

Tony groaned and leaned his head back against the carriage, closing his eyes. "I would take it most kindly if you would pray that I never do something so stupid as to encourage gossip again."

Francis coughed in surprise, his walking stick suddenly whacking Tony in the shin. "What?"

Tony nodded without opening his eyes. "I know. So, if you wouldn't mind…"

"Lord, please save Tony from his own stupidity," Francis muttered.

"Amen."

His cousin barked a hard laugh and Tony opened his eyes to look across the carriage at him. "What was that for?" Tony asked.

"I wasn't actually praying for you," Francis informed him with a sardonic look. "That was more of a curse."

"Not sure that was very helpful, then."

In truth, he wasn't entirely sure a prayer would have helped him either. He'd spent a full week learning everything he could about the Spinsters from the point of view of everybody else in London. He'd called on the Partlowes and managed to bring them up in conversation, and discovered that Mr. Partlowe, while speaking very highly of the women in general, disapproved of their group as a whole. Mrs. Partlowe did not seem to disagree, though she did not concede to anything her husband said either.

Lady Hetty found them all exceedingly agreeable and wished she'd thought of such a task at their age, though there were hardly any unmarried girls in her situation. All of them had been "poorer and plainer, and nothing worth going on about." He'd have to take her word for it, but she was most likely a fairly unbiased source.

Fairly.

Then he'd been to every sort of event the Season could manage in the course of a week. He'd followed the guide mentioned in that week's Spinster Chronicles and found it to be an accurate portrait of what Society offered. Theater, balls, card parties, soirees, luncheons, even a scholarly meeting of bluestockings and intellectuals; he'd been rather out of place with the scholars, but he muddled through well enough.

Everybody had an opinion on the Spinsters.

Fathers of daughters found them to be interfering and insufferable. Young men thought them shrewish nannies-in-waiting. Mothers fussed about the effect on their daughters, and the difficulties for their sons. Scholars thought it an imprudent rebellion against tradition, while the bluestockings found it ennobling and admirable.

The young ladies were a mixed bunch, depending on which side they took. The fairer, more experienced ones thought it a ridiculous venture by embittered old maids to make the rest look foolish, while the plainer, sometimes younger ones found great delight in applying the lessons to their own lives. Old women fussed and bothered. People in the streets used their name as a joke or an insult. The cads and wastrels at gaming tables cursed them regularly.

And then there were the few girls who spoke of them with an almost reverence, their eyes soft at the mention of them. They spoke of gratitude and enlightenment, of finding their own strength, and two who were now happily married spoke of the Spinsters as being the reason that they were so.

Nothing correlated, and everything was subjective.

Which made perfect sense to him, as it was all gossip.

And he hated gossip.

His leg was suddenly kicked, and he jerked his head up to look at Francis again, unaware that he had begun to drift off. "What?" Tony demanded, wanting to rub his eyes of the bleariness that they currently held.

Too much social interaction in a short amount of time had left him sleep-deprived and agitated. And as his interaction with Georgie or any of the other girls had been very limited during that time, he was also sorely lacking in decent conversation.

"Would you care to tell me why you are engaging in gossip mongering of late?" Francis asked with all the imperiousness of a peer. "After all, we are using my carriage to meet your friends."

Tony exhaled heavily and sat up taller. "For your kindness, my lord, I will oblige you."

Francis scoffed loudly but folded his arms and looked interested.

"For the past week," he began, his voice sounding almost as weary as his body felt, "I have been unusually social for the express purpose of collecting information and gossip. About the Spinsters, with a capital S."

His cousin groaned and looked out of the window. "For God's sake, man, you're obsessed with the Spinsters."

"Everybody is obsessed with the Spinsters," Tony protested, crossing an ankle over his knee. "You should have heard the way everyone jumped at the chance to talk about them. And that was before this week's edition came out. It only got worse after that."

"I could have told you that." Francis exhaled heavily and turned back to him with an almost disgusted scowl. "Why are you doing this, Tony? And don't tell me you're bored or you're curious, I won't believe that. Something is driving you."

Tony stared at his cousin for a long moment, letting the sounds of the carriage fill the silence. He hadn't admitted to anyone what he was really doing, or why he was involved at all. Only Hugh knew the true purpose as it originally had been, and they had not spoken since their fight. He had received a very brief note with a poor attempt at an apology, but as no apology had been made therein, he did not see a need to accept it as such.

"I've been asked to investigate the Spinsters," he finally confessed.

Francis did not look impressed. "By whom, the Prime Minister?" He snorted incredulously.

"By your brother."

That drew him up, and he stared at Tony wide-eyed. Swearing under his breath, he leaned forward. "What did he ask you to do? More to the point, why are you doing it?"

Tony smiled blandly. "He asked me to investigate them and break them up."

Francis swore again and rubbed his face with both hands.

"And I agreed because... I was bored and curious." Tony let his smile spread into one of excessive innocence.

Francis dropped his hands and glared at him. "Very funny."

"It's true," he admitted. "But I didn't intend at that time to break them up, nor do I now. I've come to know these women decently well, and now I seek to support them in any way I can."

"Oh, Lord," Francis moaned leaning his head back and looking heavenward.

"Are you praying or cursing this time?" Tony inquired mildly, watching in amusement.

"Both," Francis snapped. He squeezed his eyes shut and shook his head slowly back and forth. "Why, Tony? Why?"

Tony chuckled at his cousin's distress. "Because they aren't actually doing half of what London thinks they are. Because they could use a friend on the outside. Because it turns out that being a spinster in general is not pleasant for any of them, but they're trying to make the best of it."

Francis winced at the last bit and reluctantly nodded. "All right, I concede to that, but really, collecting gossip? Surely they know what is being said."

"Not entirely." Tony shrugged and glanced out of the window. "Most things are not said to their faces or in their presence. Georgie asked me to look into it, not thinking I truly would, but I said…"

"Georgie?" Francis interrupted sharply.

Now it was Tony's turn to muffle a curse and he waited for the fatal blow to fall.

"Would that be Georgiana Allen?" Francis continued, drawling now, his interest further piqued. "Widely speculated as being the leader of the Spinsters?"

"She'd never put it that way," Tony insisted, shaking his head, "but she probably is, if any of them must be called such."

"I see. And you've spent a good deal of time with her, yes? If you call her Georgie…" The suspicion was blatant, as was the suggestion.

Tony scowled, wishing the earth would swallow him up at this moment. "I spend a good deal of time with most of them, Francis. I call them all by their Christian names, at their request."

Francis laughed heartily, too heartily for Tony's taste, but it was to be expected. "And Georgie is your favorite."

"What?" Tony almost barked, whipping his head around to look at Francis. "Why would you say that?"

The dark eyes of his cousin sparkled with humor. "Because she's the only one you mentioned by name. But if that wasn't it, your reaction just now would prove it."

Tony lowered his head in abject misery, wishing he'd never opened his mouth about any of this. His cousin would be insufferable about it now and would tease him to the end of time about Georgie, and he wasn't prepared for that. He had no defenses against it.

Because it had only just occurred to him days ago that Georgie *was* his favorite. Hers was the company he had missed the most in the last week. She was fairer in his memory than he thought she'd been in reality, but he couldn't be sure, as he suddenly considered her to be rather fine in all respects.

She was beautiful, and somehow, he'd missed that before.

He had no rebuttal against accusations about his feelings for her, his relationship with her. He wasn't sure what they were himself. All he knew was that he wanted to pursue whatever it was and see how it played out.

The Spinsters were all friends of his, and he would protect and defend them for life.

But Georgie…

That was entirely different.

"Don't worry about it, Tony," Francis said calmly with a sniff, as if he hadn't just discovered a great secret. "Miss Allen always was Janet's favorite one. Introduce me at the ball this evening, will you? I want the pleasure of a dance with her."

Tony looked up at him in surprise. "I've not even danced with her. I don't know if she's any good at it."

Francis shifted a little. "That doesn't matter much, does it? You hate dancing, so she can dance with me instead."

There was no possible explanation for the madness that had just overtaken his cousin. A fever would not have him looking so well, no delusion could take hold so quickly, and Francis did not possess acting skills proficient enough to be pretending at this. He must have simply taken mad.

Tony would have a hard time explaining that to Janet.

"You hate the Spinsters," Tony reminded him weakly.

"I do not." Francis shook his head firmly. "I find the discussion of them to be an annoyance. You think well of them, so must I do. You hold Miss Allen in some great regard, so must I do." He lifted one shoulder. "Simple as that."

Tony gaped at his cousin for a long moment, curious that Francis should shift his perspective so suddenly on his word alone. Something Hugh had not been capable of in his limited knowledge of the situation.

"Ah, here we are," Francis said as the carriage rolled to a stop, preventing Tony from expressing his gratitude in whatever way he could manage.

He nodded and climbed out of the carriage, blinking hard in the bright sunlight.

Of all days for London to not be its usual dreary self, it had to be a day when he was already pained by nearly everything.

Tony looked around the coaching station as Francis disembarked behind him. Henshaw and Morton ought to have been easy enough to find, having yet to resign their commissions. Unfortunately, scarlet was a popular color this Season.

Or so the Fashion Forum had stated the other day.

"There," Francis pointed out, gesturing with his walking stick. "Is that them?"

Tony looked, and sure enough, Henshaw's broad shoulders and wide grin met his gaze. Morton stood next to him, more reserved, as usual, but seeming pleased to see him. He moved swiftly in their direction and shook both their hands warmly, introduced them to Francis, and then followed them into the inn.

Francis ordered a luncheon for them all, and they sat in a private room together, regaling each other with stories from their past and reminiscing on former comrades. Henshaw told most of the stories, which suited his nature, and Tony and Morton were left to defend themselves as much as they were able, with Francis not believing anything they said.

Once the meal was finished, Henshaw leaned back in his chair, scratching at the pale scruff along his jaw. "Oh, it is good to be with a group of lads again. I've had no one but my sisters for days, and they are so much noisier than I remember."

Morton chuckled at that, his wide eyes flicking to his larger friend. "You're the one who wanted to go, Henshaw. I offered to have you come stay with my family, as it is only Kitty and me, but you insisted."

Henshaw gave him a sour look. "Your sister would be terrified of me, Morton. According to you, she is too shy and sweet to tolerate my roughness."

"Yet you have seven sisters," Tony mused aloud.

"Nothing shy or sweet about my sisters, Sterling," Henshaw grunted, though he smiled. "Just surrounded by females all the time."

"Poor lad," Francis mourned, raising a glass to him.

Henshaw sat forward suddenly. "Speaking of being surrounded by females. I've heard you're associating with spinsters now."

Tony groaned and shook his head as Francis began to laugh. "Please don't ask."

Oddly, Henshaw didn't laugh. "I've heard they're quite the group. Do you know if they are recruiting? Or if they even do that?"

"Sounds rather ominous," Morton murmured as he sipped his drink.

Tony ignored him. "You know a spinster?"

Henshaw nodded once. "Yes. Well, no, not exactly. She's a widow, but she was only married for about five minutes. She's without family or friends, and she's fresh out of mourning, I believe, and coming to London."

Tony looked at Morton, who shrugged helplessly, and at Francis, who only made a face. He returned his attention to Henshaw. "How do you know her? Personal interest?"

"Protective interest," Henshaw corrected, blue eyes flashing. "I met her brother doing some training with the Highlanders. He asked if I might look after her when I returned."

"Scottish girl?" Tony was surprised by that, as it was hardly a common thing to have a Scottish woman in London these days. "And you agreed?"

Henshaw glared. "He knew I had many sisters. He asked me to do so, brother to brother. I take that seriously."

Morton seemed to consider that, then turned to Tony, his disheveled dark hair disheveling further. "I would, too, for my sister."

"So would I," Francis added softly, surprising him. Francis might not mention it often, but he was remarkably protective of Alice. There were more than ten years between them, but they were unusually close. Had she not chosen to spend a year abroad, she would have been flitting about with the other young women of the Season, no doubt being carefully guarded by one or both of her brothers at every turn.

He faintly wondered how Francis would feel about the Spinsters had Alice been about.

Tony nodded at his friend, smiling a little. "I'll see what I can do. They may not take my suggestion to heart, but if there is a young woman in need of friends and associates, I think they just might. Tell me her name, and I'll see to it."

He wasn't exactly in the mood for the theater again, not after the week he'd had, but he had promised to be there, and to attend the ball at Charlotte's afterwards.

There was no refusing the Spinsters when they set their mind to something.

Besides, it would be better for him to tell Georgie exactly what he could before he forgot it all or had a chance to think too much on it. And he now had a task for her to see to as well, and he thought she might need the diversion, given what he had to tell her.

It was destined to be an unpleasant night, and he hadn't even seen the play yet.

But at least he would see Georgie and the others, and there was some comfort in that.

Oh, he had seen them from time to time at various events, as they really were invited to many things individually, but he had kept his distance. None of them had said anything about it, so he assumed that Georgie had told them, at least in part, what he was doing.

Or she'd flat out lied to them all.

He could never be sure with Georgie.

He hid a yawn behind a gloved hand, then moved into the main of the theater. He hadn't bothered securing a box or anything of the sort. His cousins had begged off but would attend the ball later. He fully intended to snooze during the bulk of the show in the hopes that it would allow him some energy for the ball.

But for now, he would smile and nod at all who acknowledged him, making all manner of small talk, and generally being a congenial gentleman, as his reputation had indicated he was. If word was getting out that he was associated with the Spinsters in some way, he would need to present a persona that was above reproach. The perfect gentleman, a warm acquaintance, and a good sport, if it came down to it; proper and respectable at all times.

Surely he could manage that.

"Tony!" Charlotte's voice called out to him.

He bit back a groan.

So much for proper and respectable.

He turned to face her, bowing politely. "Miss Wright."

She grinned at him, her dimple making an appearance, and

winked. "Don't think me forward. I call everybody by their first name in public, so I might as well do the same with you."

"If you like," he replied, nodding once. "You look lovely, Charlotte."

She truly did, in a gown of deep pink that heightened her rosy complexion and made her dark hair and eyes richer. The cut was bold, but not to the extreme. It was very flattering, and very Charlotte.

Charlotte beamed up at him. "For that, Captain Sterling, I shall take your arm. Come and sit in the box with us."

He could not bear the thought of enduring more than a quarter of an hour with her bevy of suitors vying for her attention. He would not last the night if he did.

"Charlotte..."

"We're all going to be in there," she overrode. "My parents, Izzy, Prue, my brother, Mrs. Lambert, Georgie..."

"Really?" he said with interest, his ears perking up.

She gave him an odd look, which shouldn't surprise him. He practically jumped at every mention of Georgie's name now, and he could not understand why.

"I would have thought your admirers would want to be close to you this evening," Tony explained, giving her a knowing quirk of a brow.

Charlotte rolled her eyes and scoffed. "Lord, no. I get enough of them at everything else, I want to spend the evening with my friends."

Tony chuckled and inclined his head at her. "I am privileged to be included in the group."

"Charles will probably want to talk to you the entire time," Charlotte warned him. "He is dreading the number of females in the box, none of them of any interest to him."

"That shows what an idiot he is, if you'll forgive me."

"I do." She grinned up at him without shame. "This is why I like you, Tony. A proper sense of humor."

He shook his head with a laugh. "Thank you, I think. Why were you alone when you found me, Charlotte? Surely you weren't wandering about alone."

"And what if I was?" she demanded, looking perturbed. "I am an independent woman!"

"Charlotte."

She scowled and waved a hand at a man in eveningwear nearby. "Michael followed me."

"And he is…?" Tony asked, not sure he liked the idea of her being followed.

"Old friend. Very old. Practically my brother."

But not her brother. No, he didn't like that one bit. "And why was he following you?"

Charlotte huffed and frowned at him. "Because I wouldn't let him escort me properly, now are you going to be my nanny?"

Tony raised his hands in surrender and led her to the box, Michael following behind yet again. They arrived and heard sounds of jubilation from the girls. Even Prue seemed delighted to see him, and he found a great comfort in that.

"Mr. Wright, Mrs. Wright," Tony said as he bowed to them. "A pleasure to see you both. I hope you don't mind my joining you, Charlotte insisted when she saw me just now."

"Not at all, not at all," Mr. Wright exclaimed. "The more the merrier! Michael, find another chair, will you?"

Michael nodded without speaking, then left the box again.

Remembering his duties, Tony turned to bow to Mrs. Lambert. "Mrs. Lambert, what a pleasure to see you again."

She didn't look entirely convinced, but she smiled politely. "Captain." Her eyes flicked to Izzy, who had only waved at him and was now talking with Prue again.

Tony greeted Charlotte's brother with a handshake, but he was preoccupied arguing with his sister, so paid Tony little mind, which suited him well enough.

"You look rather ill," came Georgie's voice in her usual straightforward manner.

He turned to look at her and found himself suddenly without words or breath.

However he had imagined her in his mind over the last week, it had not been remotely like this. She was an absolute vision in a cream muslin with a pale green panel extending from the square bodice, gathered at her waist, and falling the length of the dress. Elegant gold embroidery fashioned vines and flowers along the bodice, and the green ribbon in her hair bore a similar embroidery. Her eyes seemed somehow more green, more vibrant thus, and her hair was fairer than gold, but only just.

"You look extraordinary," he replied, somehow managing the breath to say it, though his sense returned to him the moment the words escaped. If only his control had done the same.

Georgie's brows rose in surprise, but her lips curved into a small smile that teased at his heart. "Why, thank you, Tony." Her brow puckered, and her smile turned almost coy. "You did mean that as a compliment, yes?"

"Yes," he rasped, nodding fervently. "I did."

Her smile grew, and she gestured to the seat beside hers. "Sit here, if you like."

He did like, and he did so. It was a trifle difficult to see the stage from behind Mrs. Lambert, but he did not mind that much.

"This way you can fall asleep without offending anyone," Georgie whispered, holding her fan up to shield their conversation.

Tony smiled as he looked at her, still somewhat blinded by her stunning beauty. "Is it that obvious?"

She shrugged a little. "Not wildly, but I know you, and I've never seen you look so fatigued. Trouble?"

He shook his head at once. "No. Gossip."

Georgie wrinkled up her nose at that. "I don't like the sound of that. Do you have much to report?"

He nodded, unable to stop looking at her.

She heaved a little sigh. "Very well. Don't tell me now. Wait until the ball. We will probably be less likely to be overheard there."

Michael returned to the box then with another chair and set it down beside Charles Wright and began conversing quietly with him.

Tony watched for a moment, then leaned closer to Georgie. "Who is Michael?"

She looked over, then back to him, trying not to grin. "That is Michael Sandford. He was at the Galbraith's garden party, remember?" At his shake of the head, she smiled again. "He holds the distinction of being the first person to propose to Charlotte."

That was not what Tony had expected to hear and he looked back to the man. "And he is still here?"

Georgie nodded, giggling just a little bit. "He is still here. Can't stay away, even though Charlotte doesn't see him romantically at all. And he has never courted anyone else. Isn't that something?"

It certainly was, though he wasn't sure if it were something mad or something admirable.

Tony looked at Georgie with a fond smile. "How do you know so much?"

Her smile turned sly as she looked back at him. "Being a spinster has some advantages, one of which is knowing far more than anybody thinks about things nobody knows about."

He couldn't keep his smile from turning to a full-on grin as he stared at her. "I am very impressed, Miss Allen. What else can you tell me about the members of Society?"

Georgie laughed, then looked towards the stage. "So much. So very much. But don't you want to spend the time here sleeping, Captain Sterling?"

As she glanced back at him, Tony shook his head slowly, smiling rather stupidly. "Not anymore, I don't."

Chapter Eleven

The most extraordinary things can happen at balls. Whether they be good or bad is entirely up to the parties involved. And whether or not those things have witnesses.

-The Spinster Chronicles, 2 April 1816

Being profoundly labeled a spinster by all who knew her didn't preclude Georgie from deriving pleasure from certain things just as she had when she was first out.

Attending a ball was one such thing.

She'd always thrilled with the excitement of it, despite the fact that she rarely danced anymore, particularly at a ball as fine as one held by the Wrights. They were among the wealthiest, most influential members of Society, and all of London begged for an invitation to anything they hosted. The Wrights were adored by most, revered by some, and widely regarded as some of the friendliest, most delightful people that had ever graced high Society.

Georgie could only be grateful to be on such good terms with them as to always be assured of her own invitation.

The ball tonight did not disappoint.

The Wright's ballroom, usually a very elegant room on its own merits, had been transformed into what had to be a glimpse of heaven itself. Candles dotted every chandelier and sconce, swaths of sheer fabric were elegantly draped along the walls, and dozens of flowers had been brought into the room, all of them pale shades and blossoming brilliantly. Charlotte had warned them that her mother had taken things to the extreme, but never had Georgie imagined anything so ethereal.

Mrs. Wright had outdone herself, that was certain.

Georgie release a breath she'd forgotten she held and had to smile.

"My sentiments exactly."

She glanced over at Tony, who was escorting her as well as Izzy into the ballroom. They had just finished greeting the Wrights at the entrance, which had seemed superfluous, as they had just been at the theater together, but it was the custom, so they followed along.

"What?" Georgie asked him, curious as to what he thought she was feeling.

He looked down at her, his dark eyes warmer in the light of the candles, and his mouth curved on one side. "This room. These people. This night. It's all rather breathtaking, isn't it?"

"It's perfectly magical," Izzy exclaimed, almost dancing on the other side of Tony. "Oh, it's just lovely! Have you ever seen anything so lovely?"

"No, I have not," Tony replied.

But he had not been looking at the room, as Izzy had been.

He was still looking at Georgie.

Oh, lord…

Georgie swallowed hastily, looking around for any sort of distraction while her mind reeled at the implications. Something had come over him tonight, and she wasn't sure what it was. He stared a great deal, and smiled even more, though not with the same teasing edge she had grown accustomed to. Oh, they had talked and laughed a great deal at the theater as she had imparted some of her best information concerning particular members of Society, and his responses had been just as sharp and witty as before.

But something was different. He was different.

And yet…

"Oh!" Izzy suddenly cried, blissfully unaware of everything going on beside her. "There is Grace! Oh, doesn't she look marvelous? Tony, thank you for escorting me, but I am going to see her now."

"Of course, Izzy. Save one of your dances for me, will you?" he asked, finally turning to her.

Georgie didn't need to look to know her cousin would be beaming up at him for that.

"You could have your pick of the lot, Tony," Izzy said with a giggle. "Just say the word, and the dance is yours."

She departed then, and Georgie was left to be escorted by Tony alone, which, oddly enough, did not bother her in the least.

"What about you, Georgie?" Tony asked, his voice almost lost amidst the hum of voices around them and the musicians that had begun to play.

She waved at Prue, who looked much better tonight than she had at the last ball. Her mother had fallen ill, which everyone was quite relieved about, and Prue looked very pretty in a pale blue gown. She was such a tiny creature, and delicate in more ways than one, but the smile on her face this evening brought her to life in a charming way. She likely wouldn't dance, but she would keep Lady Hetty company, and she did so love the music.

If only...

"Georgie."

She jerked to look at Tony, who was giving her a too-polite smile. "Yes?"

"Will you dance this evening?" He raised a quick brow, and she wondered at the equally too-polite tone in his voice.

"If I am asked," she replied slowly as she attempted to surreptitiously determine the cause of his behavior. But no one was looking at them, and they were not speaking loudly enough for those nearby to overhear. "I am a touch out of practice."

"No one dances with you?"

Georgie shook her head, then inclined it with a warm smile as she caught sight of Lady Hetty, who winked boldly at her. "No, they fear what I will do to them."

Tony chortled a little and seemed to straighten up. "I'm not afraid. I will dance with you."

"My hero," she muttered blandly. "Don't put yourself out."

"Trust me, Georgie," he replied with more warmth than she anticipated. "Dancing with you would not put me out in the slightest. I rather think I will ask you."

She glanced up at him with narrowed eyes. "Now?"

Tony returned her look, then let a slow smile spread across his face, which somehow stirred an equally warm sensation to slowly course through her. "Not now. When you least expect it."

Georgie's breath caught in her throat and she wrenched her gaze back to the safety of the mingling guests. It was too much. She was losing her mind and had somehow taken leave of her senses. She was not this silly sort of creature, always blushing and agitated. She could not be so fluttery when she was on the arm of the handsomest man in the entire room. Alone.

Her heart lurched quite forcefully at that thought.

Oh, that was enough, now! Tony was a friend of hers, and only recently so. He was a very good man, and an excellent companion, given his wit and intellect. He was not a man that ought to possess her thoughts so completely as he seemed to be doing, and she ought not to dwell on the current changes in him with such wonder. He was exhausted, that was all. She had given him an assignment and he had taken it up with great energy. He was undoubtedly unaware of the way his words sounded, or how his behavior could be portrayed.

There was absolutely no reason for him to be treating her in any respect other than that of a good friend.

That was all.

"Come, Georgie," Tony said suddenly, his tone markedly brighter than it had been all night. "I want to introduce you to my cousin."

Georgie's heels began to dig into the ground as she whipped her head around to stare at him in horror. "What?"

He nodded quickly, smiling with all the excitement of a little boy. "He asked to be introduced to you this evening."

"But… but…" she stammered, wondering why her feet were still moving when she expressly bade them to stop. "Why would he want to be introduced to me?"

Tony slid a sardonic glance her way. "Because he knows I know you."

"Tony!" She huffed in irritation and tried to find her words, though her throat suddenly burned in distress. "That doesn't mean a blasted thing! Loads of people know you know me, and they…"

"Aren't relations of mine," he finished easily, guiding her around a small group of people. "He knows that I have become acquainted with the Spinsters, and today when he asked about it, he also asked to be introduced to you."

Georgie chewed on her lip with a distressed whimper. "Why?"

Tony stopped and looked at her closely, his brow furrowing. "Because we're friends. Because I've been spending time with you. Because he's a good man who prefers to make his own impressions of people. Because he's my cousin, and what is important to me is important to him."

She couldn't bear to ask the question that was in the forefront of her mind and clamped down on her lips to keep it from escaping.

And I'm important to you?

She stared at Tony for a long moment, her heart pounding somehow harder still as she began to lose herself in the darkness that swirled there. Had he always been this handsome? Had his voice always rippled down her spine as it did now? Had his smile always turned her knees this way?

"Also, he may expect you to insult me or be quick-witted," Tony said at last, the intensity of his look only slightly abating as he gave her a crooked smile, leading her forward once more. "I am sure he is destined to be disappointed there."

Georgie swallowed and fought for control. "No more than he undoubtedly is attempting to banter with you."

Tony laughed once and nodded. "That's much better. I thought you would faint for a moment, and I have no idea what I would have done then."

"You could have been heroic and carried me to safety," Georgie pointed out, grateful that she was feeling more herself. "Think what that would have done for your reputation."

He gave a mock shudder. "No, I thank you. Women might begin fainting all over the place just so I might save them."

Georgie snorted once and looked around the room derisively. "I doubt it would get that far. It's not *that* tempting a prospect."

Tony made a face as if she had wounded him and shook his head slowly. "Not kind, Miss Allen. Not kind at all."

She tilted her gaze up to him. "Still wish to introduce me to your cousin?"

He met her gaze without any hint of reserve. "Yes."

Curses...

She forced her attention straight ahead and exhaled slowly. Surely it meant nothing. One made new acquaintances all the time, especially at events such as this. Why, she had introduced Tony to dozens of people in the recent weeks, purely to expand his social circles.

Lord Sterling was reportedly a good man, and a fine gentleman. His wife was more opinionated and certainly a beauty, but very well thought of. They had attended some of the same events, and she knew them by sight, but their paths had never crossed.

Now they would.

"Why does that bother you?" Tony murmured, as if he could read her thoughts.

"I never know what people think of me, or what they have heard," she whispered through her teeth. "Not knowing which side they take bothers me."

Tony covered her hand with his, then dropped it quickly as they approached more people. They were in public after all, and it would not do to be overly familiar here. "My cousin will be polite with you, and stern with me," he told her quietly. "Just as you'd prefer. His wife, as I understand it, thinks highly of you and the girls, so you have no cause for concern there."

"And you?" she replied almost briskly, her fingers tightening on his arm. "What do they think of you?"

He grunted softly. "I am a necessary evil."

Georgie managed a smile. "I doubt that."

"Which part?" Tony asked, sounding intrigued. "I'm not evil?"

Georgie shook her head, her smile turning into a smirk. "Necessary. Entertaining, perhaps, but not necessary."

He hissed and craned his neck as if uncomfortable. "A bit harsh, Georgie, even for you."

"Prove me wrong, Tony Sterling," she taunted, smiling pleasantly as they approached his cousin. "Prove me wrong."

"If you insist," he muttered darkly. Then he brightened. "Francis, Janet, may I present Miss Georgiana Allen?"

Lord Sterling, not quite as handsome as his cousin but certainly handsome enough, smiled with surprising warmth. "Your servant, Miss Allen." He bowed very politely, then indicated his wife. "My wife Janet, Lady Sterling."

Georgie curtseyed, as did Lady Sterling, who was positively beaming as she came forward to take her hands. "My dear Miss Allen, it is a pleasure to make your acquaintance at last. I've heard so much about you."

"From whom, my lady?" Georgie asked, unable to help smiling in return. "For that will determine your opinion of me. And if Tony is the one informing you, there is no telling what your thoughts and impressions will be."

Lady Sterling threw her head back and laughed, while her husband grinned, flicking his eyes to Tony. "Oh, Miss Allen," Lady Sterling said, once she'd recovered, "I liked you before Tony ever said a word, not that he said much to me, but now I positively adore you. Come and take tea with me this week, hmm? Bring whomever you'd like, or no one at all. I'll send a coach for you."

Georgie stared at the lovely woman in disbelief, sure there was some mistake, but smiling all the same. "I would be delighted, my lady, if you are quite certain."

"She's always certain, Miss Allen," Lord Sterling assured her, still smiling himself. "She prides herself on it."

"Pity about her marriage, then," Tony offered with a heavy sigh.

Georgie widened her eyes at him meaningfully and jabbed him with her elbow hard.

Lady Sterling smirked a little at Tony. "Careful, Tony. You know how Francis can be."

"Ahem," Lord Sterling interrupted with a scolding look at each of them. "How Francis *is*, my dear. Come, Miss Allen, will you dance the next with me? My cousin is obviously giving you a poor impression of the Sterlings. Allow me to make amends." He held out his hand and smiled in a very sincere apology.

Tony made a noise of playful outrage, but Georgie ignored him and put her hand into that of his cousin, returning his smile with one of her own. "I wish you would, my lord."

As it happened, Georgie found herself growing enormously fond of Lord Sterling and his wife. Lord Sterling had the same sort of wit and humor as his cousin and expressed it in such a droll way that one could miss it if not paying close heed. He danced well and kept up a steady stream of conversation without plaguing her with unnecessary commentary. He'd instructed her to look delighted no matter what he said and to laugh on occasion so that Tony might have some fear and trepidation about their topics of conversation, and Georgie had played along.

Sure enough, the moment they had returned, Tony had demanded to know what they spoke of, and her aloofness made him even more agitated. The look on his face when he behaved so was particularly endearing, and he continued to give her consternated looks the rest of the evening, no matter where she was.

At the present, she was enjoying herself by watching the dance in the company of Lady Hetty, who always had the most delightful things to say about whatever she was witnessing. And as Jane Wilton was currently dancing with a particularly fine man in uniform that they did not know, the speculation from the older woman was utter perfection. Georgie laughed so much her sides began to ache, and she had difficulty containing that laugh in a ladylike fashion.

Tony, however, wasn't watching the couple. He was dancing with Grace, who looked the picture of the goddess she was. He would make her laugh, then they would send speculative glances in Georgie's direction.

When she could manage, Georgie would stare just as boldly back.

"What are the two of you playing at?" Lady Hetty suddenly asked from beside her.

Georgie turned to look at her in surprise. "I beg your pardon?"

Lady Hetty had never looked so derisive in all the years Georgie had known her. "Come now, Georgie. I've seen the two of you together, and now I am seeing you stare at each other across the ballroom. There is a connection there."

Heart suddenly pounding in her ears, Georgie tried to swallow and look completely baffled by this insinuation. "My lady, Captain Sterling and I are friends, and we have been for some weeks."

"Friends don't look at each other like that," the older woman asserted bluntly, her wrinkled visage somehow turning more severe.

Georgie laughed a false, grating laugh. "Oh, no, Lady Hetty, I am teasing him. I danced with Lord Sterling, and Tony believes we spoke of him. He's been trying to get the details out of me all night, and I am playing coy. There is nothing in it, I promise."

Lady Hetty suddenly gave her a smug smirk. "Tony, is it? Well…" She returned her gaze to the dance, then made a noise of disapproval. "And there he is dancing with that charlatan."

"Grace?" Georgie coughed and shook her head. "She is lovely, Lady Hetty. And one of the Spinsters."

Lady Hetty shook her head. "I don't trust a girl so fair and fine to be a spinster for the right reasons. Mark my words."

Georgie bit back a groan and shook her head. "I'll mark them," she conceded dismissively.

There was absolutely nothing wrong with Grace, aside from the fact that she was a spinster and ought not to be. Lady Hetty could look for the remaining years of her life, but she wouldn't find a single blemish on the person or character of Grace Morledge. It was one of the most irritating things about the girl.

It was the *only* irritating thing about her, actually.

The dance concluded to general applause and Prue suddenly nudged her from the other side. "Tony's coming over," she whispered. "Why is he looking at you so fiercely?"

Georgie almost groaned again. She couldn't bear any more speculation, and certainly not from Prue. "I had an assignment for him," she confessed as she fanned herself more quickly. "He's been trying to find an opening for us to confer about it privately."

"Well," Prue muttered with a very small smile, "my very ill mother just came into the room wearing a vibrant shade of yellow, so your window of opportunity might be now."

Georgie looked up and saw Mrs. Westfall parading around as if miraculously cured and drawing far too much attention to herself. The gown was both unsightly and unflattering, which would not necessarily correlate, but certainly did on her particular person.

"Prudence Westfall," Georgie muttered, leaning close, "did you just suggest something unkind about your mother?"

Prue's cheeks flushed brilliantly, but she smiled a little. "No. But you may infer it, if it helps."

Georgie chuckled and covered Prue's hands with her own. "It certainly does." She looked up then as Tony arrived, Grace having been deposited somewhere else, apparently. "Captain."

He bowed. "Miss Allen. I wonder if perhaps…"

"Yes," she said with a prim nod. "Quickly, before the shock of Mrs. Westfall's canary impersonation wears off."

He choked out a laugh and gestured for her to lead the way.

Georgie threw a wink at Prue over her shoulder, then quickly moved through the people nearest them towards the gardens. She knew this house well, having spent much time here with Charlotte and the girls, and the gardens, while not as extensive as some others, were particularly well shielded from the windows of the ballroom.

It would have been an ideal setting for any sort of tryst, come to think of it, but most guests would have entered them from the main doors of the ballroom. Most of them did not know the passage that led to the servants' door into the gardens, and that it was fairly easy to make one's way there without witnesses.

One could only hope word of this particular architectural insight had not spread far.

The Spinsters would live up to everybody's declarations if that were true.

But tonight, it served its purpose, and they made a clean escape from the ballroom without incident.

"That was some of the best strategic maneuvering I have seen outside of clandestine services," Tony said with a quiet laugh as they moved further into the gardens. "Please tell me you sent Mrs. Westfall the dress just to be a distraction."

Georgie shook her head, laughing herself. "I am not that clever, but I so wish I had. Such a flattering shade, don't you think?"

"I do," he agreed as he pushed a small tree branch out of the way. "I would have added more feathers, though. Much more birdlike."

"With that nose? People would have expected her to burst into song, and trust me, that would not be pleasant." Georgie threw him a knowing look that had him chuckling more.

They reached an opening in the garden, the lights of the ballroom only barely visible, though the upper windows of the house were clear.

Georgie frowned up at them. "We'll have to hope there are no spies, or we will really be in for it."

Tony looked up at them as well and shrugged. "We'll tell them I've recruited you for covert operations and refer them to the Foreign Secretary."

"Would that work?" she asked dubiously. "Do you know him?"

He shook his head and waved her onto the stone bench. "No, but it would take them several weeks to even get through to him, so we'd have sorted everything out by then anyway."

Georgie snorted softly as she sat, shaking her head. "Well, Captain Sterling," she sighed, lacing her fingers together in her lap, "what is everybody saying about the Spinsters?"

Tony seemed to hesitate, then his shoulders sagged, and he began to tell her.

She sat still for the entire telling, nothing particularly shocking or upsetting being revealed. The extremes were laughable, certainly, but not truly offensive. If any of them had been possible by a small group of women, it would have been a miraculous feat. And given such supposed extremes, it was clear that the general populace thought themselves far less moral than they actually were. The comments by mothers and fathers of girls who enjoyed their column stung somewhat, but she could hardly be blamed for the misguided actions based on interpretation.

Could she?

According to Tony, the very people crying for an end to the Spinster Chronicles were the ones who could quote particular passages, indicating that they were devoted readers of it. Would they find themselves regretting their retraction of the clever commentary on Society when it was gone? Or would they take pride in removing an annoyance from their presence, and consequently find that absolutely nothing had changed?

The gentlemen of London seemed to have the most complaints,

which was strange as they, as spinsters, rarely interacted with them at all. She could not take any responsibility for the behavior of young women who spurned certain men, and the very few times they had actually done anything by force had been directed purely at the women involved. The one exception had been Tony seeing to Mr. Delaney, but she hadn't heard anything on that score.

Tony watched her almost expectantly as he finished, but she only nodded as if it were nothing more than she expected. She suspected he had kept the details of the complaints from her to spare her, but she could imagine what they were. They would revisit her tonight as she lay in bed, and her mind would twist each until her doubts and guilt overwhelmed her.

Tears would be shed, breathing would grow painful, and she would vow to end it all and live quietly in the country forevermore. Then sense would return, fatigue would set in, and she would fall asleep while telling herself she would fix it all tomorrow. Waking the next day would be only a faint echo of the night before, and she would proceed as she had done for years without moving one way or the other until her good humor returned.

She knew the pattern well.

Georgie smiled up at him faintly. "Well then. What do they say about me?"

Tony blinked at her, brows furrowing. "Georgie…"

"I already know what they say about us collectively," she told him a bit sharply as she tugged at one glove. "I want to know what they say about me."

Clearly, he did not want to tell her, and she didn't blame him for that. But she had to know, and if he could not tell her, who could?

"Please, Tony." She tilted her head, softening her smile and her tone. "Please."

He shook his head slowly, then exhaled. "Many people think you are choosing not to marry."

Georgie blinked in confusion. "I'm what?"

His mouth formed a tight line as he nodded once. "Not marrying intentionally. To become the voice for spinsters and make yourself more influential. Rather like Charlotte, but without the fortune or romantic notions."

"Am I?" Georgie spat, her fingers gripping each other tightly. "Well, when you find the line of men queuing up to ask for my hand that I am apparently so adept at refusing, kindly inform me so that I might live up to that assumption."

Tony's gaze on her remained steady. "Georgie..."

"What else?" she demanded. "Tell me more."

"Georgie." He sat on the bench beside her, shaking his head. "Georgie, it's enough. You don't have to hear it."

She glared at him with all the venom she felt for the rest of them. "Tell me."

He exhaled through his nose in irritation, a strange fire in his eyes now. "They say that you are a proud woman without redeeming qualities, a shrew in the making, and that the reason you remain unmarried, apart from the refusals, is because no man can get close to you without being verbally assaulted. You are too independent and too filled with your own self-importance. You have never needed anyone, so those who might have been brave enough to bear the vitriol saw no reason to try."

Any breath in Georgie's lungs seemed to simply vanish as she stared at him. There was no air to inhale or exhale, and hardly any to keep from swooning off the bench entirely. Her fingers seemed numb in her lap, yet she felt them shaking against her.

"What do you mean I never needed anyone?" she whispered. "How can anyone know I never needed anyone?"

Tony's face softened, and he took one of her hands. "That's only what I've been told."

"Of *course* I needed someone," Georgie insisted, her voice catching. "I could have used someone at any given time! But that doesn't mean I was going to wallow about it. I had to get on with life, didn't I?"

"Yes, you did," he replied, squeezing her hand hard. "And you have, Georgie."

She could barely hear him over her own thoughts. "I don't mean to be unpleasant," she admitted roughly. "I didn't mean to make anybody hate me."

Tony shook his head and took her face in his hands. "Look at me, Georgie. Nobody hates you."

The firmness in his tone made her eyes shift to his. "No?"

"No," he repeated. "They just don't understand."

Georgie tried to nod and managed a weak swallow. "They might if they tried. As you do." She inhaled a shaking breath, the feeling of his hands on her cheeks somehow both weakening and strengthening her. "Help me, will you, Tony? Help me not be so unlikable to them."

He stared at her for a long moment, no sound or breath between them. And then his lips were on hers.

She couldn't gasp, couldn't move, could barely think her own name. His kiss consumed every thought and sensation, keeping her grounded yet making her soar. His mouth was soft and sweet, gentle in his caress, and far too soon, it was gone from hers.

Georgie blinked at him stupidly, watching him stare back at her, feeling her face flush. "You kissed me."

"I did," he murmured, keeping just as still as she was, his hands still on her face.

Georgie swallowed once. "Why?"

He wet his lips quickly. "It… seemed appropriate."

That made her smile a little. "I thought it was a bit bold."

There was a faint shake of his head. "It wasn't."

She tried to find some semblance of outrage, however weak. "You took a liberty."

"Georgie…"

"Yes?"

"Don't panic…" he murmured slowly, "but I'm going to kiss you again."

A sigh of relief escaped her, and she nodded weakly.

This time she kissed him back.

She'd never kissed anyone before, and suddenly it was one of her chief regrets in life. But kissing anyone else couldn't possibly be the same as kissing Tony. His attention was entirely focused on her, his lips caressing hers with an eager gentleness that stole her breath. She gripped at his coat with her fingers, afraid to do anything else, but desperate to cling to him somehow. She hadn't even known she wanted him to kiss her until he had done so, and now she only wanted more.

More kisses. More caresses. More him.

More.

He broke off and chuckled softly, touching his brow to hers, one of his thumbs grazing her cheek. "Georgie..."

She reached up to grasp his wrist, smiling breathlessly. "Well..."

"I've wanted to do that all night," he confessed, brushing his nose against hers.

Georgie dipped her chin shyly. "I did too. I just didn't know it."

They shared a wild grin. Then Georgie's eyes widened, and her heart dropped to her stomach. "We can't tell anybody about this."

Tony reared back, shaking his head almost violently. "Good heavens, no." He made a quick face. "Not that I'm regretting it, because I'm really not..."

"Charlotte would be beside herself," Georgie overrode, horror setting in.

Tony gaped for a moment. "Oh, that's a terrifying thought..."

Georgie nodded quickly. "We need to get back inside. Now."

They rose and hurried towards the house without speaking, though she was now painfully aware of his hold on her arm. Those fingers had cradled her face so tenderly, had stroked her skin in featherlight caresses, had held her...

"Georgie."

"Hmm?"

Tony pulled her to a stop and kissed her a third time, this one quick and hard. Then he grinned at her without reserve. "I just needed to get one more in."

Georgie looked up at him in disbelief, then laughed at them both. "Oh, we're in trouble. What am I going to tell them? They know we we're out here."

"I've got something," he said, holding out his arm. "It will distract everyone sufficiently and happens to be true."

"Tell me."

"There's a young woman I need you all to see. A replacement for Emma, if you will. She's a widow just recently come to London..."

Chapter Twelve

———— ◦⟨∞ ∞⟩◦ ————

Some secrets must be shared with others for the good of all involved. Aid can be given, as well as advice; experience shared may save a world of heartache; truth confessed may enlighten minds; guilt expressed may soon be wiped away. But there are some secrets that absolutely, positively, irrefutably must remain untold.

-*The Spinster Chronicles, 19 March 1817*

"You did *what?*"

"Shh! Do you want the entire street to know?"

"I just… You never said anything… Are you sure?"

"Positive. It's the right thing to do."

"Georgie…"

"Izzy. She's a woman in need, why shouldn't we offer ourselves to her?"

Izzy looked unconvinced, wincing in what had to be a painful manner. "She's not a spinster, Georgie."

Georgie stared at her cousin for a long moment as the carriage rocked slightly. "Who are you and what have you done with my nice cousin?"

Somehow Izzy's wince grew briefly, but then her face relaxed completely. "You're right, I know you're right. But I didn't think we were taking on any new girls for the group."

"Perhaps we won't." Georgie shrugged one shoulder and plucked at her bonnet ribbons, retying them quickly. "It may be that

Lady Edith wouldn't suit. But we can still befriend her, can we not?"

Izzy softened somehow further still. "Of course, we can. The poor dear, I couldn't imagine coming to London without a husband once I'd had one. How long has she been a widow?"

Georgie glanced out of the window as they rolled on into Cheapside. "Tony didn't say."

There was silence in their carriage, and Georgie reluctantly looked over at her cousin, who watched her with a speculative look.

"What?" Georgie demanded, practically begging her cheeks to remain devoid of any telling color.

"Tony said we should?" Izzy was very firmly *not* smiling as she spoke, which seemed a miracle. "Tony is making recommendations for our membership, is he?"

"Yes…" she replied slowly. Was the idea really so foreign? Tony had been of great help to them, had livened them all and supported them, and never seemed to mind their distinctly feminine topics of conversation. He had been nothing but kind and respectful and saw to their welfare more often than not. Why shouldn't he make recommendations about potential members of their group?

Izzy appeared unconvinced, watching Georgie carefully. "I find that hard to believe."

"That Tony could make a recommendation that I would take?" Georgie asked, the beginnings of irritation setting in.

Her cousin grinned briefly. "Well, there is that. The two of you fight like a pair of misbehaving siblings."

Guilt flared within Georgie and began to gnaw at her stomach. They did fight often, and quite well, purely for the sport of it, but now…

Now…

"But no," Izzy went on, blissfully ignorant of Georgie's torment. "I was speaking more of Tony's knowing anybody we should consider. He doesn't know anybody, does he?"

Swallowing was a trifle difficult, but somehow Georgie managed. "He knows more than he used to," she reminded her cousin. "We've introduced him to a great number of people."

In fact, Georgie was regretting that she had taken such an interest in expanding his social circles. It had only put him in closer proximity to her, which had undoubtedly led to her having a more favorable impression of him than she ought to have, and, ultimately, for his opinion of her to be too warm in return. He couldn't possibly be as inclined towards her as he seemed to be two nights ago, it was pure folly.

No one had ever been interested in Georgie in *that* way, and as she was only growing older and more set in her ways, it was not likely to change now.

She was used to it by now. If anything had changed... If he really was... Well, that would have been the most terrifying prospect she could have imagined, and one for which she had absolutely no frame of reference. She would never be able to cope properly and would likely never be at ease again.

This would all play out soon enough, and they could get back to their normal way of living.

"But we know those people, too!" Izzy exclaimed, bringing her back to topic. "And we didn't know anyone that we were considering bringing into the group, did we?" Her gaze sharpened on Georgie then. "Did you?"

"Did I what?" Georgie asked roughly, wishing they would arrive already. She hadn't thought Cheapside so very large, nor that Lady Edith would be so difficult to track down. This was all supposed to have been very simple and straightforward, and her cousin was certainly not supposed to be interrogating her as they went along.

Izzy seemed rather put out by Georgie's response, and huffed. "Did you know somebody that you had been considering and didn't tell us?"

Georgie shook her head quickly. "No, not at all."

"Then how did Tony?" Izzy demanded. "And why did he tell you and not the rest of us? We meet together all the time, and he never said a word."

"Tony has other friends," Georgie reminded her with more patience than she thought she could manage. "From before he came to London. As I understand it, one of those friends, a Lieutenant Henshaw, informed him of Lady Edith's situation and that she was just recently come to London. Tony thought she could use some support and acquaintances to aid her in settling here, so he brought it to our attention."

"Your attention. Not ours." Izzy folded her hands and gave Georgie a knowing look that frightened Georgie somewhat. "Since when do you accept Tony's word so easily?"

When? Georgie almost laughed. Since he had kissed her senseless. Since he had become the sight her eyes longed to see. Since he had defended her, stood by her, respected her more than any other person had. Since he had proven himself her equal in wit and banter, and somehow was still the best of men.

She settled for shrugging one shoulder instead of offering a confession that would have startled her cousin. "He has proven himself, don't you think? He's been a good friend to each of us and has not given us a moment's cause for alarm."

"True…" Izzy said slowly, her brow furrowing.

"He would have told the rest of you," Georgie assured her, reaching over to take her hand, "but he had been busy investigating what the gossips were saying about us and making worthwhile connections all last week, and this information only just came to him. We have Writing Day at our next gathering, so he knew he wouldn't be able to share it then. Last night at the ball, he took the opportunity to share his report with me and spoke of Lady Edith then."

Izzy sighed heavily and nodded. "Very well, I concede that he had good reason for sharing it with you. After all, you are our fearless leader…"

Georgie broke out into a relieved smile, satisfied that her concocted explanation was taking root. It was reasonable to assume that those had been his reasons, even if it were not entirely true.

She gave a mock shudder of revulsion. "I am not. Don't call me that."

Izzy returned her smile easily. "I rather think you are. You are fearless, and you are our leader. We can all see it, why can't you?"

"I never wanted to be the leader," Georgie answered, looking out of the window once more. "There's nothing to lead."

"Georgie, what's wrong?"

Izzy's tender tone, which she ought to have been quite accustomed to, seemed to drive tears into her eyes. It was all she could do to keep them contained, and somehow manage to smile, still keeping her face firmly set towards the window. "Nothing, Izzy. I'm only having one of my melancholy spells. It'll fade once we meet Lady Edith. I have no doubt she will be perfectly agreeable."

"Georgie, you haven't had one of your melancholy spells since we started the Spinsters." Izzy reached forward and took her hands, squeezing gently. "What is really the matter?"

Georgie chewed the inside of her lip for a moment, then, once she was sure any trace of tears was gone, turned to face Izzy. "Do you ever wonder if this is it for us?" she asked with the sort of raw honesty she usually avoided.

Except, of late, with Tony.

She couldn't think what that meant, not while she was filled with this turmoil and daydreaming about their kisses.

She cleared her throat awkwardly. "What if we don't marry, Izzy? What will we do with ourselves? My mother will undoubtedly cast me out, and I cannot impose upon your mother forever. I will be a burden to my father until his dying day, and then my burden will be passed to Thomas, and while he is fond of me, I cannot see him being overly generous with my income. Charlotte and Grace need not worry, they have a fortune entirely their own. I barely have enough to be admitted into Society. What if this is it?"

Izzy's eyes were wide, no doubt confused as to what had driven Georgie to express such extremism about their futures. Georgie had always taken care to move forward without showing any fear or apprehension about their situation, as she was desperate to avoid being put in the same category as other spinsters who constantly bemoaned their fate. She would be a different sort of spinster, set a new tone for the name, and do something with her life.

Only she hadn't.

And still she cried over the neglect she'd felt in her life. The dreams she'd let fade. The ache that never seemed to subside.

She was exactly like the other spinsters.

She only hid it better.

And now Izzy knew that.

"Forgive me," Georgie murmured, sliding her hands from Izzy's grasp, lowering her eyes to them. "It was a foolish question, forget I said anything."

"I cannot tell you," Izzy suddenly said, keeping her voice low, "how delighted I am to hear you say that."

Georgie jerked her head up to give Izzy a bewildered look. "You what?"

Izzy smiled a breathless, very relieved grin. "Oh, Georgie, I had no idea, but I can tell you that I have those exact same fears on a regular basis. Not for you, but for me. I have even less to offer than you."

Georgie gave her as derisive a look as she could while still feeling that she wanted to hug her tightly. "You have *more* to offer than me, Izzy. People actually like you, and that includes men. You have a kind heart and a sweet temper, and there's still an air of liveliness about you." She snorted and spread her hands slightly to indicate herself. "I am dull, sharp-tongued, and rather cynical."

"Oh, stop," Izzy laughed. "You put on at least half of that for show, and you know it."

Georgie shrugged again, not seeing the need to explain what her cousin already knew. She might not have known why Georgie did it, but she didn't need to know that either.

"So, what will we do?" Izzy went on, smiling so widely it seemed as though it might touch the edges of her bonnet. "We'll get a cottage in Oxfordshire with the income our fathers set for us, and live quietly within our means, saving everything we can and teaching all of the children in the village how to write clearly and succinctly."

The thought made Georgie laugh aloud. She doubted she would have much more patience with children than she had with people her own age, but it was certainly within the realm of possibility.

"Or…" Izzy tilted her head from side to side as if considering options, "we go to work at a finishing school and work our way up to becoming headmistresses. We are very accomplished, surely someone would want to hire us."

"And who would give me a reference?" Georgie asked with another laugh.

Izzy smiled with an impish glint in her eye. "Tony. And you know he would do it."

Georgie's desire to laugh faded and her smile became forced. Would he? There was no way to know what Tony would do anymore, considering he now apparently enjoyed kissing her. Would he have strong opinions about her leading a reclusive life?

Probably.

Would she take that into account?

Probably.

Because she enjoyed kissing him as well, and she couldn't help feeling anticipation to do it again.

"Lord Sterling might," Izzy rambled, completely missing Georgie's reaction yet again. "Lady Sterling. Lady Hetty..."

The carriage pulled to a stop, and Georgie breathed a sigh of relief. "Oh, we've arrived," she said quickly, not bothering to wait for the servant to help with the door. She pushed it open and climbed down on her own, looking up at the rather simple edifice before her.

"You did send a card or something, right?" Izzy asked as she disembarked. "Lady Edith might prefer propriety."

"I sent both of ours," Georgie assured her, brushing off her dress. "And a note. She should be expecting us."

"Should be?" Izzy squawked. "Should be?"

Georgie strode forward and rang the bell, stepping back just as Izzy reached her side.

"Sometimes, Georgie Allen," Izzy muttered, "you are simply too much."

Georgie nodded once. "Thank you."

The aged black door swung open and a bald, bearded man of some stature answered. "Yes?"

Georgie bit back a laugh and handed her card to him. "Miss Allen and Miss Lambert to see..."

"Herself's expectin' ye," he growled in a thick Scottish brogue as he stepped back to let them in. He was dressed as a butler, though he hardly seemed the part, and the clothing seemed a little tight in places. But he bore the token somber, if glowering, expression a butler would, so he must have been qualified.

Izzy whimpered in apprehension but took Georgie's arm anyway. They proceeded into the dark house, the interior seeming to be dated at least a good hundred years, and yet without any of the grandeur of that era. And given the layer of dust on the currently empty sconces on the wall, without any of its cleanliness.

"Mind tha' step," the servant said brusquely. "Don't need any turned ankles."

They avoided it dutifully, then followed him into a small drawing room, which was much better cleaned than the corridor had been, and in surprisingly brighter colors. It was still rather old and faded, but far more pleasant than Georgie had expected.

"Herself's comin'," the servant grunted, giving the slightest bow ever known to man before leaving the room.

"Georgie…" Izzy whispered, pulling her arm tightly.

"Hush. It will be all right."

Just then, a woman of moderate height and slight frame entered the room, startling them both with her beauty and her small smile, her dark hair neatly pulled back, green eyes sparkling. "Miss Allen, Miss Lambert," she greeted, her brogue delightfully present in the soft tones. She curtseyed, then clasped her hands before her. "I hope you weren't put off by Owen. He's very fond of me, but not entirely trained as a butler. Or footman, for that matter, but he tends to serve as both."

"Lady Edith," Georgie said, stepping forward. "Thank you for letting us call. I know you've only just arrived…"

"Oh, it is my pleasure," Lady Edith interrupted gently, gesturing for them both to sit, and doing so herself. She pulled a tartan shawl around her simple grey dress, smiling. "I don't know a soul in London, and while we haven't really opened the house fully yet, I felt I had to welcome you." Her smile broadened briefly, which had to be a thing of perfection itself. "The tone of your note was rather convincing."

"That would be Miss Allen's way," Izzy replied with a laugh. Then she sobered quickly. "But may we, from the bottom of our hearts, express our condolences on the loss of your husband, Lady Edith. We know you're just out of mourning, so we'd hate to impose."

Lady Edith tilted her head, her full bottom lip pulling as though she bit it. "I'm afraid, Miss Lambert, that the bottom of your heart is rather too far to go for those condolences. I didn't go that far myself. But then, as you've no doubt heard, I was only married for about five minutes." She shrugged a shoulder, again startling them both.

No hint of remorse, even the pretense of it, and nothing mournful about her. Yet she did not seem a vindictive sort, nor the kind that would wish ill on anyone. Aside from her honesty just then, she rather reminded Georgie of Prue, if Prue were a little less shy and a little more open.

She and Izzy looked at each other, then back at Lady Edith, who did not seem surprised by their confusion. But she made no efforts to explain herself and only dipped her chin. "Owen has gone to fetch a tea tray, so perhaps until he returns, you might tell me how you became aware of me? I have no great acquaintances here, and no one to recommend me."

Izzy looked at Georgie expectantly, and Georgie tucked a resigned smile against her cheeks. "Actually, it's a bit out of the ordinary, Lady Edith, for the person who recommended you doesn't know you either."

He'd kissed Georgie. Not once, not twice, but three times.

It was madness, it was absolute madness!

What was worse was that all he'd been able to think about since kissing Georgie was kissing her again.

Not that any of it had been unpleasant, or worthy of any sort of regret. Not in the least. In fact, it was probably the sanest, truest thing he'd ever done in his life.

What was mad was how consumed he suddenly was by the thought of her. Georgie. Everything she said and did, everything about her was now chief in his thoughts. Moment after moment of their association seemed to be forefront in his mind, and he was so distracted by it that he was perfectly useless. Sleep had been absolutely uprooted and disturbed by thoughts of her, by dreams and imagining future occasions with her. He was utterly exhausted, practically delirious, but not entirely aware of any of it, he was so delighted.

Not that anyone would know. Tony had determined he was not safe around those who knew him well enough to notice and inquire, and so had spent the day before cooped up in his apartments. Rollins thought he was ill, and then thought he might actually have gone mad, so he was vastly relieved to have Tony leave the place today.

He wasn't entirely sure what he was going to do with himself, but a long walk about London would do for a start.

Hyde Park was more crowded today than it had been when he had walked with Georgie, but as he still did not know many people, he was not concerned with that. Nobody would care that he was in Hyde Park today without direction or purpose. No one would be stopping to speak to him or ask him questions, and everybody would go about their merry way without noticing him at all.

"Tony!"

Perhaps it would have been better for him to go for a ride out of London and feel the fresh countryside fill his senses. It would have given him more time to think and process, and there would be less need to mind his expressions and behavior.

"Tony!"

His horse was stabled at the local mews, and it had been some time since he had taken him for a good ride. He rarely rode about London, and as he was not settled in a country house anywhere, there was nothing to call him away.

"Tony!"

That was his name. Faintly, it occurred to him that someone had been calling him, and as he processed that in his mind, he stopped in his tracks.

He knew that voice. He blinked hard and told his feet to turn towards it.

His feet would not listen.

He couldn't blame them. No one would have expected him to hear that voice in London, let alone on a day when he was feeling only slightly less tossed about than he had been the day before. That voice belonged to a person who was entirely too intuitive, and entirely too meddlesome.

His stepmother, Miranda.

Tony swallowed hard and turned his head, which decided to obey, towards the sound.

Seated in an open barouche on the lane was indeed his

stepmother, her beauty catching the eye of several gentlemen both young and old, and making her look far younger than she was, as her hair was still the same dark shade it had been in her youth. She wore a large, expensively adorned bonnet that only highlighted her perfectly sculpted cheekbones, and the ribbons danced on the breeze too perfectly. Her complexion was flawless, nearly without line, and her eyes were a brilliant crystal blue. She was graceful, poised, and the picture of utter refinement. It was no wonder she attracted so much attention, she was almost the description of perfection.

Almost.

No one looking at her would know she was the most mischievous woman he had ever known in his entire life, including any of the Spinsters.

One look in that barouche told him that he was in a great deal of trouble and would have to proceed with caution.

He'd rather not have proceeded at all, but proceed he must.

Miranda was not to be ignored.

His feet complied with his order to move this time, and he turned on his path, making his way towards the barouche, forcing himself to smile. It wasn't so difficult, as he adored Miranda, but at this moment, he wished her miles away.

Miranda smiled benevolently as he approached, and he chuckled to himself at how perfectly "Miranda" this all was. She was out for a ride in the fashionable hours in Hyde Park, wearing what seemed to be a newer gown, its sleek lines slimming her where she would wish and enhancing her favorite assets; and all the while she had spotted the stepson she found the most amusement in. She was being admired while doing something she knew could cause some trouble.

It was her dream come true, in his estimation.

"Miranda," Tony greeted, sweeping off his hat and bowing to her. He examined the barouche quickly, then raised a brow at her. "What, Rufus didn't come with you?"

Miranda narrowed her eyes at him, trying not to smile at the mention of her beloved bloodhound. "You know perfectly well that Rufus would never tolerate an open carriage with so many people about. This isn't the country, Anthony, and he might think the passing members of Society rather large foxes."

"You could get a smaller dog," he pointed out.

"Rufus suits me perfectly well, and I don't recall asking your opinion on the subject."

"This is true." Tony shook his head, allowing himself to grin freely at his stepmother. "You are looking lovelier than I recall."

She gave him a small, bemused smile and inclined her head. "Tony, dear, don't flatter me when you don't mean it."

He rested his arm on the wheel of the barouche, peering up at her. "I always mean it when I flatter you, Stepmama."

Miranda's nostrils flared slightly, and her smile tightened. "Anthony Sterling, you know better than to call me that horrible name, even in jest."

Tony adopted a would-be innocent expression. "But that's what you are. Isn't it a mark of respect?"

"It will be a mark of something if you do it again."

He chuckled and smiled up at her. "I hadn't expected to see you in London, Miranda. You've never expressed an interest in returning before."

Miranda sighed as she adjusted her kid gloves. "Well, Mr. Johnston had some business in London, and Arabella decided to join him, and I decided to join Arabella. Now Mr. Johnston has extended his business indefinitely, so we've rented a house."

Tony bit back a groan. Indefinitely was a dangerous word with Miranda, and if she was in London long enough, she would know about Georgie.

That would be a disaster.

"Don't mind me," chimed in another voice, seated beside Miranda, but barely visible at all from his vantage point. "You two keep chatting away and ignore me."

Tony made a show of peering around his stepmother and smiled warmly at his aunt, who was not and never had been a match for her sister in looks but was certainly a handsome woman in her own right even now. "Good morning, Aunt. How are you?"

She smirked at him and folded her hands primly in her lap. "With my sister attracting all of these men like bees to honey? I'm worn out and desperate for a cup of tea."

"Oh, hush," Miranda scolded, her delicate brow knitting as she looked at her sister. "They only want to look, and I'm not going to encourage anybody. I never do. I'm far too old to marry again, and I don't care who hears me say it."

Tony rolled his eyes at that. Miranda was determined to remain devoted to the memory of his father, which he approved of, but she also made a point of reminding everybody that she could marry again, if she wished to, while at the same time determining herself to be older than she was.

"Why are you walking Hyde Park alone, Tony?" Arabella inquired, pointedly ignoring her sister's proclamation, as per usual. "It's a fine day, should you not have a lady on your arm?"

"Or at the very least a horse at your disposal," Miranda added, returning her focus to him. "A gentleman on horseback is a fine sight indeed. One walking on his own a rather poor one."

"Then a poor sight I am, and it will undoubtedly do me a world of good." He gave them both a cheeky grin, drumming his fingers on the wheel.

"Of that, I have no doubt." Miranda frowned a little and turned more towards him. "Tony, could you not convince Ben to come up from Dorset with you? Surely he would be sound company for you."

Tony shuddered for effect. "One month with the good doctor was more than enough, I can assure you. He's very well set up, I'll grant you, and his house is very comfortable, even for you."

She gave him a dubious look at that but smiled in amusement.

"But no," Tony sighed, shaking his head. "Ben has no desire to come to London, nor to take up Mawbry House. He says he feels uncomfortable, as it is your house, and not our father's."

Miranda snuffed loudly, surprising him. "Fiddlesticks. I don't have any children that I have borne, and I promised your father when *we* bought my cousin's house that it would stay within the family. Ben's the eldest, it's his estate!"

Tony shrugged a shoulder, grinning at her vehemence. "Ben wants to make his own way."

"He can make his own way in a large house in Dover," she snapped. She huffed in irritation and looked at Arabella. "Don't say a word, I refuse to deed it to Simon."

Arabella raised her hands in surrender. "I didn't ask. Simon has his own inheritance, and I doubt he'll deserve that one."

Tony did not want to begin a conversation about Arabella's fat and useless son, and he certainly did not need to start a series of rumors about him and a beautiful older woman holding an in-depth conversation in Hyde Park where anybody could see them. He looked around almost apprehensively, trying to keep his pleasant demeanor. Rumors about him would not help the Spinsters, and if Miranda was about in Society as much as he feared, she would hear about his involvement with them.

She would have a great deal to say on that subject when that fateful day arrived.

Especially if she caught word of Georgie. Of *him* and Georgie.

If there was a word to be said about them.

He hoped there would be. He hoped there would be many words to be said.

But what would they be?

A low, amused hum met his ears, and he looked up into the sparkling eyes of his stepmother, now smirking at him.

"What?" he asked sharply, forcing himself not to rear back. "Why are you looking at me like that?"

Miranda still smirked and nodded to herself a few times.

"What?" Tony looked at Arabella wildly. "What is she doing?"

Arabella chuckled and gave him a knowing look. "She's your stepmother, Tony. What do you think?"

That was what terrified him. Miranda had been his stepmother since he was twelve years old, and she had always had far too much intuition where he was concerned. She had always known when he was lying, what he was really thinking, where he had been, and knew exactly how to make him laugh when he'd been determined not to. She'd always tried to be more of a friend than an authoritarian, sometimes opting not to tell his father when he had misbehaved, and it was because of that kinder hand that they had such a warm relationship now.

But Miranda's intuition couldn't possibly extend to his secrets now, could it?

He was far too old for her to analyze as she had done before, wasn't he?

Miranda laughed in a tone that he did not trust at all, then sat back against the barouche seats. "I do hope you will bring her to take tea with us soon, Tony, dear."

He reared back a little, eyes widening. "I beg your pardon?"

"The woman who has you so tangled in knots," she elaborated, her smile turning coy. "The one running rampant through your mind, no doubt throwing your life into complete chaos. It is all over your face, and I must know who she is and how she claimed you."

"I haven't the faintest idea what you are talking about," Tony retorted hotly, folding his arms.

Miranda glowered at him, a look that he knew all too well. "Don't let her know that. She'd never forgive you for lowering her to such an extent."

Tony forced himself to have a completely blank expression, despite his rapidly quickening heartbeat. "Miranda, I'm sorry to have to contradict you, but…"

"I wouldn't," Miranda interrupted with a shake of her head.

"Nor I," Arabella added, intentionally not being helpful, to be sure.

"It's too easy." Miranda sighed and adjusted her bonnet. "We are at Number 14 Mount Street. Bring your lady by, or I will be forced to make inquiries."

He shouldn't have, but he pressed his luck and asked, "And to whom would you inquire?"

The look Miranda bestowed upon him made his heart stop in his chest. "Everyone, Anthony Sterling, beginning with your cousins, Lord Sterling and his wife. I have heard remarkable things about Lady Sterling, and as we were not able to become fully acquainted at their wedding, I feel obliged to make her better acquaintance now. I must say, I am quite looking forward to the prospect."

Tony forced a swallow. "You would start rumors about me, Miranda?"

"Darling," she replied in a very pitying tone, "I am quite sure that the rumors are already started." She nodded at Arabella, who called to the driver, and they pulled away, Miranda waving her dainty fingers at him.

Tony watched them go, feeling rather tossed about by that

exchange. Miranda was meddlesome, tiresome, and altogether too clever for her own good. Unfortunately, *he* was the one that would undoubtedly suffer for it, and who knows what other chaos would ensue as things unfolded. His feelings for Georgie were too fresh, too new to be explored so thoroughly by himself, let alone anyone else.

He had to warn Georgie.

He had to *see* Georgie.

He had to…

Well, seeing Georgie would be enough. He would be at once calmer and more agitated, but only in the best of ways. There wasn't an explanation for it, but he didn't need an explanation.

He didn't want one.

Tony exhaled slowly, amazed that he could smile with ease once the thought of Georgie returned. He turned back the way he had come, thinking quickly on how the day would need to proceed now, and plotting his course to circumvent Miranda's efforts while pursuing his own agenda with Georgie. The Spinsters would need to be alerted, and a plan put into place.

The thrill of battle suddenly rose within him, a long-forgotten friend, and his smile deepened.

His stepmother might be conniving, but she had never met Georgiana Allen.

There was no telling what madness could unfold.

Chapter Thirteen

<hr/>

A group of women when banded together with a common purpose is the most terrifying thing on the planet. Unless their purpose is something foolhardy and doomed to fail, and then it may descend into the worst sort of madness. Or it may rise triumphant and surprise all who doubted its cause. One never knows from the beginning how victorious the end might be.

-The Spinster Chronicles, 1 July 1816

"Oh, you'd like her very much, Charlotte. She's got some spirit to her, despite living in such shoddy conditions."

"I don't like the sound of it."

Georgie looked at her friend in shock. "Of Lady Edith?"

Charlotte scowled. "No, not at all. Of her situation."

"I don't like that either," Grace murmured, setting down her drawing pencil. "Why should a woman of her status be living in such a place? And you said she lives in Cheapside?"

Izzy nodded quickly but did not look away from her embroidery. "Lombard Street, I believe. Charming house from the exterior. A little plain, but quite suitable."

"Lombard Street." Grace looked at Charlotte in utter bewilderment. "I don't even know where Lombard Street is."

"You're a Mayfair girl, dear," Charlotte reassured her almost condescendingly. "You wouldn't."

Georgie raised a brow as she imagined Tony doing, though she knew the impact would not be remotely the same. "Are you inclined to disapprove of those who live in Cheapside, Charlotte?"

Charlotte's cheeks flushed, a telltale sign, to be sure. "No," she said in a tone that was not entirely convincing.

Izzy laughed aloud as Georgie smiled.

"Maybe a little," Charlotte admitted reluctantly. "It's simply not fashionable."

"Perhaps she cannot afford to be fashionable," Prue suggested from the window, where she sat reading a novel, looking too pale.

Charlotte frowned at that. "She's the daughter of an earl, correct?"

Georgie confirmed that with a nod.

"A Scottish earl?"

Georgie sighed and nodded again. "Don't tell me you disapprove of that, too, Charlotte."

"I don't disapprove in general!" Charlotte gasped. "I just wanted to clarify! Shouldn't the daughter of an earl and the widow of a knight be in possession of some kind of fortune?"

"Only if her father was a well-to-do earl," Izzy commented with an edge to her voice that Georgie rarely heard. "And only if her husband happened to possess one himself and made a settlement for her in his will."

Charlotte rolled her eyes and sank back against her chair. "I should never argue legalities with the sister of a barrister."

Izzy shrugged a shoulder and smiled, now back to herself, it seemed. "David never put his books away. I tended to read whatever I could."

"Georgie," Grace broke in, her dark eyes concerned, "is Lady Edith really so badly off?"

Georgie fought the urge to huff in irritation. She hadn't interrogated the woman, for heaven's sake, she only knew what she had seen. It had been a poorer house than she had expected, not because it was in Cheapside, where a great many people of good character lived, but because of the conditions of the house itself. And she hadn't meant for her friends to pounce on that small detail so heartily. She'd only brought it up to illustrate Lady Edith's need for friends and perhaps their aid, but not in a monetary fashion.

Lord knew she had little enough to spare, and Izzy and Prue were only slightly better. Charlotte and Grace had come into their majority, but their fathers still maintained much of their control. It was not for them to offer funds to a woman such as Lady Edith, and she did not think Lady Edith would have appreciated the gesture.

One's pride was a fickle thing in that respect.

"I don't know," Georgie finally admitted. "It's entirely possible that they hadn't had time to prepare it properly. She said she'd only recently arrived, and her clothing was in very good condition. She's barely out of mourning, so it may not be the latest fashion, but the quality was there. I would hate to judge a woman purely on the state of her house when she has obviously suffered a loss and has no friends to help her recover from it."

Charlotte winced at the harsher tone Georgie had taken on by the end, and Grace wrinkled up her nose.

"Did she seem inclined to join us?" Prue asked, her book now open in her lap as she watched the rest of them.

"I didn't explain it fully." Georgie offered Prue a small smile. "I think she might take your companionship better than mine, Prue."

"Oh," Grace moaned sympathetically, "is she shy? Poor woman, I couldn't possibly imagine being in her situation and not in a position to make friends easily."

Izzy chuckled softly. "I didn't get the opinion that she was particularly shy as much as reserved. Nor did she seem to need any sympathy. She was perfectly comfortable and at ease, but soft-spoken and gentle. I liked her immensely."

"That doesn't say a single thing, Izzy," Charlotte scoffed. "You like everybody immensely."

"Not true!" Izzy protested.

"It's true," they all replied as one.

Izzy scowled and muttered under her breath unintelligibly.

"The point is," Georgie said, pulling the conversation back, "I think we should adopt Lady Edith. Perhaps not as a Spinster, given her situation, but as our friend. That's not an unreasonable request, is it?"

The others looked at her in varying levels of thought.

"I don't kn-know that I could call on her myself," Prue replied hesitantly. "Not without an invitation. And Mother would never let me have someone come to the house to see me that wasn't a suitor or heiress."

"Yes, I wondered why I could come but not Izzy," Charlotte mused aloud.

Prue's cheeks flamed, but she smiled sheepishly. "Mother likes you, Charlotte."

Charlotte looked mildly disgusted by that. "That is the worst thing you have ever said to me, Prudence Westfall, and I demand you take it back."

Prue giggled and returned her gaze to Georgie. "I am happy to be her friend, if she will have me."

"Who wouldn't have you as their friend?" Grace soothed. "You're the best of every one of us."

Prue gave her an utterly bewildered look. "I think you've just confused me for you, Grace."

Charlotte barked a laugh while the rest of them just snickered. "Hear, hear!"

"Notice she didn't say you," Grace reminded her.

"No, and why would she?" Charlotte retorted. She rubbed her hands together and looked back to Georgie. "What does Tony have to say about this?"

His name seemed to light up Georgie's heart, sending a warm sensation cascading down the length of her, and it was all she could do to avoid the guilt washing over her face.

Guilt that the mention of him had that effect on her.

Guilt that the last three days had been spent thinking of little but him.

Guilt that her friends had no idea what she was thinking, feeling, or dreaming.

And most of all, guilt that she had been listening for his steps in the corridor with every beat of her heart, more than she had ever wished for anything in her life.

She had been overcome with madness, and giddiness, and she hadn't even seen him since that night.

It was entirely possible that he regretted it.

But she wouldn't.

She couldn't.

"Georgie?"

She jerked at her cousin's voice and looked around. "What?"

"Goodness," Grace murmured, twirling a drawing pencil between her fingers. "Where were you just now?"

She was *not* answering that question truthfully. Georgie smiled with only a hint of guilt, though not for what she was about to say. "Lost in thought, I suppose. Trying to think of how to help Lady Edith rejoin Society without overwhelming her."

"And I will repeat my question," Charlotte huffed, apparently believing her. "What does Tony have to say about this?"

"What do I have to say about what?"

Georgie's heart lodged itself in her throat and breathing was suddenly a trifle difficult, as her throat constricted around it.

Tony stood in the doorway to the drawing room, looking somehow handsomer than she had ever seen him despite his clothing being fairly ordinary for a gentleman. His hat and gloves had been removed, and he was brushing down the back of his hair absently. She'd wager that was a habit of his. She tended to pat her hair when she removed a bonnet to ensure it was still in place, so it would only follow that he would do something similar.

He'd shaved this morning, but there was a very faint shadow on the lower part of his face. Had it always been there? His hair was so dark, it was probably never completely gone even with the closest shave. It was odd, but she found she liked that very much. It made Tony seem somehow less of a perfect gentleman and more human.

Yet he was a perfect gentleman.

It was too much, having him here and looking so well. She couldn't bear it, knowing they couldn't speak in privacy, knowing she couldn't let the air between them fill with unspoken words and unidentified feelings until she could barely breathe.

Knowing she couldn't kiss him.

Oh, she desperately wanted to kiss him.

But she settled for rising with the others, trying in vain to swallow, and curtseying with all due politeness.

It had never felt more preposterous in her entire life.

"Lady Edith, Tony," Charlotte went on, gesturing for him to have a seat near her.

Georgie almost bared her teeth at that.

And Tony, that idiot, did so, not even glancing in Georgie's direction.

Cad.

"I've never met her," Tony admitted with his usual carefree air. "I only had her name from Lieutenant Henshaw."

Charlotte frowned, her eyes flicking to Georgie briefly. "And what does Lieutenant Henshaw say about Lady Edith?"

Tony grunted, which Georgie interpreted to be an indication of some distress.

Good.

"As far as I know," Tony said carefully, "he has never met her either."

Charlotte blinked, staring at him without words.

That wasn't good.

"So you sent Georgie and Izzy out to meet a woman that you knew nothing about," Charlotte finally forced out, her hands fisting in her skirts, "on the word of a man you know, who also knows nothing about this woman, because you both know that she is unmarried and you happen to know a group of unmarried women?"

Georgie clamped down on her lips hard.

Sometimes Charlotte truly was an utter delight.

Tony seemed to flinch, though his expression barely changed. "No, Charlotte," he said calmly, "I did not."

She frowned at that. "You didn't?"

He shook his head slowly. "I did not."

Charlotte blinked again, then turned to Georgie with a furrowed brow. "You told me he was the one who gave you Lady Edith's name!"

Georgie opened her mouth to respond, but Tony answered for her.

"I did."

Charlotte whirled back around. "What? Tony, you just said…"

"I didn't send anybody anywhere," he overrode firmly. "My friend, Lieutenant Henshaw, told me of a young widow recently come to London. He has made a promise to her brother, whom he met in the army, that he would look after her here. He knew, as I did, that doing so would be impossible without some feminine aid, unless he wished to marry her. As he did not know her, nor her tastes, he could not assume to do so while remaining a gentleman."

"Very sensible," Grace praised, having returned to her drawing, but listening in. "Speaks highly of the lieutenant, I think."

Tony nodded at her words, though she wouldn't see it. "Lieutenant Henshaw had been made aware that I had some female friends in London and asked if I might pass Lady Edith's name along, in the hopes that they might help him see to her wellbeing and perhaps even become her friends. I agreed to do this, and I did so."

Charlotte stared at him again, her jaw tightening. Then she rolled her eyes and groaned dramatically. "Oh, very well, it is a sound plan, and I cannot find any fault in it."

"Thank you," Tony replied with a smile.

Charlotte glared at him. "No, that praise was for Lieutenant Henshaw. You had one task, and you did it. Hurrah for you."

Georgie almost laughed aloud, which would have been entirely inappropriate, even though Izzy and Grace snickered a little. She couldn't do that, though. Her laughter wouldn't do anything to add to the situation except negatively, and she couldn't let that happen.

She wouldn't have been laughing for the same reasons anyway.

Tony shook his head, smiling in a way that flipped Georgie's stomach over. "Charlotte, what do you object to? That I value the Spinsters so highly that I immediately acted on the information of my friend? Or that I didn't bring it to you first?"

Now Georgie had to laugh a little. It was too perfect a reversal of argument, and Charlotte deserved every bit of it.

Tony was too clever and too witty, and she tended to forget that in the midst of her recent rose-colored dreaming of him.

Charlotte sniffed haughtily and turned away from him, waving a hand. "I am not dignifying that with an answer. Go away now, I don't want you sitting here after all."

He didn't seem at all put off by that and shrugged, rising from the chair. "As you wish, Miss Wright." He looked around the room, then looked at Izzy.

Not Georgie.

"No Elinor today?" he asked, hands resting on his hips.

"She's taking tea with her sister," Izzy told him with a smile.

"Although why Mrs. High and Mighty Emma Partlowe can't come take tea with we low spinsters who were once her friends…" Charlotte muttered widening her eyes.

Grace groaned, dropping her pencil and turning in her chair to look at Charlotte. "You know Mr. Partlowe thinks we're all hoydens and wishes his wife well away from our influence. It's not Emma's fault."

"She married a man who disapproves of us," Charlotte shot back. "It is her fault. No man is worth it if he restricts the friends of his wife."

"Georgie's still accepted," Izzy reminded her, "and he's very polite to us in Society."

Charlotte turned her dark, flashing eyes to Izzy. "Oh, that's very good of him, isn't it?" she drawled sarcastically. "So considerate to not give us all the cut direct in front of everyone, when we're the ones who brought his wife to his attention."

Izzy had no response for that but to shrug a shoulder and go back to her embroidery, which was far better than anything Georgie could have managed.

"Worst decision we've ever made," Charlotte grumbled to herself.

"Partlowe's not such a bad sort," Tony offered, looking down at her. "I was at school with him, remember?"

"Which says nothing good about you, Tony Sterling."

Prue sighed softly and closed her book with a snap. "Don't bother trying, Tony," she told him without a hint of a stammer. "Arguing with Charlotte won't get you anywhere but in a right muddle, and there's no getting out of it."

Georgie looked over at her in shock, as did everybody else.

It was the first time in her recollection that Prue had said anything more than four syllables to Tony, without stammering, and using his name.

His response would be crucial.

Georgie watched him now, begging him to do it right.

She could see how delighted he was, though he kept it in check. "I suppose you're right, Prue," he said with a dramatic sigh. "But you can't blame me for trying, can you?"

Georgie exhaled slowly with relief as Prue smiled at him. "No, indeed," Prue replied. "She's so engaging, one cannot help but be tempted."

Charlotte gaped at her, then at Tony, then back at Prue. "I'm right here," she managed, though without any of the outrage she had intended.

"And we're so glad you are," Izzy broke in with a giggle, loving the exchange.

Georgie shook her head at the lot of them. They were certainly a silly group of girls, and Tony did not exactly bring them up to any higher standards than what they had held before. But he did add a certain something that made them more than what they had been. More complete, perhaps, and well-rounded.

Balanced. That's what it was; he brought balance to their group.

It was a satisfying feeling, to be sure, though at the moment she felt anything but balanced herself.

He wasn't looking at her. He wasn't addressing her. She might not have even been here for all the attention he was paying her. It was bound to be obvious soon. He and Georgie always sparred verbally when the group assembled, it was just the natural way of things. But without engaging in conversation, they couldn't hope to maintain a sense of normalcy.

She could say something, she supposed. He might have responded, and then all would be well.

But what if he didn't?

What if he deliberately ignored her?

No, that would make things all the more obvious and draw attention to his behavior towards her. That would raise all sorts of questions, and then the truth would come out, and everybody would be horrified. After they lost Emma to marriage, there had been a sense of foreboding about them.

They all wanted to marry, but they didn't want things to change.

It was a complicated paradox.

If they admitted what had passed between them, and Tony had to leave because of it, they would all resent Georgie and feel the loss keenly.

Perhaps they could go back to the way things had been. Before that night at the ball, when they had all simply been friends, when everything had been right.

Georgie looked at Tony briefly as he and Grace discussed her drawing, which he seemed pleased by. She didn't want things to go back. She wanted things to go forward.

The trouble was that she didn't know what going forward meant.

And the anxiety was eating at her.

She couldn't stay here and endure his presence without knowing what was going to happen or why he was ignoring her, couldn't bear his warmth for the others and not for her.

Georgie rose quickly, the book in her lap toppling to the floor. She had completely forgotten it had been there, and her action was even more obvious for it.

She managed to smile, though it felt forced. "It's such a warm day, I thought I might take a turn about the garden. Anyone is welcome to join me."

She didn't wait for anyone to respond and nearly fled the room. The corridor was long, but she passed down it quickly, shaking her head at herself. Could that have possibly been a more inelegant exit? She was growing increasingly hopeless, and there wasn't anything she could do about it. Clearing her head would help, but it wouldn't solve anything.

She moved out to the garden and inhaled deeply, tipping her head back. The sun was warm, and its rays felt heavenly upon her skin. Her aunt had so many flowers in the garden that the fragrance from them was almost intoxicating, but not at all overwhelming. It was the most pleasant breath of spring one could ever hope for.

It was exactly what she needed at this moment.

She wandered along the stone path slowly, meandering without thought or purpose. The shrubs and bushes seemed rich in their colors, vibrant and bold against the commonplace grey of the path beside them. Birds overhead called to each other and sang sweet songs in the afternoon light. It was tranquil and comforting to be out in nature.

If only she could find such feelings in herself.

Voices suddenly reached her, and she looked up to see the others coming out as well.

Tony was with them.

Georgie moved to the small bench nearby and sank down, watching them all with trepidation.

Charlotte, Grace, and Prue chose to stay by the house, settling themselves in chairs the servants set out and Grace began to draw something in the garden while the other two watched.

Izzy and Tony continued towards her, Izzy holding a basket and shears while Tony walked beside her.

Then suddenly Izzy stepped off the path and moved towards a bright collection of flowers.

Tony watched her go, then slowly turned his gaze to Georgie.

When his eyes met hers, Georgie felt a soft gasp well up within her. She gripped the bench tightly beneath her, desperate for some sort of footing to steady her.

He came towards her almost carefully, nothing eager or anxious in his step, nothing to draw anybody's attention. Yet his eyes were fixed on her with such intensity that she couldn't move.

"Georgie," he said as he approached, and her name sounded soft on his lips.

She swallowed hard. "Tony."

His chest moved on an inhale and she watched it do so, waiting for the accompanying exhale.

"That was some exit you made," he told her.

She looked up to see a gentle smile and couldn't find one to return. "I had to. I was about to go mad."

He tilted his head at her, brow wrinkling. "Why?"

"You didn't say a word to me," she heard herself admit before she could stop herself. "You didn't even look at me. Not once."

"I couldn't," he admitted with a rasp to his voice. "I was afraid of what I might say, or what you might see. What they might see." He laughed breathlessly. "Georgie, I was afraid that if I looked at you for too long, I might kiss you again right in front of everyone."

Georgie stared at him in disbelief, then found herself laughing as well and releasing her death grip on the bench. "So, you don't regret it?"

Tony scoffed almost too loudly. "Regret it? I've thought of little else since then, and I've been counting down the moments until we could do it again."

"So have I." She bit her lip and looked behind him at the others, who were not paying any attention to them. She couldn't even see Izzy, which was comforting. She glanced quickly down the path, where the larger hedges began. She nearly jumped to her feet. "Come with me."

"Absolutely," he replied, following without hesitation.

The hedge was just barely tall enough to hide his height completely, and once they were behind it, Georgie turned to him with a wild grin.

He returned it with one of his own, and then cupped her face, stroking her cheeks gently. "I missed you," he whispered.

Georgie grabbed his coat in her hands, her fists clenching the fabric. "I missed you, too."

He kissed her then, long, slow, and leisurely, and she responded in kind. Her skin tingled where he held her, and the rest of her itched with excitement and the thrill of his kiss. Her hands slid up to his neck and pulled him closer, seeking more of him and more of their connection.

Her head swam with delight, caught up in the intensity of the sensations and emotions swirling within and around her. She felt the restraint in his kiss, in the way he held her, and she nearly smiled at it. He kissed her as though she were a treasure, a delicate creature, as though she might break with his touch.

She would not break, and yet she felt as though she could safely crumble in the hold of a man such as this.

It was a humbling, terrifying, exhilarating thought.

Tony broke the kiss before she was ready, and shushed her whimper with a soft laugh, touching his brow to hers. "Georgie, we have to be careful," he whispered.

"You're not about to compromise me in my aunt's garden, are you?" she teased with another laugh. "You're bound to be disappointed, I'm determined to have towering control."

He pulled back with a wry expression. "No, I was not going to compromise you, and yes, I am sure you do. I only meant we have to be careful, as there are four friends of ours not far from us, and if we don't make an appearance soon, they are bound to wonder..."

Georgie rolled her eyes and groaned. "This is so inconvenient."

"I know." He sighed and stroked her cheeks, kissing her quickly again. "I could court you, you know."

Her heart skipped in her chest, and she looked at him dubiously. "After what Charlotte said today? You think that would go over well?"

"So, we continue to steal moments together whenever we can and hope nobody notices?" he asked. He shook his head. "It's not going to last long, I have a hard enough time hiding my feelings for you just looking at you."

"What are your feelings for me?" she inquired, rising up on her toes with helpless excitement.

He chuckled and brushed his nose against hers. "Nothing easy to define. But everything good."

She barely restrained a sigh and released her hold on him. "I feel the same way." She held out her hand, which he took instantly. "Come on, we must be seen or be suspect. Look as though I've just said something ludicrous, and I will scowl at you."

"You scowl so beautifully," he praised as they moved on down the path.

She dipped her chin in a modest way. "Thank you. I have worked hard to perfect it."

The moment they were in sight, their hands separated, and they adopted the aforementioned expressions.

"I have something you need to know," he said as he shook his head at her.

"What's that?" she responded, looking all too superior.

"Miranda, my stepmother, is in London, and she is anxious to meet you."

Georgie tripped on the cobblestone, but caught herself, glaring at Tony without having to act. "How does she know about me?"

"She doesn't," he assured her, trying not to laugh. "She has determined that there is a woman plaguing my mind and tormenting my emotions. She's not wrong." He gave her a knowing look that made Georgie bite on her lip again. "And she wants to meet whoever it is."

Georgie shook her head quickly. "You can't tell her."

"Obviously." He snorted. "You don't even know Miranda. It would be horrible to give her your name this early on. Yet I need to introduce her to all of you. Most especially you."

"Lovely." She could sense that Tony adored his stepmother, and yet his reluctance amused her. Something she could play at, then. Marvelous. "I would love to meet her."

Tony jerked to look at her, his expression horrified. "On second thought, no."

"No?"

"Very much no. You don't understand, this is very much not a good idea." He shook his head very firmly. "No, Miranda isn't like other women, Georgie. I can't promise she'll behave."

Georgie almost laughed, shrugging. "I can't promise I will either. I'm taking tea with your cousin's wife on Thursday. Have her invite your stepmother along. Then we will see if it's a good idea or not."

Tony only groaned in response.

Chapter Fourteen

—⸿⸎⸿—

Men are not useless creatures, despite any evidence to the contrary. They do have a purpose in this world, and can offer something of value, if they so choose. They have thoughts, feelings, and impressions, same as the rest of us. Whether or not they decide to employ any of those things is entirely up to them.

-The Spinster Chronicles, 23 October 1817

"I have a very bad feeling about this."

"Hush, it will be fine."

"You can say that? You, who knows Miranda personally."

"It will be *fine*, Tony. Janet is in there, so you are safe."

Tony barked a hard laugh. "Janet is in there with Miranda and you find that comforting." He shook his head and pinched the bridge of his nose. "You have absolutely no idea, Francis."

Francis grunted softly, moving around the corner of the billiards table, eyeing the balls carefully. "How bad could it possibly be? You like Miranda."

Tony leaned his head against his stick, sighing. "I adore Miranda. She was both mother and friend to me after Mother died, and she brought Father back to life. She's eccentric, she's refined, she's witty… Miranda is wonderful. But even I can admit that Miranda can be too brash, too bold, too inquisitive, too rough around the edges…"

Francis leaned over the table and looked up at Tony with a quirk of his brow. "And all of that reflects on my wife how, exactly?" He struck his cue ball, narrowly missing Tony's, but sending the red ball into the pocket easily.

"Janet has a sharp tongue, which is what I like about her," Tony told his cousin as he moved to fish the balls out of the pocket. "She'll say exactly what she thinks, no matter the consequence, and argue her point to the death."

Francis went to the sideboard and picked up his glass, taking a quick drink. "Tell me about it. We've been having a discussion on the same topic for three months now, and absolutely no progress has been made one way or the other because she refuses to budge."

Tony found that to be an amusing thought and wondered what the topic of discussion was, and whether such discussions belonged more into the class of arguments. He couldn't have said one way or the other, nor was he about to inquire. The dealings of a married couple within the walls of their home were certainly no concern of his, especially when he happened to be related to them.

But Francis had never been very good at arguing, so he was willing to bet a great deal that the only reason the discussion, or argument, had gone on as long as it had was because Francis was actually right this time.

"And who will win that discussion?" Tony asked, setting up the cue balls once more.

Francis smiled, leaning against his cue stick. "Probably Janet, though she'd be wrong. Makes no difference, really."

Tony shook his head and leaned across the table to align his shot. "So, she's stubborn and opinionated. Just what Miranda needs to start a fire." He took his shot but missed the red ball and hit Francis's cue ball instead. He hissed as Francis chuckled.

"Poor strategy, Captain," Francis said as he fished his ball out. "It's a wonder you ever hit your mark. Ten to nine."

Tony scowled, straightening. "I'd be happy to prove my skills with firearms at any time."

"Not in London, you won't." Francis grinned and took his shot, missing both balls completely. "Save it for your invitation to Crestley Ridge later in the year. We are overrun with pheasant."

"Happy to oblige." Tony looked towards the door, unease

gnawing at his stomach.

Just a few doors down, Georgie was taking tea with his favorite female relations. They'd not come to Sterling House together, as he'd wished to, because Georgie had insisted that they approach this event as if they were nothing more than acquaintances.

It made no difference to her that Francis knew Tony was attached to her in some way, which meant that Janet probably suspected more than that, and that all would be sniffed out by Miranda sooner rather than later. There was nothing to tell, she'd insisted, and nothing to lose, so why should they be worried?

Nothing to tell? There was certainly a great deal to tell. Miranda did not need much information to make a fuss, and make a fuss she would if she discovered that the woman who had captured Tony's affections was having a second helping of cake.

Nothing to lose? Nothing could have been further from the truth. One wrong word from Miranda, and Georgie could be hurt or offended, insulted, appalled, and who knows what else. There was no guarantee that she would like Miranda as much as he did, or that she would understand her the way he did.

He couldn't lose Georgie. Without having a definition to place on what exactly he felt for her, or what she meant, or where this all might go, he could not lose her.

But Miranda wasn't going anywhere. She was his stepmother, and he would not be able to wound her by cutting off his association with her.

Just down the hall, two of the most important women in his life were meeting.

One of them knew of the significance.

The other had no idea.

Yet with her rested all the power to make Tony's future all the more secure, or all the more uncertain.

And Francis thought he had no cause for concern? His wife could sway the meeting one way or the other as her tastes and preferences would allow. She liked Georgie already and was disposed to make this gathering a rather fortunate one.

But what if Janet liked Miranda more than Georgie?

"Are you planning on taking a shot or would you rather go press your ear to the door of my wife's parlor?"

Tony glanced at his cousin, who looked all too smug in his shirtsleeves and waistcoat, grinning at him.

"You find my discomfort amusing, do you?" Tony asked as he took up position again for his turn.

Francis shrugged nonchalantly. "Always have. It's one of my favorite sights."

Tony grunted under his breath, sending the cue ball ricocheting off Francis's to hit the red ball squarely into a corner pocket. "Then I hope Miranda asks Janet about the arrival of your firstborn child and when she should prepare for the christening."

He straightened and looked at his cousin to find Francis staring at him with wide eyes.

"Janet's not with child," Francis stammered. "She's... and I..."

"Then she will ask about that," Tony commented in an offhand manner as he moved to take a drink from his glass on the sideboard. "She's really very interested in the progression of the Sterling family, but you're the only cousins she cares about."

Francis swallowed with difficulty and completely botched his next shot. "That's not her business."

Tony turned to his cousin. "That's never stopped her before." He took another drink and set his glass down, coming back to the table. "Or perhaps she will ask her about Hugh. That's undoubtedly a much safer topic."

He knew he'd hit upon a sore spot, but he didn't particularly care at the moment. He needed to deflect the questions and focus from Georgie and his anticipation for this meeting of theirs to quite literally anything else. Or else he just needed Francis to understand the true gravity of the situation as it stood.

Either outcome would suffice.

Francis glowered as Tony surveyed the table. "I might actually prefer the other topic to that of my brother. He is determined to ruin himself in any possible way, and if he had more money, he would lose that as well."

Tony shook his head and aligned his cue stick. "Hugh never was much of a card player."

"And he cannot hold his liquor." Francis snorted softly and

watched as Tony sank the red ball again. "I can only be grateful he has yet to debauch anyone, so at least we don't have indignant fathers banging on our door demanding satisfaction."

That wasn't much of a comfort. "Is it as bad as that?" Tony asked with a wince.

Francis exhaled and took another drink from his glass. "He's been spending most of his time with Simon Delaney and George Hastings and Daniel Lyman. I rarely see him now, but when I do, he smells of the gaming tables and looks like a drunkard. His funds are his own, and he never gets in too far over his head. I can only hope that he still has some sense and retains some shred of dignity."

Tony stared at him for a long moment, then felt himself smile. "I'd wager he is rather enjoying my involvement with the Spinsters, eh?"

That earned him a groan and dramatic roll of the eyes. "Please. If I'd known what he wanted you to do, I'd have stopped him long before it got anywhere. The Spinsters may be an annoyance with their popularity, but they've never done anybody harm, and it's certainly not anybody's business if they want to continue writing. Their Society commentary is usually spot on."

"You read them?" Tony laughed aloud, covering his eyes briefly.

"Of course, I read them!" Francis countered hotly. "It's sometimes the best part of the newssheets! And once I'd spotted your name in the Society Dabbler, I had to keep reading to see if you appear often." He looked at Tony thoughtfully. "You really don't. Is there some reason for that?"

"If you're implying that I somehow have any kind of power over what goes into those columns, you are sadly mistaken." Tony shook his head and gestured for Francis to take his turn. "I am not permitted entrance on Writing Day, so I don't see the articles until the rest of London does."

Francis chuckled easily, moving back to the table. "Ah, so you are still an outsider to them, eh? And what does Miss Allen think of that?" He sank Tony's ball easily, missing the red.

Tony smiled at his cousin's ignorance. He obviously did not know Georgie at all, and he was to be pitied for that. "It seems to be at Georgie's insistence, actually."

"I knew I liked her." Francis cast a teasing grin over at him. "So, if Miranda approves of her, will you court her officially?"

"That is my business, not yours."

"I could say I've got an interest, having met the girl and danced with her." Francis leaned on his cue stick again. "You haven't even danced with her yet, have you?"

Tony scowled at that. No, he hadn't, and Francis knew it well. He hadn't danced with her the night she'd confided her thoughts about disbanding the Spinsters, and he hadn't danced with her that night he'd kissed her. All the other events they'd been at together had been too small to consider doing so, unlike the safety of a grand ball. He wasn't sure he could dance with her and be safe from himself.

Enough was said about her already, why enflame things with a different sort of talk?

But if he courted her, that would stir things up as well.

He could court her quietly, he supposed, and take care not to attract attention by it.

Except he wanted to court her for all the world to see. He wanted everyone to know that he was not afraid of their opinions of her, that he would take her just as she was and not find anything wanting, that they were all fools for having missed it. He wanted to be done with the secrecy and pretending he only admired her for the attitude with which she had managed her spinsterhood.

Georgiana Allen was an impressive woman who had chosen to get on with her life despite not having it turn out the way she had wanted, and without any of the bitterness and spite that other women in her situation might have done. She might not have had an alternative future set as a precaution, nor would she be able to manage a comfortable living on her own, should she never marry. But she had come to terms with her situation in life, and with her own temperament, and she was making the best of things. She did not simper or whine, and she did not look to anyone else to find completion in her life.

There wasn't another woman like her, he was sure of it.

He was feeling very much that he was on the edge of something, though what it was escaped him.

So again, he would seek safety in distraction.

"Your wife," Tony began as he took his shot, "my stepmother, and the woman widely believed to be the leader of the Spinsters are all having tea together. Three very determined, very unusual women. Either they are going to battle with each other vehemently, or they are going to get along splendidly. Which outcome would you find more comforting, Francis?"

His cousin suddenly seemed to blanche and looked towards the door with a great deal of apprehension as Tony watched his cue ball sink both Francis's and the red ball into the far corner pocket.

"Your turn."

"So, Miss Allen, you are a spinster."

Georgie turned to Mrs. Sterling with a bland sort of smile. "So it seems."

Mrs. Sterling narrowed her strikingly blue eyes and lifted her teacup to her lips. "Do you disagree?"

She shook her head slowly. "Not at all. At twenty-seven, there really is no better way to define me. I own up to it, ma'am, though it sounds rather dreadful."

Lady Sterling... Janet, she reminded herself... choked back a laugh and set her own teacup down. She smiled at Tony's stepmother, who was still a woman of astonishing beauty at her age, and dressed perhaps too finely for this occasion, but only in the most tasteful ways. Both women were impressive to Georgie, and far more refined.

They were also far better dressed, but as their fortune was substantial by comparison, that went without saying.

Besides, Georgie had neither the coloring nor the figure to look half so well in the same clothing. Dark colors had never been a friend to her, but both women had dark hair, very richly so, in Janet's case, and they looked simply marvelous.

Mrs. Sterling seemed to smile without actually smiling. "I was married at twenty-five, dear, and I never considered myself a spinster before I was wed."

Georgie considered that, wondering just how honest she ought to be with Tony's stepmother. She was a different sort of woman than Georgie had expected, and yet somehow fit the part perfectly. This was the woman who had helped to raise Tony to be such a perfect gentleman. She was every bit as fine as Georgie had anticipated, but without any of the airs. There was a light in her eyes that Georgie liked very much, though she was fairly certain it was also capable of a great deal of mischief.

"I didn't consider myself a spinster of my own volition, madam," Georgie informed her politely. "I was informed that I was one. Rather resoundingly so."

"And what is wrong with you, dear?" came the quick retort.

Janet coughed again, this time without any laughter. "Miranda!"

Mrs. Sterling held up a hand. "It is a legitimate question. This woman, who is still young, I might add, is rather pretty. Her clothing is in neat condition, suits her well, and she arrived promptly in a rather fine coach. Surely there is a fault I am not seeing, or else she would be married by now."

Janet clamped down on her lips and closed her eyes, obviously mortified by her guest's behavior.

Georgie wasn't, however. She found it to be very refreshing. "I've never been entirely sure what is wrong with me, Mrs. Sterling. I have always gone about my life with the determination to make the best of any situation, and to devote myself to the future I imagined would lie ahead of me." She shrugged a shoulder and sipped her tea. "This isn't exactly what I'd thought it would be, but it seems a poor use of my time to wallow in despair."

Mrs. Sterling's brow wrinkled, and she frowned a little. "Yes, but *why*, Miss Allen, are you unmarried?"

Georgie smiled at her. "If I knew that, Mrs. Sterling, I'd have changed it by now and be on my way to church this instant."

Mrs. Sterling suddenly broke out into a grin, then laughed rather heartily. "Oh, you were so right, Janet, I adore her." She reached out a hand to cover Georgie's free one. "You must call me Miranda."

"Thank you, ma'am," Georgie replied with a dip of her chin. "You may call me Georgiana. Or Georgie, if it pleases you."

"It certainly does," Miranda said as she sat back and reached for a cake. "Now who was idiotic enough to inform you that you were a spinster? That's nigh unto a death sentence for a young lady."

Georgie shook her head. "Just a passing gentleman, ma'am. He had come over to meet me, and was introduced by a cousin, who felt it polite to announce my age as well, at which point the gentleman said, 'What? A spinster? Not worth my time,' and he promptly left to find a girl of considerably fewer years to acquaint himself with." She smiled forcibly at them both. "He married her two months later."

"Good riddance," Janet said with a disapproving shake of her head. "He'd have made you a worthless husband, I am sure."

"But is a worthless husband better than no husband at all?" she asked them, looking between them.

Miranda sighed a little, seeming to consider the notion. "I don't think so. You might be more secure in having a husband than not, but it wouldn't add to your happiness. Is there peace of mind in being secure if you are miserable?" She frowned again. "When I married Thomas, Tony and Ben's father, I did not love him. He was a very good man, and I was fond of him, certainly, but it was not love until years later. Yet I was never happier than in marriage to him, even more when there was love."

"But Thomas was not worthless," Janet pointed out.

"Well…" Miranda said with a wince, though her eyes twinkled.

Georgie laughed aloud, as did Janet.

"I jest, of course," Miranda explained, smiling at them both. "He was never worthless, though there were times I wondered at his intellect or common sense."

"I have the same trouble with Francis," Janet sighed, sipping her tea. "That man…" She shook her head.

Georgie chose that moment to take a bite of crumpet, as she had nothing to offer about men. She wasn't about to say a word about Tony, knowing what sort of a mess that would bring about. Besides, Tony wasn't her husband. It was hardly the same thing.

But she was honest enough with herself not to deny that the thought of him as such made her heart quiver just a little.

"Now, Georgie," Miranda said, breaking into Georgie's sudden imaginations of veils and bells, "Janet has told me of your Spinster Chronicles and I have read the most recent issue."

"Did you?" she responded, grinning in outright delight. "And which part was your favorite?"

"The main article, to be sure." Miranda nodded quickly. "It was witty and tactful, yet contained all the wisdom in the world. I've had similar thoughts on the idiocy of vapid women, but never had the talents to put it into words. Were you the author of it?"

Georgie was pleased to deny it, shaking her head. "No, I wrote the Fashion Forum this week."

Miranda looked at Janet in thought. "Was that the piece about lace gloves?"

"It was," Janet confirmed, smiling at Georgie. "They are pretty enough, I agree, but as far as functionality goes, they are perfectly useless. I had a pair some months ago and they were quite done for within three uses."

"Exactly," Georgie stated with a firm nod. "If one is only to be decorative, then by all means, wear them. But if any sort of activity is to be engaged in, they are hardly worth the price."

"Sound judgment," Miranda praised. She leaned forward a bit, looking intrigued. "How did you all manage to get a printer to agree to articles written entirely by women? That's hardly a good inducement for a businessman."

Georgie shook her head, grinning. "No, it is not. But my uncle Lambert has a cousin that is a printer in town, and my uncle has always been very indulgent with me. He got us a meeting with his cousin, who refused to publish anything unless it was worth reading. When we showed him our articles, he accepted at once and published them in the paper three days after."

"It's a wonder one of you does not become a writer," Janet offered. "It is possible to be published as a woman, as Mrs. Radcliffe and Miss Austen have proved."

"Oh," Georgie protested, raising a hand, "none of us would ever claim to have their level of talent, even collectively. My cousin may consider such a task, though, if she doesn't marry. She enjoys it very much."

"And you?" Miranda pressed none-too-gently. "What will you do? If you do not marry?"

Georgie grew restless in her seat and fought the urge to shift. "I've thought about going to be an instructor at a girls' school, if they'd have someone as stubborn and opinionated as I."

"You should have met some of the teachers I had at finishing school," Janet told her with a grimace. "You would be a breath of fresh air compared to those trolls. And any school would be hard pressed to find anybody who did not have a face of worn wood applying for their positions."

Miranda eyed Georgie carefully, saying nothing.

"Georgie," Janet said suddenly, not noticing Miranda's behavior, "everybody says that your group interferes with the nefarious intentions of certain gentlemen with young ladies. Is this so?"

"No," Georgie replied at once. Then she winced a little. "Well, it is not entirely true, I should say. There have been two or three times, perhaps, where one or more of us has been able to prevent something that could have been disastrous. But it is not as though someone in London is being compromised every five minutes."

"That we know of," Janet scoffed.

Miranda still said nothing.

"We have taken some girls aside that we had noticed certain behaviors in," Georgie went on. "We've given them some council, either on the man they were choosing to be so free with, or with their behavior in general, but they have always had their own way. Nothing has ever been forced, we are not knights of feminine virtue in petticoats."

Miranda's lips curved into an amused smile, but she was still silent.

"All I can say for us," Georgie said, sighing a little, "is that we are trying, and have been trying, to give young women more to consider, more to think about. We'd known a few girls that had been married under less than ideal circumstances, either due to their desperation to marry or their naïveté about a man's intentions. Or his character. We didn't want to lose any more girls that we cared about just because marriage seemed the only way to have a fulfilling life." She swallowed with a little difficulty, wondering at her emotions. "It isn't. There can be a very fulfilling life regardless of one's marital circumstances."

"Why do you intervene?" Miranda asked quietly, her eyes fixed on Georgie. "Why do you make it your business?"

Georgie smiled back at her. "Someone has to look out for them. I know that not every girl we stop wants to be stopped, or lectured, or influenced. But if I can give her a chance to reconsider, to choose better, to think just a little, maybe it will be enough."

Miranda nodded slowly. "And while you are running around giving second chances and finding happy endings for them, who is finding yours?"

"I think this is mine," Georgie told her without any of the despondency those words once might have carried. "Or it could be. Not exactly what I had in mind, but there it is."

Janet smiled at her proudly, then turned to glance at Miranda with a coy grin. "Well, Miranda, what do you say to that?"

Miranda fiddled with one dangling gold earring absently, still staring at Georgie as if for analysis. Then she lowered her hand back to the table with a firm nod. "You'll do."

"Do?" Georgie asked with a laugh, looking at Janet in bewilderment. "Do for what?"

"My stepson," Miranda said simply.

Janet, having taken up her teacup again, coughed none-too-delicately. "I beg your pardon?" she managed to squeak out.

Miranda ignored her. "I have it in mind to see that my stepsons are situated well in their lives, and as neither of them have any interest in taking up the house we lived in while I was married to their father, I am left to meddling in some other way. So, tell me if you would prefer Dorset or the great unknown for your future?"

"What's in Dorset?" Georgie laughed, finding this all terribly amusing, despite the quick lurch of her heart at the initial suggestion.

"Benedict," Miranda told her. "He's the elder of the two, but only by a year and a half or so. He's a doctor, trained at the Royal College of Physicians. Top marks. He's a sweet lad, very considerate and noble, the perfect gentleman, though he moves in lesser circles by choice. A fine rider and a great reader as well. You'd liven him up creditably."

Georgie had to fight hard to avoid bursting out into giggles. She wanted her to marry Tony's brother? Oh, he would perish the thought!

"Not as handsome as Tony, though," Miranda mused,

drumming her perfectly manicured nails on the table. "And Tony is in London at present." The drumming stopped, and she looked at Georgie again. "But I forget! You know Tony already."

Georgie nodded, biting back a smile. "I do, yes. A fine man. A credit to his family, to be sure."

Well, it had sounded like safe enough praise in her head, but at her words, Miranda gave her a slow and very devious smirk of a smile.

"Yes," Miranda replied in a tone Georgie wasn't sure she cared for. "Yes, he certainly is. Very well, then, my dear. I will see what I can do to make Tony forget whoever is running around in his head and vie for you instead. And if I don't see you married by autumn, one of you is a very great idiot."

Janet looked beside herself, but it could not possibly compare to what Georgie was feeling.

Miranda wanted Tony to forget the woman in his head, who was Georgie, so that he could devote his attentions to Georgie, officially, so that he could marry Georgie before the summer was over.

He was never going to believe this.

Then again, considering the way Miranda was looking and knowing what Tony had said about her, perhaps it would not surprise him at all.

Chapter Fifteen

------------ c∞∞ɔ ------------

There is nothing so changeable as one's feelings. Families are no exception.

-The Spinster Chronicles, 8 January 1816

"Oh, isn't this lovely? What a perfectly masterful arrangement of rooms! What taste! What elegance! Where are the hosts? I must congratulate them."

Tony lifted his eyes heavenward. "Miranda, we are to be presented shortly. You haven't even seen the ballroom yet."

Miranda peered up at him suspiciously, her navy and gold earbobs glinting in the candlelight. "And why should that be any less magnificent than what I am currently seeing? Is the family inclined to leave that room to be an eyesore? I think not." She reached down and flicked her navy silk skirts, the gold detailing on the hem dancing with the motion.

Tony shook his head and pulled her along as gently, yet firmly as he could. "Miranda, please do try to behave yourself."

She gave a mock gasp of affront. "When has my behavior ever been less than perfection in public?"

"Shall we compile a list?" Mr. Johnston blustered good-naturedly from behind them.

Tony looked over his shoulder with a quick grin. His uncle by marriage had always been an amusing fellow, if a bit slower than one might have expected from a business man such as himself.

"Oh, Mr. Johnston, how droll," Arabella chuckled, wrapping her husband on the wrist.

"And too cruel," Miranda pouted. "After all the kindness I've shown you."

Mr. Johnston had no chance to respond as they were suddenly before their hosts.

Tony bowed politely. "Lord Kirby, Lady Kirby, may I present my stepmother, Mrs. Sterling?"

They both inclined their heads with warm smiles. "A pleasure, Mrs. Sterling," Lord Kirby said with genuine fondness. "We are most delighted with your stepson here. Such a credit to you."

Miranda curtseyed graciously. "He is a credit to his father, sir, I can take no credit for his goodness myself, but I thank you for the compliment of thinking so."

"You are so familiar, ma'am," Lady Kirby broke in, shaking her head slightly. "I am sure I know you from somewhere."

Miranda looked surprised. "I haven't been to London in some years, madam. But I was once Miranda Keyes, if that helps at all."

Lady Kirby beamed at her suddenly. "Of course! You sang at a musicale hosted by the Gregsons some years ago, an Italian aria."

Now Miranda seemed positively bewildered. "I did, madam. Were you in attendance?"

She chuckled at that. "I was indeed, though half a world away. Lord Kirby asked for my hand that night, and your song seemed the song of my heart. I have never forgotten it."

Miranda beamed and took Lady Kirby's hand. "I am glad it touched someone, at least. What an honor, madam. Truly." She turned to indicate the Johnstons. "My sister and her husband, Mr. Johnston."

"Charmed," Lord Kirby greeted, nodding to them. "Charmed indeed. Please, enjoy the ball."

They all nodded and proceeded into the ballroom, Tony feeling a little windswept.

"You sang?" he asked Miranda quietly as they entered. "In public?"

"Every now and then," Miranda said through her teeth, smiling for all the world, "I do behave as a proper lady ought. When asked to sing, being in possession of the necessary skills and talents, I complied. And in case it escaped your notice, I touched a few hearts."

"Well, one, at least," Tony reminded her.

He received a sharp elbow in his midsection for that, but it might have been worth it.

"Oh, look at this room!" Arabella exclaimed from behind them. "It's a fairy land! Everything is gold! Oh, I shall be too afraid to touch anything. Fred! Fred, isn't it a fairy land?"

"Just when I think the two of you couldn't be more different," Tony muttered, "something reminds me that you really are very alike."

Miranda bit back a laugh and pulled his arm tighter.

Tony exhaled audibly as he looked about the room. He knew several people in attendance now, and most of them seemed to be here. He hadn't thought the Kirbys so very popular, but the evidence was before him. He saw Charlotte in the midst of her admirers, Grace in conversation with her brother, who looked all too superior in these surroundings, and Prue, situated in her corner, as usual.

"Goodness sakes, is that Lady Hetty Redgrave?" Miranda suddenly asked, her voice ringing with delight.

Tony turned to her quickly, eyes wide. "You know her?"

"Of course! But I haven't seen her in years, I had no idea she was still..." Miranda trailed off, tilting her head meaningfully.

"Alive?" he offered.

Her cheeks colored. "Well, yes, to be frank."

"Be frank. She is alive, and she's undoubtedly the best company you'll find tonight." He gave her a crooked smile. "Outside of yours truly, of course."

Miranda gave him a pitying smile and patted his cheek. "It's adorable that you think so." She released his arm and started off towards Lady Hetty. "Save a dance for me, Tony. And one for Miss Allen. I insist on that."

She insisted? He glanced around. At least six people had heard her say that.

There was nothing for it, then. To obey his stepmother, he had to dance with Georgie.

How unfortunate.

"Oh, Tony's here, what a relief. All of the young women are safe."

Tony turned at the sound of Hugh's voice. "You object to my interference?"

Hugh looked at him blearily, looking rumpled, despite having just arrived. "I object to anything that doesn't suit me."

"Might I remind you that it was you who asked me to get involved?" Tony hissed, fighting his own revulsion at seeing his cousin thus.

"I didn't think you'd go so far," Hugh whined, blinking with difficulty. "It's making me look dashed foolish before my friends."

"Well, we couldn't have that," Tony drawled with a derisive snort.

Hugh missed the nature of his tone. "Give me something to tell them, Tony. Please. Anything."

Tony stared at him, desperate to tell him off, to end the charade, to tell him the truth… He exhaled in irritation. "Tell them not to question me. I know what I am doing."

Hugh brightened and thumped Tony's chest almost jubilantly. "Brilliant, Tony. Absolutely brilliant. I'll go straight away to the gaming room and tell them." He half-stumbled away, struggling to recall the manner in which gentlemen usually walked.

"If you can remember it in five minutes," Tony grumbled, shaking his head.

A twinge of guilt caused a pain in his chest, but he brushed it away. He hadn't said anything that wasn't true. They didn't need to question him, and he did know what he was doing.

It simply wasn't what Hugh or the others thought it was.

No harm done.

"What was that about?" Francis asked, suddenly coming to his side.

Tony shook his head. "You do not want to know, believe me." He nodded at Janet with a smile. "Janet, you look beautiful."

She curtseyed in acknowledgement, the burgundy of her gown bringing out the dark richness of her hair and eyes. "Thank you, Tony." She glanced around, then back up at him. "Where is Miranda?"

Francis groaned, and Tony chuckled. "She spotted Lady Hetty, and decided she was better company."

Janet laughed at that and looked towards the corner, where Miranda was now being introduced to Prue, who looked mildly terrified at the prospect.

Tony looked back at Janet with a frown. "Did you tell her about my association with the Spinsters, Janet?"

She turned back in surprise. "No, not a word. I presumed you would tell her if it became relevant. Considering she's already decided on a woman for you…"

"She's *what?*" Francis and Tony said together.

Janet giggled to herself, then clamped down on her lips. "Never you mind, it will all come out soon enough." She waved her fan at the pair of them, then sauntered off in search of better company herself.

"Do you get the feeling that we have been left utterly abandoned and uninformed by our family?" Francis asked, sighing a little.

"All the bloody time," Tony replied as he shook his head. He nodded towards Miranda and Lady Hetty. "Who knows where that will take me? I should probably make myself scarce."

Francis made a soft sound of amusement. "Probably. Go find someone to dance with. They can't criticize you if you're dancing."

That was probably true, Tony considered.

But whom would he dance with? Miranda wanted him to dance with Georgie, but he hadn't seen her yet, so that was not an option. He glanced around the room, wondering how to spend his time until she did arrive.

Then suddenly he had it, and he smiled to himself.

Hugh and the other annoyed pups were upset that he was too involved with the Spinsters? They would absolutely despise him after this.

He strode across the room with all the purpose in the world, not caring who saw or what they would think about what he would do.

He stopped in front of Grace, who turned to face him in surprise. "Miss Morledge, would you dance the next with me?"

Grace smiled at him in confusion. "Of course, Captain Sterling."

Tony held out a hand, and she took it with a laugh. "Good," Tony praised softly. "Smile and laugh the entire time."

"I can manage that," she replied. "Why?"

"I'm going to dance with all of the Spinsters," he informed her with a proud grin. "And I want everyone to see you all happy."

Grace unleashed the full force of her smile on him, and he blinked at its brilliance.

"Right," he said, slightly unsettled still. "Just like that."

She nodded at him, took up position with the other ladies, and the dance commenced.

Grace smiled and laughed the entire time, drawing the gaze of a great many people, as though suddenly seeing her for the first time.

Charlotte followed suit, smiling and laughing gaily, though with none of the false airs she played at with her suitors. This, too, left the general public stunned and confused.

Prue was more restrained than the others, as was her nature, but by then everyone was wondering which lady would be delighted by dancing with Tony next, so her smiles and giggles had much the same effect. Even her mother was smiling, which was something of a miracle.

He allowed himself a rest after his dance with Prue, having been too distracted by the dance to notice if Georgie and Izzy had arrived, but he had seen Janet and Francis grinning at him, giving their nod of approval.

Miranda watched with interest from her seat near Lady Hetty but had remained where she was and as she was.

"You look fatigued."

Tony smiled before he could stop himself and turned to face the voice he craved to hear. "Miss Allen."

Georgie was a vision in a gown the color of lavender, her eyes the sort of brilliant green that would inspire poets and artists until the end of time. Her lips seemed fuller than he recalled, drawn up in a small smile that weakened his knees. She tilted her head at him curiously, her eyes asking a question that she did not voice.

"You are the most beautiful sight I have seen all day," he told her in a ridiculous rush of breath.

She seemed surprised by that, then wrinkled up her nose in delight. "That's a very lovely thing to say, thank you."

"I mean it."

"All day?" she asked, her mischievous glint returning.

"All day," he said again. "Including this room, the park this morning, and anyone I saw in passing. Maybe even more than some flowers."

"Well," she replied, pretending to be impressed, "apparently I have a misconstrued idea of my own beauty."

He nodded quickly, taking on the same sort of air. "I am sure you do. It is your one failing."

Georgie heaved a sigh. "I knew there was one. What a tragedy."

"But surely now that I have brought you into this new awareness, you are saved from it." He tried to look hopeful, and it made Georgie giggle, which would forever be his favorite sound.

"I suppose so." She smiled up at him. "I have no more failings."

No, she did not.

But then, he wasn't certain she ever had any to begin with.

That would remain his secret, though.

"So," Georgie said in a suddenly bright tone, "your stepmother."

Tony groaned and turned to face her with a shake of his head. "What did she say? I didn't see you after you left, and she didn't say a word. Nobody said a word."

Georgie pretended to pout. "Aw, are you feeling left out?"

He gave her as severe a look as he could manage. "A little, yes. I am greatly concerned about everything surrounding Miranda."

"I can see why." Georgie watched the dance, seeming to laugh to herself.

Tony followed suit but couldn't manage to smile. "Now what in the world does that mean?"

"Miranda is very… direct," Georgie said, smiling still.

"Georgie, you know this is killing me, right?"

She nodded once. "I had gathered that, yes."

He growled softly with his irritation. "And? Are you going to take pity on me or torment me?"

"Decisions, decisions…" She gave him a distinctly impish look, and he had the wild urge to kiss her senseless.

"Georgie," he ground out.

She giggled to herself again. "She's decided that I will do for her stepsons."

Tony blinked at her once, twice, and then… "She said… what?"

Georgie gave him a sidelong look. "I'll do. She gave me a choice of Dorset or elsewhere."

Tony's heart began colliding with every single one of his ribs. He wet his lips carefully. "And how did you reply?"

"Oh, I didn't, really," Georgie said, scoffing a little. "I didn't have to. Miranda's already decided."

So help him, if she said anything remotely resembling his brother's name or county at this moment…

"Apparently, we're to be married by autumn." She gave him a mock apologetic look. "I'm terribly sorry about this."

Now he desperately wanted to kiss her senseless. But he opted to adopt a doleful expression. "I suppose I shall have to deal with it. But perhaps there is someone else you might wish to marry? I am hardly a fair prospect. Elinor could tell you that. I don't even have a house."

"This is true." Georgie sighed and looked around the room. "Surely we can find a more suitable candidate."

Tony pretended to help her look. He spotted a dashing looking young man who was too eager for his own good. "Why not marry him?"

Georgie snickered softly. "Not that one."

"Oh, poor lad," Tony pitied. "Why ever not?"

"Because he's an idiot and I'd find a better husband on the docks."

Tony tsked and shook his head. "You are rather selective."

Georgie gave him a bewildered look. "No idiots, no old men, and no cads. What in the world is selective in that?"

"You just ruled out the entire right side of the room," he told her, gesturing grandly.

Georgie coughed a laugh, covering her mouth quickly with her pristine white gloves.

Tony snickered beside her, barely maintaining his composure.

"Oh, if only it were so simple," she mourned, still smiling. "But there are too many factors to consider, and everything gets all muddled. Look at Grace. Was there ever a better picture of perfection? Yet there she sits, no suitors and no prospects beyond her own fortune."

Tony shook his head sadly. "I don't know why any of you are unmarried. Except for Charlotte, but she's peculiar."

Georgie grinned briefly at that. Then she sobered. "I tried, you know. The first five Seasons, I did everything right. I should have been just as sought after as any of the other girls. But I never had anything. Not even once. And after a while, you just stop trying. Not because you've given up or you no longer want it, but because it's easier. Why put forth the effort when there are no results? Trying only leads to disappointment. So, you lower your expectations, and instead of being disappointed, you become comfortable. Because it is all you've ever known, and it becomes what you expect. And yet... somehow you still hope."

"Do you?" Tony asked, holding his breath.

Georgie dipped her chin in a brief nod. "Every ball. Every start of the Season. Every time Elinor brings information about a new gentleman. It would be easier to stop, to accept my fate as it is. But I still have hope." She smiled almost sadly and looked over at him. "Does that make me pathetic?"

He shook his head at once. "No. No, not at all. In fact... You're terrifying."

That took her by surprise and she reared back. "What? Why?"

"Because you're impressive." He shrugged as if that explained everything.

Georgie frowned at him. "That's not terrifying."

"Not to you," he replied. "But to a gentleman tasked with approaching you to ask for a dance? To court you? To marry you?" He shook his head again. "Utterly terrifying. You walk into a room and know exactly why you are there and what you are going to do. You handle every obstacle without fear and with a firm step. You are no damsel in distress, and you never will be. You, who are in possession of a fairly dismal prospect for your life, can still find a way to hope. That is both impressive and terrifying."

Georgie stared at him silently for a moment, then returned her gaze to the dance, blinking rapidly. "I should very much like to be alone with you right now, Captain Sterling."

His stomach lurched, and his toes began to tingle. "Indeed?"

She nodded very firmly once. "There is a rather enthusiastic kiss just begging to be claimed. Possibly more than one."

He groaned very softly. "Oh, for an abandoned alcove."

Georgie smirked at nothing in particular. "A closet, a closet, my kingdom for a closet?"

Tony managed a laugh. "Yes, something to that effect."

"Well," she said slowly, nodding in thought, "if we go along with this idea of Miranda's, we could, perhaps, be permitted some time to ourselves every now and again."

He liked this plan already, and he didn't mind showing it.

"It is possible, yes," he agreed, keeping his tone mild. "Miranda is a very determined woman, and if she has decided on you…"

Georgie winced. "She did seem rather certain."

"Then it would only be fair to indulge her." Tony pretended to consider it reluctantly. "For her sake, if nothing else. She does so want to be helpful."

"And no one need know what we are about," Georgie offered. "Miranda doesn't know many people, and there will be no formal courtship or outings, so who is to know?"

Well now, that didn't sound nearly as appealing.

"Actually," he said slowly, dropping more than a little suggestion in to his tone.

Georgie whipped her head around to look at him. "What?"

He smiled rather smugly. "Miranda insisted that I dance with you."

Her eyes widened, and she blinked hard. "She insisted you what?"

"Dance," he repeated. "With you."

Georgie's throat worked on a swallow, and Tony watched it move.

"I must say, I was rather pleased about the suggestion," he went on, keeping his eyes steady on hers. "After all, it is going to be difficult to find a moment alone with you without being seen or someone thinking we're being improper."

She stared back at him, her breathing just the slightest bit unsteady.

"This way," he continued, dropping his voice, "I can be close to you without being remotely inappropriate. I can be near you and touching you in front of all these people, and no one will think anything of it. I can hold your hand, Georgie. And it won't be a kiss, but it will be the closest thing we have."

Georgie seemed to tremble before his eyes, and he smiled knowingly at her. He felt the same sort of tremor, though his was not visible. It thrummed through his body with energy and vigor, filling him with the need to act, to seize whatever opportunity he could.

"Must we?" Georgie whimpered. "Everyone will think…"

"At least six people heard her command me to," he assured her, gentling his smile. "They and their friends will consider me fulfilling a duty."

She nodded once, swallowing again. "And the rest?"

"I thought of that, too." He winked at her. "I have at least four more dances I must engage in tonight."

"Truly?" she managed. "With whom?"

"Well, I've been making it a point to dance with the Spinsters tonight," he informed her with a smug smile. "I've enjoyed a dance with Grace, Charlotte, and Prue so far, so the next must be with you and with Izzy."

Georgie began to smile at him, her eyes crinkling a little. "And the last two?"

"Miranda begged a dance for herself, and I think Janet deserves one as well. They're not Spinsters, of course, but they are family. Duty must be upheld, after all."

"Of course." She smiled so warmly at him that he could scarcely breathe, and whatever power he'd felt from Grace's smile seemed insignificant by comparison.

There was no telling what he would do for such a smile, but he suspected it would be a substantial effort.

He held out his hand as he tried to find his voice.

Georgie wordlessly put her hand in his, smiling at him still. "You're right," she murmured.

"About what?"

She looked down at their hands, then back up at him. "It almost feels like a kiss."

If he somehow avoided dying this evening, it would be an

absolute miracle.

He steeled himself, nodded politely, and led her out onto the dance floor, the room watching yet another Spinster dance with too much interest.

What they did not realize was that this was the one that mattered most.

Chapter Sixteen

———⁂———

A courtship, if properly pursued, should be something formal, sedate, and supervised by the appropriate chaperones. If pursued informally, it should be public, simple, and properly chaperoned. If pursued in haste, it should at least be properly chaperoned. Anything else is absolute madness and a certain path to disaster.

-*The Spinster Chronicles, 2 December 1816*

"Did they see us? I don't think they saw us."

"I don't see how they could have. You were far ahead of me, and I happen to be very quick."

Georgie grinned, holding out her gloveless hand.

Tony smiled back, still breathless from their running, and took it. "I missed you."

His words lightened her heart, and somehow, she smiled further still. "I just saw you yesterday."

He shook his head slowly. "That was much too long ago." He tugged on her hand, pulling her against him and kissed her, his lips slowly devouring hers with soft, gentle caresses that made her spine tingle and her toes ache.

"Georgie! Tony! Where did you get to?"

Georgie broke off, moaning weakly. "Why can we not hide?"

Tony kissed her nose, then the corner of her mouth. "Because we have very inquisitive friends and family, and we are only secretly courting to please Miranda. If we want any real privacy…"

Georgie shook her head, then dropped her brow to his shoulder. "Yes and no. No and yes... Tony, I don't know what I want or what to do."

He kissed her hair quickly and rubbed her back. "Well, if you keep running, I'll catch you again. There's another stand of trees over there, and it's far more shaded."

She smacked his shoulder, raising her head with a scolding look. "Really, Tony? Really?"

He grinned unabashedly. "What can I say? Chasing you is an inordinate amount of fun and sneaking around is rather enjoyable."

She scoffed and pushed off him, pulling her glove back on. "You should have gone into covert operations, Captain Sterling."

"Who's to say I am not?" He raised a brow at her with perfect alacrity.

She gave him the sort of look that said exactly what she thought of that.

He hefted his blue pall mall ball and chuckled at her. "You better start your march to your own ball, Miss Allen, or face the questions of our friends."

Georgie narrowed her eyes at him, stuck out her tongue, and then trudged on up ahead.

"Oh, there you are, Georgie!" Izzy called from the other side of the bushes. "I didn't see you. Where's Tony?"

Georgie scowled and pointed at him. "He decided it would be amusing to stand on his own ball once it was next to mine, and then hit it so that my ball went soaring into the distance while his stayed put!"

Izzy laughed aloud while Charlotte cheered. "Good strategy, Tony!"

"Not helpful!" Georgie bellowed down to her. She turned and continued her way up the lawn, now grinning to herself. The truth of the matter was that she had thrown her ball as far as she could the moment she had been out of sight from everyone else to give herself time away.

They'd all driven out to Janet's family home, situated outside of London, for a picnic and games, and the first thing Janet had insisted upon was a game of pall mall. Georgie hadn't played since she was a much younger girl, but any chance to be competitive was something she would jump at. Prue and Grace hadn't come with them today, nor had Elinor, who seemed more disgruntled than usual, despite her recent absences, so it was left to Izzy, Charlotte, and Georgie to represent the rest of the Spinsters in their game.

Tony had come, obviously, as had Lord Sterling, Lieutenant Henshaw, Mr. Johnston, his wife, and Miranda. Mr. Johnston and his wife had opted to remain at the house, though they watched from the terrace, and Miranda, though not playing, was following along to observe.

She was undoubtedly trying to watch Tony and Georgie interact, what with her plans for them, but up until this point, they hadn't given her much to see aside from their bickering and too-competitive nature.

Not that either of them was focused on the game overly much. They were having too much fun putting on a show for her and for everybody else. Ever since the ball at Lord and Lady Kirby's, they had been practically inseparable. They'd taken up sending each other missives throughout the day, arranging to meet up in the most innocent places.

The bookshop on Wednesday, though Tony had never been a great reader. Outside of the milliner's on Friday, though Georgie had no need for more headwear. Tattersall's on Thursday, though neither of them needed a new horse. Hyde Park nearly every morning with a servant in tow, as Georgie had suddenly developed a taste for early morning walks.

They never behaved in a manner that would rouse comment, staying strictly within the confines of good behavior. Everything was polite and proper, with absolutely no touching unless it was deemed necessary by good manners. Georgie had begun growing purposefully clumsy, so Tony would be forced into taking her hand or holding her arm to steady her, but the moments never lasted long enough for either of them. He could help her in and out of carriages as often as he liked, but it wouldn't change anything.

It was madness, what they were doing. Absolute madness.

She was only growing more and more fond of him, more and more attracted to him, and more and more desperate to be with him above all others.

Yet the betrayal that had been felt when Emma had married Mr. Partlowe and left the Spinsters weighed heavily upon her. Would they feel the same way if Georgie left them all for Tony?

She blanched at the thought. The word marriage had never been shared between them except in jest, so there was no reason to think that this infatuation could lead to that extreme. This could all be nothing more than a temporary romance to entertain them both for a time.

It didn't feel temporary, though. It all felt rather consuming and wild, yet with a depth that was fast taking root within her.

Neither of them had uttered the word love, and Georgie wasn't certain she could.

Was she in love? Was that what this madness all amounted to? Or was she so desperate for the future she had always envisioned that she was not seeing things clearly, not as they truly were?

These were the thoughts that kept her awake at night, when she was not dreaming of Tony and his kisses. She had never been in love before, had never been courted, either for the public or in secret, so she had no idea what to expect.

She had witnessed several courtships from the outside perspective, including Emma's. She knew how those had looked, and what had been said about the couple in particular from those watching. She'd seen courtships that had floundered, courtships that had surprised her with their swift success, courtships that seemed doomed to fail yet thrived, and courtships that would have bored her to tears. Long courtships, short courtships, and courtships that had been all show and little substance.

But she knew nothing about being *in* a courtship. How would someone court her? What would make a courtship of Georgie Allen successful?

Tony seemed inclined to try, though she couldn't say to what end. She did not doubt that he had good intentions, nor could she doubt his sincerity. He was not the sort of man to prey upon a woman's heart and tender emotions. He was a good man, and a handsome one. He had honor, valor, and good judgment. He was witty and charming, kind and considerate, and his smile made one wish for wings to fly.

He was exactly the sort of man that Georgie had always wished herself to fall in love with but had not managed to find.

She glanced back down the green now, where the others followed, including Tony, and he looked up at her. His eyes warmed, and he cast a very faint wink at her, causing her heart to skip a beat.

Was Georgie turning into one of those silly creatures she had always disapproved of and pitied simply because a handsome man was paying her attention?

Probably.

But was it unfounded?

That was a far more difficult question to answer.

Georgie shook her head and took up position next to her green ball, waiting for her turn.

Tony stopped several feet away, propping his mallet atop his ball and turning to look at the others. "Charlotte, if you would like to take your turn before the autumn sets in…"

Charlotte scoffed loudly, making a face at him. "My strokes are far more accurate than yours, Tony Sterling, as you will notice by my proximity to the wicket. You will have to backtrack to get through it, and if you continue to whack away at it like a madman, you'll be here until Michaelmas, not me."

"Tony, do behave with gentility," Miranda scolded, her tone one of mild offense. "What will the ladies think of you?"

Lord Sterling chuckled and propped his mallet on his shoulder. "That he's a sportsman despite his gentility?"

Miranda threw a dark look at him. "Not helpful, Francis."

He grinned at his aunt and shrugged. "Terribly sorry, Miranda, but it is true. And Miss Wright was not at all offended, was she?" He looked at Charlotte with inquiry.

Charlotte shook her head straightaway. "No more than anyone could be with Tony at any given time. It's truly the lieutenant who needs to work on his aim."

Lieutenant Henshaw coughed in mock distress, putting a hand to his heart. "Miss Wright, you do wound me so!"

"Yes, I have that effect on people," Charlotte sniffed, tossing her dark curls. "You'll grow accustomed to it."

Henshaw grinned at her, and his smile was one of warmth and friendliness rather than adoration. "Would you care to wager, Miss Wright?"

"Oh, no," Izzy moaned, putting her head in one hand. "Lieutenant, you shouldn't..."

Georgie looked heavenward. "Please, no..."

"I always care to wager, Lieutenant," Charlotte said with a mischievous note in her voice. "What are we wagering on?"

"Five strokes," Henshaw said firmly, his mouth curving. "Our balls are in a near proximity at the moment. Whoever can be the most accurate with their five strokes and the remaining four wickets wins."

Tony was shaking his head, laughing to himself. "Henshaw..."

Despite Miranda's command for Tony to be more genteel, she watched this particular interchange with interest.

Georgie thought Miranda and Charlotte would get along famously, if given the chance. Or else they would clash like titans and leave a destructive path in their wake.

"And the stakes?" Charlotte asked Henshaw, tilting her chin.

"A dance?" he suggested.

Charlotte sputtered in disgust. "Too simple."

"She'd dance with you anyway, Lieutenant," Izzy informed him with a laugh.

"Money," he suggested.

"Too mercenary," Janet scoffed, warming to their game. "And I think she has more to offer than you, Lieutenant."

Henshaw considered that, then smirked at her. "Dessert, then. At the picnic. If I win, I get your desserts. All of them. If you win, you get mine."

Georgie grinned swiftly at that and eyed Charlotte carefully. There was nothing Charlotte loved so well as her dessert, and it would be a true test of her honor to see her give them up.

Charlotte nodded at once. "Agreed." She gestured at Tony, taking up her position. "Move, Sterling. I have desserts to win."

Tony chuckled and bowed as he stepped aside.

Charlotte hit her yellow ball and watched it roll almost directly to the next wicket, then grinned proudly and turned to her competitor. "Your move, soldier."

Henshaw raised a brow at her, then stepped forward and sent his red ball directly at hers, knocking it aside of the wicket.

"Foul!" Charlotte cried with a stomp of her foot.

"That's pall mall, Miss Wright," Henshaw told her with an easy smile. "One stroke down, four to go." He twirled his mallet over his shoulder and whistled as he headed for their balls, Charlotte glowering darkly as she marched behind.

"I resign," Lord Sterling said with a laugh. "I want to watch this play out."

"Me too," Janet offered, setting her mallet aside and taking her husband's arm. "I'll place a guinea on Charlotte."

Lord Sterling chuckled. "And I'll put mine on Henshaw. Miranda, may I escort you?" He offered her an arm and a smile.

Miranda looked at Charlotte and Henshaw in speculation, then glanced over at Georgie briefly with a raise of one brow before striding forward. "Yes, Francis, that would be lovely."

They moved away, placing their own bets and making an analysis of the rest of the course.

Tony watched them go, then looked up at Georgie with a teasing smile.

Naturally, she had already been watching him, and something about his eyes on her made her smile. Just a soft, warm, contented smile, something familiar and easy, and all the frantic emotions of late faded before her.

She could very easily love this man.

She might already.

Again, he gave her a faint wink, and then struck his ball with the mallet in the direction of the others, though nobody was paying attention to anyone else now.

He followed it, leaving only Georgie behind.

With Izzy.

Georgie's eyes widened as she realized that she'd forgotten all about her cousin still being behind with her and Tony. And she'd just been smiling so fondly at him, and he'd winked at her! For all intents and purposes, that might have been as bad as an embrace!

She looked over at Izzy, who was very quietly standing by her ball, her copper hair glinting a little in the sunlight.

Izzy gave Georgie an unreadable smile. "Your turn, I suppose."

Georgie frowned a little. With what Izzy had just witnessed, she was still intent on playing the game? Hesitantly, Georgie hit her ball and sent it in the direction of the next wicket.

Izzy watched the ball, then nodded with a proud smile. "Excellent shot." She lined her ball and mallet, and made a similar shot, but winced this time. "That wasn't as good. Oh well." She grinned at Georgie and tilted her head in the direction of the others. "Shall we?"

Georgie nodded absently and started to walk when she felt Izzy link their arms and sigh.

"I don't know why the two of you are being so secretive," Izzy commented with an airy note. "We all know."

Georgie nearly stumbled in shock, but Izzy kept her upright. "You... what?"

Izzy's wide eyes took on a pitying look. "Oh, Georgie, you didn't think we were as blind as all that, did you?"

"I..." she stammered, wondering if this sensation of being completely tossed about and without words was what Prue endured. "I don't..."

"We've all discussed it," Izzy went on, "and we're tired of pretending we don't know. You and Tony deserve to court for all to see, and none of us know why you aren't."

This was beyond anything Georgie could have imagined. "You all... Who?"

Izzy looked surprised. "The Spinsters, of course. We've decided that if you two don't start a proper courtship, we're going to start rumors about secret liaisons to force you to start one. The choice is yours, really."

"Then you approve?" Georgie asked, hardly daring to hope.

Now Izzy was bewildered, and she laughed. "Of Tony? Good heavens, Georgie, absolutely yes. We all adore him, so snatch him up before somebody else tries to."

Georgie laughed breathlessly, her heart lighter than air, and she pulled her cousin closer. "Oh, good, because I really hate morning walks, and I'd rather not keep doing them."

"Yes, I wondered about that."

Charlotte rather enjoyed her additional desserts but surprised them all by not lording over Henshaw about her victory.

In fact, at this moment, she was sitting quietly on her corner of the blanket, smiling quite proudly to herself as she finished her second one.

Henshaw, ever the good sport, had admitted defeat graciously, and announced that he could best her in shooting once they had concluded their picnic.

Tony wasn't going to underestimate Charlotte again, but he wouldn't dare tell his friend so.

Luncheon had been delightful, if a bit much, and they all sat or laid about rather sleepily on the lawn at Linley, nobody feeling particularly inclined to engage in activity for a time.

Francis had his head in Janet's lap while she played with his hair, Henshaw was laid out flat on the grass dozing, Miranda had gone up to the terrace to chat with her sister and Mr. Johnston, and Izzy and Georgie lounged nearby, still picking at the remaining strawberries.

Tony watched Georgie for a moment, wondering at the ease he saw in her now. She always tended to hold herself almost stiffly when they were in company, though an outing such as this would induce her to let her guard down a little. She was determined to always be the strong image of herself everybody saw her as, but he sensed that the pressure to continually be so weighed upon her.

She'd opened herself up to him, and he'd never quite been able to put his finger on the reason. Perhaps it was because he was an outsider who had no pre-conceived notions of her, perhaps it was desperation to confide in anybody who wouldn't judge her, or perhaps she had seen something in him that prompted her to do so. Whatever her reason, he would always be grateful that she had.

He could not have imagined his time in London without her. Well, without any of the Spinsters, to be sure. He held them all in high esteem and had great affection for each one of them. Even before he'd grown close to Georgie, he'd felt that for her.

But now…

Everything was changed now. He knew her well, despite their relatively short acquaintance, and the prospect of coming to know her better filled his soul with anticipation and delight. He wanted to share so much with her, the details of his life, even the things that were inconsequential, and the memories he hadn't shared with anyone. He wanted to take her to Mawbry and Engleford, where he had grown up, and show her all the best trees to climb, the secret way to the kitchens, and the tree house he and Ben had fashioned as boys.

He wanted to tell her about his time in the army, the good and the bad, and everything that filled the spaces between. He wanted to dance with her more than once at a ball. He wanted so much and yet he couldn't bring himself to move.

Georgie had to be sure. She never did anything unless she was, and this could not be an exception.

Time would be his ally. Time and patience. If Georgie was the result, he had an eternity's supply of both.

"Tony?"

He looked over at Janet, who seemed to be watching him in amusement. "Janet?"

She smiled at him. "Will you be a dear and round up the remaining pall mall equipment? I don't believe everything was brought down. The servants will be setting up the shooting for Henshaw and Charlotte, and I'd hate to take them away from it."

He nodded and sat up, brushing his hands off. "Of course. I could use the exercise, anyway, after such a splendid meal."

Janet squinted up at him in the sunlight. "Cook will be delighted to hear that. She may send you home with a basket."

"One can only hope," Tony laughed, climbing to his feet.

"I'll come with you," Georgie offered with a groan as she rose. "I'm likely to fall asleep if I don't do something with myself."

Tony's heart lifted in excitement.

Georgie didn't look at him as she turned to look at Izzy. "Do you want to come, too?"

What? Why would she ask that? He liked Izzy as much as anyone else, probably more than most, but to invite her along when they had a chance to be alone? If he had the freedom to express himself as he wanted to, he would have glared at Georgie rather ferociously at this moment.

Izzy shook her head and tilted her face back more fully into the sun. "I'd rather enjoy a nap in the sunshine at present. I am perfectly content to remain just as I am here."

Izzy was now his favorite person in the entire world, including his own family.

Georgie nodded and started towards Tony, who gestured in the direction of the pall mall course and scattered equipment.

They walked side by side in silence, enough space between them for another person besides. Every now and then, one of them would stoop to pick up a wicket and loop them over an arm. Tony picked up a ball, Georgie a mallet.

"Sorry about that," she suddenly murmured as they picked up more wickets. "I thought it best to keep up appearances."

Tony exhaled roughly, relief washing over him. "Was that what that was?"

Georgie cast a look at him. "I could hardly squeal in excitement at the prospect of five minutes alone with you in front of the rest, could I?"

He chuckled and allowed himself to grin without reserve. "I suppose not. Was that your inclination?"

She shrugged with a teasing smile. "It might have been."

"I'll take it." He held out a hand for the ball she picked up, and she gave it to him, their fingers brushing.

Georgie suddenly blushed and ducked her chin.

Embarrassed, was she? He found that perfectly endearing and utterly charming. His strong and witty Georgie was bashful about her feelings for him.

That was a good sign.

He chose not to comment on it and continued forward, looking for the next wicket. "So, what do you think about Charlotte and Henshaw?"

Georgie laughed once. "Oh, they are a formidable pair, but she's not for him, nor he for her."

"No?" Tony asked, truly curious. "I thought they would make a rather good match."

Georgie shook her head very firmly. "No. Henshaw is far too nice a man to be paired with Charlotte, even if he can provoke her so well. I rather think they will just be good friends." She looked over at Tony with curiosity. "He's a rather good friend for you, I think."

Tony nodded, picking up another mallet and handing it to her. "He is, and one of the very best. A good heart, strong convictions, endless amounts of courage, and a devilish sense of humor; I cannot tell you how often he lightened the hearts of those in his company."

"I believe it," Georgie replied, sidestepping a puddle. "I like him immensely."

"I hoped you would." He smiled over at her with all the warmth he couldn't express with words.

She caught it and surprised him by returning it in full measure. "I have had a thought," she suddenly said, still smiling.

"Oh?" he inquired, picking up another wicket. "Should I be worried?"

Georgie hummed a little. "I don't believe so. You know that my mother and father are abroad this Season."

He nodded, deciding, probably for the best, to avoid criticizing parents who abandoned their daughter so easily.

"But Uncle Lambert is charged with my care and guardianship in their absence," Georgie went on, suddenly finding the ground of particular interest.

"Yes, so you've said," he replied a bit slowly, wondering at the point she was trying to make.

Georgie's lips quirked, and her gaze shifted his way, although it never rose enough to meet his. "He thinks very well of me and is very good. I believe if someone with a particular interest in pursuing any sort of arrangement to keep company with me within the public eye…"

Tony stopped and stared at her in wonder.

"… might find himself rather welcome to avail himself of my uncle's presence around three in the afternoon tomorrow, when he will be returned from his business, and during which time he is most accommodating. Should any requests wish to be made." Georgie had stopped now as well and bit her lip, the corners of her mouth pulling as if she would smile.

214

"Georgie," Tony began slowly, unable to keep from smiling, not daring to hope, "are you saying that… I may court you? Officially? For all the world to see?"

Georgie grinned and nodded eagerly. "If my uncle agrees, which Izzy assures me he will."

"Izzy knows?"

"They all know." Georgie shrugged with a laugh. "I had no idea, Tony, but they've known all along. And they approve."

"They approve?" he echoed in disbelief.

She nodded again, now all-out giggling. "Tony, Izzy threatened to expose us if we don't go public. They would start rumors about us just to get us to court properly."

Tony shook his head, staring at this wonderful, beautiful, incomparable woman before him. "If we weren't in full sight of the house right now, I would kiss you like there was no tomorrow."

Georgie smiled at him tenderly. "I'd let you." She held out her free hand, and he took it in his, holding as tightly as he dared.

"This will suffice," he whispered with a wink.

Georgie nodded and stroked his hand with her thumb. "For now."

And they continued to walk along the green, hands only parting when they must, and joining again the moment they could.

Chapter Seventeen

———⟨∞ ∞⟩———

There is nothing to make a soul so fulfilled as finding purpose, and nothing to bring as much joy as searching outside of one's self for it. Being consumed with one's own affairs overly much is a sure way to invite misery and discontent. A good heart is a fine thing to possess indeed.

-The Spinster Chronicles, 20 February 1818

The evening had begun over half an hour ago, and still Lady Edith had not arrived.

Georgie barely avoided wringing her hands together as she paced the floor. She had delivered the invitation to Lady Edith personally, and had been assured she was coming.

The evening was specifically designed with her in mind, for pity's sake!

"Georgie, do calm yourself," Aunt Faith murmured with a hint of scolding. "It is not attractive to behave so. What would your mother say?"

"That an anxious woman never gained a thing," Georgie uttered without thinking. "I know that one."

Her aunt harrumphed and nudged her husband, whose almost bored expression hardly changed. "What, Faith?" he grumped. "I'm wondering where the lady is, too. All the other guests have arrived, including Georgie's new beau." There was a suggestive note in his voice, and Georgie turned to look at him with a raised brow.

Her uncle chuckled easily. "I'm only saying, Georgie, that it is hard to sustain a courtship from separate rooms."

"Tony doesn't mind, Papa," Izzy broke in helpfully. "He's a good sort, and he wants Lady Edith here as well."

"Hush, Izzy," Aunt Faith scolded quickly. "He is Georgie's beau. When you have one, you may speak of him."

Izzy rolled her eyes and shook her head at Georgie as she headed for the front of the house.

Georgie was not going to comment on that, for fear of lashing out at her aunt, and that would not help anyone, least of all Izzy.

But where *was* Lady Edith?

Had Georgie and Izzy intimidated her? Had they somehow misunderstood when they visited her? Did she not want their friendships? Had they gone too far?

So many questions, so many mixed emotions, and absolutely no answers.

The evening would not be a loss if she didn't come, but the disappointment would be crushing.

At least her courtship with Tony had begun officially, and she could be seen going to him for comfort, though it would have to be more composed than she would have liked.

Flinging herself on him wouldn't do if she wanted to keep above rumors and speculation. She wasn't prone to dramatic displays as it was, so the odds of her doing that no matter the circumstances were low.

Still, it might have been an entertaining spectacle, and Tony would have no idea what to do, or that it was coming. His expression would have been rather hilarious and imagining it might have been enough to satisfy her.

"She's here!" Izzy suddenly squealed as she dashed back to them.

"Oh, good," Aunt Faith said under her breath. "Though it is rather deplorable manners to show up so tardy."

"Don't tell her that, Faith," Uncle Lambert told her. "We are warm and welcoming, and grateful to have her here."

Aunt Faith glared at him briefly. "Yes, of course, we are. But the fact remains…"

Georgie ignored them both and smiled as Lady Edith finally appeared, looking enchanting in a green muslin that enhanced her eyes so perfectly. She hurried down the corridor towards them, an apology no doubt on her lips.

"Lady Edith," Izzy said quickly before any apology could come forth. She curtseyed and held out her hands. "We're so delighted that you could join us."

Izzy's warmth could have thawed an entire winter, and Lady Edith looked both bewildered and delighted by it.

"Thank you, Miss Lambert," she replied, smiling prettily. "It is a pleasure to be here. I pray you'll excuse my tardiness…"

"No need, no need," Uncle Lambert told her with a congenial smile. "My daughter is quite right, we are delighted to have you." He bowed, and Georgie could have kissed him for his goodness.

Aunt Faith curtseyed and smiled as best she could, gesturing for her to proceed into the drawing room where the others had gathered.

Izzy took Lady Edith's arm, and Georgie followed, smiling in her relief.

The night would be well now, no matter what transpired.

"Are you settling, Lady Edith?" Izzy asked, rubbing her arm. "We descended upon you so suddenly after your arrival."

Lady Edith chuckled easily. "Oh, yes, we're quite settled now. You'd hardly recognize the place if you saw it. And please, do call me Edith. I've never enjoyed formalities."

"That's fortunate," Georgie replied. "We hate them ourselves."

"What do you hate?" Charlotte queried as she approached them. "I adore hating things, do tell me."

Edith looked intrigued by that but said nothing.

"Formality," Georgie informed her.

Charlotte shuddered delicately. "I despise formality. I never use it if I can help it. No point to it at all."

"Some would disagree with you," Izzy broke in, shaking her head.

Charlotte shrugged. "No matter." She looked at Edith with interest. "You must be Lady Edith Leveson."

Edith inclined her head, smiling a little. "I am."

"This is Charlotte Wright," Georgie told her quickly, knowing that Charlotte despised protocol almost as much as formality. "She's one of the Spinsters, too."

"Charmed." Edith bobbed a quick curtsey, then tilted her head in question, as if she could sense that Charlotte was not through.

And, of course, she wasn't.

Charlotte nodded thoughtfully, her lips curving slightly. "I've heard that you were only married for about five minutes."

"Charlotte!" Izzy gasped, pulling Edith closer to her. "Don't!"

"It's all right," Edith said, patting Izzy's hand. "I've heard it all in Derby. I was not married long at all, Miss Wright, but married I was, so the status remains."

Georgie gnawed the inside of her lip, watching the exchange carefully. Charlotte could easily get out of hand, and she had no idea if Edith had enough mettle to endure such a thing. If she needed to act, it would be easiest to remove Charlotte, though how she would accomplish that, short of bodily means, was beyond her.

"And how was being married?" Charlotte inquired.

"Charlotte," Georgie warned in a quiet voice.

Edith smiled just a little. "Quick."

Charlotte grinned. "I like you, Lady Edith Leveson." She tossed her head back and laughed a deep, throaty laugh. "I think I shall like you immensely. Play a hand of whist with me later, once you've made the rounds."

"If you like," Edith replied with a much warmer smile.

Charlotte nodded and made her way around the room.

"Well done, Edith," Izzy praised, laughing in disbelief. "You handled Charlotte marvelously."

Edith exhaled softly, shaking her head. "Let's hope not everyone will be so suspicious."

"They won't," Izzy and Georgie said together.

Georgie waved a hand at Tony, who nodded and came to them with Henshaw in tow. "Edith, this is Captain Anthony Sterling, a very great friend, and Lieutenant… I'm so sorry, I don't know your given name."

Henshaw smiled at that. "Not to worry, Georgie, it's Edward." He returned his gaze to Edith and bowed. "Edward Henshaw, at your service, Lady Edith."

"You must be the man Lachlan wrote me about," Edith replied with a bright smile. "You sent over supplies to stock our kitchens."

"I did, yes," Henshaw confirmed, his eyes twinkling. "I hope you didn't take offense."

Edith reared back a little. "From a brace of pheasants and vegetables? Not at all, we were most grateful for them. It was very generous."

"Well," Henshaw blustered, looking embarrassed, "I did promise to look after you, Lady Edith, and I am a man of my word. I didn't want to impose on you without a formal introduction, lest you think me presumptuous."

"That didn't stop Georgie and Izzy," Tony brought up with a small wink.

Edith giggled while Henshaw scowled. "That is not the same thing and you know it, Sterling."

"Georgie's all imposition," Izzy laughed with a meaningful look at Georgie. "We've never been able to fix that."

"Yes," Georgie admitted with a dramatic sigh, "it is all I ever hear about."

Edith looked around the group with a sort of wonder, then looked back at Henshaw. "Well, it will be no imposition henceforth, Lieutenant."

Henshaw smiled broadly. "I'm glad to hear it. Please, do send for me if you should have any need. I'll give my information to your manservant and see that he knows it as well."

Edith nodded, a sudden strain appearing in her face that Georgie wasn't sure she cared for. But it was gone so quickly she couldn't be sure it had really appeared.

"I'm grateful to you for that," Edith murmured, her voice not quite steady. "I hope, however, that we'll have no cause to meet other than a social one."

"Agreed." Henshaw looked at Edith another moment, then shook his head. "If you'll permit me, Lady Edith, you're far prettier than your brother led me to believe."

Izzy giggled while Edith simply smiled at the handsome lieutenant. "And what did my brother say on that subject?"

Tony seemed to be fighting laughter, and he watched his friend with interest.

"He said you were a fair enough lass, I believe." Henshaw

shrugged his broad shoulders. "I find it a poor description."

Edith snorted softly, her smile turning wry. "And yet it is one entirely worthy of Lachlan. I am glad to surpass expectation."

Henshaw chuckled and moved aside. "Don't let me keep you from making acquaintances, Lady Edith. There's a fair group here, every one of them a connection worth maintaining."

"Why, Lieutenant," Izzy said with an air of surprise, "I had no idea you thought so fondly of us."

"I'm in your presence, Izzy," he responded with a slight bow. "I think very well of everyone you admit into your circles."

"Down, Henshaw, down," Tony coughed with a wave at his friend. "You'll make somebody swoon."

Izzy and Edith laughed, then moved away to greet others in attendance. Henshaw watched them go, then took himself in the opposite direction to speak with Grace's brother, having not yet learned that expecting intelligent conversation there was a fool's errand.

"I'm not going to swoon," Georgie informed Tony proudly.

"No?" he inquired, his gaze darkening. "Then perhaps I ought to stand closer."

Georgie's toes tingled, and she looked up at him. "Perhaps you should."

Tony had to laugh at Georgie's suddenly impish behavior. They'd only been officially courting a day, and already the change in her was extraordinary.

He didn't think he could find her any more agreeable than he already did, but this side of her, this playful, flirtatious part, might become a favorite.

"Well that was well done," Tony murmured as he came to stand beside her. "Henshaw and Edith? What do you say to that?"

Georgie looked up at him with a smirk. "Since when have you turned matchmaker? Henshaw has tasked himself with her care, you cannot think he would think more of her than that."

Tony shrugged and accepted a glass of punch from a passing footman. "She's a beautiful woman, and you heard him just now. He's enchanted."

"Yes, and I heard him with Izzy," Georgie pointed out. "And with Charlotte. And Grace. And Prue. And myself. And a score of other women in London. Tony, he's a very charming man, and he flatters. Not in a scoundrel's way, but flatter he does. I gather he feels a responsibility for Edith, and for that he may pay her a degree of attention, but I think we will both find he will be more like a brother and less like a lover."

Tony watched her for a moment, feeling rather skeptical. "You want her to be yours for a while longer before giving her up to anyone else."

Georgie scowled and elbowed him swiftly. "That is not true. Not in the least."

"It's a little bit true, Georgie. Admit it."

"Shh," she shushed, trying not to smile. "I like Edith a very great deal, but I would not stand in the way of anything she wished to pursue. For pity's sake, Tony, I've only known her a short while. You make me sound like a tyrant."

"Says the woman who began a newssheet devoted to reaching out to the females in London making poor choices with the men in their circles," Tony said under his breath.

Georgie made a soft noise of disgruntlement. "That was never about preventing marriages. Just because I apparently can't have a marriage doesn't mean nobody else should. I'm not preventing anything. I have no authority. I just wanted to give them the best opportunity possible."

"You sound like the headmistress of a girls' school." Suddenly he wasn't playing anymore, and he found himself peculiarly invested in the conversation.

"If I really don't marry," Georgie told him in a soft tone, her smile gone, "that's exactly what I plan to do with myself."

She could not have surprised him more if she'd announced her intention to be prime minister.

A headmistress? She'd hate being cooped up in a school all the time, managing the lives of many little girls and their instructors, meeting with parents regularly, keeping up with the duties of the school itself and its running... She would have done it all rather impressively, but it would drain the light out of her, and she would have been miserable.

And what did she think he was courting her for? He had a personal stake in her and in her future, whatever it would be, and if he had his way...

Well, she wouldn't wind up as a headmistress of a crumbling school in Chester if he had anything to say about it.

"You don't mean that," he said, trying to scoff.

Georgie looked out over the company, expression unreadable. "Perhaps not, but I do have to think about my options, and they are few." Her voice had taken on a suddenly dour tone, and he hated the sound of it.

"I could help you come up with a few options, if you like," he suggested brightly. "Certainly, something more creative than a school headmistress."

She smiled at that and looked over at him. "Oh, really? Feasible ones, or all funny imaginings?"

Tony coughed in mock outrage. "Oh, ye of little faith! I can concoct feasible occupations for you, should you never find your way to the marriage altar."

Her lips quirked, and she turned to face him more fully. "Can you? Do go on, then."

"Circus rider," he said at once.

Georgie snickered and looked away. "I don't think so."

Tony cocked his head, frowning. "No? You're a very good rider, it would not be difficult for you."

"It's not respectable," she reminded him, still laughing. "I'd never be able to see my parents or brothers."

"A very great loss, to be sure," he quipped.

Now Georgie snorted and covered her mouth, looking back at him over her glove.

"But family connections must be kept," he went on with a reluctant sigh. "I concede your point. Very well, then. Book keeping."

Georgie dropped her hand and shook her head. "I'm dreadful with figures."

Tony made a face at that. "Oh, I don't know, I think you have a rather remarkable figure. I'm quite fond of it."

She rapped his arm sharply, her eyes widening. "Tony!"

He gave her a swift grin, relieved to have his spirited Georgie returned to him. "Governess."

"No," she laughed with a weaker swat. "I'd be so dreadful at that. I'd let the children run all over and never mind their lessons."

Tony shrugged a shoulder. "So, we send you to the home of a country squire who would love that sort of thing. It is all about perspective, you see."

Georgie shook her head at him, smiling in a way that made him want to hold her. "Oh, Tony."

"Or you could be a printer and publisher yourself," he went on, losing some of the playfulness in his tone. "Take the Spinster Chronicles further. Print an entire paper of it. You could collect unmarried women from all over to submit articles. Think of what Lady Hetty could offer."

"There's a terrifying prospect," Georgie muttered, still smiling.

Tony nearly took her by the arms, the idea suddenly had such merit. "It could be an overthrow of everything that currently defines the publishing world. Stories, news, gossip, advice… Georgie, the Spinster Chronicles could become the most widely read paper in London."

Georgie considered him with an almost sad air. "And who would finance it, Tony? Who would let a group of women take on an entire paper on the off chance that Society wants more than what it already has? You think we are hated now? Imagine what an entire paper written by spinsters would do." She shook her head and took his hand, keeping the clasp hidden from anyone that may have been looking. "It's an entertaining thought, and maybe it would work, if things were different. But not with us. Not in these times." She looked out over the group again, not seeming to see any of them. "I should have more purpose. I should have done something more with my life."

"And what is preventing you from having a purpose now?" he asked, taking a chance, and stepping closer to her. "You are not at the end of your life, nor anywhere close to it. Your future is still before you."

"But to what end?" Georgie's brow wrinkled, and she turned to look at him, her eyes almost stormy. "What can I do that will be meaningful? If I'm not to have the life I imagined, what sort of life can I have? What do I do with it, Tony?"

What did she do with it? Could she not see what he was seeing? She was so lost in her own cares and concerns, so worried about her future, that she neglected to see what she was currently doing; the effect she had on people, the energy she brought wherever she went, the smiles she brought about, the courage she bolstered, the weakened souls she lifted, and the goodness she shared.

How could she not see this?

"Georgie…" Tony murmured quietly, squeezing her hand. "Help Edith. Help Izzy. Help Grace and Charlotte. Help Elinor, for heaven's sake. You need a purpose? You have one. And it's incredible. You are capable of so much."

She tilted her head slightly, her lips parting in wonder.

Tony swallowed hard, rubbing her hand with his thumb. "You can't see yourself, Georgie. You're too close. But I see you, and it's quite a stirring sight."

She was silent for a long moment, and he could feel each exhale escaping past her full lips in that silence. Then her throat worked, and she smiled at him. "That's it, you are coming with me everywhere all the time."

He hadn't expected that, and he laughed in surprise. "What?"

Georgie nodded. "You are too good for my self-confidence, and yet can stop me just short of getting an inflated ego." She brightened, and her smile widened. "There's a purpose for you, Tony Sterling. Steady me so I can do mine." She laughed at that and turned to check on Izzy and Edith's progress, though she still held his hand in hers.

Steady her? He stared at her fixedly, observing the turn of her throat, the golden curls of her hair, the natural flush on her cheeks, the exact shape of her eyes.

Steady her.

"I'd love to," he nearly said aloud.

But he couldn't.

Because the truth of the matter was that he had another idea in mind. Another purpose for himself. One that would allow him to accomplish her suggestion and more while giving his own life more meaning.

More fulfillment.

More everything.

One purpose he could see himself living for every day for the rest of his life.

Loving Georgie.

His breath caught in his chest with such swiftness that he thought he might be the one to swoon after all.

He loved her. Fiercely and with a depth that startled him beyond measure. How long had he loved her and not known it? How long had he been blind enough to ignore the greatest truth he had ever known in his entire life?

Of course, he loved her.

And he intended to make it perfectly clear that she wouldn't need to find an occupation with her life to make it have purpose and meaning.

He had the perfect solution for her.

He couldn't tell her yet, not until he had thought this all through and made necessary arrangements. He needed a plan, for her, for him, for them both. He needed to feel this exhilaration of loving her for longer than three minutes before acting on it.

But she would know soon enough.

"Georgie," he said quietly, loving the taste of her name on his lips.

She knew that tone and looked at him with a curious tilt to her chin.

Saints above, how he loved her! He shook his head to himself, and murmured, "Oh, for an abandoned alcove!"

Georgie's eyes lit up and she grinned swiftly. "Actually, I know of one. Give me three minutes, and then follow down the corridor you came through, and you may just get a kiss before we go in to dinner."

He nodded at that, squeezing her hand. "If you're very quick, you might get two."

Georgie winked, wrinkled her nose, and left the room at a

surprisingly sedate pace.

Tony looked around, counting the time in his head, and waiting.

At two minutes and twelve seconds, he decided he'd waited long enough and followed.

There were three kisses before dinner, and no one was any the wiser for it.

Chapter Eighteen

⸺⧼❧❧⧽⸺

There is nothing so dangerous as a musicale. There are no guarantees that those presenting their musical abilities are truly in possession of musical abilities worth sharing, and as such, there is much risk involved. If you truly must attend a musicale, do be sure that the host and hostess have taste and knowledge of music. If that is not secure, then sit at the very end of a row. A swift exit may become necessary.

-The Spinster Chronicles, 21 May 1816

"I don't understand why I must accompany you to this."

"Somebody has to, it might as well be you."

"You know how I feel about these things."

"It will be good for you. A little more taste and refinement to bolster your reputation."

"I wasn't aware that it lacked anything of the sort."

"Military men are always in want of taste and refinement. They are dashing, to be sure, but a woman wants something more than a uniform."

Tony looked over at Miranda dubiously. "Are you telling me that I am nothing more than a uniform?"

Miranda sniffed and swatted her fan at him. "I would never be so crass as to include you in that assessment."

"Which brings me back to my original point," Tony stated firmly. "Why am I here?"

She tossed her hair and stared at him rather frankly, her blue eyes raking him over coals. "Because you adore your stepmother and she did not wish to come alone, so you have lent her your arm and your company until she sees fit to return to her sister's house for the evening."

Well. That answered *that* question.

Tony adjusted his cravat and craned his neck. "There, you see? I only needed a reason. Shall we go in?"

Miranda scowled and looped her arm through his, her dark cloak swishing behind her. "You are so impertinent sometimes, it's a wonder Georgie lets you court her."

"Georgie likes my impertinence," Tony assured her with a smile. "She says it keeps her entertained."

"Wonderful," Miranda replied, widening her eyes meaningfully. "You're an impertinent performing monkey."

Tony laughed and leaned over a little. "You told her she would do for either of your stepsons. Have you changed your mind about that?"

"Not at all. Although, I rather think I should have given her to Benedict."

Tony hooted in disbelief. "She would have eaten Ben alive, Miranda, and you know it. Ben needs a sweet wife who is as devoted to his patients as he is, and Georgie would never do."

"That may be," his stepmother huffed as they ascended the stairs, "but she's far too good for you, and I trust you are well aware of that."

He nodded in the affirmative, not seeing the need to expound on that point.

He was fully aware of it. He was all too keenly aware that the only reason he had a chance with Georgiana Allen was the fact that there was a shocking lack of intellect in the eligible men of Society. She should have been made someone's wife ages ago, but their loss would be Tony's great fortune, if he could manage it.

He had spent the last several days arranging and planning. He'd written to her father in Switzerland to ask for permission, he'd secured a country house in Essex, and he'd arranged to examine a London house by the week's end.

It had occurred to him to wonder what Elinor Asheley would

think of his prospects now.

He'd seen her since his decision to propose to Georgie, of course. He'd seen all of them, and several times. He walked with Georgie every day, with his stepmother acting as chaperone, and often with Izzy for company. He'd been to the theater, to tea, to Bond Street, and had even managed to borrow a phaeton from Francis to take Georgie for a ride.

Everything was proceeding very properly, though it felt like the pace of a rather sleepy turtle.

But he had needed the time to set his affairs in order, so it was all well and good.

Miranda had accepted his insistence on not taking Mawbry from her, but he wasn't entirely sure she had forgiven him for it. But, as he'd told her, she was already settling more than his father's inheritance on him, and to have the estate also pass to him would feel too much like charity.

Time would tell what revenge she would concoct for him, but he hoped he could bear it, whatever it was.

They entered the house, removed their outerwear, and were shown in to the too-grand music room of the Trenwick family, which had been transformed to accommodate a rather large gathering of people. He'd had few encounters with the family outside of Grace, but he understood that the entire family's allotment of good sense seemed to only exist in mother and daughter. The son was a peacock, and the father, currently absent, a cantankerous codger who would rather spend money than time on his children.

Grace and her mother were close, though, and it did them both credit.

Tony and Miranda greeted both with politeness, and Grace smiled warmly at Tony, inclining her head towards the rest of the guests. "She's already here," she whispered, seeming too delighted by the idea.

He shook his head and nodded his thanks before escorting Miranda in.

Grace really was a sweet girl, and a good match for any man worth his salt. Once he and Georgie were settled, he would have to look out for her. It wasn't right that she should be so neglected.

"Oh! Lady Hetty is here!" Miranda chirped happily. "Can we go and see her?"

Tony raised a brow at her. "Why ask me? I am only your escort, and entirely at your service. Lead on as you will."

Miranda rolled her eyes. "You poor, longsuffering man. How nobly you bear your burdens."

"Thank you. I do try."

They approached Lady Hetty, who was seated by Georgie and Izzy, as it happened, which made Tony very pleased.

"Now he's happy," Miranda muttered when she, too, noticed.

"Don't be prickly, Miranda," he scolded. "You like Georgie and Izzy, remember?"

She harrumphed to herself, then fixed a warm smile on her face. "Lady Hetty! I didn't think you'd be here."

Lady Hetty gave Miranda a bewildered look. "Why wouldn't I be? You think I don't like musical evenings?"

Miranda laughed easily and situated herself on the other side of her. "Not at all, I remember how fond you are of music."

"If it's well done," Lady Hetty clarified. "There's nothing so intolerable as poorly performed music. I don't even clap for those poor souls."

Georgie seemed rather amused by that. "Why not, Lady Hetty? Surely their bravery for performing deserves to be commended."

Lady Hetty made a disparaging noise and thumped her walking stick on the ground. "Nothing commendable in being an embarrassment afore all Society."

Izzy giggled even as her face flushed. "Lady Hetty! What would you say when I sing, I wonder?"

The older woman gave Izzy a sharp look. "You've never sung, Isabella. Can you?"

"A little," Izzy admitted with a lift of one shoulder.

"Then you shouldn't perform tonight," she said rather simply. "Even if you have the ability, you should own to it with confidence, not timidity. No one wants to hear from someone who only sings a little."

That seemed harsh, even for Lady Hetty, but Izzy didn't seem to find it the slightest bit abrasive. "I wasn't intending to sing tonight,

231

Lady Hetty," Izzy told her with a fond smile. "I never perform for an audience. I only sing to myself or to children."

Lady Hetty smiled back at her and patted her hands. "That is because you are a good, sweet creature, Isabella Lambert, and if you had any backbone, you'd be a wife by now."

Tony took a step towards Lady Hetty, ready to defend Izzy, but Izzy only sighed with a sad shake of her head. "I know. It is so unfortunate."

Miranda laughed in surprise, but eyed Izzy, obviously impressed.

Tony was no less impressed himself. Lady Hetty had insulted her to her face twice, though she claimed to be fond of Izzy, and Izzy had not only borne it, but had done so with kindness and humor. There had not even been a hint of pain or hurt in her expression.

She'd actually agreed with the woman.

He thought he'd known the extent of Izzy's goodness, of the 'nice' quality everybody claimed she had, but until now, he'd never witnessed just how far it extended.

He glanced over at Georgie, who had a forced smile on her face, and she looked up at him with steely eyes.

"But the music is destined to be lovely tonight," Izzy said brightly, looking towards the front of the room. "Lady Trenwick is musical herself, as is Grace, so we can be sure they will have secured some very promising performances."

"We shall see about that," Lady Hetty muttered. She looked at Miranda suddenly. "Didn't you sing, Miranda?"

Miranda nodded with an encouraging smile. "I did, Lady Hetty, yes."

"Perhaps they should have asked you."

Miranda waved a dismissive hand. "No, I think not. The performances are better left to the younger girls. I shall remain in the back of the room with the rest of the old women."

"No!" Izzy protested, looking around Lady Hetty at her. "Please, do perform!"

"I don't think it's open to suggestion," Georgie broke in. "Knowing Lady Trenwick, she's already decided on everything."

"Quite right," Lady Hetty grunted. "Can't have just anybody going up there." She looked at Izzy with another fond smile. "But

232

you would look very fine up there, if you could sing, Isabella. That green does suit your hair so well."

Tony looked at Georgie again, whose widened eyes told him that she was just as lost by Lady Hetty as he was.

Age was a fickle thing, it seemed.

Charlotte was suddenly with them, exhaling great pants of air. "You'll never guess," she gasped.

"You'll never breathe," Lady Hetty countered. "In and out, Miss Wright."

Charlotte flipped a hand quickly. "I can breathe later. Lady Trenwick has lost all sense, and she's asked Eliza Howard to sing."

Izzy gaped openly while Georgie seemed to freeze in place.

"That's unfortunate." Lady Hetty frowned and shook her head. "I suddenly find myself unwell and must go home." She tapped her stick on the ground and rose, shuffling off towards the door.

Tony watched her go, then turned back to the group. "She's that bad?"

"Oh, she can sing well enough," Izzy managed between shocked giggles. "She's just a horrid person, and even Lady Hetty cannot abide her." Izzy gasped suddenly and looked at Charlotte in horror. "Is Prue here? You know Eliza will do something if she is."

Charlotte shook her head quickly. "Grace intervened there. Prue is very unwell and cannot attend. But really, she's just at home reading."

Georgie and Izzy exhaled in relief, while Miranda looked utterly bewildered. "Well, I will endure it, if I must," Miranda stated firmly, a sour note in her voice, "though I am not inclined to think well of anyone who abuses sweet Prudence. I'll study this Eliza Howard and see what I make of her."

Charlotte grinned at that. "I'm sitting by you, Mrs. Sterling, if only to hear your delightful commentary." She brushed by Tony and took the seat that Lady Hetty had abandoned.

There was no possibility that Tony was going to enjoy a musical evening in the company of his stepmother and Charlotte if they were going to gossip the entire time. He looked at Georgie, imploring her to do something.

She caught his look and rose gracefully. "I'm going to visit the terrace," she told the others. "I'll come back in after Eliza's through."

"I'll join you," Tony offered, coming around the chairs to offer his arm. "The night is chilly, and you shouldn't go alone."

Georgie took his arm with a smile, nodding in acceptance. "Thank you. I rather hoped you'd come along."

"Kindly remember we can see you through the windows," Miranda warned them, smiling mischievously.

"Mrs. Sterling!" Izzy's cheeks flamed, even as Charlotte howled with laughter.

Tony looked at his stepmother. "Duly noted, Miranda, thank you. Kindly remember that your voice carries, and what you say in London may haunt you for life."

Georgie pulled him away as the others laughed, leading him out to the relative safety of the night.

"What has gotten into everyone tonight?" Georgie asked, taking in a deep breath of the cool night air. "It's as though nobody has any sense or manners."

"My thoughts exactly." Tony leaned his forearms on the railing, looking out across the well-maintained garden beyond. "I didn't expect Lady Hetty to attack Izzy like that."

Georgie sighed and rubbed at her brow. "She doesn't do it often," she said, as if that helped matters. "And she truly does like Izzy. She just… doesn't want her to be so nice."

Tony looked over at her with a sardonic brow lift. "Nobody who cares about Izzy wants her to be nice enough to be taken advantage of. But going about it this way? It only enhances that part of Izzy's nature that wants to please everyone. To put everyone at ease." He winced and turned back to the garden. "Does Izzy realize that she probably ought to be hurt or offended?"

"I don't know," Georgie murmured, watching Tony with too much interest. It wasn't often that anyone understood her cousin on this level, let alone expressed it. And there were fewer people who cared enough about Izzy to say or do anything about it.

"You don't know?" he repeated, giving her a sidelong look.

Georgie shook her head. "We don't discuss it. Every time I have tried, and I do mean every time, Izzy changes the subject or makes explanations that cause me to doubt the argument I intended to make."

Tony exhaled and shook his head. "And now we have Eliza Howard to deal with."

We. Not you, not they, but we.

Georgie stared at Tony with increasing wonder, the inkling over the past few days now pressing harder and harder against her heart. She had avoided giving in to it, or letting herself dwell on the sensation, fearing that it might weaken her further still.

But now she wondered if the opposite might be true. This feeling just might give her strength.

Tony turned to her expectantly, and she realized she hadn't answered him.

"Yes," she said quickly. "Eliza Howard."

Apparently, her response amused Tony and he straightened, smiling at her.

"What?" she asked him, suddenly feeling warm despite the cool breeze.

He smirked, looking far too handsome when he did, and said, "I was under the impression that having Eliza Howard in Town was not good for us."

Us. There he was again, using words that made her go weak despite already feeling too favorably inclined towards him.

"We can manage Eliza," she managed, her throat suddenly dry. "We always have. It's not particularly pleasant, but we'll rally around Prue."

Tony nodded slowly, still smiling in that odd fashion. "That is good. I'm glad to hear it. What is the plan? Do we hire others to be a distraction? Do we send spies to make sure Eliza and Prue are never at the same event? I'm not above poisoning if it will keep Prue from harm. Henshaw would help, and I think I could get Morton, too. He's the quieter one, not nearly as social, but he would be very good with Prue."

"Stop," Georgie begged, torn between laughter and tears. "Tony, stop."

He cocked his head, folding his arms. "Why, Georgie?"

She bit her lip, shaking her head. "Tony, it's too much. You're saying the most perfect things, and I can't have you be this perfect. It… makes me hope. It makes me feel things, Tony, and I just can't…"

Tony started towards her, his expression softening. "Georgie…"

She tried to step back, but she was already at the edge of the terrace.

Tony stopped just before her, his breath dancing across her brow. "Georgie," he said again, his voice a tender caress.

"They can see us," she whispered, her voice catching. She tilted her head towards the window beside them.

He glanced to look through, then smiled and looked back at her. "No one is looking. The music has begun, and everybody is quite transfixed."

Georgie exhaled, whether in relief or nerves she couldn't tell. She nodded once.

Tony surprised her by pulling her gently against him and wrapping his arms around her.

She laughed despite herself. "This isn't what I anticipated."

He chuckled, and she pressed her cheek against his chest, loving the sensation of feeling him laugh. "We'll get to that, I have no doubt," he rumbled, his arms pulling her more tightly against him. "But right now, I just want to hold you. I've wanted to hold you for a very long time."

The tears welled up, and she had no willpower to resist them. She slid her arms around his waist and tucked herself as close to him as she could, letting the last of her defenses fall away in his arms.

This was what she had been missing. She hadn't realized it, and wouldn't have without him. She'd been wanting someone who would hold her just like this, despite a room filled with other people just beyond, but wouldn't mind stealing this moment with her. She'd wanted the comfort of someone's arms holding her close, of feeling a steady heartbeat thud against her cheek.

But not just any heart, or any arms.

The arms that would lift her when she was weak, hold her when she was frail, and lead her when she was lost.

The heart of the man she loved.

His heart.

Georgie sighed at the sensation rippling through her frame, searing her heart and soul.

She loved him. That feeling pressing against her heart, that inkling that had tugged at her for days, was now wild and free, filling her with light and life.

She had known loneliness, sometimes to a depth she couldn't bear to explore, and now it was fading. The darkness was turning brighter and brighter, and the flame of hope she had kept steadily burning was now roaring to life in a blaze of brilliance.

"I mean what I say, Georgie," Tony whispered, pressing his lips to her hair. "I will do whatever I can to help our friends. Anything in my power."

"Shh." She turned her face and kissed him right where she could feel his heart beating. "I know." She rested her brow against him, exhaling slowly.

"What is it, love?" he asked tenderly, placing a finger under her chin, and tilting her face up to his. "What troubles you?"

Her heart caught at the endearment, and she smiled up at him. "At this moment, nothing troubles me. Nothing in the entire world."

Tony grinned at that and stroked the underside of her jaw. "Good. That's as it should be." He leaned down and kissed her as though she were a delicacy he savored, taking his time, giving the task his due attention and enjoyment, driving her mad with the thrill of it.

Georgie slid her hand from his waist and up to his neck, tugging at him, pressing his lips more fully against hers. He complied without resistance, his kiss turning deeper, more insistent, more captivating. This was no mere kiss, this was a claiming, though who was claiming and whom was being claimed seemed rather unclear.

It didn't matter.

Nothing mattered but them. This moment, this night, this man…

What she wouldn't give for eternities of this.

Tony broke off with a series of gentle kisses, nuzzling against her, then pulling her into his arms once more.

She felt him tremble a little, and she smiled. Knowing she could bring him to this filled her with a heady sense of pride. She, who had never so much as turned a head before, could weaken Tony Sterling into a trembling tower.

What a perfectly delightful thought.

Tony cleared his throat and released her, his hands trailing along her arms. He backed away, staring at her with an odd, heated sort of look.

Georgie frowned in confusion. "Tony?"

He turned and walked a few paces, looking up into the night sky, then turned back around to face her. "Georgie, I have to be perfectly honest with you."

She tried for a smile but couldn't manage it. "That sounds ominous."

Tony stared at her with the same look. "It might be." He took in a deep breath, then released it. "…I'm in love with you."

He was… *what?*

Georgie was entirely beyond words, staring back at him, her mouth gaping wide open.

Tony swallowed and nodded once. "I've been in love with you, probably from the beginning." He gave a breathless laugh. "I've never met anybody like you, and Lord knows, I wasn't looking. But you came into my life, and it took me all of five minutes to decide that you were my idea of perfection."

She was sure her heart was beating, she could feel it pounding against her chest, but she wondered if it hadn't taken flight and joined itself with the heavens. She wasn't sure she was even awake, but in her dreams, nothing this sweet had ever occurred.

"Georgie, I love you," Tony said again, and his tone made her ache somewhere deep inside.

He loved her. She, who had only just admitted to herself that she loved him, was now to accept that he loved her in return.

How could she manage to comprehend anything so miraculous?

Tony swallowed with some difficulty. "Well?"

Right. She had to respond. She had to tell him…

She wet her lip carefully. "We all strive for perfection in some way," she managed. "It's a pleasure to know I've attained mine."

His brow furrowed, but a small smile made itself known on his lips. "Does that mean…?"

Georgie smiled at him, a grand, beaming, adoring smile. "I love you, too," she whispered.

Tony stared at her for a moment, then laughed again. "You do?"

She nodded almost frantically. "Yes."

He strode to her and hauled her into his arms, picking her up off the ground and burying his face against her. "Oh, my love," he murmured, laughing, and twirling her. "Oh, thank God."

Georgie clung to him, giggling wildly, and feeling the desire to squeal like the little girl she had once been.

Tony set her down and cupped her face, kissing her deeply, but briefly. "Georgie, my love, will you be my wife?"

She gasped and choked on a laugh. "Say that again?"

He smiled a slow, delicious smile. "Georgie. Marry me."

"I don't mind if I do," she replied, her tears returning to the surface and spilling onto her cheeks.

Tony wiped one away and kissed its place, then kissed her lips with such tenderness more tears began to flow.

He touched his brow to hers, grinning madly. "You have no idea how happy you've made me."

She nudged his nose with hers. "I think I have some idea." She pulled back and gave him a wry look. "What am I going to tell the others? What will they say?"

Tony snorted softly. "They shouldn't say much. The only complaint before was that I didn't have a house, and I've just procured one. Even Elinor would call me a good match now."

Georgie laughed and shook her head. "I don't care what Elinor would say. I think you're a good match, and I intend to take you for myself."

"Go ahead, my love. I am yours for the taking." He glanced through the window again. "Do you think Eliza Howard has finished yet?"

Georgie shrugged. "It's entirely possible she will perform another. We'd better stay out here, just to be safe."

Tony chuckled and leaned closer. "If you say so, Miss Allen."

She smiled up at him, wrapping her arms about his neck. "I say so, Captain Sterling."

"Then stay we will," he whispered just before his lips claimed hers once more.

Chapter Nineteen

———— ❦ ————

One should always say the right thing at the right time. Saying the right thing at the wrong time will always cause strife, saying the wrong thing at the right time will only bring confusion, and saying the wrong thing at the wrong time… Well, how wrong does a person need to be?

-The Spinster Chronicles, 28 January 1817

"I knew it! I knew it! I simply *knew* it was going to work!"

Tony rolled his eyes, but smiled with all the good nature he had ever wished himself to have. "Miranda, you can hardly take credit for my engagement."

"I can too!" She clapped her hands, twice, squealing to herself. "Oh, this is the most blessed news! What can I do? Let me do something, Tony!"

He sat back in his chair, laughing to himself. "I have no idea what you can do, Miranda. We've only just received the news from her father that the engagement may proceed, which is why I didn't tell you sooner. Her parents will arrive in a few weeks, and we will be able to be married shortly thereafter. We've already submitted the banns, and they were read on Sunday. You have a little over a month to do whatever you like."

Miranda spun in a circle clapping her hands again.

Rufus, her adoring bloodhound, who had been dozing by the fire, suddenly sprang to life, barking a chorus to her applause, following her as she turned.

"Yes, Rufus, yes!" Miranda cooed, reaching down to pet the eager dog. "It is a most joyous thing!"

"I'm fairly certain he thinks you want him to do something," Tony remarked as he crossed an ankle over his knee. "He doesn't care one way or the other about my engagement."

That earned him a sour look, then Miranda returned her attention to the dog, cupping his face. "You do care about my insensitive stepson's engagement, don't you, darling? You want him to be happy, even if he doesn't reciprocate."

Tony dropped his head back against the chair with a groan. "I want Rufus to be happy, Miranda. He's an excellent dog, and a fine hunter."

"Ha!" Miranda cheered, patting her dog soundly. "Did you hear that, boy? He loves you! Go and see him!"

Rufus was either the most brilliant dog in the world, or followed gestures with perfection, for he trotted over to Tony at once and put his head directly within petting distance of Tony's dangling hand.

Tony shook his head and scratched the dog's ears. "How do you survive having such a woman as a mistress?"

Rufus gave him a distinctly doleful look, made even more poignant by his slightly drooping features, as if to say, "You have no idea."

"I take my hat off to you, sir," Tony murmured, moving his hand to scratch under the dog's chin. "You are nobler than I would be."

Miranda laughed and put her hands on her hips. "You're a fine pair, both of you. I'd send him to live with you if I wasn't so terribly fond of him."

Tony smiled warmly at the animal, now arching his neck for more attention. "Well, if you decide to breed him, I'd happily take one of his offspring. Someone ought to carry on these magnificent bloodlines." He cupped Rufus's drooping face in his hands, forcing the sagging skin forward. "Yes, indeed, look at these features!"

"Oh, stop," Miranda laughed again, settling herself on the sofa. "Rufus, down."

Rufus looked over at her, seeming to beg against it, but at her look, he licked his face loudly and hunkered down to the ground, resting his head on his paws.

Miranda nodded primly, then looked back at Tony. "Have you written to Ben of your news?"

Tony nodded, easing himself back against the back of the chair once more. "I did, though I have yet to hear a response. If he can part with his idyllic country life, I'd love for him to stand up with me. If not, I'll ask Henshaw."

Miranda tilted her head with a fond smile. "Dear Henshaw. We must find a good match for him next."

"Whatever you say, Miranda." He waved a hand at her dismissively. "Marry off Henshaw, and Charlotte, and anyone else you like."

"You make it sound so interfering," she protested in a wounded tone. "I am not a busybody."

He pinned her with a sardonic look. "Are you not?"

She smirked in response, rolling her eyes at herself. "Oh, all right, so I am, but only in the best sense."

"That was the only way I meant it." Tony smiled at her warmly. "You know what you mean to me, don't you, Miranda? You know that marrying you was the best thing my father did."

She seemed surprised by that, swallowed once, giving him a misty smile. "You are very sweet to say so, Tony. I don't know if I can accept such a statement, but marrying your father was certainly the best thing I did. He married well the first time, and I don't mean by Society's standards. There was real affection and love between your parents."

Tony shook his head regretfully. "I barely remember my mother. I was so young..."

"He adored her," Miranda told him. "We spoke of her often after he and I wed. How she had behaved, what she was like, her tastes, the silly games she used to play with you boys... I've done my best to help mold you and Ben into the men I felt she would want you to be, and sometimes... I think she and I have conversations of the heart." She smiled at him then, and he could see the sheen of tears glistening in her fair eyes. "She would be so proud of you, Tony. Of you and Ben. And she would adore Georgie."

Tony's throat constricted, and his eyes burned, feeling suddenly awash in memories and feelings long forgotten. "She would, wouldn't she?"

Miranda nodded repeatedly, one tear making its way down her cheek. She was quick to swipe it away and sniffed loudly. "Well, while we are on that subject… I don't suppose you have given much thought to a ring for your bride, hmm?"

He jerked. "No, not really. Georgie said she didn't need one until the wedding, and I'd thought just to obtain a simple band. Georgie's tastes are not very extravagant."

"That may be so, but the girl does deserve more finery than a simple band." Miranda rose and moved to a desk in the corner of the sitting room. "I found this when going through some of your father's things at Mawbry, and I intended to give it to you or Ben simply to keep until the time was right, but now…" She opened a drawer, pulled out something small, and closed the drawer quickly, turning to him.

Tony frowned, rising. "What is it?"

Miranda came towards him and gestured for his hand.

He gave it, and she turned it over, then dropped a small item into his palm.

"Tell me if this would do for your lady love," Miranda said softly as she patted his hand, stepping away.

Tony looked down and, in his palm, he saw a small ring with three emeralds set in it. He picked it up and looked more closely, taking in the faint marks of age on the gold band, yet the precious metal somehow still gleaming as if freshly gilded. Small diamonds bracketed the emeralds, and the setting was so fine, so delicate, that a passing eye would almost not notice it.

Yet as he stared at it, he felt a tug at the back of his stomach, a knot that refused to dislodge, and he found himself nodding, smiling at the token.

"Yes?" Miranda asked from the sofa where she sat once more.

"Yes," Tony repeated, looking over at her. "It's perfect."

Miranda smiled knowingly. "I thought so as well. Your mother's ring, Tony. It's a sweet reminder for you both."

Tony tucked the ring into his waistcoat pocket and nodded again. "Yes, it is."

They smiled at each other for a moment, then the clock on the mantle chimed the hour.

Miranda glanced at it, then back at him. "When do you meet Georgie?"

"Soon," he replied with a sigh. "We're to look at a town house, and then walk Hyde Park." He tugged at his coat sleeves, brushing off any remnants of Rufus's attentions, and then gestured at himself, looking back at Miranda. "What do you think?"

She made a face and an indifferent noise.

Tony coughed at that. "I beg your pardon?"

Miranda rose, wrinkling her nose up in apparent distaste, and took two steps towards him. "If I may…?"

"Please," Tony replied drily, beckoning her.

She came to him, smoothed his hair, took his chin in hand, and turned his face one way, then another. "Well," she sighed, "I suppose you'll have to do."

He batted her hand away with a frown, making her laugh. "You are incorrigible."

Miranda acknowledged that with a dip of her chin. "But you love me."

"God help me," Tony replied, leaning down to kiss her cheek quickly. "I'll give Georgie your love."

"Please do," she said as she took his hand and led him out. "And invite her for dinner on Thursday. Mr. Johnston insists."

"He does?" Tony queried mildly, looking down at her. "Or you do?"

"Ta ta, darling!" she airily called, letting go of him and returning to the drawing room.

He had to laugh at her antics. For all her quirks, Miranda was the most lovable woman on the planet, and he feared what he would have become without her.

"Going out, Mr. Sterling?" the surprisingly young butler inquired.

Tony nodded at him. "I am, yes. Is a hack available?"

"It is, sir, if you'll wait just a moment." He signaled to one of the footmen, who left the house for only a minute or two before returning.

Tony nodded at them both, then exited, climbing into the hack with ease and giving the address to the driver.

He felt for the ring in his pocket and grinned at the weight of it against him.

Georgie would not be expecting a ring like this, and certainly not one with any meaning attached to it. For all her years of dreaming of marriage, her expectations of the wedding itself were not high. She was fully cognizant of her financial situation, and that of her family, and she saw no need to push anybody to their limits in that way.

She'd even told him she would wear one of her Sunday dresses for the wedding rather than procuring a new one.

That seemed a bit stringent, even to him.

Perhaps Miranda could help him with that one.

Georgie wouldn't take kindly to receiving charity or anything resembling it, but Miranda was generous, and she was impossible to refuse.

The Lambert residence was not far from the house the Johnstons were renting, so the drive was not long. Tony disembarked from the carriage almost the moment it halted, and strode his way up to the door proudly, oddly hoping that the neighbors would see.

Word of his engagement likely hadn't spread very far, nobody knowing enough of him to care, but Georgie's was a name that everybody knew, and once word got out that *she* was engaged, everybody would be watching from windows.

He found a great deal of satisfaction in that thought.

He wanted people to watch for him and Georgie. He wanted others to take notice of their good fortune, more on his side than hers. She would gain respectability by their marriage, and lose the unfortunate title of spinster, but nothing else would change. She would be the same woman she always had been, he would insist on that, only now she would be a wife.

Would her mother think and speak more warmly of her once she was wed? He hoped so, for Georgie's sake, but she didn't seem to have much hope on that score. Apparently, her mother would only move onto the subject of children and the management of their house, which prompted Tony to consider inquiring after houses in Northumberland rather than Essex.

But Hazelwood Park would do well enough, he was certain of it.

Georgie would have the full running of it, from top to bottom, and he would focus on the management of the estate and tenants. He'd already set up a meeting with the existing agent, who seemed relieved that someone had taken an interest in the place. The family who had once lived there had long ago left it empty, only making a passable effort to support the tenants.

Tony could do better, he was sure of it, and there was real possibility for the area.

He'd been at a loss to know what to do with himself when he'd resigned his commission, not knowing anything beyond the fact that his time in the army was done. Others had told him it was a foolish notion, considering he was a younger son without much hope of improvement in status from when he'd begun his service. He'd seen the wisdom in their suggestion, but there was no future for him in the army either.

Now he had found a purpose and opportunity for his future, and there was an excitement that filled him with that thought. He was only beginning on the path that would set the course for the rest of his life and having Georgie by his side would make all the difference.

He raised his hand to knock at the door only for the door to swing open as Georgie exited, bonnet and spencer in place, looking bright and fresh in a pale muslin. She tugged on her gloves, widening her eyes meaningfully.

"Are we meant to make haste?" he inquired mildly.

Georgie glared at him and took his arm, forcing him to turn around. "Yes," she hissed.

Tony looked behind her and saw Bessie coming out, frantically tying the ribbons of her cloak. "Oh, good. I was concerned we would be unchaperoned."

"If only," Georgie muttered. "Aunt Faith had determined that she would chaperone us on this errand, but I managed to steal Bessie away before Aunt Faith had seen the hack. So yes, we really must make haste!"

Tony laughed and hurried both women to the coach, giving Bessie an apologetic look. "So sorry, Bessie. I know you're not the usual sort of chaperone under these circumstances."

Bessie shrugged, smiling. "Not the usual thing, sir, but I can't see anybody raising a fuss over it. I'll ride atop with the driver, sir, if you don't mind."

He inclined his head politely, knowing Bessie had been his favorite maid for a reason. "Whatever you prefer, of course."

The driver hopped down and assisted her up, then nodded at Tony, who entered the coach, taking the backwards-facing seat.

"Were you watching for me out the window?" Tony asked Georgie as the hack pulled away.

Georgie gave him a coy smile. "I might have been. What girl isn't so invested in seeing her intended?"

"Or so desperate to be away from home?"

She grinned outright. "Or that. Now tell me about this house."

"Tony, I think we should take it."

"But the garden is small."

"That's not so very important. Besides, we could always have it done over eventually."

"Eventually, indeed. Do you have any idea what a renovation like that would cost?"

"But we are to become wealthy landowners, you forget. In a few years, the cost will be nothing."

Tony threw his head back and laughed. "Oh, well, in *that* case."

Georgie snickered and turned to face Bessie behind them, somehow still maintaining a decent walking pace though walking backwards. "Bessie, what did you make of the house?"

"It's not my place to say, Miss," Bessie replied obediently.

"No, go on," Georgie insisted, smiling at her. "You're bound to notice things that Captain Sterling and I do not. I insist, share your thoughts."

Tony shook his head in amusement. Asking a servant for an opinion on a house? It was a singular notion, and one that was entirely worthy of Georgie. He didn't disapprove in the least, in fact, it was a rather good idea; he was just certain he would never have thought of it.

Then again, Rollins might have had a very worthwhile opinion on the subject.

Perhaps he would have to revisit the place with his valet in tow.

"The servants' quarters were of a good size, Miss," Bessie told her, seeming to choose her words with care. "The corridors are easily navigated, and the kitchen was spacious enough to host a fair party, if you were so inclined. It was a bit drafty, but not in an obvious way. I think you could make it over nicely, Miss."

Georgie nodded very firmly and turned back around, joining her arm with Tony's again. "There, you see? Bessie thinks we should take it."

"Did she say that?" Tony asked with interest. "I didn't hear those words at all."

"Men never hear what women hear," she assured him. "It's a well-known truth."

"And which edition of the Spinster Chronicles is that gem from?"

She elbowed him hard but smiled at him. "You are so rude."

"I know."

"Tony!"

Tony looked up to see Hugh riding towards them, looking only slightly more put together than he had when he'd last seen him.

"Oh, blast," Tony muttered under his breath.

"What?" Georgie asked quietly.

He shook his head. Now was not the time to explain the complicated nature of his relationship with this particular cousin. "Hugh," he greeted, trying for a smile.

Hugh reined the horse in, taking in the pair of them with some interest. "Walking the park, are we?"

Tony nodded once. "We are, yes. Hugh, do you know Miss Allen?"

Thankfully, Hugh had the good manners to tip his hat in greeting. "I do, a little. How are you, Miss Allen?"

Georgie bobbed a curtsey and smiled with all friendliness. "I am very well, thank you, Mr. Sterling."

Hugh nodded, but was already looking back at Tony. "I've heard a rumor about you, Tony. Can you guess what it is?"

Oh, to be miles and miles away from this conversation.

"Undoubtedly, it was that I am to be married," Tony replied with a bland smile. "To Miss Allen here."

Hugh nodded, smiling a little as though it were all a very fine joke.

"As it happens," Tony informed him, "that's no rumor. It's the truth. Which you would know if you spoke with your brother at all."

"Tony," Georgie muttered beside him.

For once, he ignored her.

"I am to be married to Miss Allen," Tony went on, enjoying the stunned expression on his cousin's face, "and we would be pleased to have you attend in a few weeks."

Hugh blinked several times, his horse snuffling in agitation, then looked at Georgie with disgust. He shook his head and shifted back to Tony. "Good lord, Tony, what have you done? I told you to break up the Spinsters, not join them." He snorted in derision and dug his heels into his horse, riding off quickly.

Tony closed his eyes in abject horror, feeling how still the woman beside him had suddenly become.

"Georgie…" he began softly.

"Don't," she clipped, jerking her arm away from his hold. "Don't you dare." She walked a few steps ahead of him, her fingers clenching tightly, then unclenching as she paced a little, her bonnet obscuring her face.

Or perhaps that was simply the way she was turned.

Her steps were clipped, harsh, and it was as if he could feel every one of them himself, each making him jump a little. His anxiety heightened the longer the silence stretched on, the back of his neck growing heated and damp with perspiration.

He looked to the heavens, praying for some semblance of mercy in this moment.

Georgie stopped pacing, then moved directly in front of him, fury rolling off her in waves. "What did he mean by that, Anthony Sterling? Break up the Spinsters?"

"That was what he wanted, yes," Tony admitted, knowing he would never survive unless there was complete honesty in this. "When I first arrived in London, he approached me and asked me to intervene."

Georgie laughed once in disbelief. "And you accepted that? You agreed to it?"

"Not at first, no," Tony insisted, looking around to see if anybody marked them. "I told him I would never interfere in the affairs of a group of women."

"And yet, here you are," Georgie snapped, folding her arms. "Interfering."

Tony exhaled shortly through his nose. "I was curious after reading the articles. After hearing what was said. I wanted introductions, and I needed him to make them."

Georgie was nodding, though there was nothing at all agreeable in her expression. "Introductions. To the women terrorizing London with their wild ideas and moral stances, preventing marriages because they can't manage one for themselves. You saw the need to insert yourself into something that we worked so hard to set up purely because your pompous peacock of a cousin found it inconvenient to not have a naïve girl to ravish at his pleasure?"

He'd never seen high dudgeon like this before, and it rankled him. "That wasn't it at all."

"Oh no?" She nodded again, almost shaking with indignation. "You sought out Prue, the sweetest, shyest creature in the world, and you made her trust you. You, who were tasked with dismantling the only group of friends she has ever had, manipulated her into liking you."

"Now wait one moment," he countered, raising a finger.

But Georgie wouldn't stop. "You convinced my cousin, who hates absolutely no one, to give you introductions and take you under her wing, knowing she was a nurturing soul. You took advantage of her goodness. To what end? To get to me?" Her eyes widened, and her nostrils flared. "That's how they told you to break us up, isn't it? They thought that if I was gone, the rest would crumble and fade away."

Tony's temper flared, and he lifted his chin. "Georgie," he ground out, his teeth aching with their clenching.

"Well, let me tell you something, Captain," she overrode, spitting his title out with venom. "The Spinsters are not going anywhere. If I was gone, they would rise up in defense and become an even greater annoyance than anyone would anticipate. But I'm not gone. Not in the least."

"Georgie," Tony barked, not caring if anyone could hear him now. "Stop."

She scoffed loudly. "I'm not one of your inferiors, Captain. I don't have to obey you, nor do you have any control over me."

"And you think I obey any command given me, no matter who issues it?" he demanded, flinging an arm out. "For heaven's sake, Georgie…"

She shook her head, not willing to listen, it seemed. "I should have seen it. I knew I shouldn't have trusted you from the start, but the others were so convinced. And I believed you so easily after… I believed everything you said. Simple little spinster, just as naïve as everyone else…"

Tony's heart lurched, and his eyes narrowed. "Georgie."

Georgie looked up at him then, her jaw set. "If this is how things really are, we should not marry."

The breath seemed to vanish from his lungs and he looked down for a moment, his hands going to rest on his hips. Then he glanced up at her. "Are you finished?"

Her jaw shifted to one side, then back to center, and she nodded once.

He exhaled shortly, fighting for control. "How many times have I stood by you? All of you. Or gone to some young woman's aid because she seemed in need? When have you ever seen me converse with any men that would make your list of unfortunate candidates? Or behave in any way that would be deemed disreputable? I've earned the scorn of many eligible men in London, just for associating with you, because all of them wanted me to interfere with the Spinsters. And in case it has escaped your notice, I haven't done anything remotely resembling their plans for me."

Georgie shrugged one shoulder, not at all convinced. "Perhaps you just wanted to get on my good side. Even gentlemen can have nefarious intentions."

Her coldness shook him, and he felt the fight go out of him. "If you truly think that I am incapable of acting in any manner other than what you deem my own self-interest, then you're right." He shook his head slowly, his eyes trained on hers. "We shouldn't marry."

She stared back at him, her breathing unsteady, her gaze piercing. "It's settled, then." She nodded at him and swept passed him.

"Where are you going?" he asked her, moving to follow.

"Home, Captain," she called over a shoulder. "To my family who loves me. Do not call on me again, we have nothing to discuss."

Bessie stared after her, then looked at Tony in horror.

He nodded at her. "Go with her, Bessie. See that she gets home safely."

"Aye, sir," she whimpered with a curtsey. She turned and dashed after Georgie, who did not look back at him even once.

He stood there in the lane, faintly aware of his heart pounding, but wondering at the sensation.

She hadn't shed a single tear. She'd just broken their short-lived engagement, crushed his heart underfoot, and been too enraged to cry or to even appear remotely disposed to tears.

Was that significant?

What was he supposed to do now?

Tony inhaled a shaky breath, finding it all too painful, and began the slow journey back to his apartments, the weight of the ring in his pocket greater than anything he'd ever felt in his life.

Except for the suddenly crushing weight of despair settling in his chest.

Chapter Twenty

———— ❦ ————

Unsolicited advice is sometimes the best sort. Provided one is open enough to hear it.

-The Spinster Chronicles, 1 May 1817

It was a wonder how dreary England could be at times, even for one who had never been outside of it. She ought to have been accustomed to the resident gloom that pervaded her home and thought she had been.

But nothing could compare with the dreariness at present.

Georgie sat in the window seat of her room, staring out at the streets below, hair unbound and loose about her shoulders.

Tangled and knotted, surely. Yesterday had been a day of ranting and raging about her room, pulling at her hair, and knotting it with her agitation, and she hadn't taken a brush to it since then.

The day before, she'd been almost herself and had even succeeded in descending the stairs for breakfast properly dressed. It had been close to luncheon and there was no breakfast to be had, but she'd done it.

She hadn't managed since, though.

What would be the point?

Today was a meeting of the Spinsters. It was Writing Day, even, and here she sat. She was dressed, if her oldest, most faded, and most comfortable calico was considered being dressed, but that was all. Her feet were bare, and her toes cold, but no more than the rest of her.

She wasn't going down; she'd decided on that hours ago. She couldn't face them like this.

Not after what happened.

There would be questions and demands for explanation. There would be judgments and advice, pity and sympathy, and probably some exclamations of her own idiocy. Some would be on her side, but she could not account for all of them.

She couldn't confess that she'd been wanting to end the Spinsters herself, and then had admitted a man into their company whose sole purpose had been that exact thing.

The shame was too much to bear.

Her mortification knew no ends.

But that had nothing to do with the Spinsters.

She'd loved him. She had given her heart to a man who had come to them under false pretenses. She could not trust anything about him, knowing now what had brought him to them. She should have trusted her first instincts and sent him away, saving herself this misery and heartache.

Love. What a foolish, pathetic notion that had been. A man worth loving would have been honest with her. He would have proceeded properly with courtship and paying proper addresses, not sneaking her away to steal moments alone.

You went willingly, her heart reminded her. *You ran without any prodding.*

She hissed and wrenched her gaze away from the window.

She knew she'd been a fool, that she'd been so overjoyed with the newfound sensations that she hadn't managed a moment of sense. She ought to have seen what a mockery it was, what a waste of her heart and energy.

Except it hadn't been anything of the sort.

It had been wonderful and delicious and heady, everything she had ever wanted love to be and more. He had been witty and charming and real, proper and perfect without being stodgy, and he had worshipped her.

He'd sparred with her better than either of her younger brothers had managed to, and with far more intellect, but he had worshipped her.

That ought to have been the first sign of trouble for her.

No one felt that way about Georgiana Allen. They never had. All his compliments and flirtations, all the looks and smiles and kisses…

She bit back a combination of a sigh and a whimper.

Those had all been part of his plan to seduce her away from the Spinsters. To make her forget herself and revert to the silly girl she had once been and take up once more the dreams she had long ago set aside.

He had made her feel things again.

Wish for things.

Hope.

A weak sob escaped Georgie, accompanying tears suddenly filling her eyes. She buried her face into her knees, wrapping her arms around her legs.

How could anything as blissful as the way she had felt only days ago result in the tearing apart of one's very soul?

For this agony was nothing less than that.

Tony's betrayal, however sharp, had been nothing compared to her own betrayal. She had betrayed herself in this, blinding herself to the reality of her situation, and his intentions. For a woman who prided herself on her good sense and judgment, she'd had none of it here.

There was a soft knock at her door, but as it was not mealtime, she did not acknowledge it. She'd only been taking trays the last few days, unable to bear her aunt's tirade any longer.

She did not need to hear how disappointed her mother would be when she returned to England, or how she had given up the honor of the family by ending the engagement. It made no difference that there had been no formal announcement of its dissolution, she stated, the word would get out.

Georgie did not care.

If everything she had heard about herself was true, she could not be more disliked than she already was.

The knock sounded again, and again she ignored it.

She was not coming down. She was not seeing anyone.

The door opened without her consent, and she turned her head to glare at whoever dared enter without permission.

Izzy stood there, her brow furrowed, her wide eyes confused. "Georgie."

She ought to have snapped at her, the way she wished to. She ought to have yelled or screamed, thrown a pillow, or said any number of things designed to hurt or offend.

But this was Izzy.

She could not.

"Izzy, please," she pleaded, her voice breaking.

Her cousin's brow cleared, and she came into the room, closing the door quickly.

"No," Georgie protested, tears rising. "Please..."

"It's no use protesting," Izzy said lightly as she came to her, sitting opposite her in the window seat. "My cousin and best friend is in need, and I am going to sit here and be loving for as long as it takes."

Georgie managed a watery smile at her. "As long as it takes? For what?"

Izzy shrugged, smiling. "For you to be happy once more."

Oh. That.

She shook her head slowly. "I fear that will take a very long time, Izzy. Despondency is all I know."

"Why?" Izzy cocked her head and placed a hand over hers. "Why so despondent? Because Tony's gone?"

Georgie's face crumpled and a sob broke free. "No. And yes." She inhaled sharply. "Oh, Izzy, I don't know what to believe. Do I listen to my heart, which may betray me, or my head, which seeks to know truth?"

"Ideally," Izzy prodded gently, "I believe you listen to both."

Somehow, Georgie laughed and shook her head. "I cannot listen to both. They are at war, and with good reason on each side. I must choose one or the other, and I'm not sure I can bear to."

Izzy squeezed her hand tightly, seeming close to tears herself. "What happened, Georgie? You haven't said a word about it except that you were no longer engaged, and you've hardly left your room. This isn't like you. You always march forward with a purpose, your head held high."

Georgie jerked her hand away from Izzy and sprang to her feet, shaking her head frantically. "No, that is *not* the woman I am. It is only the woman everybody thinks me to be. Does everybody seem to think that I have no heart? No real emotions of my own?"

Izzy sat in stunned silence, her hand slowly returning to her lap.

Georgie grabbed at her hair, tilting her head back as tears leaked from both eyes. "Do you think that I should not have loved a man so deeply that the loss of it makes the thought of living unbearable? That I am not capable of such passion? I have no sense of who I am anymore, no idea how to proceed, how to act, how to breathe…" She suddenly wrapped her arms around herself, moaning weakly. "I can't breathe, Izzy."

Her knees unexpectedly weakened, and she began to crumple, but Izzy was suddenly there to steady her. Together they sank to the ground, and Izzy held her close.

"Oh, sweet Georgie," Izzy soothed, brushing her hair back gently. "Of *course*, you should be miserable for a time. I know what a fierce heart you are in possession of, and how much you love Tony."

Even in her state, Georgie did not miss Izzy's choice of words.

Love. Not loved.

Present. Not past.

Her heart keened, and she leaned against Izzy feebly.

"Why this misery, dear?" Izzy asked as she ran her fingers through Georgie's hair. "Why did you break it off?"

Georgie stilled and slowly pushed herself off Izzy, staring at her in disbelief. "Why would you think that I am the one who cried off?"

Izzy frowned a little and began fiddling with her skirts. "I just… Well, Tony is a man of honor, and I cannot see him jilting anybody, least of all someone he loves as he does you."

"Oh, but I would jilt him?" Georgie scoffed loudly and got to her feet. "I would cast aside a man so honorable and good purely because of my own pride and out of spite?"

Izzy's eyes widened. "Georgie, don't… I didn't mean…"

"Is that what people will think?" she demanded, somehow suddenly beyond tears. "They will blame me, won't they? They will sympathize with Tony, for who could bear to marry someone as heartless as me?"

"Georgie," Izzy whimpered as she reached for her. "Come

downstairs with me. Come see our friends and let us comfort you."

Georgie shook her head and went to her bureau, fishing out stockings and quickly slipping them on. "No, I thank you," she spat, tearing a hole in one stocking as she pulled it up. She shook her head, not particularly caring at this moment. "I don't need comfort or pity. I need a walk. A very, very long walk."

"Georgie, no," Izzy pleaded, coming over to her. "It's raining, and you don't want…"

"I do want!" Georgie cried, slapping her hands away and reaching for her boots. "I do want. Did that never occur to anybody? I do want, and I want many, many things. And right now, I do not want to be reminded that I am still a spinster and going to remain a spinster until I can convince some other poor man to offer for me, or until I am dead in the ground." She frantically tied the laces of her boots. "All I want is to go for a walk in the rain!"

Izzy sank back onto the bed, nodding. "All right, Georgie," she whispered.

Georgie moved to the door in quick strides, then chanced a glance back at her poor, sweet cousin. "I'm sorry."

She saw Izzy nod, but couldn't stay. She moved down the corridor quickly, calling for a coat, bonnet, and umbrella as she plaited her hair.

She would not look respectable to anyone looking, and she knew that she was pale and drawn, but the dreariness of the day and dismal downpour would make any woman so.

Not that anyone would care.

Georgiana Allen did not need to look well.

Her coat and bonnet were given her, and she donned them quickly, not bothering to tie the ribbons. She held her hand out for the umbrella, and marched out the door, without calling for any sort of servant.

She was old enough to be a spinster to everyone. She was old enough, therefore, to go unaccompanied wherever she liked.

The rain pounded on her umbrella, and she was grateful for the noise. It kept her from having to heed her own thoughts, or to let them form words that would open her wounds continually.

She did not care to have her own company just now. The solitude found in the sound of the rain, the cool breeze as it rushed passed her, and the increasing dampness of her skirts were all the sensations she needed. These were real, these she could feel without pain, comprehend without struggle.

There was nothing to think of or decipher.

Nothing.

Hyde Park was empty but for the occasional hurrying person, but Georgie took her time with her pace, slowing now that she was free to do so. The lanes were clear, the streams of water flowing into the sodden grass, the gurgling sounds almost lost in the symphony of raindrops. Her footsteps added an odd cadence to the sounds about her; slow, steady, an echo of her heart as it pounded within her.

She inhaled deeply, letting the crisp air fill her lungs, then released it in a heavy sigh, feeling some of the weight she'd been carrying release with it.

She would manage to find her usual spirit and wit again. She would be able to smile without pain. She would be able to laugh again.

But it wouldn't be the same.

It couldn't.

"Georgiana Allen?"

Oh, Lord have mercy on her soul, she couldn't bear it…

Georgie shook her head, picking up her pace and lowering her head.

"Georgie! I know it is you, girl, and if you do not stop this instant, I will call your name louder until the entire street can hear it!"

She knew that voice. How did she know that voice?

She stopped and turned towards the sound of it, her brow furrowing.

A carriage was stopped in the lane, it's occupant staring fixedly at her through the lowered window, her singularly blue eyes rather bright against the grey of the day.

Miranda Sterling.

"Oh, damn," Georgie muttered with a rough exhale.

There was no way she could avoid this confrontation, and it was destined to be ruthless.

For all of Tony's generous kindness, his stepmother did not feel the same compunction if it did not suit the circumstance.

She rather expected this to be such a circumstance.

Still, she managed to smile a little and force her feet to move in the direction of the carriage.

"Wise notion, my dear," Miranda praised when Georgie was close enough. "Now get out of that dreadful rain and into this carriage before you catch your death."

"What?" Georgie squawked, tilting her umbrella away from the coach. "Mrs. Sterling…"

Her brow knitted darkly. "You know better than to call me that, Georgie, dear. It is Miranda."

"Yes, madam, I know, but…" Georgie stammered, twisting the umbrella in her hold anxiously.

"But nothing," Miranda insisted firmly. "I am offering my carriage, and it would be terribly rude of you to refuse me."

Georgie was willing to risk rudeness if it would save her the trouble of facing Tony's staunchest supporter.

Miranda opened the carriage door, nearly hitting Georgie with it. "Get. In."

She almost refused, her indignation rising again, but she was so very tired of being indignant. She closed the umbrella and climbed into the carriage, averting her gaze from that of her companion.

"Wise notion, Georgie," Miranda muttered again, tapping the ceiling of the coach, which suddenly lurched forward.

Georgie nodded in acceptance, feeling rather conspicuous as she was dripping wet in this pristine carriage. She knew Miranda was looking at her, but she couldn't bear to think on it. She couldn't raise her eyes enough to see above the rich color of Miranda's skirts.

And, oddly enough, a dozing bloodhound on the floor.

"Rufus adores carriage rides in the rain," Miranda said lightly, reaching down to pet him. "And he's a wonderful companion and confidante. I tell him all my secrets, and he's never shared a one of them."

Georgie was inclined to believe her, and was instantly tempted to scratch the dog at her feet.

But she couldn't. Tony would scratch the dog. Pat his head. Take him on the hunt.

Not her.

"Georgie, look at me."

Miranda's words echoed her thoughts too perfectly, and Georgie was unable to refuse yet again.

She looked up and, to her astonishment, found Miranda smiling softly at her.

How could she do that? Knowing what Georgie had said and done, she could smile at her?

"You don't look well, dear," Miranda said gently. "And it isn't the rain, I can see that."

Georgie shook her head, her throat working on a swallow. "I'm not well, Miranda. I'm not well at all." She bit back a cry and looked out of the window, covering her mouth to stifle her tears.

Miranda tutted softly and handed her a handkerchief. "Oh, pet, don't hide your tears. Let them out, for goodness sake! They'll drown you if you hold it in."

A watery chuckle escaped Georgie and she dabbed at her cheeks and eyes. "I've been drowning for days, I'm quite used to the sensation."

"Yes, I wondered if you might be." Miranda sighed and leaned over, taking Georgie's hand. "It will be all right. No matter what happens."

Georgie looked back at her, dubious amidst her tears. "You can say that to me? You who are Tony's stepmother?"

Miranda smirked. "Darling, I may be his stepmother, but I am my own woman. And I am your friend. For your own merits, not because of him. I care about you both, and this mess of things affects us all. I refuse to take sides."

"Thank you," Georgie whispered, her chin quivering.

Miranda winked and nodded, sitting back against the sheepskin behind her. "Not that I know what the pair of you fought about to begin with. Tony's refused to say anything about it, and if he's said anything to Rufus, he's not sharing that with me."

Georgie couldn't smile at that, not even the light quip. "How is Tony?" she asked in a shaking tone.

"Distressed," Miranda replied on a sigh, smiling sadly. "I haven't seen him smile in days, but he's not come around for some time. Says he needs to think things over, make other arrangements... I think he might be considering giving up the house in Essex after all."

Georgie closed her eyes, her heart dropping into the pit of her stomach. Not Hazelwood Park. He'd spoken of it with such eagerness, describing every detail he could recall, though he'd only seen it once. Georgie had begun to imagine it herself, picturing the tranquil setting in the beautiful countryside, seeing herself accompanying him on visits to the tenants, proving herself to be an accomplished and able wife.

But she wouldn't be mistress of such a house or have those tenants to tend to.

He could, though. He could still have that future.

"He should keep it," Georgie rasped, her throat burning. She forced her eyes open and looked at Miranda with an attempt at a smile. "He should."

"I said the same thing." Miranda returned her weak smile and shrugged. "He said he didn't want it without you."

Georgie clamped down on her bottom lip hard. She forced back a tide of emotions and exhaled slowly. "What will he do?"

Miranda made a soft noise of derision. "Probably take up his commission once more. There were many who asked him to remain, and they would be only too happy to give it back."

That was exactly what Georgie had feared the response would be. Tony had been a good officer, a stalwart soldier, and he would do well to return to an occupation he was so well suited for. But the thought of him in such danger struck ice in her heart.

"Do you love him, Georgie?" Miranda asked pointedly as the carriage jolted around a curve. "After whatever has passed?"

Georgie whimpered and dropped her head, looking at her bare hands, still wrinkled from the rain, clenching at each other.

Rufus whined and sat up, shifting over to lay his head in Georgie's lap, his soft eyes peering up at her.

She reached out to stroke his head, the weight of him in her lap soothing, giving her strength.

"I'm afraid I do," Georgie whispered in answer to Miranda's question.

"Why afraid?" came the response. "Dear girl, if you love him, and he loves you…"

"Does he?" she interrupted. "I cannot be so sure."

There was silence for a long moment, even from Rufus.

Miranda shifted in her seat, leaning forward once more. "Georgie, of *course* he loves you still."

"Did he really love me at all?" Georgie wondered aloud. "I've never been in love before, and I've never had a man in love with me before. I don't know how to feel, or anything about it. What can I trust? What can I believe? I'm afraid of all of it." She shook her head, surprised to still find more tears at her disposal. "I'm even more afraid that my fear has made me act rashly in the face of something true and honest."

"Ah," Miranda murmured with understanding. "If that is the case, why would Tony let you go? You cannot tell me this is all on your part."

Georgie nodded, still petting Rufus absently. "I overreacted and seem to be doing a lot of it lately. I did not let him explain, and I don't think I would have believed it if I had. I lashed out at him, and he returned the favor. Just this morning I screamed at Izzy, my cousin and best friend, who was only trying to help. I am apparently not in control of my own emotions, Miranda, and Tony is quite right to be rid of me. I can now see what everyone else has known all along... I am not fit to be any man's wife."

Suddenly, Miranda plucked Georgie's hand from Rufus's head and squeezed it tightly. "If I hear anything so disgustingly self-pitying from your lips again, Georgie Allen, I'll ship you off to Bristol in a trunk on a mail coach."

Georgie hiccupped softly, smiling again.

"You are not unhinged, you are in pain." Miranda gave her a pitying smile. "Your heart is broken, dear, and that is not madness. Marriage is not a union of two perfect people who will never offend and upset each other. It is made up of two very imperfect people who have chosen to live their lives together, and if there is love in the union, it is all the more precious. If you marry Tony, your problems will not vanish. Indeed, I rather think he will give you more problems than you deserve."

Georgie laughed in surprise but nodded.

"But even with love, Georgie," Miranda continued, "marriage is difficult, and you will argue, and cry, and scream. But you will also laugh, and dance, and love… You cannot run from every trial in a marriage. You stand and face it together."

The tightness in her chest began to ease a little, and she managed to give Miranda a wry smile. "Did you give this speech to Tony?"

Miranda chuckled and released Georgie's hand with a pat. "Of course. And I won't tell you how he responded, your ears may never recover."

Georgie giggled easily at that, the tightness easing further still. So, she was not the only one behaving out of sorts. There was comfort in that.

She looked at Miranda with interest as an errant thought occurred to her. "When did you know that you loved your husband, Miranda? After you married him, I know, but when?"

Miranda's brows rose, and then a soft smile crossed her lips. "When I lost our second child. I'd already lost the first, and then we lost the second, and it became apparent that I might not be able to bear him another child, despite both of our wishes." Her throat worked, and her eyes turned misty. "He held me in his arms and told me that if it wasn't meant to be, he would still be the most contented of men. So long as he had me, he needn't wish for anything else. I did not fully comprehend the character of the man I had married until then, but I loved him fiercely from that moment on."

Such an intimate response was not what Georgie had expected, yet she could not regret asking. "He sounds like a remarkable man."

"He was," Miranda replied with a smile. "And I love him still, though we are separated now. He will always be the man of my dreams, and having had that love, I do not feel the need to seek out any other. He is still mine, and I am still his. And that is enough."

Georgie could not speak for a long moment, the emotions surging through her too raw for words. Could she ever find such a love for herself?

Had she found it and lost it?

Had any of it been real?

Miranda cleared her throat sharply. "So. You pet Rufus for as long as it takes to make you feel better, and I'll take you home when you do. You marry whomever you like, whether it be my Tony or not.

I will always be your friend, dear. On that you can depend."

Georgie smiled warmly at her, sure she did not deserve such kindness.

She wanted to hope that this woman might yet be her mother-in-law.

But hope had wounded her before. She could not allow it to do so again.

Chapter Twenty-One

A little bit of mischief can go a very long way...

-*The Spinster Chronicles, 10 June 1817*

"I still don't know why you pressured me to come. I'm not feeling quite up to it."

"Because you love balls, and you know how much Anna loves having us attend her family's events."

"If your sister-in-law thinks that we will ever forget that her brother trod both our toes so badly we bruised at the ball four years ago, she is sadly mistaken."

Izzy giggled and looked around at the grand ballroom at Maxwell house with all the eagerness of a seventeen-year-old. "But I do love this room, Georgie! It is the best and brightest in all of London!"

Georgie eyed her cousin fondly. "Only because you are practically glowing, Izzy. You look positively lovely."

She was not exaggerating, either. Izzy wore a white muslin that gave her an air of innocence yet suited her so well that the look was more elegant than anything else. Her ribbons and earrings matched, but around her neck she wore only a simple gold chain, and that seemed the most perfect accouterment for her appearance.

It was a testament to Izzy's perfect nature that she was once again so warm and familiar with Georgie after her outburst. Upon her return the other day, Izzy had only wrapped her in warm blankets and sat with her by the fire, sipping hot tea until they were both warm and sleepy, giggling like they had as children. Forgiveness came far too easily for her cousin, and she was never more grateful for it than now.

And truth be told, she did rather want to be here. Not to be eyed with speculation when she and Tony avoided each other, provided he would be in attendance, but to be out among people and behaving with as much normalcy as she could manage. She frequently attended the balls that were held at various houses in London. She was one of the regulars who could be counted on, even if she rarely danced.

The slow progression into her typical activities and behavior had been good for her, and after her conversation with Miranda in the carriage the other day, she had been determined to pick up the pieces of her life and move forward.

The Spinsters had been surprisingly silent on the topic, but she could only presume that Izzy had warned them off, and for once they had heeded it.

Georgie looked around now, sighing to herself. This would be good for her. She could manage it.

Izzy rubbed her hand, then walked with her over to the corner where Lady Hetty was sitting.

This could be dangerous on far too many levels.

"That's a very pretty gown, Georgiana," Lady Hetty said with a fond smile at her. "It's almost pink, isn't it?"

Georgie smiled and looked down at the dress, a very pale rose-color overlaying cream underskirts and trimmed with gold. "Yes, ma'am, it is. Izzy persuaded me to have small flowers in my hair to match it." She turned to show her the hair accessories, dotted among her pinned braids.

"Isabella has such fine taste," Lady Hetty praised, reaching a hand out for Izzy. She beamed up at her, then looked at Georgie with equal warmth. "I hope you will dance tonight, Georgiana. A pretty girl like you must dance, indeed you must. Don't sit over here with an old woman."

"Perhaps I like sitting with old women," Georgie suggested with a tilt of her chin. "I am near to one myself."

Lady Hetty scoffed loudly. "Pish tosh. You are as young as spring tonight. I will see you dance." She thumped her walking stick loudly. "Greensley!"

Mr. Greensley, who was just passing, stopped and bowed to Lady Hetty swiftly, looking resigned, but already amused. "Lady Hetty, you look rather charming this evening."

"I look old and feeble, and this shade is not my color," Lady Hetty retorted. "But at my age, I no longer care. Dance with Miss Allen, Greensley. Give her the next two."

"Lady Hetty!" Georgie protested, her cheeks flushing hotly.

Izzy, however, looked highly amused.

Greensley nodded, too much a gentleman to refuse, and turned to Georgie. "Miss Allen, may I have the pleasure?"

She restrained the urge to sputter in irritation and placed her hand in his. "Of course, Mr. Greensley." She speared Lady Hetty with a scowl as he led her to the floor.

"Come now, Miss Allen," Greensley teased as they took their positions. "Surely you can dance with me. I've known you since we were six."

Georgie gave him a look as the music struck up. "Yes, and your dancing has not improved since the last time it was permissible for me to call you Everett."

He chuckled and bowed to her. "You've not danced with me since then, Miss Allen. I think you will find I am much improved."

"We shall see," she replied with a curtsey.

Truth be told, it was rather nice to dance with him. Mr. Greensley had always been a good neighbor and friend, though their friendship had lapsed somewhat in their adult years. Theirs was a family connection, not one necessarily of their own making, but he could always be counted on if she had need.

He'd never said anything against the Spinsters, but he also had never given her any reason to suppose that he supported them. It did not make much difference, she supposed, as he was destined to be supportive of her specifically no matter the situation. She could not imagine that everybody would look on the Spinsters with the same understanding that Tony had done.

If Tony had done.

Despite what she had seen and felt, she could not know for certain that the man she knew him to be was the man he truly was.

It was destined to make a marvelous column in the Spinster

Chronicles once she had the clarity and distance to adequately describe it. There was much to learn from such an experience, and several other girls deserved to benefit from it. There were lessons to share now, though she would keep the details to herself, and if she could find a way to use her personal tragedy as an example, perhaps it would not have been for nothing after all.

It hadn't been for nothing at all.

She had learned firsthand the feelings of love, of loss, and betrayal. The vulnerability she had allowed herself, the trust that had been broken, the never-ending doubts that had surfaced and swirled since it ended…

Georgie hardly recognized herself, though she was much the same in many ways. But she was better now than she had been days ago, and while her heart was still feeling tender and fragile, her defenses were beginning to rally.

And here she was dancing, managing to smile, and recalling the thrill of such an act.

Greensley was a much better dancer than she had feared, which made everything more enjoyable, and nobody would presume anything by their dance, as Greensley tended to dance with a great many young women without any serious pursuit. It was probably the greatest kindness he had ever done her, though he probably had no notion of it.

She passed Greensley in the dance, her heart lighter with each step and turned to circle about with the other ladies.

Then she saw him.

Tony.

He hadn't seen her, he was talking with Henshaw and Morton, who were dressed in their uniforms, but he was here.

He was there.

He wasn't in uniform. Had he decided not to go back into the army, then? Had he simply not had the opportunity yet? He looked well. He looked very, very well, and her arms suddenly ached to hold him. Her feet continued in the dance, and the rest of her followed, but her attention was fixed on him now.

It had to be.

The first dance ended, and there was some applause from the

dancers and those watching.

Tony applauded absently, then looked out at the dancers.

At her.

Georgie's breath caught in her chest, a flash of agony slicing across her heart. Those eyes had stared at her so many times with heat, with love, with adoration, and even with mischief.

Now there was only pain.

The dancers changed positions, some new ones joining while others departed. Greensley took her hand and moved her to another place on the floor, but Georgie couldn't pay attention to any of that.

Not now.

The music struck up, and Tony turned away, speaking with Henshaw again.

That was it, then. There was nothing to expect from him, nothing to mend, nothing to prove.

He hadn't loved her as much as she'd believed.

If he had, surely he wouldn't... He couldn't...

Why the pain, then?

Well, perhaps he was gentleman enough to regret wounding her, but it could not be more than that, she was sure. She regretted giving so much of herself that she was left wounded. Regrets were not useful to either of them. It was time to let it go, put it all behind her, and move forward with her life.

She nodded to herself and forced a smile as she danced the next with Greensley, trying in vain to take as much pleasure from it as she had the first one.

When it was finished, he returned her to Lady Hetty, who had now been joined by Prue and Elinor, though none of the others. Prue looked almost as pale as Georgie had been, but that was undoubtedly due to her cousin, who had already proven snide and vindictive. She smiled rarely but was bravely making an effort.

If Prue could withstand her difficulties, so could Georgie.

Elinor stood behind Prue with a glower, no doubt looking for Eliza or any other person so willing to abuse one of their own.

Georgie looked around the room with a frown, wondering where Izzy had gone. She was not dancing, and she could not find her amidst those watching. Charlotte had her usual collection of admirers, though it seemed somewhat diminished, for whatever reason. Grace was also conspicuously absent, though she was sure she had seen her enter.

She situated herself beside Prue, not feeling particularly inclined to seek out either of them. She was not their nanny, and they certainly did not need to stay together. But it was though they were all refusing to dance on a principle. She rather hoped that they would choose to dance instead. Why should any of them refuse to dance simply because nothing would come of it? They had every right to life's enjoyment exactly as they were, and she would see to it.

The Spinsters would continue on exactly as they had been, only she would find a way to make them more relatable, more likable, and more of a welcome sight. There was nothing shameful in being a spinster, with or without a capital S, and she was determined that everyone should know it.

It might not have been a favorable outcome of life, but there were many worse situations to be in.

"You've decided something," Prue murmured, watching her. "You look very determined."

"I have," Georgie informed her. "A determination to make the best of my situation, whatever it is."

"That's very brave." Prue smiled weakly. "When you have done that, share your wisdom with me, won't you? I've never been determined about anything."

Georgie made a sympathetic noise and covered Prue's hands with hers. "Sweet lamb, you are determined to be here, are you not? Despite all the adversities?"

Prue looked unconvinced but nodded. "That and Mother forbade me to stay at home."

Georgie winked at her. "We'll just pretend you made the decision on your own."

That made Prue smile more naturally. "If you insist."

"I do," Georgie assured her. "In fact…"

"Georgie!"

They both turned to see Grace and Izzy rushing over to them, taking care not to draw too much attention to themselves. Both girls appeared strained, if not outright agitated, and Georgie's senses suddenly seemed to heighten.

"What is it?" Georgie hissed, rising as they approached.

Grace shook her head quickly, her dark eyes wide. "Jane Wilton can't find Lucy."

Georgie's heart sunk. She looked at Izzy for confirmation.

Izzy nodded frantically. "She says Lucy has been secretive for days and refuses to talk to any of them. And nobody has seen Simon Delaney since the first set." Izzy bit down on her lip, wringing her hands together.

Georgie looked between them, her mind whirling. "Any idea where they might have gone? Does Anna know any ways out of the ballroom that might be easier for them?"

Izzy shook her head. "No, I've asked her, and she says they would have been seen if they'd gone through the house. The terrace and gardens are the only way." Izzy shook with anxiety. "Georgie! She's only fifteen!"

"All right," Georgie said, thinking quickly. "Izzy, we'll go to the terrace. Grace, fetch Jane Wilton, but tell Charlotte to keep up appearances so there is less likely to be a fuss. Prue and Elinor will stay here with Lady Hetty."

"What's going on?" Lady Hetty asked, leaning forward.

"Nothing," replied at least four of them, which made her harrumph in disgruntlement.

Georgie nodded firmly, heart racing, but her mind made up. "Right, maintain discretion, but make haste. Let's go."

Overall, this wasn't as terrible as he'd thought a ball at the Maxwell's would be. He hadn't been sure of his attendance, as the eldest Maxwell daughter had married Izzy's brother, but Francis had assured him that the families were not that close, and there should be no awkwardness on that quarter.

And there hadn't been.

But there had been Georgie.

He couldn't stop watching her, whether she was dancing or

sitting, talking or laughing. His attention was continually being brought back to her.

It was too much, seeing her and knowing he had lost her.

But he had to endure it. He could hardly avoid her forever in London, and time would eventually cause the pain to fade.

Or so he told himself.

"Of what do you currently disapprove, Captain?" Henshaw asked from beside him. "The dance or the fashion?"

Tony looked over at him with a raised brow. "Pardon?"

Henshaw returned his look with one of his own. "You're glowering at a ball, Sterling. Hardly appropriate. Would the card room be more to your taste this evening?"

Tony shook his head, turning back. "Hardly. I'm in no mood to gamble, and have nothing to gamble with even if I did."

"Tony!"

He looked to his right to see Francis heading towards him, brow furrowed, making his way almost roughly through the closest guests in his efforts to get to Tony. A few people scowled, but nobody seemed to mark him.

Tony looked at Henshaw, who shrugged, but watched with interest.

"Francis," Tony greeted suspiciously when his cousin had reached him. "Is Janet in a right temper again?"

Francis did not smile. "The youngest Wilton girl is missing, and so is that Delaney fellow. Janet's just been talking with one of the sisters, and they're beginning to worry."

Tony bit back a curse and looked around the room. "Are you sure? Are they sure?"

Francis gave him a bewildered look. "How sure do you want them to be at this moment?"

It was a fair point and Tony bobbed his head in acknowledgement. "Where would they go? Are there any other ways out of here?"

"No," Francis told him firmly, all business. "Maxwell says just the gardens, if they wanted to be secretive."

Tony nodded. "Henshaw, with me. Morton, check the gaming tables for Delaney, just as a precaution."

He did not wait to see if Morton would do as he ordered, but turned towards the terrace, Henshaw and Francis on his heels.

He'd warned Delaney what would happen if he tried anything, and he'd been quite sure that the Wiltons had given strict instructions to their youngest daughter. If those two had been foolish enough to try something again, especially with Lucy now having some idea of what could transpire, then perhaps they deserved each other. But he could not face the Wiltons knowing he could have done something to help.

If there was anything left to help. It was entirely possible that it was already too late, and he would have just been another member of Society who knew too much, now bound to keep a secret for the sake of sparing the family's reputation. It would never recover fully, but perhaps there was still a chance the older two girls might manage sensible marriages, though not nearly to the heights they might have done otherwise.

The terrace was suddenly before him and he pushed the doors open, scouring the gardens beyond.

All looked dark, despite the occasional torches set along the stone path, but he couldn't hear any footsteps, hurried or otherwise.

"Francis," Tony barked, whirling to face his cousin.

But he never got that far.

On the other side of the terrace, bent over the rail and now slowly straightening, eyes trained on him, was Georgie.

"Izzy," he heard her whisper, but Izzy only stood there, watching Tony with surprisingly steady eyes.

Tony swallowed once. "Francis," he said again.

"We knew the only way to get you fools together was if someone was in trouble," Francis replied, his tone perfectly at ease now. "Miss Lambert's maid was kind enough to relay the nature of your argument when pressed, and we're all agreed that this should be simple enough to clear up."

Georgie turned to Izzy, her expression full of betrayal, but Izzy had already moved towards Francis, smiling smugly.

"So," Francis went on, nodding at Izzy, "we will return to the ball and take Henshaw here, and the two of you will kindly reconcile, or at the very least refrain from killing each other."

"And Lucy Wilton?" Georgie pressed, her brow furrowing. "Is she all right?"

"Oh, she's perfectly fine," Izzy said with a laugh. "She's still confined to their house until she's learned how to behave appropriately in society, Jane's just told me."

"And before you can ask," Francis continued as Tony opened his mouth, "Delaney is in the gaming room. You can check with Morton when he returns, he will undoubtedly see him there."

Francis bowed, Izzy curtsied, and Henshaw looked utterly lost, but chuckled as they all turned for the house once more.

Tony cleared his throat quickly. "I thought you said there would be no grand gestures from you for the Spinsters, Francis."

Francis turned back, raising a brow. "If you think I could face my wife after doing nothing under these circumstances, you are grossly mistaken. I would have done exactly as I did, had the situation been real." He gave him a wry smile. "But in this case, cousin, it was not for the Spinsters at all, but for you. And every now and again, I may find myself accomplice in a grand gesture for that purpose."

He and the others left them then, leaving the door open, the music of the ball mingling with the night air.

Tony looked back at Georgie, who gripped the terrace railing behind her, staring at him as though he might disappear.

She was a vision tonight, somehow lovelier out here in the starlight than she had been only moments ago. Her gown was the color of a blush, and it only heightened her own healthy glow, the gold details somehow drawing out a similar shade in her tresses. She was perfectly adorned, perfectly situated, and perfectly pleasing to look upon.

Perfection in every respect.

Her slender throat worked on a swallow. "You... you thought Lucy was in trouble again. And you came to save her?"

Tony nodded, his eyes locked with hers. "If I could. I had to do something."

"Did you see me come?" Georgie's voice quivered, as did her arms. "Did you know we were doing the same?"

"No," Tony insisted, shaking his head. "No, I didn't see you. But... I would have come anyway. For Lucy."

Georgie swallowed again. "You can't stand Lucy."

He smiled a little. "No. She's a petulant child who needs more time in the schoolroom, but I would have come for her anyway."

Georgie inhaled a shaky breath, then released it much the same. "You weren't trying to break up the Spinsters at all, were you?"

He shook his head at her. "No."

"You wouldn't."

"I wouldn't."

"You… you meant what you said, then?" she pressed, her voice rising in pitch. "About me?"

Tony's throat clenched involuntarily, and he was unable to speak for a long moment. "Every blessed word."

Georgie's lower lip trembled dangerously, but still she clung to the railing. "And your c-cousin?" she stammered, rather like Prue would have done. "The younger one?"

"I haven't spoken to him since that day, and I may never speak to him again." Tony sighed as he looked at this woman he loved so dearly. "I would never hurt you, Georgie. Even if I didn't love you, I would never, and I could never do anything like Hugh suggested…"

"You still love me?" Georgie interrupted, her voice a gasp.

Tony stopped, his mouth working soundlessly. "Yes."

Her gaze somehow grew in intensity, the brilliant shade more enhanced for it. "After everything I said and did?"

He nodded once. "Yes."

Georgie went completely still, as did the night, and then she heaved a wrenching sob, covering her face with one hand. "Oh, Tony, I'm so sorry!"

He was to her in an instant, hauling her against his chest and pressing her face against him. "Shh, darling, it's all right. It's all right."

She shook her head against him. "I'm so sorry. I was so blind, it was unforgiveable to doubt you so easily. I should have known you were not like him, that you were sincere and true…"

"Georgie, Georgie, enough," Tony shushed, kissing her hair, and rubbing soothing circles on her back. "Don't."

She pulled back, tears streaming down her cheeks. "I should have believed you. Will you forgive me?"

He cupped her cheeks gently, smoothing away her tears.

"Always, my love. Do you forgive me? I spoke harshly, and I should have told you from the beginning what had happened. Then we would never have…"

"I forgive you," Georgie interrupted, fisting her hands in his lapels. "I'll forgive you everything if you still love me."

Tony kissed her hard, sliding one hand into her hair. "I love you," he whispered against her lips as she panted in response. "I love you."

One of her hands went to his neck as another tear fell. "I love you, too," she murmured. "More than I knew."

He kissed her again, sweetly and tenderly this time, wringing pleasure and passion from them both in the gentlest manner. Her lips toyed with his, her hand gripping his neck tightly, pulling herself closer, more fully into his embrace. He wrapped one arm around her, cradling his love against him, fearful still that this all might be a dream he would soon wake from.

Her touch was all that was real to him. The feel of her lips on his, the taste of her tears on his tongue…

If this were a dream, he did not dare awaken.

Georgie broke the kiss and pressed her forehead to his, sighing in relief.

Tony matched it, stroking her cheek softly. "I missed you," he told her.

She nodded against his. "I missed you."

"Will you still marry me, my love?" he asked as he wiped away the remains of another tear.

Again, she nodded. "Yes, please."

"Well," he replied roughly, suddenly finding a lump in his throat, "since you said it so politely…" He leaned in for another kiss.

Georgie pressed off a little, giving him a teasing look. "Don't you dare compromise me, Tony Sterling. I'll never live it down."

He barked a laugh. "Do you really think you are that susceptible? What about your towering strength and control?"

"You send the whole thing trembling," she admitted with a smug little smile he desperately wanted to kiss.

An odd sense of pride shot through him and he pursed his lips in thought. "Hmm. Can we start some rumors?"

Her eyes narrowed. "Why?"

"So then you'll have to marry me faster." He shrugged as if that should be obvious.

Georgie broke into a mischievous grin. "Or... we can simply marry faster."

Tony liked the sound of that. "How?"

"The banns have already been read twice," she reminded him, her other hand settling on his shoulder. "We didn't revoke them. One more Sunday, and we can marry."

He gaped in amazement as he thought back. "Two weeks."

She nodded quickly. "If that."

Two weeks. Two simple weeks and the woman in his arms would be his. He smiled at her in wonder, the purest, most intense joy filling him so completely he thought he might burst. "Done," he grunted against the hoard of emotions. "Now to seal the deal..."

Georgie grinned and pulled him to her for a long, blissful, rather thorough kiss.

And then Tony took his intended into the ball once more, danced several times, and let the entirety of London Society be made aware that this particular Spinster, with a capital S, was his, and his alone, forevermore.

Epilogue

———— ❧ ——————

Change is said to be beneficial. A time for growth and adaptation, development, and lessons. This author finds change to be a rather annoying pest of a thing, and not entirely agreeable. Change may surprise you, and surprises are not always pleasant.

-The Spinster Chronicles, 7 April 1818

"This meeting of the Spinsters, with a capital S, is now called to order."

"You needn't make it sound so bleak."

"Isn't it bleak? We are one member short."

"And yet we've gained one."

"Thank you for the lovely reminder."

"Edith, don't be so droll!"

"You're not actually a spinster."

Edith raised a questioning brow at that. "With or without a capital S, Charlotte?"

Charlotte scowled at her across the room. "Without, of course. We've already made you an official Spinster."

"Is there a badge of some sort for that?" she inquired mildly, looking over at Grace. "Or a brooch?"

Izzy clamped down on her lip hard, biting back giggles.

"As I was saying," Charlotte pressed on very firmly, "this meeting is called to order."

Elinor sat up straighter in her chair, but she seemed the only one paying any attention.

Edith frowned a little. "Is it always this formal?"

"No," Izzy and Grace said together, while Prue merely shook her head.

"I see." Edith nodded, a small smile forming. "And is Charlotte always in charge?"

Charlotte threw her another hard look while the others giggled.

"No one is in charge, really," Izzy told her. "But since Georgie married, she seems to have taken over."

"Commandeered the group," Grace offered.

"Seized the throne," Elinor chimed in.

Prue said nothing but seemed amused by the banter.

"Oh, very well," Charlotte grumbled, sitting down on the sofa. "I just so hate change."

"We know," Grace assured her.

Charlotte hummed in irritation. "Everybody, just work on your writing, and I'll shut up."

Everybody laughed and turned to the pieces of paper they had.

Edith looked around in confusion. "What am I to write? I'm not particularly good at anything."

"I'll help you," Elinor offered, sliding her chair closer. "We'll do the Social Calendar. It's less writing and more factual."

Edith nodded, looking grateful. "Thank you, Elinor." She looked sheepishly around at the rest. "I don't suppose I'm used to being a Spinster yet. I'm not sure of the way of things."

"Oh, nobody is," a voice from the hall chortled. "We all just make it up as we go along."

"Georgie!" they all cried, seeming as one.

Georgie appeared in the doorway with a bit of flair, grinning at them all. "Good day, Spinsters, and how are we faring this fine Writing Day?"

Everybody arose quickly and moved to embrace their friend, laughing and chattering rapidly.

"Slow down, slow down," Georgie told them all, waving them back. "I've still not managed to reply to everybody at once."

"Georgie, we thought you weren't due back for three days!" Izzy squealed, her face flushed with excitement.

Georgie smiled at her. "We weren't, but Brighton is not nearly so exciting as we thought, and we grew tired of it, so we're back early. We're just getting set up in the house here, so you're all invited to call as early as Friday."

"I will be there tomorrow," Charlotte proclaimed with a prim nod.

"Of course you will," Georgie replied with a snort. "I'll warn Tony."

"And how is your handsome husband?" Izzy teased, biting her lip.

Georgie's smile turned mischievous. "Very well, and very handsome. And very underfoot as I try to set up the house."

That made them all laugh, including Prue.

"But he sends you all his regards," Georgie went on, "and to assure you that the only reason he is not here with me is because it is Writing Day, and he knows better."

"Hmph." Elinor grunted, still not quite forgiving Tony, or Hugh, for what had happened. "Too right."

"That is a lovely gown, Georgie," Grace told her, eyeing the green-striped muslin and dark pelisse with envy. "It does suit you so well."

Georgie rolled her eyes. "Thank you, Grace. Miranda insisted on providing me with a whole trousseau, and I've only just gotten around to wearing anything from it. She does have splendid taste, though."

"But your wedding dress was exquisite," Edith reminded her warmly.

Georgie shrugged, smiling in embarrassment. "She insisted on that, too." She waved her hands quickly. "Enough about me! It is Writing Day! What are we working on?"

The Spinsters looked at each other in confusion.

"What?" Georgie asked, glancing around. "What is it?"

"Georgie…" Izzy began slowly. "You're married. You're not a spinster anymore. You don't have to write for the Chronicles."

Georgie looked at her cousin quizzically. "I didn't write for the chronicles because I was a spinster, capital S or not. I did it because I loved it. And I will always be a Spinster at heart. So. Which section can I write?"

The others conferred on that, but Georgie suddenly found her attention drawn to Prue, seated further away than the rest.

"Prue," she said softly. "You're very quiet. Is anything the matter?"

"N-no," Prue replied with a quick shake of her head, more intent on her paper. "No, n-nothing at all."

Georgie frowned at that, hearing the nervous stammer, but she could hardly press her before the others.

"Take up the Quirks and Quotes," Charlotte settled, handing Georgie a sheet of paper. "You're always good at that."

Georgie took the page but gave her friend a skeptical look. "I've been away from London for three weeks."

Charlotte waved a hand. "Just quote Miss Austen and we'll see if anybody notices."

"Does your husband really know you're here?" Elinor demanded, still disgruntled.

Georgie nodded, unable to keep from smiling. "He does. It was his idea, actually."

Elinor hadn't expected that and looked at Grace for help.

But Grace was smiling in wonder. "You have married a remarkable man, Georgie."

Georgie's smile grew, and her heart warmed at the thought of him. "Oh, I know," she sighed. Then she straightened up, eyes twinkling. "And while I may be more limited in my time with you, and less involved in our usual activities, I have found something new to occupy my mind and time."

"Oh?" Izzy asked, perking up excitedly.

"Yes," Georgie replied with a firm nod. She gave them all a very smug smile. "I intend to see you all married."

Everyone exclaimed something at that, crying out their opinions, but Georgie was firm in the face of their interjections.

"No, no," she insisted. "Not to save you from spinsterhood, you know how I feel about that. But because it is a remarkable amount of fun, and I insist on you all participating."

"Done that," Edith muttered, widening her eyes.

"For about five minutes!" everyone said together, laughing at their unison.

Prue sat very still in her seat, staring at her paper, a handful of words written there, but none of them clear just now.

She'd never thought she'd marry, given her marked impediments, but she'd always thought it could have been a lovely change.

But now…

Now…

The very idea terrified her more than anything ever had.

And it was only the beginning.

Coming Soon

THE Spinster AND I

The Spinster Chronicles

Book Two

"If you give a rogue a spinster…"

by

REBECCA CONNOLLY

9 781943 048533